THE
ICE CHILD

THE
ICE CHILD

Elizabeth McGregor

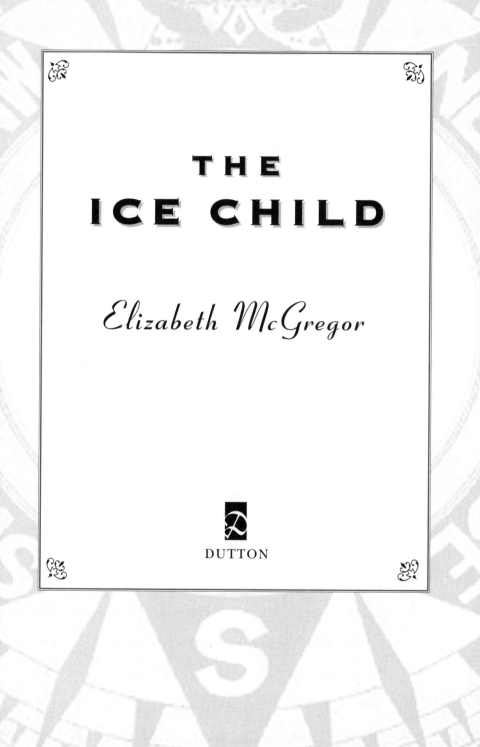

DUTTON

DUTTON
Published by the Penguin Group
Penguin Putnam Inc., 375 Hudson Street, New York, New York 10014, U.S.A.
Penguin Books Ltd, 27 Wrights Lane, London W8 5TZ, England
Penguin Books Australia Ltd, Ringwood, Victoria, Australia
Penguin Books Canada Ltd, 10 Alcorn Avenue, Toronto, Ontario, Canada M4V 3B2
Penguin Books (N.Z.) Ltd, 182–190 Wairau Road, Auckland 10, New Zealand

Penguin Books Ltd, Registered Offices: Harmondsworth, Middlesex, England

Published by Dutton, a member of Penguin Putnam Inc.

First Printing, May, 2001
1 3 5 7 9 10 8 6 4 2

REGISTERED TRADEMARK—MARCA REGISTRADA

LIBRARY OF CONGRESS CATALOGING-IN-PUBLICATION DATA
McGregor, Elizabeth.
The ice child / Elizabeth McGregor.
p. cm.
ISBN 0-525-94567-9
I. Title.

PS3563.C368117 I28 2001
813'.6—dc21   00-067703

Printed in the United States of America
Set in New Baskerville
Designed by Julian Hamer

PUBLISHER'S NOTE
This book is a work of fiction. Names, characters, places, and incidents
are either the product of the author's imagination or are used fictitiously,
and any resemblance to actual persons, living or dead, business
establishments, events, or locales is entirely coincidental.

For Kate, who can see in the dark

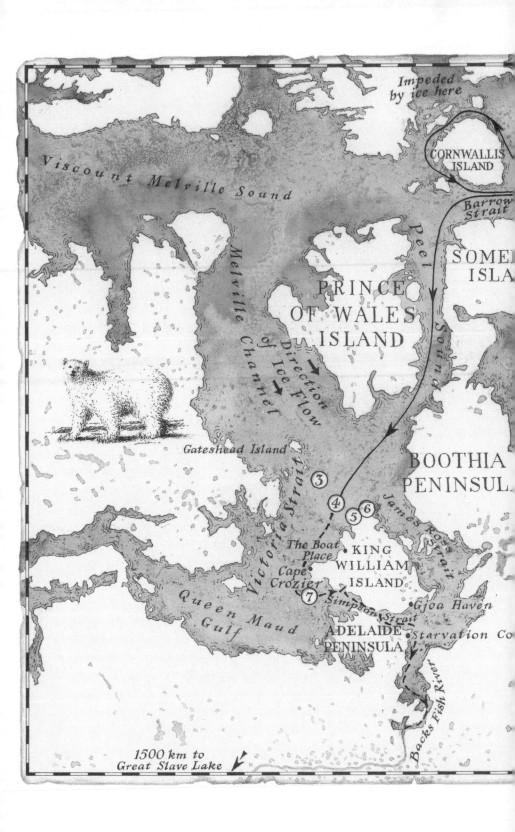

Impeded
by ice here

CORNWALLIS
ISLAND

Viscount Melville Sound

Barrow
Strait

PRINCE
OF WALES
ISLAND

SOME
ISLA

Peel Sound

Melville Channel

Direction of Ice Flow

Gateshead Island

BOOTHIA
PENINSUL

③

④ ⑥
⑤

Victoria Strait

James Ross Strait

The Boat
Place

KING
WILLIAM
ISLAND

Cape
Crozier

⑦ *Simpson Strait*

Gjoa Haven

*Queen Maud
Gulf*

ADELAIDE
PENINSULA

Starvation Co

Backs Fish River

1500 km to
Great Slave Lake

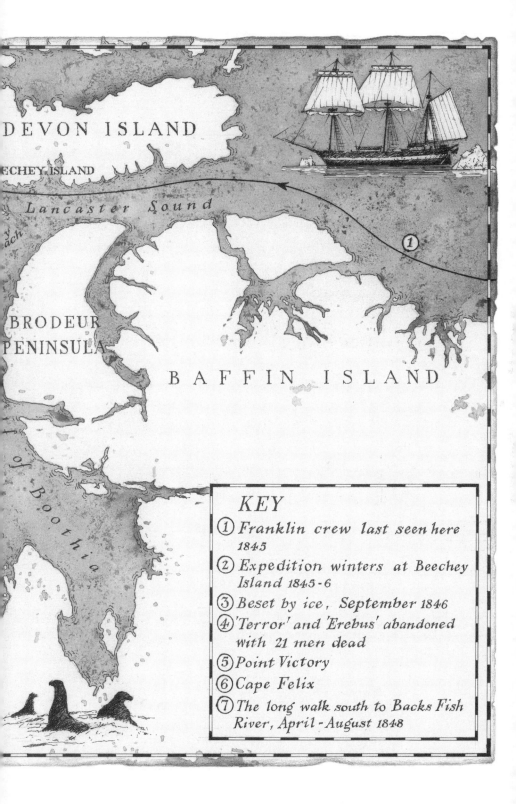

DEVON ISLAND

BEECHEY ISLAND

Lancaster Sound

BRODEUR
PENINSULA

BAFFIN ISLAND

of Boothia

KEY

① Franklin crew last seen here 1845

② Expedition winters at Beechey Island 1845-6

③ Beset by ice, September 1846

④ 'Terror' and 'Erebus' abandoned with 21 men dead

⑤ Point Victory

⑥ Cape Felix

⑦ The long walk south to Backs Fish River, April - August 1848

THE
ICE CHILD

Prologue

Summer 2000

THE great white bear lifted her head, narrowing her eyes against the driving Arctic snow. She looked back along the rubble ice to the cub that followed her, waiting for him in the white-on-white landscape.

All around her the ice of Victoria Strait groaned as it moved, compressed by the pressure that flooded from the Beaufort Sea, forcing its way through Melville Sound toward the Northwest Passage.

It was desperately cold. Colder, certainly, than a man could tolerate for long. But the bear did not register the temperature, padded as she was by four inches of fat and insulating fur. She was in her country, her kingdom, impervious to any law but her own.

The Greeks called this place Arktikos, the country of the great bear. From November to February it kept the long watches of the world's night; but in the spring it was more alive than any other country.

Three million fulmars, kittiwakes, murres, and guillemots fed in Lancaster Sound in the summer; over a quarter of a million harp, bearded, and ringed seals. In May and June ten million dovekies, with their stocky little black-and-white bodies, passed over Devon Island. And above them all, clearly bright in winter, shone Polaris, the yellowish star that never seemed to move, with the lesser stars of Ursa Major, the Great Bear, circulating around it. Most beautiful of all were the lights—lights that the Inuit said were the torches held by the dead to help the living hunt—the aurora borealis, whose pale green and rose-colored flags streamed and undulated across the skies.

The polar bear had mated on the ice floes of Peel Sound last May. She had been an exceptional and solitary traveler, even among her own long-ranging kind. Swimming all that season, rarely resting on the ice, she had crossed the Arctic Circle opposite Repulse and was spotted, though not tagged, by a marine mammal research team, as she crossed the old whaling routes, in March. On most days she could swim fifty miles without a rest, churning through the checkered ice at six miles an hour.

In December she had given birth for the first time, in a snow den deep underground.

Her single male cub had arrived complaining, mewling, flexing his feet against her within minutes. He weighed less than a pound at birth and fitted neatly into her curled paw; but by April he had grown to twenty-six pounds, and she had broken her drowsy sleep and pulled down the door of the den to the outside world.

She came out onto the snow, thin from her prolonged starvation, her cub following her. At first, she simply sat contentedly in the sun at the den's entrance, closing her eyes against the light. Even then she had no desire to eat, but she would occasionally roll backward to let her son feed, while she looked up at the endless wide sky. Sometimes, the cub would lie on her stomach, and she would rock him in her forelegs, just like a human mother rocking her baby in her arms.

But it was August now, and the light was beginning to change. And she felt—had felt for days—that the angle of the light was subtly wrong. She had, perhaps, tracked too far before denning; perhaps she was too far west. The internal mapping that ought not to fail her seemed to have done so, and in the first spell of real cold now, she stood indecisively on the freezing floe.

There was something strange here.

She felt a thread of danger—just a beat in the blood, a message transmitted in nerve impulses and scent. She wanted to turn back, to trek south, where her own kind was concentrated—and it was starting to be a command, this low-key tremor in her consciousness. But louder still was the knowledge that the cub was sick—too sick to travel far. Still watching him now, she saw him drop to the ground, roll over, and lie passively in the snow.

The polar bear raised herself up on her hind legs and, after pausing only for a second, slammed her full nine-hundred-pound body weight down. If the same mammal tracking team that had recorded her last year had seen her now, they would have been puzzled at this out-of-place behavior. With such force she was able to break through into seal dens, stealing the pups before they had ever seen the light, or break through ice to make swimming holes. But neither purpose was fulfilled here, in the whiteout of the storm.

She could feel the wreck underneath her, on the seabed below.

It smelled, even now, even after lying under the ice for a hundred and sixty years, like man. The wooden and iron bulk had left its insoluble human mark—this sense of *un*rightness, a kind of dislocation in the frequencies. The echo touched the animal above. She paused, balanced on her hindquarters, swaying, seven feet high at the shoulder, her immense forepaws extended in front of her.

Then she dropped down to all fours, and turned.

She turned back toward the cub, scenting—rather than seeing—him in the blizzard. As she drew level with him, she dropped to the ground and wound her body around him, pushing him gently into her shoulder, until she felt his faint warm breath against her.

PART ONE

Spring 1997

One

IT had begun in April, in the spring.

Easter Saturday was sunny, the first warm day of the year. All through Victoria Park the cherry trees were in flower, and the hornbeam were coming into leaf, and there was that first iridescent promise of summer showing in the dusty haze of the city.

When she thought about it now, Jo would see herself in that same café on the corner of Bartlett Street, Gina leafing through the newspaper at her side. And she would link those two: the cherry trees and the newspaper. The first day that she ever really gave more than a passing thought to Douglas Marshall.

She was twenty-six years old and had been writing for *The Courier* for four years, where Gina was her editor. From time to time Gina took it upon herself to see that Jo's life ran a more ordered, less frantic pattern, and it was this concern that had found Jo, at midday on Good Friday, bundled into Gina's battered blue Citroën.

"It'll do you good to get out of London," Gina had told her, on the way to Bath down the M4. "You can't have another weekend cooped up in that flat."

"I am not cooped up," Jo had objected. "I like it," she added, defending the three rooms she could barely be described as living in. Most of her possessions were still in boxes six months after moving there. The cupboard was very often, as in the nursery rhyme, bare. She lived on milk and cheese biscuits, from what Gina could make out.

"You want to take care of yourself."

A roll of the eyes from Jo. "Gina. I *do*."

Gina glanced over again at Jo's profile and saw a stubborn little grimace of independence.

Whenever people met Jo, they would most commonly screw up their faces, trying to dredge a name to fit the face. "Don't I know you?" was the commonest opening gambit.

Jo's photograph on the top of *The Courier*'s guest column pictured her sitting on a scattering of books and newsprint. The image had been taken from above so that, laughing, she was shown marooned in a little sea of paper, her head turned slightly away, so that sunlight slanted across her face and apparently naked shoulders.

If Gina herself had a characteristic expression, it was a sardonic smile below her rounded, you-don't-say eyes. Somewhere back along the line, Gina was both Indian and Spanish, a mixed heritage from a Jamaican port that the tourists didn't see. Her parents had come to England in the fifties. Gina's father was an engineer, her mother a nurse, and between them they had produced five lusty, forthright, hard-to-ignore children, of which Gina was the youngest. Gina had propelled herself to features editor at *The Courier* by the time that Jo was taken on as a freelance, a babe-in-arms of twenty-two.

Perhaps it was Jo's sheer outlandishness that pleased her friend; the complete refusal to be deterred. Jo's career had been checkered, to say the least. She had dumped university in favor of following a radical student theater group on tour, and had found her way into journalism by gate-crashing the rock-classics concert of Excelsis at the Edinburgh Festival. She had been spotted there by a morning TV show and hired to present their entertainment slot—and by this route, single minded and outspoken, she had arrived at Gina's desk one morning.

Gina's first thought had been that Jo hardly looked painfully young. She was, as Gina's mother would have said, five foot five of fresh air—thin, almost scrawny; antsy with impatience; quick to humor, quick to anger. Her smile hid a sharp, ironic mind. She stuck out her hand that first day and shook Gina's with a fierce grip. It had been quite a job to get her to sit down, such was her enthusiasm to get going.

Sitting now in the city center, looking at her, Gina smiled to herself behind the newspaper page. Jo was stretched out in her chair, eyes closed and turned to the sun. For a second she looked the perfect picture of relaxation. Until she opened one eye, yawned, and tapped the newspaper in Gina's grasp.

"What's the opposition say?" she asked, ruffling her hair and wriggling upright in her seat.

"Nothing radical," Gina said. "Except for that." She held open the paper at the third page. Jo shielded her eyes against the sun and looked at the article.

There was a map on the top right-hand corner—an indented coastline and contour lines of mountains that ran down to the sea.

"What is it?" she asked.

"Greenland," Gina said. "You know Douglas Marshall?"

Jo had to think for a second. "Give me a clue."

"BBC Two."

A long moment went by. "Gardening," Jo guessed at last.

"Not even close," Gina said. "Archaeology. *Far Back.*"

"Ah," Jo acknowledged. "Lots of running about with bits of pottery. Which one was Marshall?" she asked.

"The tall hairy one."

"They were all hairy."

"The smiling one. The ship expert."

"Oh, *him*." Jo vaguely remembered a tall man, habitually dressed in a battered leather jacket. Not a good color. Dirty red. Faded flash. "What's happened to him?"

"He's lost."

"What, there?" Jo asked, glancing at the map.

"In the land of ice and snow, uh-huh."

Jo took the page from Gina and took a second to skim the article. Douglas Marshall had been reported missing while on an archaeological trip in one of the most inhospitable landscapes on earth. She sighed heavily. "This guy's gone on some harebrained personal mission in a snowstorm, and now we're supposed to all go out and find him," she said. She pointed to the final paragraph of the article. "Look, they've actually sent a bloody frigate. What a waste of money."

Gina frowned at her. "You don't mean that."

"I do," Jo countered. "The expense! What has he gone there for, really? Personal glory. Some obsession or other, I bet."

"You cynic!"

"It's true," Jo retorted. "I mean, it's like these other idiots who cross Siberia in a balloon, or something. Hang gliding down Everest, whatever. It's comic-book stuff."

Gina took the page back from her. "Actually," she said, "it's an academic exercise. An expedition."

"Same thing."

"But he could be dying, Jo!"

"Did we ask him to do it?"

"We have to do something."

"Send out the fleet?"

"Yeah, send out the fleet, why not? He's a British subject."

Jo burst out laughing. "What ho," she said. "Wave the flag." She looked away, down toward the traffic.

"So . . . what's the alternative?" Gina asked. "Let him freeze?"

"Yes," Jo said. And she almost meant it.

Jo had almost forgotten the conversation when she went into *The Courier* the following Tuesday. It was ten o'clock, and the building was already busy. She put her head around Gina's door, just to wave hello.

"Hey, come here," Gina called.

"I'm going up to the clippings library," Jo said.

"In a minute," Gina replied. "Sit."

Jo did so. "What is it?" she asked. "Something good? Send me to Cannes, Gina. Look at me. I'll die if I don't get sun."

Gina was sorting through papers on her desk. "Marshall," she said. "I've been thinking about him. He's still missing. I want you to do a piece."

Jo's gaze settled on her. "You're joking. Not the madman."

"No. I want you to go and talk to his wife."

"His *wife?* Ah, Gina. No."

"Why not?"

Jo shook her head. "I can't go steaming in there. And I don't know a thing about him. And I don't really want to either. You *know* that."

Gina nodded, but briefly, the nod dismissing the objection rather than seeing its point. "We haven't heard anything at all from Mrs. Marshall, and that's why I want you to go."

"To talk to her . . ."

"To talk to someone who knows the family."

"Because?"

"Because no journalist has *ever* spoken to Alicia Marshall."

Gina found what she was looking for on her desk. "Here's Marshall's biography," she said, handing Jo five or six stapled sheets. Marshall's pretty upfront, but his wife likes to keep a low profile. Power-behind-the-throne stuff. A lot of money. She's a trustee of the Academy. Rumored to be a bit of a bitch."

Jo raised her eyebrows, interested at last. "Oh, yeah?"

"She was asked for a comment this week, on Monday," Gina said. "And she said, 'No comment.' "

"Who to?"

"The Times."

"Ha," said Jo, amused.

"You've seen the latest on him?"

"No."

"They found the GPS."

"What's a GPS?" Jo asked.

"Global positioning. The one thing you need, a kind of satellite compass. It was dropped on the ice."

Jo hesitated. "It's really not my scene, you know," she muttered. "Can't you send someone else?"

"I've got a hunch," Gina replied.

"What kind of hunch?"

"Dunno. Could be good for you."

"Hmmph," Jo responded, unimpressed. She leafed quickly through the papers in her lap. "I don't even know what he was looking for in ruddy Greenland."

"Medieval settlements. Something about Vikings and Eskimos."

"Oh, thrilling."

Gina ignored her. "The archivist at the Academy in Cambridge is called Peter Bolton." She passed a page of notes across to accompany the photocopies. "He can only see you at eight tomorrow morning. He's teaching all day."

Jo held Gina's eye for a few long seconds, before conceding. She knew the glint in her editor's eye only too well to refuse. "Great," she grumbled, as she packed the papers together.

It was a long way on the tube to Jo's flat. After a full day correcting copy and researching for another piece she was scheduled to interview for on Friday, Jo was still not really interested in Marshall. Riding the stuttering rail, crammed into a car with a hundred other commuters, she only skimmed through his biography.

> Douglas James Marshall, born Ontario 1957. Fellow of Blethyn College, professor of archaeology, specialist in marine sites, special interest Victorian ship construction, chairman Royal Commission 1989–92 Naval Heritage, author of *The Shipwreck Society* (1994), *Under the Mediterranean* (1996), *The Search for the* Caesar Augustus (1997). . . .

Over the last couple of years Douglas Marshall had become the spokesman for the University Exploration Academy, and was regularly wheeled out to comment on anything where a tame historical expert was needed. Plus, he had been a regular on the BBC 2 series. She could bring the title pictures to mind, even see the landscapes, and the stills that the Sunday supplements had used in various articles. But as for Marshall himself, she couldn't visualize him beyond a broad, blurred smile.

When she got home, the light on the answering machine was flashing, and she saw the fax waiting. She ignored it while she showered and made herself a sandwich. Only grudgingly, after she had got out, and wrapped herself in a towel, did she read what Gina had given her.

Alongside Marshall's biography was a copy of the Saturday article.

He had gone missing at a place called Uummannatsiaq.

Frowning, Jo went over to one of the moving firm's boxes, where she rummaged for a moment among the books inside. She emerged with her old school atlas and sat down with it, riffling through the pages.

Uummannatsiaq . . . she couldn't even find it. She looked across from the islands of the Northwest Passage, over Baffin Bay, to Greenland. Even from the map she could see that the coastline there was mountainous and unforgiving. Surely at this time of year there would be ice packed deep into the fjords and way out to sea. If, indeed, the ice ever broke up at these places. She shuddered involuntarily. She had never liked the cold, and the thought of spending even one day in such an unforgiving climate was horrendous. Give her a beach with warm sand, somewhere that you could kick off your shoes and clothes.

She smiled to herself and flicked back through the atlas pages.

The book was a mixed bag of memories. Inside the cover her own childish hand had written her name, followed by the address she'd had at seven: *Rheindahlen JHQ, West Germany.* Her father, a career civil servant, and already fifty when Jo had been born, had been an advisor to the MOD. The atlas pages were grainy and thick, the lettering and layout old fashioned. As her father regularly traveled, it had been her daily ritual when a child to find where in the world Daddy might be. She vividly recalled turning to those countries, known to her even now by the texture of the paper under her fingers. She'd traced her father to places in the world whose very names had become part of his identity. *Kuwait. Singapore. The Falkland Islands.* More islands. Offshore islands like these, swept by wind and current. She looked at the great green sweep of Canada now, fringed with its border of ice.

She closed the page and replaced the book.

As she did so, she paused to look at the frayed red spine of the returned atlas, so out of place among the newer paperbacks, its fabric shedding, showing the cardboard underneath. The expression on her face was impenetrable. She had lost both father and mother in the last five years, and the isolation was still fresh.

Yet people like Douglas Marshall actually chose to exile themselves. She wondered, still staring at the spine of the school atlas, what kind of family she would find, waiting for Marshall's return.

Only as she finally turned out the light did she catch sight of the fax machine again in the hallway. With a cup of coffee balanced in the crook of her arm, she pulled the piece of paper out, and managed to tear it.

Doug Marshall's face, ripped in two, stared back at her.

On the top of the piece of paper Gina had scrawled, *This is your man.*

She slotted the two halves together. It was not a great photo.

Marshall's face was screwed up against bright sunlight. Impossible to guess his age from that shot, though she might have tried at something less than the biography had told her. A frown into the camera, a

backdrop of ocean. He was leaning on a white rail and holding something in one hand. She squinted at the image.

Impossible to say what it was that he was holding. It could have
been a piece of iron, a metal rod, a wooden stick.

She sighed as she trailed to the bedroom.

"Oh, I'm going to love *you*," she muttered as she closed the door.

The Exploration Academy was housed in a Georgian building, set
back in its own gardens. It had once been a private house, whose dis-
creet black railings, ornately finished with complicated patterns of
leaves and vines, separated the residence from the street.

McCullock Road was in the heart of the city, close to Lion Yard, and
by the time Jo got there, just before eight, the traffic was already building up. Cars were backed up in the narrow street, waiting for a delivery
van unloading in front of one of the colleges. A hundred yards away
down the street Jo glimpsed an archway with a wooden door, a green
quadrangle beyond, a red coat of arms on the medieval wall above.

The double glass doors of the Academy led onto a large foyer.
Pressing the doorbell, Jo could see a reception desk, with some sort of
office behind, and glass-fronted cabinets in the hallway. To the left another door opened into a bigger room. To their right was a flight of
stairs.

A woman came out of the office. She smiled at Jo through the glass
as she unlocked the door and ushered her in.

"He's upstairs," she told Jo. "I'll tell him you're here."

She was shown to a chair in the hall.

The place was huge, the ceiling thirty feet high. Jo noticed, now,
that at some time fairly recently the whole of the back of the building
had been remodeled; beyond the flight of stairs the wall was glass, and
a room-wide corridor led to another building, a modern block that
looked like a library.

Several minutes ticked past.

Eventually she got up and walked to the cabinets that were ranged
against the far wall.

She rested her hand on the sloping glass of the first. Under her
palm lay a meaningless scatter of objects and a few sepia photographs.
There was a silver spoon with a copper repair on the handle. The tat-

tered remains of a small book, empty of pages, and what had once been gold initials faded on the front. A tiny piece of red tin or aluminum. A page with a drawing of some kind of engine.

She peered at the photographs. Four men in uniform, only one of them youthful. They had the very posed and rigid look of early Victorian daguerreotypes. Their names were underneath, but she barely read them. Not one was looking directly into the camera. Behind them in the case was a long and narrow map of a waterway.

"Miss Harper?"

She turned.

She hadn't heard him approach, but a man was standing at her shoulder. He was barely her own height, not more than five foot six, and was incredibly round. He held out his hand.

"Peter Bolton."

"Jo Harper."

She liked him on sight: he had the face of an enthusiastic schoolboy. He was overweight, probably more than two hundred twenty pounds, and breathing heavily from the exertion of walking down the stairs.

"Come far?" he asked her.

"London," she said.

"Ah," he replied, commiserating. "Come with me. I've got hot chocolate." He stopped and peered at her. "Do you drink hot chocolate?"

"Yes," she said.

"Good."

They went back to his office. In this assumption, made while she was driving here, trying to visualize both him and the institute, Jo had been right. It was a typical academic's room, so much a cliché that it might have been prepared for a film set. Shelves lined the room floor to ceiling. Books lined the floor. Dust was everywhere. They could just about get in the room by pushing hard on the door, and picking their way over to two chairs marooned in a wash of files and paper.

Bolton fished a thermos from under the desk. "We have a machine here that never works, and we have Mrs. Cropp, who does. But I don't like to bother her," he said, pouring the drink into two plastic cups.

They sipped.

"My phone has never stopped ringing," he said.

"You must be fed up with us all."

"No, no," he replied cheerfully. "I'm very popular all of a sudden."

"Has Douglas Marshall been missing before?"

"No. Never."

"But he's been on expeditions. . . ."

"Oh, yes. The Antarctic, you know. Turkey. Asia. The Caribbean."

"And the Arctic?"

"Yes, twice."

"I see," she said. She glanced around her. "Have you known him long?"

"Over ten years."

"Really?" she said. "I'm sorry. You must be frantic."

He nodded slightly. "Yes . . . it's unlike Douglas. But . . . one tries not to be frantic, exactly."

"But anxious . . ."

"Oh, yes."

"And his wife."

"Alicia?" He stopped. Paused just a fraction too long. "Yes, of course."

Jo smiled. "I would like to talk to her. Is that possible?"

To her surprise Bolton blushed. "No."

The abruptness of the reply took her aback. "A very short interview," she said. "Perhaps a photograph?"

Bolton shook his head. "Alicia never gets involved in the public side."

"Just five minutes. Do you have her address?"

"No, I'm sorry . . . if you want to ask me about Doug's journey, anything about that . . ."

She let it go temporarily. "I might as well tell you, I know nothing about Doug Marshall and I don't understand this passion for Greenland."

"You don't know his background?" Bolton asked.

"Not really."

"Qilatitsoq?"

"No."

Bolton shook his head. He stood up and took a box file from one of the closest shelves. Opening it, he took out a sheaf of papers and began removing pages from among the pile. "I was going to make a press release, if I ever got around to it," he said. "Take a copy. It's Doug's curriculum vitae . . . a couple of articles he's written. . . ."

She took the papers from him. "Thank you."

"The Inuit communities are where he started," Bolton continued. "Because of Franklin. Franklin has been Doug's lifelong passion. Of course, he's done other things—a considerable number of other things—but the Inuit and Franklin were the subject of his original doctoral thesis. That set him off on the Greenland mummies. You've heard of them?"

"I'm sorry."

Bolton ran a hand through his hair. "Six women and two children. Dead for over five hundred years. They were in a magnificent state of preservation."

"Oh . . . like these ones they found in the Andes?"

"Similar. Similar preservation. Cold and dry, you see?"

"And these were . . ."

"Inuit. What we once called Eskimo. Or Esquimaux." He spelled it for her.

"And this is why Doug Marshall is there again, because of mummies?"

"Yes."

"He's found more?"

"Not quite. Doug feels there is one other, a crucial religious site, deeper in the fjord."

"I see," Jo said. But in all honesty she couldn't see. A people living on ice. She couldn't imagine a place dominated by the dark.

"And of course," Bolton said, "there's the Franklin connection."

The phone rang. He picked it up.

Jo sat watching him. She had no idea at all who—or what—Franklin was. She felt her mind go momentarily blank and recognized it as her hitting-the-wall feeling, a sensation she habitually got when her interest in a story waned, or the smell of it left her. A good story had that speeding sensation, and the scent of revelation. There was nothing to reveal here, except a passion for the dead. And even that was an old story. She gently tapped Bolton's desk, to attract his attention.

"How long has he been looking for these other bodies?" she whispered.

He put his hand over the mouthpiece. "Six years."

"*Six . . .*"

Forget that, then, she thought. How crazy did you have to be, for God's sake, to look for six years for dead people in a place that was permanently frozen?

Bolton started to flick the pages of the diary open in front of him. His gaze drifted away, as he listened to the caller on the other end of the line. "He has a *lecture* at two-thirty. . . ."

Jo got to her feet. Taking a piece of paper from her bag, she scribbled on it, *Are you free at lunchtime?*

He glanced at it, nodded, wrote *1:30* on the page. *Perhaps.*

"Thanks," she said.

Going down the stairs, she stopped halfway, thinking.

The world was looking for a man who couldn't be found. And the press were looking for a woman who didn't want to be found.

"We'll see about that," she told herself.

She went over to the reception desk, and the same woman who had shown her in got up from a desk beyond the counter and came over to her.

Jo smiled. "Mr. Bolton's given me the address of Mrs. Marshall, but I don't know Cambridge," Jo lied smoothly. "If I take a right from . . ."

Mrs. Cropp paused only for a second before she glanced down at the map that Jo was holding open in front of her. She shook her head. "Oh, you can't get to it that way," she said. "Go down the 603. You'll come out at the highway. Cross over the bridge and carry on down toward the Eversdens."

Jo took a gamble. She glanced at the map. "And the house is at Little Eversden?"

"No. Pass the Eversdens. But don't get into Haslingfield. That's too far."

Jo gave her her broadest smile, folding the map. "That's great," she said.

"You're welcome."

Well, Jo thought, going out of the door.

Someone's going to get to the wife eventually.

It might as well be me.

*   *   *

According to her road map, which was not greatly detailed, there were maybe ten villages in those twenty square miles. She drove out into a cool, gray-on-green landscape. Roads that had been laid down centuries ago crossed the flat fens. Jo, who had an abiding passion for mountains—or at least a place where there were defined hills and valleys—always felt a little lost in the wide sweeps of East Anglia. The light was high and curious.

She passed a string of houses, bordering each side of the narrow road. The village was there and gone in thirty seconds. A fine mist of rain obscured her windshield. She put the wipers on, negotiated a right-angle turn that appeared from nowhere. The road narrowed further, to the width of a lane, and began to bump through sunken patches. On either side of the road were black-and-white markers, to show flood heights of the river that ran alongside. Ahead she could see a church.

She pulled in close to it and looked again at the map. The Marshalls had to live somewhere close. She imagined it would be a largish house, one known to the locals. Looking up, she saw a man walking his dog. She wound down her window.

"Excuse me," she called, "is Mrs. Marshall's house here?"

He shortened the dog's leash, so that the spaniel wouldn't jump up. "Marshall?"

"Alicia Marshall?"

"Don't know a Marshall," he said.

She drove on. Frustratingly, before long she found herself back at the A603 again. Gritting her teeth, she crossed the main road and headed south.

The rain began in earnest, and the light grew dim enough to need the lowbeams. Just as she switched them on, she saw a sign in the hedgerow, a little black-and-white sign at the edge of a path. But it was a full hundred yards before it registered with her, and she stepped on the brakes.

Franklin House.

It was worth a try.

It was a beautiful mellow stone building, with a steep tiled roof. She guessed at eighteenth, maybe early nineteenth century. A huge magnolia tree so dominated the front of the house that it well nigh obscured the door.

Jo rang the bell. It was a long time before she heard footsteps, and the door was opened.

The woman who had answered was in her early forties and very tall. She wore a dark suit and had dark hair pulled back from her face. She was well groomed and composed, and, if not beautiful, certainly striking.

"Yes?"

"I'm looking for Mrs. Marshall," Jo said.

"And you are . . . ?"

Jo held out her hand. "Jo Harper . . . have I got the right house?"

The woman did not reach out her own hand. "What is it in connection with?"

"I've been speaking to Peter Bolton at the Academy," Jo said.

Alicia Marshall's face clouded. Her mouth turned down in an expression of distaste. "He sent you here?"

"No," Jo replied, "but I was speaking to him an hour ago. I'm from *The Courier.*"

The mention of one of the most prestigious British newspapers sometimes eased the way into a conversation like this one; if it was anything at all, it was at least a guarantee that any story would be intelligently handled. Jo expected to see a softening in Alicia Marshall's face.

Instead the other woman began to close the door.

"I was wondering if you could tell me about this trip," Jo said. "Why your husband went . . . how you feel about such"—she hesitated for a second under the scathing gaze—"such adventures."

For the first time Alicia Marshall smiled. "Adventures?" she echoed.

"Have you heard from your husband?"

"No." The door caught a little on the flagstone floor of the hallway. Alicia pushed it hard.

"You've heard nothing at all? Since he left?"

"No. Now please—"

Jo put her hand on the door frame. "Are you separated?" she asked.

Alicia Marshall gave Jo a lingering look. Then, "You people," she said at last, contempt in her voice.

"Would you speak to me about him?" Jo persisted.

"Please take your hand from the door."

"Are you worried?"

"No."

"I'm sorry? You're not worried at all?"

Mrs. Marshall stared pointedly at Jo's hand.

"Do you think he's alive?" Jo asked.

"I really have no idea."

Astonished at her tone, Jo dropped her hand.

Alicia Marshall shut the door in her face.

For some time Jo remained where she was, staring at the heavy iron knocker. Behind her the rain pattered down through the magnolia. Turning, she glanced up and saw the drops forming on the first half-opened petals on the naked branches.

"Not worried," she murmured.

Past the tree a field stretched away to a patch of woodland. Nothing stirred in the landscape at all, not a blade of grass, nothing in the blue blur of the distant city. It was a picture book, with Douglas Marshall's house delicately penciled in the foreground.

Jo wondered what had happened here, to make a wife want to seem careless of a husband's life or death. And suddenly she felt very sorry indeed for Douglas Marshall.

And very interested indeed in what had taken him away from home.

Two

JOHN Marshall was dreaming.

He knew it, but he couldn't wake up.

He could see his father out on the ice, a long way out, a pinprick of black on a frozen ocean. The sky was a pale eggshell-blue above him. Doug was saying something to his only son—something very important—while he turned his head away, his words swallowed in the vast, flat space.

John looked down.

At his feet, outlined in the snow with curious clarity, were polar-bear prints. All four massive paws had left a closely spaced track: the claws had left long trails between each print. He stepped forward now and put his own foot inside one of the enormous depressions.

When he looked up, his father was gone.

Instead, not twenty yards from him, and rising, on her side, from the ice, was the *Jeanette.*

Shock coursed through him. *You're dreaming,* he thought. *You're at home—in bed—and asleep. It's not real at all.* And yet it did look so real—De Long's pretty little ship, bought in England, wooden hull, steam powered. He moved toward it along the line of bear prints, seeing how they circled the lifeless wreck.

How many years was it since the *Jeanette* had sailed? A hundred and thirty? She was not even a wreck now, but somewhere at the bottom of the ocean, crushed and broken . . . and yet here she was, not a man aboard her.

But him.

He suddenly felt the handrail as he came up the hatchway. He was climbing her with ease, the fluid ease of sleep. Just at the first rung, the rail was puckered and fluted, a lighter color showing in the oak. He knew that for almost two years the *Jeanette* had lived in a deadly, drifting dance. She had sailed free for only a matter of weeks, until the ice claimed her, and had held her, month after cold month, week after frozen week, as she trailed in a helpless triangular journey dictated by the polar drift.

He knew the details of the journey as if he had made it himself.

They had sailed from San Francisco in July 1879. They had passed through the Bering Strait at the end of August. They had been chasing a dream—the fantasy of a Polar Ocean. They had gone confidently north, planning to winter in the Chukchi Sea, believing that, where the Kuro Siwo Current met the Gulf Stream, the ocean would part, the ice would change to warmer water, and that there would be a straight path directly to the Pole.

They chased the dream for three years, and became finally stuck in ice in 1881. On June 11 that year the *Jeanette's* hull suddenly began to murmur—very soft and low at first—as soft as a baby's cry. Then, the ship began to grunt, like a human being receiving a blow to the solar plexus, over and over again.

John murmured in his sleep now, as if he himself were transfixed.

At four in the afternoon the ice suddenly pressed against the port side, jamming the ship hard on starboard. The *Jeanette* immediately keeled over to sixteen degrees, and the starboard ceiling opened over an inch between the beams, and De Long ordered the starboard boats down, and hauled away from the ship onto the ice floe.

The ice, meanwhile, was coming in the port side, raising the port bow and forcing the starboard bow down. In the engine room they saw that the *Jeanette* was breaking in two down its center, and water was pouring into the starboard coal bunkers. On deck the work of off-loading the dogs and foodstuffs went on with a silent desperation, every man momentarily expecting the ice to move again and the ship to split in two. She was warped, twisted like wet paper, the bolts barely withstanding the pressure, the deck slipping to a twenty-degree list, and sliding unstoppably underwater.

Then, suddenly, at five, the ice moved like a locomotive.

The spar deck buckled, and the crew was ordered to take everything—clothing, bedding, books, and provisions—off. As they ran, another broadside collided with the hull, and the ship filled fast with water. It tilted to thirty degrees, and the last of the men got down, trying to pull the whole of the ship's freight clear.

The *Jeanette* hung in the half-light, suspended in its death throes. The crew could hear it, as if it were breathing—its dying voice echoing around them.

She went finally down at four in the morning.

They stood on the floe and watched while the smoke-pipe top flooded and while the yardarms, which had been so far over that they had rested on the ice, righted themselves. *Jeanette* went down almost upright, as if she had wanted to raise her head up as she died and look around her for the last few seconds.

John could almost feel it—almost feel the cold water flooding the timber. Feel the great gulf of ice collapsing over her. For a second, ice flowed through his own bloodstream and invaded his senses. With a tremendous effort he willed himself from her.

He walked away in his dream, following the bear's track, seeing how it mingled, occasionally, with his father's own footprints. He looked at the long gray-and-white miles of the floes, and he shut his eyes tight, so painfully tight that it caused flecks of color, a starburst of blues and oranges, a sprinkling of fireworks. When he opened them, he caught a faint halo around the sun. The cold penetrated his body, through every inch of skin and bone.

He looked around once, to stare at the ghost of the *Jeanette*, the ship that could not be there again in this world. But perhaps he was not in this world.

"Dad!" he called. "Dad . . ."

His voice went barreling away across the ice, silenced in seconds. Thin trails of blowing snow, more like vapor than flakes, were already wiping away the tracks of both the bear and his father. The idea rushed in on him that he was lost, truly lost. He had vanished into the same empty gulf that his father had traveled before him, and there was no way back. No path. No guide. No exit.

He had an urgent desire to lie down on the ice itself.

"John," a voice said.

He was aware of his naked arm.

"John," she repeated.

And slowly he opened his eyes.

Amy Wickham was looking at him.

She had her hand on his arm.

"You," he said.

"Me," she agreed. "You're bloody cold."

John Marshall winced, flexing the arm that had been out of the bed. "I was dreaming," he said. "Jesus, I feel like I'm freezing to death." He grinned at her. "Warm me up, why don't you."

She put her hand under the cover and rubbed the skin of his arm. He caught her hand and turned over and she lowered her face to his.

"You smell good," he murmured.

"I wish I could say the same for you," she told him.

He smiled lazily. He worked at a college bar at night, and last night had been a busy one. He had been bought half a dozen drinks, and now his head was aching. As he lay back in bed, Amy considered his rumpled good looks with a smile. He picked up on her desire. "Get in here with me," he said softly.

She started to laugh. "Not with you stinking like a distillery," she said. "Get in."

She rocked back on her heels, out of his reach. More than pleased to tease him. "What were you dreaming of?" she asked.

He ran a hand over his face and turned away from the glare of the window, where she had drawn the curtains. The sun was pouring in. "De Long," he said. "And the *Jeanette.*"

"Him again," she retorted. "You are truly obsessed, Marshall. Obsessed." She stood up.

"And Dad," he said.

She looked down at him, her expression mixed; somewhere between concern and trepidation. She didn't know what to say to him about his father; Doug was so rarely spoken of normally that it was all uncharted territory for her. Having only known him for a matter of weeks, she felt something like a trespasser. She walked away to the window, twisting a strand of hair around one finger. He had time to watch her as he stretched, trying to shake away the *Jeannette*'s image. He put his hands behind his head and looked at her.

Amy Wickham was his own age, nineteen. She was five foot two, black haired, sturdy rather than slim. He had met her at the end of last term: seen her dancing, alone, on the tiny floor of a pub in town. She must have been wheeling about there for at least ten minutes before he stepped forward to catch her arm and pull her toward him. She had a strong little body, fists raised to the music, hair slicked at the back of her neck.

"When are you going to marry me?" he demanded now.

"Don't be daft," she told him, not even turning her head.

Which was just as well, because there was no way that he meant it.

She turned around and he saw, by contrast, that her expression was serious. The thought of continuing to tease her left him at once, to be replaced with a sudden gut dread.

"What is it?" he said. He sat up.

"It's not your father. There's no news."

Relief plucked the dread away.

"But your mother rang," Amy said.

John sighed, and dragged himself out of bed. He picked up his jeans off the floor, where they had been thrown last night. He didn't ask what Alicia had said.

"Didn't you hear the phone downstairs?"

"No."

"It was ringing when I came through the door. There's some reporter here from *The Courier*, trying to do a family piece on you," she said. She was watching him dress. "A woman. Your mother wants you to go home. Not to talk to her. She said it three times. Her name is Joanne Harper. Not to talk to her."

"I don't want to talk to anyone anyway," John said. He pulled a sweater over his head.

Amy had walked to the table with his computer on it, and was leafing through some of the printouts that he had made last night, after he had come in from work. "What's this?" she asked.

"Nothing you'd be interested in," he told her.

She was holding up a picture, turning it this way and that, trying to make out the detail.

"What is it?" she repeated. "Looks weird."

"Ice drift," he told her. He took the printed page from her and showed her the image. "Lancaster Sound," he explained, tracing the shorelines with a fingertip.

"Yeah?" she asked.

"You remember I told you about this group?" he said. "Eighteen people going after Franklin relics. The Canadian historians. This is from their Web site. This is yesterday's ice drift in the sound, and going south, down McClintock Channel."

"Right," she said.

He smiled at her. "Pretend you give a damn."

She raised her chin, returning the grin.

He slung his arm around her neck from behind, holding the page in front of her face. "Historian people looking for big story," he said, as she wriggled, her breath against his cheek. "Big historian people chasing big Victorian ship, big ship disappeared, men disappeared, whole fucking thing disappeared, never seen again. Lots of cash and kudos for guy finding wreck."

"In all that ice? No way."

"In ice," he confirmed. "Thousand mile wide, yeah. Go *sikkim*."

She feigned a yawn. "*So* boring."

He released her. "No imagination," he said. "That's your trouble."

She shrugged. "I'm mathematics, remember?" she said. "*You're* archaeology." But a second printout on the desk, a photograph, caught her eye. She snatched at it. "Oh, sweet!" she said.

It was a picture of a polar bear, way out on the ice: blue-white ice, with turquoise shadows, a slanting and blinding sun, and the bear's head lowered in the characteristic pose of listening for seal.

John sighed resignedly. "That's not sweet," he told her. "That's the world's largest land carnivore. A killing machine." He pulled the picture away from her grasp. "See the crescent scar on her face?" he said. "This maritime history crew have got a photographer with them, a guy called Sibley. He takes shots like this . . . grizzly, caribou. White bear. They call this one the Swimmer."

"Why?"

"Why d'you think?" John said, grinning. "Because she swims a hell of a long way."

"Excuse me for asking," Amy replied. She looked at the photo again. "But look at its feet. The size of them! Aaaaah. They're just cuddly feet."

This time John didn't even hear her. The enormous predator with the scar across her face, according to the Web site from where these pictures had been taken, was following the course of Franklin's ships almost mile for mile. It was eerie. He considered her, the long neck, the powerful shoulders, the intensity of the bear's look.

Amy had picked up her bag and slung it across her shoulder. She was standing with one hand on her hip, looking at him. "John," she reminded him, "your mother told you to go home. Right now. Today."

John at last tore his gaze from the paper in front of him, flung it onto the desk, and rubbed a hand through his hair. He looked pointedly at the bed, and back at her. He began to smile, a little-boy grin that lit up his face, all innocence and charm.

"But I don't want to go home," he told her.

Jo was driving back to the Academy when the mobile phone, on the seat next to her in the car, rang.

"Jo? It's Gina."

"Hi, Gina."

"Where are you?"

"Driving back into Cambridge," she said. There were traffic lights turning red ahead of her. She eased her foot onto the brake.

"Drive back out of Cambridge," Gina said.

"What?" she thought that she had misheard her.

"Come back here."

"Why?"

"I've had Mrs. Marshall on the phone."

Jo joined the line of traffic. Students were crossing the road, books tucked under their arms. A girl in a tight black T-shirt cycled past. Jo saw the man in the car ahead turn to watch her.

"And?"

"She's furious."

"Why?" Jo objected. "I was politeness itself. You should have heard me. I didn't even get over the doorstep."

"Peter Bolton rang me too."

"But he was perfectly okay!"

"Not now."

"God," Jo breathed. "She came to the door, I didn't argue—"

"She's a trustee of the Academy, remember?" Gina said. "A benefactor, no less."

"And so we aren't allowed to ask her anything?"

"It's not worth it," Gina said. "We can't press it. Private grief."

"He hasn't died," Jo pointed out. "And anyone less like a grieving wife I have yet to witness."

The car behind blew its horn.

The lights had changed.

"Leave it," Gina told her.

There was an opportunity to take a right turn, toward the M6 southbound.

Jo hesitated just for a second before she put her foot on the accelerator, and made for the city center.

She got to the doors of the Academy at one-thirty.

Peter Bolton was just coming out.

When he saw her, his face fell a mile.

"Can I speak to you?" she asked him. He had come out of the doors and was walking down the steps, without stopping for her. She walked at his side, out of the gates, turning along the street.

"I have a class," he said.

"Mr. Bolton . . ."

He did stop then, and looked at her. "You lied to my assistant."

"I'm sorry."

"I did not give you Mrs. Marshall's address."

"No."

He looked exasperated. "Have you any idea how much trouble you've caused?"

"I'm sorry. . . ."

He shook his head. "You can't walk roughshod over people."

"I didn't walk roughshod!" Jo objected. "She seemed to know nothing about what her husband is doing. Did you know that?"

He opened his mouth to say something, then evidently thought better of it. "Nice try," he said.

"Is it a state secret?"

"Yes."

"Is it, really?"

"Yes." He gave the ghost of a smile.

"Is Doug Marshall's visit to Greenland controversial?"

"No, of course not."

"Did he go unprepared?"

"No."

"Is there another issue at stake, other than finding these Inuit relics?"

"Not at all."

"It's just Mrs. Marshall's privacy."

"Yes."

She frowned. "I wasn't at all rude," she repeated.

"That's not the point," he told her. "That you were there at all, that is the point. Aren't your relationships private? Do you want strangers asking pointless questions when you have a crisis?"

But Alicia Marshall had not been in a state of crisis. She had been composed, cool.

"Is Douglas Marshall concerned by his marriage?" Jo persisted. "Has he gone missing because of his marriage?"

This time Peter Bolton laughed out loud. "Because of . . . ? No, no, no."

"He isn't concerned about the state of his marriage? It wouldn't have affected his judgment?" This was the idea that had been preying on her mind. One of those out-of-the-blue hunches, the result of adding two and two and getting five. Douglas Marshall in a life-threatening situation and just not wanting to come home. Seeing no *point* in coming home.

Bolton stared at his feet for a while, then sighed. "What is it," he said, "about his marriage that so fascinates you?" he asked. "His marriage is no different from anyone else's. His marriage in no way affects his professional judgment, and no one else in the country is the least interested in it, which is as it should be."

"But—"

"You really must excuse me," he said. "I'm now late."

She watched him cross the road and walk away.

For a while Jo followed him, not particularly intentionally, but simply because he was heading in the direction of the shopping district. After a while she lost him in the crowds. She dawdled along, irritated at his dismissal and at Alicia Marshall's having rung Gina. It was like being reprimanded by a headmistress. In fact, that was exactly who Alicia had reminded her of—Jo's own headmistress, a buttoned-up virgin, a *Miss* of uncertain age, who favored a beehive hairstyle long after the fashion had died and been buried. She had never once seen the woman smile.

Stopping outside a pub, Jo thought about Alicia. Thought of her smiling. Laughing, even. Thought of opening her arms to welcome her husband home, have a meal waiting, a warm bed.

No, it did not compute.

Alicia Marshall's face was colder than Greenland itself.

Jo shrugged. There was nothing here, other than the fact that Douglas and Alicia Marshall had a terrible relationship, which enabled him to go ice-hopping at regular intervals without a moment of regret. He probably wasn't the kind of man, anyway, to sit down in the snow and weep over his private life.

Yet she wondered. She still wondered.

Most of all, she wondered who Franklin had been, what the lure could be. Someone who, by Bolton's own admission, had been the passion of Marshall's life.

She looked briefly at the blackboard menu, propped on the wall outside the pub, and went in.

Three

THE bear lifted her head. She could hear the plane.

She was on hard-packed floe, and the weather was startlingly clear.

Space lost all perspective here, where there was nothing to measure distance or size. Alone, she was the center of a perfectly flat and featureless world, and the horizon was a line that might have been ten miles away, or twenty. Ice crystals in the atmosphere created a double sun, a central light source with a circle of glowing satellites.

She turned away, toward the dull drone of the aircraft engine.

The Twin Otter was flying low. Richard Sibley, swathed in layers of expedition clothing, sat forward, waiting to take shots through the copilot's window. He had spent the last week at Resolute, begging space from the base there both to stay over and to take whatever flights he might be able to charter now that the historians had left Beechey Island.

When conditions were right, and luck was in, it was theoretically possible to take the kind of photographs that kept him in business. As far as he knew, he was one of only a handful of Arctic specialists. Because you needed to be more than a little crazy, or bloody minded, to endure subzero work.

Still, when the rewards came, they were huge. Last year Sibley's image of a semicircle of bull and cow musk-ox, shielding their yearlings, apparently against a blue-gray blizzard—but in reality against him—made him a good income for a few weeks. The fixed, ochre-glowing eye of the bull ox, almost lost in its prehistoric mane, its brow covered by the base of thickly ridged horns, formed the entire frame of one photograph. Almost, but not quite, lost in the center of the pupil was a faint ghost of the ice ridges on which it stood. It was one of those pictures that stopped people dead in their tracks. It was almost impossible to look away from that primeval glare of endurance.

But the musk were evasive today. After making a fuel run to Prince of Wales Island, the plane was heading back. They were skimming the desolate hills, heading out for Peel.

Sibley had the edge of the island in his sight. Rippled ridges of land—much like the corrugated sand left on a shoreline by a retreating tide—swept underneath him. The colors were hypnotic—gray ridges of stunted vegetation, threadbare lichen, striped with snow. Or what had once, perhaps, been snow. Now, he knew, the consistency would be more like icing sugar or thin flour—powdery, fragile. On the ground the thermometer was at minus thirty; the wind speed about fifteen. The equivalent temperature, down on the approaching sound, was probably about minus sixty, or more. It would freeze his flesh in seconds.

It was just then, as they crossed the indeterminate border between land and icebound ocean, that he saw her.

The bear was standing stock still, though the plane was heading straight for her. As he stared down in amazement, he saw, through the lens, the crescent scar on her forehead. His heart skittered through several uneven beats; she seemed to be looking through him, without even lowering her sights in the familiar pose of aggression, let alone turning away from the engine noise.

They passed over her twice. She might have been carved from stone, her fur shimmering in the oblique light.

He had the most unearthly feeling that she was guarding something, though he knew that she had no cubs yet. There was no tag on her, and no lettering on her coat.

It was as if she had materialized from nowhere.

He ran out of film as they made the third and final pass. Cursing, he reached for another camera, and only then did he see that she had turned away. She was facing down the sound, looking south.

He had that last sight of her, her head slowly swinging from side to side, as if seeking a scent.

And then he lost her again, in the glare of the ice.

Four

JO was at *The Courier* at half past seven the next morning.

Balancing a coffee cup, the morning's edition, and her shoulder bag, she invaded Gina's office, sitting down on the corner sofa. Down the corridor she could hear a few voices, but for the main part *The Courier* was barely awake. She kicked off her shoes, glancing at the mound of papers and memos in Gina's tray. Her editor's computer screen was scrolling her own design, of an aged tortoise meandering across a five-lane motorway.

Jo smiled to herself and began unloading the contents of her bag.

Within a couple of minutes the sofa was covered, not only with the photocopied sheets on Doug Marshall that Gina had originally given her, but with several dog-eared magazines, a couple of sheaves of cuttings, and four videotapes. Grabbing the first, she crossed to Gina's TV and slotted the tape home.

As it rewound, Jo glanced to the river outside.

The day was soft, and still, and gray. The water was high, the tide rushing inland. Over Tower Bridge the traffic already flowed, a tide as constant as the Thames below.

Downstairs, in the public reception areas, *The Courier* had maps showing this exact spot on the Thames from the second century to the present day. There was an artist's impression of Caesar, perched with his legions on the narrowing of the river over the gravel beds at Southwark, preparing to cross to defeat Cassivellaunus. There was the wooden church raised in the seventh century. There were the tenth-century cargoes that in only three hundred years had swamped the whole estuary—ships, in this picture, now streamed past that same crossing.

In the fourteenth-century picture London Bridge at Southwark led to the eighty-one churches in the city, enclosed by the Tower to the east and the River Fleet to the west. The map of medieval London was the first in the group to show wharves on the river, and in Tudor London, quays filled the northern bank.

But by the eighteenth century the Thames had truly disappeared under its floating army of masts; the river was logjammed with ships from every country in the world. Riverside Wapping was congested with alleys holding every maritime trade, and the London docks took most of the country's imports—tobacco, sugar, silks, tea, china, drugs, indigo, rum, coffee, and rice. The East India Docks warehouses held palm oil, elephant tusk, wine, and fruit; the Baltic were stacked high with timber and hemp and linens. Tea and tobacco warehouses and exchanges sprang up by the Pool of London.

The videotape clicked as it reached its start point. Jo walked over and pressed play.

After a moment's static, up came the opening titles of *Far Back*, a television series that had last been shown five years before. Watching it critically, Jo frowned at the amateurish effects of city walls and the cross-section diagrams of ships. As the music died away, it surprised her to see the very image that she had just been looking at from Gina's window: the Thames on a gray morning, the water choppy as the tide turned. She picked up the tape case and checked the black scrawl along its spine. *Episode 4*, it read. *Maritime London, Douglas Marshall.*

Jo flopped down on Gina's sofa, and pressed the volume up on the remote. Doug Marshall came into view, standing on London Bridge, looking east on a winter morning. Jo considered him while unconsciously chewing on her thumbnail. She had remembered now the thick thatch of sandy hair, the tall, almost awkwardly long-limbed body. And the smile.

"When I was a kid," Marshall began, "I didn't much like boats. The thing I wanted for my ninth birthday was a bike." His grin became even broader. "A massive bike with a racing saddle, but there you go. I got a book about a boat."

He turned to lean on the parapet.

"It wasn't even a new book," Marshall went on. "I don't know where my mum had laid her hands on it. It was called *Arctic Explorations.*"

Jo pulled both knees up to her chest and wrapped her arms around them.

"Maybe the spine caught her attention," Marshall said. "There was a guy with a mustache about a foot long, and he was dressed in a fur coat and he was holding a saw, and he was using the saw to cut through a huge thickness of ice to get to a seal swimming underneath." Marshall started to laugh. "That was more like it," he said. "Going after a seal with a saw." He shrugged. "Nine-year-old boys are like that," he said.

Jo smiled in response.

Marshall was gesturing along the length of the river in front of him.

"You see an empty river now," he said, "compared to Franklin's time. Sir John Franklin, who set out from just down this same river in 1845, would have known a city within a city, where every language of the world was spoken and every commodity that could be traded changed hands. The West India Docks were half a mile long, berthed six hundred ships, and were surrounded by a twenty-foot wall. And they weren't the only ones. Farther down still was the Admiralty's Royal Victualing Yard at Deptford."

Marshall turned back to the camera, looking straight into the lens, his expression now more serious. "Vanished," he said, "like Franklin himself, and the greatest maritime nation on earth."

The office door suddenly opened. Gina paused a moment before coming in, taking off her coat. "Make yourself at home, why don't you," she observed mildly.

Jo smiled. "Hello," she said. "Sorry. Won't be long."

Gina hung the coat up. "What're you doing?"

Jo waved the tape case at her. "I got these from a guy at the BBC this morning," she said.

"He must work the night shift," Gina observed, opening a polystyrene cup of coffee.

"He does."

"Want some?"

"Um . . . no."

"Bacon roll?"

Jo grinned. Gina put a paper bag on the desk, opened it, tore the hot bacon baguette in two, and gave Jo half. They sat watching the screen. Jo had pressed pause, and Doug Marshall's face was blurred in the shot.

"Ever heard of Franklin?" Jo asked.

"Benjamin?"

"John."

"Give me a clue."

"Victorian."

Gina considered. "No. Never heard of him."

Jo finished her breakfast, wiping her fingers on a scrap of paper from the wastebasket. Then she reached for the nearest sheet from the pile on Gina's couch. "You wanted me to find out about Marshall, I found out about Marshall," she said. "You know what really drives him? Some Victorian explorer called Franklin."

"Excuse me," Gina interrupted.

"You know who Franklin was?" Jo went on. "He went to the Arctic to find the Northwest Passage. He set out in 1845 with two enormous ships and a hundred thirty–odd men, and they all disappeared. Just like that. Just vanished into thin air."

"Excuse me," Gina repeated.

"What?" Jo asked.

"Did you miss a day?" Gina said. "The one where I asked you to stop chasing up Marshall? There is no angle on this story, Jo."

Jo smiled. She shoved the papers in Gina's direction. "Look at those," she said. Gina looked down on a printout from an Internet search engine.

> Franklin, Sir John . . .
> 1–10 out of 1,264.

"Franklin, Sir John," Gina said. Her index finger traced an entry. *"Gaaad . . . "* She shook her head. "John Franklin born 1786, Arctic explorer . . . command of an expedition in 1845 . . . blah blah . . . some forty expeditions were sent to look for traces . . ."

"Forty," Jo repeated. "Victorian England went crazy trying to find him."

Gina gave her a deeply quizzical look. "And so?"

Jo sighed. "Nothing so," she retorted. "Just interesting." She flicked the tape on again. "Here he is," she said.

The picture on the screen had changed. Now Douglas Marshall was standing in central London, near Admiralty Arch, his fingers tracing a bronze plaque. The camera panned back from the close-up of the memorials to the Franklin crews.

"It wasn't only the Victorians who had an obsession with finding the Northwest Passage," Marshall said, "that elusive—and some said illusory—route over the top of the world. John Cabot started it in the 1490s, when he said that there must be a way to the Orient through the ice." Marshall glanced back at the plaque. "The hypnotic lure of tea and silk and dusky maidens was all it needed for any man worth his salt to start packing his bags," he observed.

He walked forward. Behind, the traffic of Waterloo Place could be seen threading its way along the road. "Cabot started an Arctic rush," Marshall went on. "Martin Frobisher in 1576. John Davis in 1585. Henry Hudson, in 1609, who was the first man ever to overwinter in the Arctic, and who—along with his son—was cast adrift in a small boat by his mutinous crew. Button . . . Baffin . . . Parry . . . Ross, who tackled both the Antarctic and the Arctic, and found the North Magnetic Pole."

"Jo," Gina said, "it's a detail, but I sometimes work here."

"Sorry?" Jo said, not taking her eyes off the screen.

"This is my office," Gina reminded her.

By way of reply Jo leaned forward to catch what Marshall was now saying.

"The Victorian British, with their mastery of the universe and of everything that crept on the face of the earth—including a few dark continents—were convinced that, if any generation at all was destined to conquer the route, it was them. What was the Passage, after all?" Marshall asked. "Just a few short miles of ice. What was that to the greediest colonizing nation in the world? What were the months of darkness, and the strongest sea currents on the planet? The finest nautical minds of the age talked about it as if it were an afternoon jaunt, brushing aside a few natives, bears, and bits of tundra. So"—Marshall sighed—"they sent their best. They assembled the finest ice masters, royal marines, able seamen, stokers, sailmakers, blacksmiths, quartermasters, carpenters, doctors, and engineers, and Sir John himself, a mere slip of a lad at fifty-nine, and Her Majesty's Ships *Erebus* and *Terror* sailed from Greenhithe on May 19, 1845. The best-equipped polar expedition that ever set sail."

Music swelled over the sound of Doug Marshall's voice, and his image dissolved into a shot from the prow of a masted boat.

"The ships were low in the water," Marshall's commentary now began. "Weighed down with stores and equipment, and fantastic amounts of food. They had over thirty-two thousand pounds of beef, thirty-two thousand pounds of pork, thirty-three thousand pounds of preserved meat, thirty-six hundred gallons of spirits, two hundred gallons of wine, seven thousand pounds of tobacco, and twenty-seven hundred pounds of candles. Not to mention a hand organ that played fifty tunes, a hundred Bibles, and a dog called Neptune."

Gina, who had started the process of checking her e-mail, paused, her hands hovering above the keyboard. Then she put her glasses on and leaned on the desk, staring at the screen. "That's some stack of victuals," she murmured.

But Jo wasn't listening. Her gaze was fixed on the TV.

"Although they were bark-rigged sailing ships," Marshall continued, "they both had railway steam locomotives belowdecks. Specially adapted for the trip, the trains had been stripped of their front wheels, but they still weighed fifteen tons a piece." He smiled, shaking his head at the improbability of it. "Imagine the room they took up in the holds," he said. "Partly because of them, stores were packed everywhere, above- and belowdeck. And just to add to the weight, the ships' hulls were blanketed with iron to protect them against the enormous power of pack ice."

The screen images clouded, the soundtrack rising with the noise of a fierce gale. Spray flecked the lens as the bows plunged into a stronger current. Chasing out from the Thames estuary and into the waters of the North Sea.

"On July fourth the ships restocked at Greenland," Marshall said. "They were seen by the whaling ships *Enterprise* and *Prince of Wales* on July 28, as they entered Lancaster Sound. But neither they—nor any of their crew—were ever seen again."

Finally, Jo stopped the tape.

She turned to Gina.

"It's what he chases," she said.

"Who?"

"Douglas Marshall."

"Marshall, yeah, hmm," Gina commented.

"But you see?" Jo demanded. "He's the expert on Franklin. He's been looking for those ships for years. He found a canister from one of them—" She leaned over and tapped the papers she had given Gina. "It's in there somewhere. Both ships had little copper canisters that they wrote messages for, then sealed up and threw overboard. They were a kind of marker. But only one was ever found, in Greenland. Until Douglas Marshall found another one four years back."

"What did it say?" Gina asked.

"It's in those papers," Jo told her.

Gina was tempted to look but stopped herself. "Look, Jo—"

"Do you think he went to Greenland looking for another canister?" Jo asked.

Gina crossed her arms and looked steadily at her. "Did you see the item?" she asked.

"What item?"

"This morning."

Gina took the morning copy of *The Courier* and flipped it open to the third page. Halfway down, below the photograph of a Royal Navy helicopter, was an article.

Blizzards Force Search Teams Back

The overnight search for the British scientist Douglas Marshall and his Inuit guide was last night called off until first light, following the worst weather conditions in the search area in living memory.

Marshall, 39, Professor of Archaeology at Cambridge's Blethyn College, went missing four days ago in the Uummanniaq Fjord in northwestern Greenland. . . .

Jo glanced back at Gina.

"They'll never find him out there," Gina said.

Jo said nothing. She was reading, and then rereading, the article.

"I see the angle," Gina said. She fisted her hand and pressed it to the top of her desk. "The vanishing explorer. He's relived his hero's life."

To her surprise Gina saw Jo color slightly. The younger woman turned the page and carefully folded the newspaper. Then she walked slowly to the window.

Looking at Jo's turned back, Gina frowned for a moment. Then a small light dawned on her face. For a moment her expression was all astonishment.

She got up, walked around her desk, and drew level with Jo.

"You wanted him to freeze, remember?" she said. "Only last weekend you wanted him to freeze."

Jo's expression betrayed no emotion at all—not a flicker—as she gazed at the river.

John Marshall let himself into his father's third-floor flat in Cambridge.

There was mail behind the door, almost two weeks' worth. He hesitated a fraction, then picked it up, putting it on the first flat surface to hand.

Although his father had given him a key, John didn't like to come here. The key was nothing more than a token, something that Doug had offered when he had first moved in, but it was made plain that it was only for emergencies.

He wondered if Doug would call this an emergency. He could hear him now. "What made you think I wasn't coming back?" he would say, with his concentrated, smiling stare. "What the hell made you think that?"

John smiled grudgingly to himself as he walked through the hall to the sitting room. Oh, only a couple of near-as-dammit obituaries on the TV. Only Peter Bolton's face when John had seen him last night, catching him at the lecture theater at six, and seeing Bolton's ashen look.

"Is there news?" Bolton had asked.

"No," John had said. "I thought you might have heard."

Bolton had put an arm around his shoulder and given him a ghost of a smile. "I won't tell him you were worried, and you won't tell him I was worried," he said.

John bit his lip now, walking to the window and staring out at the view.

The air in the flat smelled musty and damp. It was a three-room front in the high Victorian apartment building, looking out over Parker's Piece, and the trees in the narrow garden overshadowed the living space. There was a single bed in one corner of the main room, covered with a red throw. A couch that had seen considerably better days. A gas heater hooked onto the wall. In the corner opposite the bed, past the second floor-to-ceiling window, was a kitchen area—just a couple of counters, two small gas rings, a half-dozen cupboards.

His father had lived here for five years; although Alicia, John's mother, would deny it. She always pretended that Doug still lived at home, at Franklin House. And as though to prove it she always kept his study dusted, with books arranged on the desk. She put flowers in there. She opened the windows, and cleaned and dusted it, and turned his chair around so that the cushions didn't fade in the sun. She even had Doug's clothes on the right-hand side of the wardrobe in her bedroom. She still slept on one side of the bed, with Doug's side turned down. There were books on his bedside table; not as he would keep them, of course, in a haphazard stack that spilled onto the floor, but neatly laid out in a row of three. To one side of the books was his father's watch, the old thirties Rolex that had belonged to his own father. John always looked at that watch, which, until five years ago, had never left Doug's wrist, and now lay abandoned. Doug had forgotten it in the storm of the final morning at Franklin House. The fact that he had never come back for it, never even asked John to bring it—not that Alicia would let him—was somehow more poignant, more meaningful, than anything else. Even than his empty chair at dinner.

John walked over to the little kitchen. There wasn't much food. He checked the fridge, took out a carton of milk, opened it, and poured it away down the sink. There was a pack of bacon, still in date. Two eggs. A loaf going green. John found a shopping bag, stuffed the loaf inside, and put it down, ready to take out.

Outside, the sun was trying to come out. It cast a watery light over the room, touching the desk under the window: the computer, books, and telephone. There was no answering machine. John sat down at the desk and tilted the chair backward, running fingers over the arms with their rounded edges, the size of a man's palm. He curled his fingers over.

"He's coming back," he told the view of Parker's Piece, the few morning pedestrians hurrying across it, the dog that was running in decreasing circles, the man on the bike who had stopped halfway across.

John had gone home last night, but only after trying to get out of it. He had rung Alicia, trying to find a good excuse.

"You ought to be here."

"I have classes."

"No one would expect you in class."

In the long pause he could hear the clock in Alicia's hallway ticking.

"You ought to be here," she'd repeated.

He had gone, hitched a lift to the village.

She had been waiting for him as he opened the door. She must have watched him walk up the drive, and yet she'd not opened the door, but waited for his key in the latch.

"Darling," Alicia had said, holding out her arms.

He'd given her a kiss.

"Are you hungry?"

"Don't worry."

"I do worry," she said.

They had eaten in the dining room, not the kitchen. She had had it decorated.

"Do you like it? It's Russian red."

"It's loud." He'd smiled.

"It's actually a period color," she told him.

They had finished the meal in silence. It was an atmosphere he had grown used to in that house.

It was hard to say when the war between his parents had begun. Perhaps before he even had any memories of them. His first picture of his mother was long before they had moved out to the village. He had a memory of an enormous staircase in a house something like this one; they rented a first floor set of rooms—he could see his mother now, the flat-heeled shoes passing him as he sat, rebelling against something she had said, on the stairs.

"Stay there all night, then," she'd told him.

They had a scratchy, moquette-covered couch, a black-and-white television, and a carpet shedding long threads that he used to pull. He remembered her as constantly moving, and constantly talking. His father would be there at odd times—bleary eyed and monosyllabic in the morning, absent at night, or turning up very late, carrying his cases up those long, wide stairs.

"Your father is traveling," Alicia would say. He could still—just—recall when she said it with warmth in her voice. Pride.

From a baby—from the first time he could form a rational thought about the cases and the absences—he'd wanted to go with his father.

"Where is he now?" he'd once asked. He must have been about six. "I want to go there."

She'd brought a map from the bookshelf, unrolled it, made him sit in front of it at the desk.

"You see this island? This is where we are. This is England," she'd told him. Her finger had trailed out to sea, crossed an endless width of blue. "You see this other island? Jamaica. In the West Indies. You see where it says?" She'd rolled the map back up, pushed it onto a shelf where he couldn't reach it. "That's where he is," she'd said. And then she'd suddenly reached down to hold him, clutching him to her. "You'd want to leave your mummy?" she'd said. "Leave me all alone?"

His gaze had edged back to the rolled map. "What's he doing?" he'd asked.

She'd let him go. "Diving in water."

"What for?"

"To find buried things."

For a long time he imagined his father diving into a warm sea, over and over, for fun. Only later did he grasp that Doug's diving actually involved air tanks and endless hours of laborious work. During Jamaica—Doug had been gone for four months—John had waited with horrible impatience for his father to come back. He'd been convinced that his father would be loaded down with pirate booty. They had waited at Gatwick, John almost overcome with excitement at the idea that Doug would have gold cups and rings stuffed in his case, things that he would give to him, things that John could keep in his bedroom. He had even cleared a space for them on his bookshelves, for the treasure that he would show his friends.

But Doug had come back empty handed. "You can't take anything away," he'd explained to his son. "It has to be recorded. And it doesn't belong to me, even if I find it."

Ten years later, of course, he'd kept the Franklin cylinder.

Cheat.

There were trips in the UK that Alicia had visited. Portland, Lyme Bay. What age had John been then? Seven? Eight? No more. Memories of sitting in a windswept cliff hotel. Of The Cobb at Lyme slippery with seawater. Of dark seaweed on Lyme's beach, and a tearoom perched on the very edge, through whose steamed-up windows John had peered anxiously.

Doug had taken his son out on the dive boat one day at Lyme. It was John's initiation into marine work. A gift and a test. John had read all the books about Lyme's dozens of wrecks, all the dates, all the positions. He could name them and the dates they had foundered. He could even name some of the cargoes. He'd been fired up to show his father what he could do. He'd promised to help check the equipment, watch for his dad's times, look at the tank's air supply. Even make the tea. Alicia had showed him at home how to brew the kettle and fill the thermos. He'd practiced. He had wanted his father to be proud.

It could not have gone worse. He'd thrown up for five solid hours and had been returned to Alicia like a wet rag. He didn't even know about seasickness when he'd set foot on that boat, but he sure as hell knew all about it by the time that it was five hundred yards from shore. He'd gripped the boat rail while the tide heaved. Watched his father's descent into the gray-green murk, the trace of slithering bubbles on the waves. And suffered the complete soul-burning disgrace of being curled up on deck, feeling that the world had come to an end—or at least had been reduced down to a few yards of spattered planking that wouldn't keep still even in a stiff breeze—by the time Doug finished the dive.

"We've got to make a sailor of you," Doug had told him, frowning at the sight of him. "Jesus, J., look at the state of you." He'd put a hand over his mouth, then laughed. "You stink, my man."

I hate you, John had thought, eight-year-old grief welling up in his chest.

"I dived with my dad," he'd told the kids at school. He never told them he'd puked up over most of the crew and been sent back to Mother by midday.

When he was ten, Doug had offered to take John to Port Royal. But Alicia had drawn the line at Jamaica. It was too long, she said. Two weeks, in the height of summer. What was she expected to do with herself for two nights, while they sunned themselves?

They went to the Royal Dockyards at Portsmouth instead.

"It rains in Jamaica too," Doug had told him, trying to cheer John up the first morning. They were standing in line to see the *Victory*. John was vastly disappointed: the glamorously painted black-and-gold timbers were too much like the pirate ship in Disney World. He wanted to see the kind of ships his father worked on: he had looked for hours at report photographs, and knew that the only really interesting stuff was a raft of carefully numbered fragments.

The wreck of the royal yacht of Henry VIII was more like it.

"I knew some of the crew who raised her," Doug had told him, as they went through to the *Mary Rose*. They looked in the museum at the registered remains: the worsted clothing, the bronze muzzle-loading guns, the mattress packing, powder scoops and powder flasks and arrows and yew longbows.

His father had stood for some time, deep in thought, before one of the displays. John had wanted to hold his hand. He tried hard to resent him and all the times he had not been at home, and all he could find in his heart that day in Portsmouth was this overwhelming hope that his father would put his arm around his shoulder, or grasp his fingers. He wanted his hand to be gripped, to feel his father's skin. He wanted to bring Doug back from wherever he had drifted to.

But his father never really came back to them at all. Even when he *was* home, even when John was sitting next to him in the car or watching TV, or at the dinner table, he would look up and see a familiar expression on Doug's face: he wasn't with them. He would be immersed, instead, in some private, inner picture. He would be at the wreck of the *Lord Western* in British Columbia, suspended in a murky tide over the ship's log cargo in Sydney Inlet. Or near Nice, in the middle of the Baie de Villefranche-sur-Mer, fifty feet down, the wreck leaning forty-five degrees to port in sand and mud sediment, the wreck that had been sunk in a hurricane in 1516 with her transport of artillery. Or he would be in

Aboukir Bay in Egypt, on the body of *L'Orient,* which went to the bottom in August 1798, blown to her death by Nelson off the beaches west of Alexandria.

Nowhere that he could ever be reached.

By the time John reached sixteen, he no longer wanted to go anywhere with Doug. He'd given up on ever commanding his father's true attention. He'd accepted, with adolescent bitterness, that he was somewhere in the sidelines of Doug's life. That he came maybe second. Maybe third. Maybe fifth, sixth, or worse, after dozens of sea-covered ships. He came after Franklin, he suspected. The Franklin enigma that constantly preoccupied his father, especially after Greenland. He suspected that he meant less to Doug than Franklin or Crozier, Franklin's first officer. Crozier, the one that supposedly survived for a long time after Franklin, who had lived out on the ice after the ships sank. The hero Crozier, trying to command over a hundred dying men after *Erebus* and *Terror* went down. He grew hot, stifled, at the idea of these men who lived in his father's heart.

"I'm fucking alive," he wanted to say. "I'm not a dead hero. I'm alive. . . ."

That was where the first thought of eclipsing his father's achievements had begun, he supposed. It was a secret he had silently nourished for some time now. Years. Maybe all of five or six years. The thought had grown in his head until it seemed it had always been there, a kind of preordained quest. He dreamed of finding what his father had never been able to find. Some relic of the Franklin expedition. Some astonishing clue. Maybe even a last journal from the ships. Perhaps then his father would give him some respect, for the first time.

Much as he tried to keep the bitterness out of this picture, he found that whenever Doug was the center of attention, as he was now, a mean little voice would inhabit his head, a voice full of teenage grief that would build itself to a fury. He leaned his head on his hands now, picking at the leather seam of the chair. He had an incredible, irrational urge, sometimes, simply to punch his father's face. Just to get him to look . . . really look. The pain between them might almost be worth it, he thought, if he could see a flash of realization in that older face. See something like *My God, I've hurt him. Like this. Like blood on the fist. Blood in the mouth.*

He sighed deeply now, rubbing his hands over his hair. He stood up, stretched. He looked around at the bookcase, stuffed full of site reports. His eye trailed along the titles on the spines, the names of excavations.

The year that John was sixteen, there had been an excavation in Turkey at Serçe Limani, a Hellenistic wreck that had been carrying a wine cargo when it had gone down in the eleventh century. That name—the very name he could see right now, in Doug's handwriting on one of the reports—held a crucial meaning for them both.

Doug had arranged for John to go with him to Turkey. It had been done as a birthday present. A coming of age.

"I don't want to go," John had told Doug.

His father had been surprised. He had already bought the flight tickets, and had been holding them in his outstretched hand.

"Don't worry about your mother, I've spoken to her about it," Doug had said.

John knew. He'd heard the argument.

"I don't want to go," John had repeated.

Doug had stared at the tickets, then back at his son. "It's three weeks in Turkey, in the summer," he said, still mystified. "Look, we go from Gatwick—"

"I'm not going."

Doug had put the tickets, slowly and carefully, on the table between them. "Why?" he'd asked.

"Does there have to be a reason?"

"Yes, John. There does."

"Because you've spent the money," John said.

Doug had frowned. "Well, yes, I've spent the money. . . ."

"I didn't ask you to."

"No," Doug said. By now it was obvious that he was trying to keep his voice level and calm. "But the money doesn't matter. I want you to dive with me, John. I want to teach you to dive."

"Well, I don't want to dive."

"You don't?"

John had leapt up from his chair, blushing at his own lies and the inexpressible fury that coursed through him. He had wanted to go with Doug for years, of course.

"I'm going to Cornwall this summer," he'd said. True, but only a loose arrangement.

"To do what?"

"To surf."

There had been a long pause. "I didn't know you liked to surf," Doug told him.

"Well, that's just it," John had retorted. "You don't know a fucking thing about me, do you?"

John clenched his fists now, as he stared at the site report, tears tight in his throat.

There had been other invitations, and John had accepted them. But they were not surprises, and he and his father were never relaxed together. Serçe Limani always came between them.

The doorbell rang.

John looked over his shoulder in surprise. He took a deep breath, shook his head at his memories. He went over to the window and looked out.

A girl was standing on the step below him. He couldn't make out much of her. He opened the window. She stepped back, reading from a scrap of paper in her hand.

"Yes?" he called.

She looked up.

"I'm trying to find John Marshall," she said.

He stared down at her. The first thought that came to his mind was that the upturned face was not English. In fact, it was like no other face he had ever seen. Not here. Not in this country.

"Wait there," he called.

He ran down the stairs two at a time, his heart thudding with anticipation, and opened the door to her.

She was smiling a little, standing half on and half off the step.

"You . . ." he said.

"I'm sorry?"

"I've seen you," he said.

She adjusted the bag on her shoulder.

He could do nothing but stare at her. She was tall, perhaps a little taller than he. She must have been five foot ten, maybe eleven. She had dark hair, tied back. A loose ponytail draped over her shoulder. He suddenly felt incredibly awkward and stupid. How could he say to her, "You're like the women in the books." She wouldn't know which books. She wouldn't know about De Long, or Kane, or McClintock, or any of the others. And yet . . .

"Where do you come from?" he asked.

"I'm at King's," she said. She held out her hand to him. "My name is Catherine—"

"John Marshall," he replied, grasping her fingers.

He held on too long; she glanced down at his grasp on her hand. Releasing her at once, he did a thing he could never recall having done before. He blushed beet-red. This was what it was like, then, he thought, to be faced with your own fantasy. Here was a woman from the McClintock and Kane journals, an Inuit girl with a black snake of hair down her back, looking at him with the same kind of slightly knowing expression that he had seen in photographs from the last century.

Fantastic. Impossible. He actually blinked, half expecting her to have vanished when he reopened his eyes.

"I'm sorry," he said. "You really remind me of someone. People. Some people I've read about."

Stop gabbling, he told himself silently. *Stop that, for God's sake, before she turns tail and runs.*

But the girl did not run. Instead, she calmly finished her original introduction. "My name is Catherine Takkiruq," she told him. "Could I talk to you," she asked, "about your father?"

At eleven that same morning, Jo was in Westminster Abbey.

She had intended to go to the House of Commons—there was a contact there, a journalist for one of the tabloids, who had promised her useful background for an interview with an MP that she had scheduled next week. But at the last moment she found herself outside the doors of the Abbey, standing in line at the ticket desk.

The place was heaving with tourists. Standing looking up at the ornate doorway, Jo had realized that, despite working in London for the last four years, she'd never actually been inside the Abbey. She'd never been inside St. Paul's, or the Tower of London, for that matter. She didn't know anyone who lived in London who had either.

The queue moved forward, into the relative darkness of the

church, and Jo asked the attendant behind the counter where the John
Franklin memorial was.

"Around to your left, first on the left."

She followed the crowds, slowing down as they slowed, surprised by
the atmosphere. Probably more than a thousand people were inside
this church, but it still dominated them. The roof soared above a
wealth of gilt and marble; the voices were hushed by the sheer size. Jo
stopped when she had gone a few yards, and fished the papers about
Franklin out of her bag. She had run off some sheets from one of
the Web sites, and shuffled them now, looking for the description
of the memorial.

There was a lot she didn't need—the muster lists of the crew, for instance. Her eye traveled rapidly down them.

The printout was from an American university; their history faculty
was apparently manned by Franklin obsessives. They had listed every
single name from the *Erebus* and *Terror.*

Next to each name was a brief biography, compiled, the Web site
had noted, from O'Byrne's *Naval Biographical Dictionary,* published
1849. Just four years after they sailed, Jo thought. The faces and voices
and careers of these names would have been fresh in people's minds
when their portraits were drawn up.

Lieutenant Graham Gore, entered the Navy in 1820.

Jo tilted the page to the side, to get more light from the high chan-
cel windows.

Took part in the Chinese war . . . portrait in the Royal Naval Museum . . .
"He plays the flute dreadfully well, draws sometimes very well, and
sometimes very badly. . . ."

Jo smiled. She drew pretty badly too. She couldn't even sketch a map.

Lieutenant James Walter Fairholme . . . captured by the Moors in
April 1838 when second-in-command of a captured slave-ship. . . .
Harry Goodsir, acting assistant-surgeon and naturalist . . .
Captain Francis Rawdon Moira Crozier, born in County Down in 1796,
second-in-command, an authority in terrestrial magnetism . . .

James Reid, ice master, a whaling captain, "rough, with a broad North Country accent, but honest hearted . . ."

And there were boys, two on each ship.

She bunched the papers together and walked on, looking to the left to see where the small chapel would be. When she found it, she saw that a vast marble monument to General Wolfe dominated the entrance. Jo glanced up at it, and read its inscription.

Slain in the moment of victory . . .

She looked at Wolfe, lying in the arms of his men, under the flag.

Did anyone die like that anymore? she wondered.

Perhaps in battle. She thought of Bosnia, of muddy erratic trenches through a hillside. Were there any great national causes anymore? She had interviewed so many people who saw their country only in terms of their own success or failure. She hardly ever heard anyone—even those in government—refer to their country's glory. And yet men like these had died for exactly that, the greater glory of an idea.

She went into the chapel and passed Franklin without seeing him. She turned at the end and came back. Only then did she notice the modest little portrait halfway up the wall.

A marble bust of the commander, in uniform and wreathed in what looked like a fur cape, stared out into the main body of the Abbey. Below him *Erebus* and *Terror* were carved in marble. The ships were shown with their rigging weighed down with ice and icebergs encroaching onto the decks.

As she stopped and looked at it, tourists pushed past.

"Franklin," said an American voice. "Not ours."

She smiled to herself. Like her, all anyone knew of the name belonged to another man on another continent. She read the small, neat lettering.

To the memory of Sir John Franklin
Born April 16, 1786, at Spilsby, Lincolnshire, Died June 11, 1847, off Point Victory in the frozen ocean, the beloved Chief of the Gallant Crews who perished with him in completing the discovery of the North-West Passage.

She edged around the side, trying to get out of the way of the crowds. There was another carved inscription on the edge of the marble, almost hidden from view.

This monument was erected by Jane, his widow,
Who, after long waiting, and sending many in search of him, Herself departed to seek and find him in the realms of light July 18, 1875, aged 83 years.

Jo felt a lump come to her throat. Jane Franklin, his wife. Who had waited for him for thirty years.

Frowning, she looked down again at the papers she was carrying. She couldn't find a mention of Franklin's death. How did they know the date of it, if he and the ships had gone missing? It was so precise too. July 11, 1847. That was two years after they'd left London. He had died in the Arctic, in the ice, and someone knew the exact day.

"Frozen ship," a voice said, as they edged past her. A small boy traced his finger along the picture of the icy hulls.

"Looks like they got caught somewhere," his father said, as they walked on.

Jo followed the line of the boy's finger, and farther down to the base of the memorial, where a second plaque had been added.

Here also is commemorated Admiral Sir Leopold McClintock
Discoverer of the fate of Franklin

She looked at the name for some time.

McClintock, she scribbled on the top of the photocopy of the crew list.

Retrieving her bag from the floor, she edged out into the main aisle again, where there was more room. She got herself out of the crowds as best she could, and glanced down again at the photocopied sheets.

There were so many names.

Graham Gore . . . Harry Goodsir . . . Francis Crozier . . .

She glanced back again at the Wolfe monument at the chapel entrance. All those people, she thought, dying for England. She felt something rise in her chest, a claustrophobia, a reaction against the waste of life. They took boys too . . . two boys, for God's sake, in subzero temperatures for years on end. And for what purpose, to what end? No ships ever went north of Canada or Alaska now, from west to east, or vice versa. You just couldn't. It was all blocked off with ice. It was pitch black half the year. You couldn't fight down one of the world's greatest natural forces. You couldn't defy it with a couple of ships. Even the few Russian icebreakers who could get through were nuclear powered. And yet the Victorians had filled their ships with their best men, men like Graham Gore. Who couldn't paint.

"What the hell did he need to paint for, anyway?" Jo muttered. "Poor man."

She turned away, into the crowd.

Five

AUGUSTUS Peterman was twelve years old in 1845.

He stood at the dock at Greenhithe and shivered. Not because he was cold; it was May, and the day was warm, and there was a breeze like summer coming up from the Channel and traveling here from his aunt's house in Kent. He had come down lanes between orchards where the last blossom was still on the trees.

It was the sight of the ship that had set him trembling. The _Terror_ towered over him, wide in the beam, with its almost two-foot square ribs rising out of the water. She was massive, breathtaking, beautiful.

Augustus knew her name. Every boy in England did. When he had first come onto the dock that morning, he had dared to run right to her mooring, to touch the only part of the stern that he could reach. This was the ship that nine years before, when he was only three, had gone to the Antarctic, the bottom of the world, and been heaved completely out of the water by ice, and lain on it like a helpless toy, dismasted, until the will of God and the skill of the crew had released her.

He leaned hard on _Terror_'s side, in the shadow of the great ship, his heart pounding with ecstatic pleasure.

"Is she big enough?" a man asked him.

He leapt back, ashamed at having been seen. "Yes, sir."

It was an officer. More than that he didn't know. He daren't look up from the breeches to the face. But the voice had an Irish accent.

"Seen the bow?" the man asked.

"No, sir."

A firm hand landed on his shoulder, and its pressure walked him forward. Augustus caught sight of the *Terror*'s armoring that reached back twenty feet from the stem.

"Know what's under that?"

"No, sir."

"Three inches of English oak doubled with two layers of African oak, laid diagonal," the man told him. "Overlaid with two inches of Canadian elm, diagonal again. Five belts of timber ten inches thick." The man slapped his back. "That is *Terror*," he said. "That is what a British ship is made of."

Augustus grew hot. His mother would be looking for him. She would be furious, and she had a quick temper. But he couldn't say that to this officer. No sailor here had a mother looking for him. That wouldn't make him a man.

"Who are you?" he was asked.

He spoke his name.

"Look up at me, lad."

Augustus obeyed. He saw a round but handsome face, with sandy-colored hair. Gold fringing on the jacket. A double row of buttons. A black stock below a white collar. Clean shaven. Blue eyes.

"You are Thomas Peterman's son. Your uncle recommended you. And Mr. Reid, the ice master."

"Yes, sir."

The man nodded. "Your father was a fine seaman. A brave man."

Gus said nothing. His father had been dead for four years, and he could not remember him. He only knew the story that his father had gone down by Home Bay in the Davis Strait. The harpooner of number two boat had delivered his blow, and the whale—the crew said the same whale that had passed several times under the ship, as gentle as you could please—had suddenly lunged upward. Her enormous bulk had struck the harpooner boat, capsizing it, throwing the crew into the water. The other boats killed her by lances as they tried to get the men out of the sea, and his father had been found still holding on to an oar, floating quite dead in the mess of blood and foam, killed instantly, they said, by the first strike of the fish.

The officer suddenly squatted down now on his heels. He looked up into Gus's face. "I knew of him, Gus," he said. "We met Esquimaux on the Whalefish Islands who had sailed with your father's ship out of Hull one summer."

Gus looked into the blue eyes.

The man held out his hand. "I am Francis Crozier," he said.

Gus stared down at the open hand. He knew who Francis Crozier was, and the realization dried the words in his mouth. There was no way to reply. Crozier was second-in-command of the expedition, and captain of the *Terror*. If *Terror* was every boy's dream of a ship, Crozier was every boy's dream of an explorer. Only James Clark Ross was better known to him, and Ross was Crozier's friend. Crozier had spent ten winters in the frozen seas. He had sailed at the right hand of Ross and, on those voyages, gone farther south in the world than any other man. Before that he had sailed with William Edward Parry, and gone farther north in the world than any other man. He had survived the loss of the *Fury*. He had been at sea since he was thirteen—thirty-six years. He had sailed the Atlantic, the Pacific, and the Indian Oceans as well as the Mediterranean Sea.

It was unusual for a captain to notice a boy, less still—unheard of—for him to offer to shake his hand. Gus extended his own small palm, to see it not quite swallowed up in Crozier's grasp.

"I am indebted to you, Augustus," the Irishman said softly, "for coming with us on this adventure."

Gus tried to say something. It came out a blur, a few stumbled syllables. He stood open mouthed as Crozier walked away.

He was still standing like that when his mother found him. The first he knew of her was a stinging blow to the side of his head. Then she grabbed him by the wrist. "I've been searching high and low," she muttered.

She took him to the long row of warehouses. There his name was taken, and he was given a pack, and she leaned down and kissed him roughly, just once.

As he stood on the dock with the feel of the swift kiss still on his cheek, waiting to board, he wondered about the great white bears.

Although Augustus had been out on nine whaling voyages, he had never seen a polar bear. All he knew of them, he had from his uncle. He would shudder at the dream of them, the unreal beasts that lived where nothing else could live. It was rumored that they could sleep in storms, covered with snow. That they could swim through ice. That they could be ten feet high at the shoulder and weigh as much as eight men.

Would they see one now, on this voyage?

Gus knew that it was hard to kill them. A bullet could be put through one, and it would still live. They were the white ghosts of the seas, creatures that could dive and stay underwater for inconceivable lengths of time. They were silent, patient killers, stalking the seal for hours, lying in wait for them above their breathing holes, or listening for the sound of the pups in the ice dens below them.

His father had never caught one, but his uncle had.

Gus knew the story by heart.

The female had come right up to the ship across a floe, and had started licking the whale oil from the wood. They caught her with lassoes, with the rope heaved through the boat's ring on the stem, and the rest thrown over her head. They had to be quick to take in the slack, drawing her tightly to the boat. It was a work of seamanship and art to pull her, ten men at a time, into the boat, while she thrashed, throwing her head from side to side for air. Her huge claws dug into the ice, the boat, and the sides of the ship. She was made fast to ring bolts in the deck, with ropes on each foot and around her neck.

The men had argued whether to keep or kill her. Alive, she might be taken back to England and sold, and fetch a fine price for exhibition, although her kind did not live long once captured and caged. Or they might kill her for the rich food she could provide, better than venison, and so much better than black whale-skin, with its coconut flavor, or even the gums of the whale with bone still embedded, which could be delicious. Better even than the mess of green from reindeer's entrails, that the natives called *mariyalo*, and certainly better than boiled seal or walrus meat, which was always tough and tasteless.

They decided on slaughter.

She took the first blow, by a whale lance, with barely a shudder, still standing, her head a little lowered. At the second blow, which severed an artery and streamed blood, she turned her head in an almost full circle, and looked back over the rail, out onto the ice that she had left behind. While she swayed, they moved in on her and overcame her quickly, and she finished with her front paws folded under her, her back legs still straight.

It wasn't until the cook's fires were lit that they noticed the cub.

He was not far from the ship, on the ice, pacing forward, and then running hesitantly back. They all hung over the side and watched him, taking bets when he would run and when he would stand still and look up at where his mother had been taken. His uncle said that he stayed there for hours, and they threw bread down to him that he didn't touch. Every now and again he would cry, and it was a sound like a dog chained and unfed. Eventually, sick of the noise, they lassoed him easily and hauled him up.

He was small and easily chained to the deck where his mother's blood and skin still lay. As they broke free of the ice and sailed, the captain ordered the deck swabbed, and the cub pulled hard on the chain while the water ran under him.

He choked on the chain for a whole week, his uncle said, pacing up and down as the ship endured a five-day storm. They tried to get him to eat, but he refused everything, all the while vomiting a thick, oily, fish-smelling milk from his stomach.

On the eighth day when they came up on deck, the cub was dead.

It was a pity and a shame, his uncle told him.

All the money they could have made by selling him in Hull.

It was midmorning when Gus was taken down onto *Terror*'s lower deck.

Only half the crew were there, but it was already crowded.

The officers had cabins—tiny rooms, six feet long and five feet wide, it was true, barely enough room for a man to stand and dress—but the seamen were more cramped still. Their quarters were forward, at the bow, taking up less than half the deck. Right in the center of the smoky, dim berthing was the galley, where the cookstove belched. Above Gus's head swung the galley tables, suspended on pulleys that were winched down when the crew ate. Forward of the galley was the sick bay, although as Gus came down he could already see that all the floor of the berthing space and the sick bay was packed with boxes of provisions.

The man who had brought him below was called Torrington.

"New to the navy," he said, as the first men looked up at them.

The nearest sailor looked them both up and down. "You're a pair, then, Torrington."

Torrington grinned at Augustus. "I worked a couple of coasters. Steam, you see. I worked steam engine, not sail."

"And you, boy," the other asked. "What of you?"

"Whalers," Gus said. "Out of Hull."

"Gone to Lancaster Sound?"

"No, sir. Frobisher Bay."

The man walked over to him. "You're the boy the captain knows. Knows the men on your ships."

"Yes, sir."

"Handpicked, you are."

"Yes, sir," Gus said.

The man leaned down. He smelled of coal dust. Gus saw the black dust ingrained in his neck and fingertips, and realized, too, that it was over his clothes.

"You can call me Mr. Smith," he said. He jerked his thumb at Torrington. "You know what a stoker is?"

"Yes, sir."

"I'm a stoker, see? And this here"—he nodded at Torrington—"this here's a stoker. So they say. Only difference between us is that he's a leading stoker. Younger'n me, mind. By eight year. Not used to frozen latitude neither. Not served under Crozier neither." He stared John Torrington down. "Not been with Crozier for four years in the ice, like me. But that's a leading stoker. And I'm a stoker, plain, understand."

The two men faced each other before Smith, spitting out of the corner of his mouth, turned away.

Torrington squeezed Gus's shoulder. "Pay no heed to the sound of wind," he whispered, and smiled. "Find yourself a berth."

Gus looked, but the men had commandeered the hinged-lid boxes to stow their gear, and there was nothing left for him to do but to put his canvas roll down in a corner. He pushed it hard up against a stack of cartons, all with the stenciled marking, *Soup and bouilli—Goldner's Patent Preserved Provisions—137 Houndsditch, London.*

"They cans got here yesterday," another man told him. "Supposed to have been here and stowed a month ago. But got here yesterday," he repeated, grumbling. "Now can't get them below."

Gus didn't care. The high boxes were proof against drafts, at least. He could make himself a bit private if he were careful, curled up. And the thought that this was a true navy ship, and down the deck only a few feet away were true navy officers—the captain only just past the ladderway—and the idea that this ship would not smell of whale oil like all the others he had known, but have men aboard who knew botany and medicine and magnetism and trade, and had sailed to the southern spheres—well, that made it a floating palace, a kingdom of the favored and few. Franklin himself—whom Gus had not yet seen—had been governor in the Australian colony of Tasmania, and was refined and religious and soft voiced, they said, and a man of many talented parts, and a gentleman, and of respectable age and figure. No such man ever went to sea in a whaler and stank of grease. No such man would talk to crew like his uncle's.

While he scrubbed the deck—his daily task—he thought of the difference between Crozier and Franklin. Crozier was a plain-speaking working seaman, they said. He could be relied upon, and he knew the Arctic and the natives who endured their lives upon it, the Esquimaux. Crozier, Smith told him after barely a week at sea, was a hunter who could bring down the caribou and trap foxes. Crozier was a singing man, Smith said, with a fine Irish voice, quite fair and light. And Crozier could dance, and did dance, with the Esquimaux women, and he could play a penny pipe, and he could tell good stories, and he arranged theater plays and helped the men act in them. And he was a jolly sort, Smith said—all this information imparted while Smith hung in a hammock bunk above him at night, and the ship heaved and rolled—yes, the captain was a true jolly sort when he was not black dogged, as all men were black dogged sometimes without light or women or change of company.

"Course," Smith told him one night as they ate at the galley table, "he'll never take command of a voyage, like Franklin."

Gus had stuffed the last piece of bread greedily into his mouth. "Why?" he asked.

"Never command an expedition. He ain't no gentleman."

"He is too," Gus objected.

Smith just laughed. "He weren't brought up with a silver spoon in London," he said. "He's like the rest of us, ballast. Be he the best that ever were on the sea, bring his ship through fire and storm and monster, even find the Orient—you'll see. They'll not give him a knighthood like Ross. They'll not have him to see Her Majesty. Not him."

There was a silence around the table.

"I'm not ballast," Gus finally said.

"We all are, boy," Smith retorted. "Think we'll partake in the glory when we get home? Think that? Think you'll sit down with fine ladies? Think Parlyment will grant yer a living? Think they'll hold any parade for yer?" Smith began to laugh. "No, they won't. And neither will they for he."

A couple of the seamen opposite nodded assent as Gus glanced around the table.

"Ballast," Smith repeated, wiping his tin plate with his sleeve. "Needful for a ship, boy. Make no mistake. But not one of them, like Sir John. Not us, lad. And not Crozier. Not him."

The voyage across the Atlantic was stormy.

The *Erebus* carried heavy sail, and the ship roared on through high seas, occasionally losing sight of the *Terror.* On June 27 a thick fog came down as they rounded Greenland. On board the *Terror* they could see nothing, not even the sturdy little *Baretto Junior,* the transport that accompanied them.

Gus was allowed up on deck that morning. Alongside him at the rail was Wildfinch, a boy of nineteen from Woolwich, who had suffered terribly with seasickness and was able to stand, in the little swell of the fog, for the first real time.

"Are there Esquimaux here, Gus?" he asked.

"Yes," Gus said. "All down this shore, and Danish."

"And where we dock, in Disko?"

"Yes."

Wildfinch turned to look at him. He had a broad, flat, open-looking face, very thin hair for a lad, and skin with little red lesions, like red fleabites. Torrington had said that Wildfinch came from Whitechapel, a place that Gus knew only by reputation. There was a rumor that Wildfinch's mother was a pure-gatherer, scouring the streets at night for animal droppings to sell to tanneries. The other men said it as a joke, but Gus thought it a better living than others in Whitechapel. At least Wildfinch's mother wasn't a whore, or a thief.

He felt sorry for the lad, who, at seven years his elder and a good foot taller than him, nevertheless seemed lost.

"Are they wild?" Wildfinch asked.

"Who?"

"The Indians."

Gus smiled. "Not as wild as anything in Whitechapel," he said.

Wildfinch reddened.

"They are good hunters," Gus said. "They'll come alongside. They'll barter. You can give them something, a piece of soap, or candles, or cloth, and they'll give you maybe a tobacco pouch. It's all in skin, Robert. They sew skins something perfect, they do. Furs and the like."

Wildfinch looked out in the direction of the coast, east of them somewhere in the drifting gray mist. "Hunters," he said to himself.

By next day the fog had cleared. The ships sighted each other, and they ran in a fine show up the Greenland coast. They saw the first ice, all they ever hoped to see, bergs floating in open water. The ice masters of each ship were out in navigation; Crozier was up on deck for hours.

On June 30 they crossed sixty-six degrees north.

A small case was brought up from Crozier's cabin, and the first of the cylinders unpacked. Gus saw it tossed into the sea, a little copper rod that soon faded away.

By July 4 they were in Disko. It was bedlam in port. Everything from the transport ships was unloaded and reloaded again onto *Erebus* and *Terror*. The ten bullocks that they had brought from Stromness were taken out of the hold of the *Baretto*, led blinking onto the dock, and slaughtered before the ships. Gus went down with a contingent of men and helped butcher the meat, stripping out the bone and tendons and parceling it up for freezing in the hold. As soon as they left port and headed west, the ships would become natural refrigerators.

Gus didn't mind the guts and bone and blood. He was well used to it from the whalers, where they flensed the carcasses on deck and stood knee-deep in warm fat and flesh. It never entered his mind to question the necessity, and he held the bullocks' ropes and beat them about the head to stun them when they pulled against the tethers. There was nothing to it. Life was meat. Meat was survival. That was the only equation that mattered.

When it was all done, the ships were weighed low down in the water, groaning with foodstuffs and coal and barrels. The weather turned fair; the sun beat down on them. Word went around the ships that the ice was far open to the west; it was very warm, the sea would be warmer than usual, the passage easier than anticipated. The bergs that floated in the Baffin Sea were testimony enough. All the Passage lay waiting for them, its gates unguarded in the Arctic summer. In less than eight weeks, they said, they would be in Alaska.

They sailed from Greenland on July 12.

The atmosphere in the *Terror* was unlike anything that Gus had known in the hard business of whaling. There was a recital on the open deck one night; there was singing; there was a service and prayers. There was even a little dancing. They felt the sharp stream of the ice-laden wind, like a small painful blow to the chest when first breathed in. And the seas were bright, and the icebergs beautiful, and the sails dazzling, and they felt they were God's ships in God's ocean, on the highest mission, with God's mercy and blessing. They were the most fortunate of men.

And the only thing that spoiled Gus's sailing in these few summer days was the sight of Crozier himself.

The officer stood late in the day, every day, looking forward from the very edge of the bow. And on the very day that they entered Lancaster Sound, and hailed the whaler *Enterprise* as they passed, Gus saw a strange expression on Crozier's face.

He hid it well as he came down and passed the boy.

Crozier even smiled then, and nodded toward him, making a show of pulling at his cuffs and wrapping his coat closer around him. He went below, and Gus watched him, worried for the first time, more worried than he had ever been on any ship.

For the look in the captain's eye had not been confidence in God's mercy and grace, nor pleasure in the ship, nor excitement at the conquests they were about to make.

It was less complicated than any of that.

It was fear.

Six

THE phone rang in the early hours of the morning.

Jo struggled up from sleep. "Hello?"

"Jo, it's Gina."

"God, Gina. What time is it?"

"Nearly one."

"Where are you?"

"At work. Listen . . ."

Jo rubbed her hand over her face. "What the hell are you doing at work at this time?"

"You call this late?" Gina replied. "You want to work on a real newspaper." Jo made a face into the receiver. "Listen, they found him."

"Who?"

"Who d'you think? Marshall."

Suddenly, Jo was wide awake. "Doug Marshall?"

"Your very man. Frozen like a fish finger, but alive."

Thank you, God, Jo thought, and surprised herself at the rush of emotion. "And his guide?" she asked.

"Marshall broke a leg," Gina told her. "It was the Inuit guy that got through. Big hero stuff. They picked Marshall up an hour ago."

Jo stared out through the curtains that didn't meet. She saw nothing but cloud, the low sky yellowed by the light of the city.

"Are you there?" Gina said.

"I'm here." She swung her legs out of bed. "When's he due in England?"

She could almost hear Gina smile. "I'm going home," she said. "Chase your own story, girlfriend."

The night was beautiful.

John thought that he had probably never seen a night so beautiful, and then, slipping as he came around the corner of Trinity Lane, just past the gates of Caius, he thought that probably it wasn't so much that it was beautiful, but that he was drunk.

He steadied himself on the wall, and ahead of him she stopped and looked back.

"Got a stone in my shoe," he said.

Catherine Takkiruq laughed softly, not fooled.

"Hey," he said.

"What?"

"Come here."

He could hardly make her face out in the shadows, but he could see that hair. She had taken off the fabric band as they had come out of the bar, and in the streetlights he had seen the blue sheen of it.

"Stand up and walk straight," she murmured, half laughing, half reproving.

He did as he was told. Or the best he could.

They emerged at last in his road and stopped by the door to his flat. He gazed up at the sky and saw the stars between scudding clouds.

"I'm going home from here," Catherine said. She held out her hand.

"Going," he repeated. He looked down at the hand, shook it with a sense of ridicule. He wanted to kiss her, not shake her hand. "You can't leave me," he said. "I was going to show you the Franklin stuff."

"Maybe another time," she said.

A little bolt of panic shot through him. She would turn up this street, and he would never see her again. "I never thanked you properly," he said. "For the news and everything."

This time she did laugh, out loud. "You thanked me twenty times, John," she said, "and bought me four drinks. You thanked me all night, every time someone bought *you* a drink. Now I go home, okay?"

He caught her arm as she turned. "I'm going there," he told her, abruptly.

"Where?" she asked.

"Where you come from. King William Island."

She prized his fingers from her wrist. "I come from Arctic Bay," she reminded him. "And I haven't lived there since I was six years old, remember?"

"I'm going there," he repeated. "My secret. Now you know it."

She leaned against the wall. "Thanks for telling me."

"No," he said, trying to sober up. "Thank *you*. Your dad, and all that. E-mailing you to tell me about Dad's rescue before the papers got it."

"That makes twenty-one times," she observed. But she was not impatient at all. "François is Dad's cousin."

"Yeah. Brave man. Saved Dad's life."

"Maybe," she said. She looked at the ground, smiling to herself.

He straightened up. "Come upstairs just a second," he said. "Just want to show you. I know all about your country. All those places. Got a whole mass of stuff. Just a minute, that's all. Then I'll come with you to your door, see you home. Promise."

She paused. "One minute," she murmured. "Okay."

She followed him up the two flights of stairs. When he got to his door, he looked back at her, his heart making a lazy little flip of desire. He fumbled with the lock. Then the door opened from the other side.

Amy was standing there.

She looked him over, then Catherine. She flushed deeply at the sight of the other girl. Then she stepped back. "Come in," she said. "I'm just going."

John spread his hands. "Amy, this is Catherine Takkiruq," he said. The sight of Amy's face had had the effect of a bucket of cold water: he felt suddenly dead sober.

"Is it," Amy said. She had walked across the room and picked up her bag.

"She heard about Dad and came to tell me," he said.

"Did she," Amy said. "Jolly good."

"Now, look . . ." John began.

Amy waved his protest away. "I thought I'd drop by and see how relieved he was," she commented, stony faced, looking directly at Catherine. "I guess you beat me to it."

"I'm sorry," Catherine said.

"Don't be," Amy said.

"Come on," John said. "Sit down."

Amy turned her gaze, at last, on him. "I've been sitting down for the last three hours," she said. "Waiting."

"I didn't work tonight," he muttered. "I was celebrating."

There was an awkward silence. Catherine looked as if she wanted the floor to open up and swallow her.

"I ought to warn you," Amy said. "You'll wait around a lot here. You'll never find him, because he's always out there." She gestured toward the desk and the books stacked on it. She paused, almost out of the door. "You're welcome to him," she added.

John strode across the room toward her, but Amy was out of his grasp in two seconds and already running down the stairs.

"Amy!" he called. "Amy!"

The slamming of the street door was the only reply, and a grumbled complaint from behind the door of the opposite flat.

"Shit," John muttered.

"I think I'll go," Catherine said.

"No," he said. "Look, please. Please come in. It's not like it looks. I didn't ask her here."

"She has a key," Catherine observed.

"Yes, look . . ." He paced back into the room, exasperated. "Come in, shut the door. I'm sorry. I'm sorry for all this. . . ."

Catherine's gaze was taking in the room. The desk flooded with paper, spilling onto the floor. The Canadian Hydrographic maps above the desk. The photocopied picture of *Erebus*, cross-sectioned, that was taped to the wall by the bed.

He followed her look to the picture. "She was a warship before they took her to the Arctic," he said.

"I know," she murmured.

He sat down on the bed. No girl had ever known what he was talking about before. The fact that Catherine Takkiruq knew exactly what *Erebus* was struck something basic in him.

"You have hurt your friend's feelings," Catherine said. She closed the door, but she still didn't sit. Instead she walked to the desk and picked up the first book to hand. She inspected it, opened it, flicked through the first few pages.

"The Barren Ground of Northern Canada," she said. She picked up another. *"A History of the Canadian West to 1870–71; Being a History of Rupert's Land (the Hudson's Bay Company's Territory) and of the North-West Territory. . . ."*

"I buy them," he said.

"These are antiquarian books."

"It's—it's my thing. What I like."

She sat down on the edge of the desk, looking at him without commenting.

"I meant what I said," he told her. "One day I'll go there. I'll find Franklin."

She laughed suddenly. "Find Franklin?" she echoed. "How are you going to do that?"

"Maybe your father could help me."

Her face clouded. There was a silence of some time before she spoke again. "So this is why you talk to me all night," she said finally. "But Arctic Bay is nowhere near Gjoa Haven. Gjoa Haven is on King William Island, the Franklin island. So you have wasted your time. My father couldn't help you."

She made a move to the door. He sprang to his feet. "No, that's not it," he said. "I'm not trying to get to your father through you."

"My father hunts narwhal," she said. "He doesn't hunt Franklin. He lives hundreds of miles from the Franklin sites. He's no good to you. You wasted your time."

"You've got the wrong end of the stick," he objected. "Forget I said anything about him helping me. I'll get there on my own."

"Oh, yes?" she said. "How?"

"Some way."

She stood looking at him, one hand on her hip. "People don't do that on their own," she said.

"I will."

She shook her head. "Now I know you're crazy."

"So," he said, "I'm crazy."

"And when are you going to go, exactly?" she demanded. "In April, like now? Thick snow, John. June, maybe? The runoff. You know what that is? The ice melting. Can't keep your footing in that. July, August?"

She shook her head. "I go in August. You have to tolerate mosquito, if you go then."

"I will find them," he said. "I'll find something that no one else has ever found. That is what I'm going to do. You can laugh all you like. I'll find a way."

"John," Catherine said, "no one will ever find them. They are gone, all those Franklin crews, and the ships." Her gaze went briefly to the picture of the *Erebus* and back to him. "You know what King William Island is?" she asked in a lower voice. "A piece of land in the middle of nowhere. It takes days to trek from Gjoa Haven to the west shore. And then what? You're going to walk, dive, what? Through ice, by yourself? It's ridiculous."

"Well, maybe I am ridiculous," he said, wounded, turning away.

He went back to the bed, and looked at the picture. In the silence Catherine could hear someone passing along the street. Footsteps came and receded.

"Ever since I was a little boy," he said, still without looking at her, "I just wanted to get there ahead of him."

"Who?" she asked.

He didn't reply.

"Ahead of who?" she prompted, again.

He shook his head, but still didn't answer her.

She went over to him, touched his shoulder. He looked around at her.

"John," she asked, "who is it that you are really looking for?"

By way of reply he took her hand. Then, very gently, he pulled her toward him, and kissed her.

"Oh," he said. And his eyes were full of tears. "You really are so lovely."

She smiled, moved by the sight of the tears, and yet not quite understanding them. "No," she said.

"Of course you are."

She looked down at their still-linked hands. "I think maybe exotic. That's the way you see it. Different."

"Who do you look like?" he asked. "Your father, or your mother?"

She had already told him a little of her background that evening. Her father was pure-blood Inuit, her mother an American working with an oil exploration company. They had been married for four years, separated when Catherine was six, when Catherine and her mother had moved to London. Since Catherine had won a place at Cambridge, however, Catherine's mother had gotten a promotion and had moved back to Washington.

"My father is not very tall," she murmured, answering John's question. "And my mother is very tall." She smiled. "They are an odd couple."

"Do they ever see each other?"

"Not now," she told him. "They e-mail a lot, I guess. To argue."

He smiled back at her. "Like mine," he said.

She considered him. "You are like your father." To her surprise the expression on his face closed, became guarded. "You have the same eyes, I think. The smile. Very handsome."

But the compliment had no obvious effect. He looked away a second, then asked, "What's it like in Arctic Bay now? Is it light?"

"Yes," she said, momentarily thrown by the change of subject.

"Isn't it colder after the sun comes back?" he asked. "That's what I read."

"Sometimes."

"And sometimes it looks as if the sun's come back early, the Novaya Zemlya images, like illusions of light. . . ."

She slipped from his embrace. He couldn't read her face.

"Is that right?" he asked.

"How would I know?"

"But of course you know. You were brought up there."

"I was brought up, since I was six years old, in this country," she said.

"But you go back every year. You told me."

"Yes . . ."

"Then you know," he said. "You know more than I do. Didn't the children go around the igloos, when the sun came back after winter, blowing out the flames of the lamps, and taking out the old wicks, to put in new ones? Didn't they have to relight them from a single flame?"

She was now looking narrowly at him. "If you say so."

He was taken aback. "Didn't you?" he asked.

There was another silence, for a moment. "I think I will go," she said. She moved swiftly to the door.

"Wait a minute," he said. "Wait." He tried to catch hold of her elbow. "What have I done?"

He could plainly see that she was angry; a muscle flickered at the corner of her mouth. "I shouldn't have come in the door," she finally said. "Or stayed when I saw your girlfriend. That was embarrassing."

"I'm sorry . . ." he began, "but she's not a regular girlfriend. I mean, I didn't know she'd be here. . . ." And he at once colored, at how that sounded.

"And what she said to me," Catherine went on, more thoughtfully. *"You'll never really find him, because he's out there."* She nodded slowly. "She is right," she said. "I am just your way through to where you want to go."

"No," he said. "No."

Opening the door, she suddenly rounded on her heel. "You want a nice Eskimo girl?" she said. "Maybe like the ones that Crozier used to know, to dance with?" John started protesting. "The crews all liked Eskimos, right?" she said. "They had no morals like Christian women."

She had opened the door fully and was now at the head of the stairs. John had to get around her, and stand on the first stair down, to bar her way.

"You're wrong," he said, yet deeply thrown by her accusation.

"Oh, yes?" she replied. "Then maybe you just get off on the whole fantasy, John. Your world where you can solve some mystery. Whatever. Go hunting alone. Iceman."

"That's not it," he said.

"No? Then what is it?" she asked. "You want me to tell you *irinaliutit,* make you an Inuit?"

"No—"

"Teach you the half smile, to welcome the sun?"

"No, I—"

"I have American citizenship, John," she said. Her color was very high now, the flush touching her neck. "Yes, sure, once a year I go to see my father, who is like all Inuit now, not so much like the old ways, nothing at all like Franklin's Esquimaux. He even forgets some of the things that his own father taught him. He belongs to this century, John. Not part of your dream you have here." And she briefly inclined her head back to John's room. "Okay, he had a sled, and he hunts, but he is vegetarian," she said. "You know why that is? Because ten years ago he had an alcohol problem, and now he has a gut problem. So you take your fantasies, and . . ."

He stepped up and put his hands on her shoulders. She was breathing heavily from her outburst.

"Forgive me," he said.

She looked away from him.

"My head is just full of this stuff," he said. "It's not you. I don't want a part of you. I don't mean to disrespect your father, take a piece of his world, ask him for anything."

She closed her eyes for a second. "You don't know how tired I am," she whispered, "of guys here that . . ."

"I know," he said.

"You don't know."

He lifted her hand and kissed it.

He had meant to step aside and let her go, but the sensation of her skin against his mouth made him stop. It had sent a charge through him. He took the hand from his lips, not daring to look into her face, rubbing his thumb gently, exploringly, over her long fingers, turning her palm over.

"You don't want to go to that cold, John," she murmured, very softly. "I think maybe there is a cold in you, and that is what you want to cure. The cold in your heart. A father and son . . ." she guessed.

But he stopped her words, by suddenly looking directly into her face.

"My father doesn't have a heart," he said.

Seven

THE bear was out from Prince Leopold Island, close to Cape Clarence.

When the ships came past the Borden Peninsula in 1845, passing out of Lancaster Sound, Franklin would have seen the thousand-meter mountains that almost walled in Arctic Bay. It was an area full of narwhal, killer whale, bowhead, seal, and walrus, in season.

It was cold and clear today, minus thirty, but feeling more in the sunlight. The Swimmer had a male a kilometer behind her, a mature male of eleven hundred pounds, who had avoided her when he had not picked up a trace of estrus.

The team had come out to tag her.

Richard Sibley sat behind the lead biologist, with the biologist's assistant and their researcher alongside him. The idea was to put radio telemetry collars on young females who had not yet had cubs. They would tranquilize her from the air, the biologist explained, once she had moved past open water. They didn't want their infamous Swimmer returning to the sea while sedated.

As they passed above her, the bear suddenly began to move, front paws outstretched and the rear paws flexing outward and back. She was faster than a snowmobile, steady over the rucks of ice that would have forced a vehicle to maneuver.

They used a dart from a .22 caliber, leaning out of the side door.

The Swimmer barely looked up, propelling herself faster, weaving a little as if to avoid the gun. When the dart connected with her flank, her speed never altered. She kept up the same even rhythm, a moving cloud against cloud, hypnotic in her unchanging, shimmering pace, her blue shadow matching her.

And then she began to slow, her hind legs first showing the effects of the drug. She tried to keep running, the front paws pulling and the rear legs dragging, until she finally succumbed, suddenly lying prone on the ice, flattened to it, sunk into a deep sleep.

On the blinding white-blue of the snow they took blood samples from her, and ran an electrical current to test the reserves of fat. She was four on the Quetelet Index, an average covering of fat rising to five. She had hunted well, fed well.

They noted the extraordinary development of the hindquarters and shoulders. If she had been human, she would have been an athlete, honed to fighting weight, supple and flexed, the delineation of the muscle obvious even at rest.

They tattooed her lip for permanent identification and painted a number on her back.

As this was done, Richard Sibley stepped back.

He was experiencing the usual problems of taking photographs in subzero temperatures: his breath had coated the back of the camera with frost, and the lens itself was in danger of icing over. He put the camera under his armpit and backed away, staring down at the collar on the bear. They had rolled her onto her side temporarily, and her neck was extended along the ice, her front paw raised. Her strength and beauty moved him.

He looked away, closing his eyes against the snow streaming along the ground. He tried to see a photographic pattern. He focused on the shape of the human body against the bear, the tableaux they made with the emptiness of backdrop. He snapped off a reel of pictures, moving in to take the detail of her head, ears, and feet. Claws against ice. Collar against fur. Hand on her coat. Gun, bear, ice. The tattoo.

He could no longer feel his feet or hands. There was a warning numbness in his face, around his mouth. He got back in the helicopter, pressing his face into his coat sleeve, heaving warm breath into the angle of his curved elbow. He suddenly wanted to be gone, out of the sound, back to Winnipeg.

He couldn't explain the congestion, the pressure, in his chest until

they were airborne again, and he looked back at the female, now stir-
ring on the snow.

He felt he had invaded her, been party to a swift assault.

And more than that.

He felt she was better than they were. Moving in a world he would
never really know, possessor of some more permanent truth.

He shook the irrationality of the thought away, mentally preparing
the text of the update he would put on the Web site, and the response
that he would write to a boy called John Marshall, as they crossed Barrow Strait and made for Resolute.

Eight

THE sea was clear, but Jo couldn't look at it.

It was later that same week, and she sat directly behind the pilot in the Dauphin helicopter, wedged between John Marshall and the leading medical assistant. She spent most of her time with her fingers crossed, looking steadfastly at the portion of control panel that she could glimpse between the pilot and his observer.

It was a bright day over the North Atlantic, the visibility limitless. In all directions white-tipped waves rolled; the wind was low, the sky empty of cloud. A charitable weather system was sitting square on the southern tip of Greenland, giving them effortless flying.

"You're lucky to see it like this," the pilot had told her as they first swung out over the sea.

She had shrunk back. "I don't want to see it at all," she had told him, her words mercifully sucked away in the roar of sound as the Dauphin dipped to one side and reeled out in the direction of the *Fox*.

She glanced across at John Marshall. If anything, he looked sicker than she, his head tucked down. She nudged his arm.

"Like flying?" she asked.

He shrugged. She considered him obliquely. He looked very much like his father: tall, rangy, sandy haired. She wondered if Douglas had this same expression in his face, this guarded look. Doug's public persona seemed to be full of charm and humor. Perhaps, she thought, that was all it would turn out to be. A public face.

When she had first met John that morning, he had been accompanied by one of the most beautiful girls that Jo had ever seen. Introduced to her by John, Jo had found herself self-consciously tugging down on the bulky parka she was wearing, and standing very upright. Then, almost in the same moment, she had grinned inwardly at herself. No amount of standing up straight was even going to bring her up to Catherine Takkiruq's shoulder. To make matters worse, she couldn't even find it in her heart to hate the girl for her astonishing good looks. Catherine seemed to be sweetness itself.

She nudged John's arm again now, raising her voice above the helicopter noise.

"Is your girlfriend Russian?" she asked.

"What?" he said.

"Siberian?"

He smiled, and shook his head. "Canadian. Inuit," he said.

Of course, she told herself. *What other kind of girl would a Marshall man be interested in?*

"She's amazing," she told him.

He nodded, his eyes saying it all.

The Dauphin roared on, lost, it seemed to Jo as she caught glimpses of the sea, in an endless blue space. After a while she dug into her pocket. She brought out the crumpled photograph of Doug and, holding it down against her leg to stop it flying away, showed it to John.

"This photograph . . ." she said. She pointed to it. "Is this the canister he found?"

John seemed to look for a very long time at the image. "Yes," he said finally. And he closed his eyes and turned his head away from her.

She looked from him to the photograph, puzzled at his continuing silence. She folded the paper and put it back in her pocket, frustrated.

In the last few days she had found out about Doug Marshall's discovery, a find so momentous that it had made his professional name. She had found an article he had written for the trade press: how he had stumbled across it, almost literally, while on a previous Greenland trip. How only two canisters from Franklin's ships had ever been found: one in Egedesminde, on the west coast of Greenland, in July 1849; one by Doug Marshall, at Sarfannguag, in August 1990. The canisters, thrown overboard, supposedly, at regular intervals during the journey—a kind of metal-wrapped paper trail—noted the ship's positions and the dates. The fact that the paper trail had gone completely dead had puzzled historians for years, until Douglas Marshall had picked up the second canister, one of so many others that had been lost, and found the note from Crozier, Franklin's second officer, inside.

More than anything, Jo wanted to talk to Marshall about that note. Crozier's cryptic, lone message, thrown from the second ship, the *Terror*, in July 1845. The ships were in Lancaster Sound, past the northern tip of Bylot Island, heading west at speed. Heading straight for oblivion. Heading for hell.

Jo shivered now, involuntarily.

The sound of the engines was overpowering. Even with ear protectors the thump of the rotors seemed to have invaded her whole body, shuddering and thudding, rattling her spine. The flight had lasted fifty minutes now, with Jo continually checking her watch. The LMA gave her a crooked grin. He had an insulated pack of blood in a cool box on the floor between his feet. Now and then he rested his foot on it.

She wished it were over. Beside her John Marshall seemed to have gone to sleep.

The only other time that Jo could remember being afraid of flying was one summer when she was eighteen, coming back from Corfu on a package flight. Then, they had been caught by a thunderstorm over the Adriatic. The plane had lurched and rolled, dropping thousands of feet between air pockets, lightning dancing along the wing right next to her window.

But as far as she was concerned, the Dauphin had the plane knocked into a cocked hat.

She glanced up to see the pilot looking back at her, with a thumb raised. Then he pointed down at the sea.

Jo looked down in the direction of his finger and suddenly saw, far below them, the slim gray line of the *Fox*, a Type 23 frigate of the UK Royal Navy, heading south-southeast through the flat sea. Her heart lurched. *Thank God, at last.* The Dauphin swung low, promptly dropping Jo's stomach a few hundred feet. She clenched her fists in her lap and gritted her teeth.

Minutes later they were shepherded out onto the deck under the still-turning blades. Buffeted by the wind, and steadying herself against the slight pitching of the frigate's deck, Jo took the outstretched hand of the officer stepping forward to meet them.

"Good flight?"

She mimed enjoyment, a kind of slack grin. "Great," she lied.

Inside the hangar she pulled off the wool hat she had been wearing. The principal medical officer smiled at her. "Anthony Hargreaves."

"Jo Harper," she replied. She looked behind her for John. "And this is Doug Marshall's son, John."

The two shook hands. John said nothing.

"We've tidied him up for you," Lieutenant Hargreaves told them.

"Is he okay?" Jo asked.

"We reset the leg last night." Hargreaves hesitated a moment, glancing at John. "Nasty break," he said.

"Can we see him?"

"Anytime."

Jo looked at John. "You first."

"I don't mind," John told her.

There was a moment of awkwardness. Jo felt strongly that Doug's son should be ahead of her, and she was embarrassed for his apparent— she hoped feigned—lack of concern. She wasn't quite sure, even now, if it were she that he disliked, or the whole idea of getting to the frigate. She had moved heaven and earth to get them both here, and from the first his attitude had surprised her.

She had reached him in Cambridge the day after Doug had been found.

His voice on the other end of the phone had been wary.

"You don't know me . . ." she had begun, after saying her name.

"My mother told me," John had replied.

From this difficult start he didn't make it any easier for her.

"I'm trying to get a flight to the ship," she'd said. "I know someone in the department, and . . . well, if anyone should go it would be you and your mother. . . ."

The line had remained silent.

"I'd like to go," she said. "I'd like to interview your father."

"They won't fly us there," John said flatly.

"It's true that it's very unusual, but—"

"They won't take us," he said.

"I'm still going to try," Jo said. "I just wanted to know if you'd come with me."

Another silence. "I might," he said.

"And Alicia."

"No," he said.

She'd put the phone down with the conviction that John Marshall loathed her.

Still, less than twenty-four hours later, she rang him again.

"Someone on board needs blood," she'd said. "AB Rhesus Negative. We can hitch a ride."

"Fine," John had replied.

She had put the phone down thinking, *If your father isn't more talkative than you, I'm sunk.*

They went down the ladder now to the deck below, walked aft, and turned left into the sick bay. It was a small cabin with barely enough room for its desk, cabinets, and the screened-off double bunk in a nine-by-five recess.

Jo's eyes strayed to a notice board on the wall. There was a photograph of a young girl there, not more than eight or nine years old. Seeing her glance, Hargreaves tapped the image with his index finger.

"Daughter of one of the crew," he told her. "The whole ship was tested by the Norberry Trust when we were in port. Blood test."

"For what?" she asked.

"Bone-marrow donation. She has leukemia."

"Oh," Jo murmured. "I'm sorry."

Hargreaves walked over to the bunk and drew back the curtain.

Doug Marshall had evidently been asleep, one hand propped behind his head. As they moved up to the bed, however, he opened his eyes.

Jo's first thought was that he looked different from the photograph in her trouser pocket.

"You look younger than your publicity shot," she told him, smiling and holding out her hand. "Jo Harper."

John stepped forward and briefly touched his father's shoulder, before moving back to the end of the bunk. "All right?" he asked Doug.

"Been better," Doug replied.

Jo looked from one to the other embarrassedly.

Doug turned back to her.

"How's the leg?" she asked him.

"Fine. Dunno how I did it. It was flat where I fell," he said. "Flat as a pancake."

"Oh?"

"I slipped on the easiest terrain in the world, and fell a hundred and fifty feet."

Jo smiled at him. She had half expected a show of bravado—*I was negotiating a really hard climb, and . . .*

"Into snow?" she asked.

"Snow over rock."

"Ouch," she said.

"Actually, the landing was soft," he told her. "But the fall wasn't."

Jo nodded. "And this was a week ago?"

"Eight days," he said.

She knew all this already, of course. But as she made the small talk, she listened for her angle. "You've lain for eight days in snow?"

"I walked a bit. We found a place to shelter."

Out of the corner of her eye she saw John take off his coat. She heard him sigh heavily. She turned to look at him. He had slumped into a chair and was looking away from her.

She turned back to Doug. "You *walked* on the broken leg?" she repeated.

"I got off the shore out of the water," he said. "That was all."

She frowned. "Now you're losing me," she said. "When did you get in water?"

"When I tried to get off the rocks," he said.

She stared agape for a second, then started to laugh.

"It wasn't so bloody funny at the time," Doug retorted.

"You fell from a flat straight track a hundred and fifty feet onto rocks by water, and then fell in the water," she said.

Doug started to laugh himself. At last she recognized the TV face, creased in a fan of fine lines. Laugh lines. "Just dress it up a bit for the paper, will you?" he said. "I don't want everyone knowing."

"I'll do my best," she promised.

Hargreaves had gone to the door to answer a knock. He came back carrying a tray. "See if you can take this now, Doug," he said to Marshall, holding out a cup of tea. "And don't throw up on me again."

Sitting back from Doug temporarily, Jo saw his eyes flicker to John again. She caught John looking at her and saw a rebuffed expression. She had come between them, she suddenly realized. This was an opportunity for John to talk to his father, and she had stepped in the way. "John," she said, "come and take this chair next to your dad."

He didn't move. He drank his tea. "I'm all right," he mumbled.

Meanwhile Doug drank slowly, with Hargreaves holding his head like a child's. Jo saw how much of an effort it was for him, and registered that same glance, again, to John when he was finished.

To cover the silence she found herself saying the first thing that came into her head.

"What do you think it meant," she said, "—the note in the cylinder? The copper canister."

Doug Marshall had balanced the cup unsteadily on his chest, and looked at her. "Cylinder?" he repeated.

"I've been reading your article. 'Finding Franklin.' "

"Well," he said. "Thanks."

"What did it mean, the note inside?" she asked. "Crozier's note."

Doug nodded at Hargreaves to take the cup.

"Don't talk to me if you feel unwell," she said. "I can easily come back in a while."

He shook his head slightly. "Stately ships," he murmured.

There was a pause. Jo glanced at Hargreaves, who moved at Marshall's side. At this Doug lifted a warning finger. "If you give me one of those bloody shots again I'll lay you out cold," he said.

Hargreaves turned back to Jo. "I'll be back in a minute," he said. "See that buzzer on the wall? Ring it if you need to."

After he'd gone, Doug raised his eyebrows at Jo, as if despairing of the fuss.

"Stately ships," Jo repeated. She wondered if she was pushing him too much, but the color had come back into his face a little.

As she watched him, he smiled at her, as if really seeing her for the first time. "Are you interested in Franklin?" he asked her.

"Yes," she said.

"I don't believe you," he said.

"Why not?"

"Women aren't."

She was affronted. "Let's say I was hooked," she told him.

"By a Victorian in a frock coat?"

"No," she said. "By a man in Greenland."

Their eyes met briefly. He narrowed his gaze.

She glanced at the blanket with the cradle beneath it, and wondered about the leg. A small shot of adrenaline pumped through her system, surprising her. She had suddenly remembered Hargreaves's apology to John about the injury, the seriousness of the break.

She tore her gaze from the bed and looked again at Marshall. "Crozier's note . . ." she began.

"Poor Francis," he murmured. "And the interest of women."

"Was he married?" Jo asked.

"Crozier? No. Except to the sea."

"He was second-in-command, and . . ."

"You wouldn't have believed that note," he said. "We took the canister to the National Maritime and opened it. You wouldn't think that a piece of paper could survive weeks at sea and then over a century in the ice, but it did." He passed a hand over his forehead. "No foxing by damp, no discoloration at all," he said. "Just Crozier's handwriting on the Admiralty sheet, as if it had only been written yesterday."

"It must have been eerie," Jo observed quietly.

"It was," he agreed. "Crozier seemed to be standing there with us, willing us to understand." Doug put his hands to his face, then crossed them over his chest. "They wintered the first year at a place called Beechey Island," he said, his voice beginning to drop very low. His speech was slightly slurred. "Then it started to come true."

She frowned. "What started to come true?"

"Crozier's note. Dead days."

She leaned forward in her seat. "Dead days?"

"They wintered in Beechey Island. . . ."

The door opened again. Hargreaves was back. Jo walked over to him. John, she noticed, hadn't moved an inch from his position at the foot of the bed, and was now staring at the floor.

"I don't understand what Doug is saying," she whispered to Hargreaves.

The PMO went over and looked at his patient. "Hey, Douglas," he said. "Tired?"

"Three died," Marshall said.

"Nobody died," Hargreaves reassured him.

"Three died and they buried them."

Hargreaves looked back at Jo. She shrugged, *I don't know.*

Marshall gave a labored sigh. "They tried to sail along Lancaster Sound and into Barrow Strait. But the ice was there. They turned around, went back. The ice stopped them again. Three died that winter . . ."

Jo stepped back to the bed, alongside Hargreaves.

"I gave him morphine," he said. "It's okay."

"The stately ships go on," Doug murmured. "But it came true. They were dead men. . . ."

And while they watched him, he fell asleep.

An hour later Anthony Hargreaves loaned her his cabin to write and e-mail the article.

"Come with me," she told John. "Maybe you can help me."

Doug's son followed her grudgingly, it seemed. Like a sulky child. Jo wondered if it were she, or he, or the fact that he was an archetypal teenager. He was still in his teens, wasn't he? she wondered as she closed the door of the cabin and watched him perch, all folded up awkwardly like a crane, legs tucked under himself, arms looped over knees. Nineteen was still teenage. Just.

"How do you think Doug is?" she asked him.

"He'll survive," he responded. "He always does."

She had been in the act of booting up the laptop. The comment stopped her. She turned in her chair and looked at him. "Is everything okay with you?" she asked.

"Sure," he said.

"I feel I've got under your skin, John. Annoyed you some way."

"No."

She made a stab in the dark. "I bet you don't see much of him," she said.

"Other people see more of him than I do," he answered.

Their eyes met.

Ouch. There's the nerve.

"You're doing archaeology too."

"Yes."

She glanced at the glowing blue screen in front of her. The blank page. "Where should I start?" she asked.

There was no reply.

"Do you think your father identifies with Franklin?" she asked.

A spark of interest at last showed in John's face. "Franklin?" he echoed.

"Yes."

He grinned. "No."

"Someone I know thought that might be it," Jo observed mildly. "Why is that funny?"

"Because it's Crozier," John said. "That's the one he'd like to find."

"Crozier, who wrote the message in the canister?"

"Yes."

"A message in a bottle," Jo mused. "Sort of romantic."

John made a dismissive, huffing sound.

"Not romance, then?"

"Oh, yeah," John replied. "That's what some say. The bit he wrote at the bottom of the page, *The stately ships go on,* they think that was for Sophia, Franklin's niece. Crozier proposed to her and she rejected him."

"Oh," Jo said. "Poor man."

"Do you know what that poem says?" John asked. "The one where that line comes from?"

"No," Jo admitted. "Who wrote it?"

He raised his eyebrows. "You're a journalist, and you don't know Tennyson?"

Jo held up her hands. "Look at me, I'm a philistine."

John managed a small smile.

"Tell me," Jo prompted.

John leaned back against the bulkhead of the cabin. The ship was rolling; the light outside was fading. They could hear the routine of the ship going on all around them—the sound of running feet, the raised voices. On Hargreaves's desk a picture of a middle-aged woman was taped to the tabletop. For a second Jo wondered about being at sea for a long time. How much was put away, put on hold. Lives of the men. Of the wives. Children. Salted away, literally, for months. Or years.

John began to speak. His voice was low.

> *"And the stately ships go on,*
> *To their haven under the hill;*
> *But O for the touch of a vanished hand*
> *And the sound of a voice that is still!*

> *"Break, break, break,*
> *At the foot of thy crags, O sea!*
> *But the tender grace of a day that is dead*
> *Will never come back to me."*

They looked at each other. She saw it then, briefly, acutely, in his face; saw that he had tried to hide it. Rejection.

"Who did you lose, John?" she asked.

He hesitated. For a second she thought that he was going to reply; then, to her surprise, he suddenly got up, almost banging his head on the low ceiling. He wrenched open the door.

"John," she said.

He went out, without looking back.

She turned back to the computer screen and stared at it.

She drummed her thumb against the space bar on the keyboard.

Nine

IN October, the moon was a beautiful thing to see.

She had reached her greatest northern declination and swept around the sky, bold and luminously bright with a color like cream. Sometimes Augustus stood on *Terror*'s deck and watched her. It reminded him of the milk cart that came around the streets in Hull, grass splattered high on the wheel rims, but the board scrubbed nearly white and the churns brushed to mirrors; and when the dairyman lifted the heavy lid, that first glance at the frothy milk head was exactly this moon's color.

It was strange to think of them being so far north on the surface of the earth that the moon never set, but rolled around the sky. And the snow and water and the shore of Beechey Island itself were lit by the same glorious glow, until the ships, sealed motionless in their winter harbor, seemed to be merely flat pen drawings on a page. As the daylight failed and there was more moon than sun, Augustus wondered why he was not afraid. He had always hated going to bed in the dark, and waking the same, and he had always wanted candles, for a long time, even when first at sea. But somehow that old fear—of being in the dark—had left him. Thank God. Because he was going to be in the dark now—twenty-four-hour, relentless dark, with only this occasionally luminous moon—for weeks to come.

It helped that all the crew were so cheerful, even in the face of the winter. By October they had arranged the ships marvelously well for the winter ahead. The mooring was sheltered. The fires and ventilation fixtures below were able to keep a mean temperature on both *Erebus* and *Terror* of nearly sixty degrees, which was comfortable and warm, like a summer room at home. And even on deck, under the housing, they had still not reached freezing point.

Augustus had been thrilled by the summer. Since July they had sailed along Lancaster Sound and into Wellington Channel, farther north than he had ever been. As they had navigated past Devon Island, that huge barren outcrop rose up like a fortification.

Aboard *Erebus* Commander Fitzjames was keen, as keen as Sir John, to skip forward at a good pace, because he believed that Wellington was a route westward. A rumor flew around the crews that Fitzjames had said they might find the Passage most presently, and be through it in less than three weeks. The wind charged through the rigging, booming through the sail fabric and plucking low notes from the tightened ropes. Standing on deck was like being at the heart of a primitive orchestra, in the percussion, inside a drum.

It was on August 8 that they saw the first walrus.

And the first icebergs.

Augustus was sitting below with John Torrington when John Bailey came down to tell them.

"We'll have a storm," Bailey said.

Torrington smiled. "It'll push us farther on," he commented.

Augustus was worried for Torrington. John had not seemed right to him for more than two weeks, and for the last four days he had not worked at all. Gus thought he was thin, although Torrington was already a slim, tall man by nature. It was the sight of the bones on Torrington's face, highlighted white as he turned his face in the evening light at table, that Gus had first noticed. It had been at prayers on Sunday, and Torrington did not get up, and nor did he kneel. But he sat very upright and bowed his head, and turned it toward Crozier as the long chapter from Isaiah was read out. And it was then, as Torrington inclined his face while praying, that the bones showed: a white ridge under each eye.

"Go up and see the walrus," John said to him now.

"I've seen them before," Gus said.

Torrington smiled and gave him a heavy nudge with his elbow. "Go,

Gus," he said. "I'll be here when you get back. I shan't run away to marry."

It was a strange sort of joke he had. He had told Gus it was what his father always said. "I shan't run away to marry." He delivered it in his flat, wry Manchester accent, with its faint lilt at the end of sentences.

Gus ran up on deck.

A large number of walrus were within twenty feet of the ship, shaking their heads, as if mowing through the water with their tusks.

"Bad weather drives them in so close to land," another man said, as they watched. He pointed past the stern, to a great low brow of clouds on the southern horizon. "Storm," he added.

But it wasn't the walrus that caught Gus's attention. It was the sight of the sea ahead of them, which before had been flecked with small floes, and was now—only two hours since he had gone below—streaming with denser ice. And, bearing down on them quite clearly, high bergs— a whole horizon of them. There was no open sea now.

When he went below, Gus didn't tell John that Bailey had been right. Torrington had already gone to his bed, the hammock slung past the galley, in the sick bay that measured less than five feet square. Torrington's knees were curled in to his chest. Gus could hear the rattle of his breathing.

The gale came up fast.

He heard it as he slept, the noise waking him. He lay on the little bed of boxes that he had constructed for himself, and saw the whale-oil lights swaying. Soon they were put out. Men ran up on deck. The officers were all awake. The ship heaved, dancing curiously in the current, as if unseen hands were tugging at the stern. Both the wind and the current had changed, and *Terror* did what ships were not supposed to do—shook itself as if alive, tripping and falling, tripping and falling. He lay in the dark and thought about it, deciding, in the rapidly rising scream of the wind and battering of the waves, that *Terror* was constructed as no other ship, and so would sound like no other ship, and behave like no other.

By three in the morning it was blowing like a hurricane, and ice was driving through the strait. There was no more sleep at all. The gale tore through them. The sea was furious; the feel of the ice-laden air scythed through both ship and man. They lost sight of *Erebus*, which disappeared in the indigo-green mountains of the ocean, and it was as if the whole of the summer sailing along Wellington had been a dream, a mirage promising stillness and relief, and yet luring them into a dead end.

There was no chance of fastening themselves to one of the huge bergs for safety; the captain was of the opinion that, in such a gale, even a ten-inch-thick Manila cable would snap, and the hawsers break, and so they put in the hawse bags and blocks to make her as tight as possible against the sea, and *Terror* was allowed to scud, under canvas enough to keep her ahead of the sea, her main topsail and foresail close-reefed.

All hands watched as the enemy closed.

It was eight in the morning when *Erebus* came back into view, ahead of them still, between enormous bergs. Augustus whispered a prayer to himself. They were God's ships, after all. Surely God would not let them die before they had really begun. But at the same time, even while whispering Christ's name, his blood raced. This was really living, even if it were only to live before dying in the storm. It was *living*.

On the shore side the ice tables were grinding up together in masses, and they had no choice but to helplessly slip alongside the floes, each mass of ice running at an alarming rate, and depositing ice on deck as they were buffeted. They saw *Erebus* ahead between two enormous banks of ice, and each man waited in silence, expecting at any moment to see their sister ship crushed, as the bergs pushed in opposing directions on a collision course.

Only the appearance of a sudden passage of clear water saved them both; the *Terror* managed to make fast to the sconce of a low water-washed berg, and the ice hauled them forward like a racehorse, the sea crashing over it and the boat, running at high speed down the channel. Augustus thought then of a game he had played in the long steep channel between the houses at home. When he had been five or six, one of his friends' father had made them a flat plywood trolley with a roller at each end, and they had tied their dog to the front and gone careening down the hill, bouncing from the cobbles and against the alley walls, thrown into mud, battered by falls, trampled upon by the maddened dog, only to carry the cart and rope and dog back to the top of the hill and start again.

Augustus thought of that poor crazed dog now, leaping about, driven by their sticks, as he felt *Terror*, in all her weight and majesty, pulled by the current and a block of ice. And they bounced along the ridges of the sea, just as he had bounced, hundreds of times, along the cobbled alley.

Never had he seen ice come so rapidly.

Only the day before they had been talking of three weeks until they saw the other side of Canada; now they were driven at the mercy of the oncoming winter. It was as if their optimism had been months before; this was another landscape, another world. Quite suddenly, almost at midday, an old floe took them. Honeycombed and yellowed, it had a top that rose out of the water thirty feet high, but it sheered away under the ship at an angle, presenting what looked like a cold white shore of ice. All at once *Terror* was lifted up and pushed forward onto this shelf, just as if she were being forced into dry dock. They held on as the ship lurched, and Augustus wondered if the whole of *Terror* would be lifted up and pushed over the other side of the berg.

But the ice dropped. The ship leaned back again and righted herself, all within the space of five minutes.

Augustus looked at the man alongside him. He seemed not to care at all. "Ice has its relaxations," the fellow said, and gave a shrug. "Nip and relax, nip and relax. 'Tis all one."

Gus stared at the berg, with its old man's face, a complexion full of weathered lines and creases, as it towered alongside them. He surreptitiously pressed his palms together and held them tightly to his chest, to thank God for relaxations.

And for hearing all his other prayers, making him a seaman and not just a whaling man. Making him a part of this expedition, and not merely a hand on a blood-filled deck, cleaning blubber from bone, calf-deep in oil and salt water.

And so it was decided to make back for Beechey Island, to the little bay that would protect them for the winter.

What Sir John and Fitzjames made of the shock of the sea change, the boy did not know. Perhaps they took it philosophically, as the men had to.

Anyhow, nothing more was said of running to the Pacific in three weeks. They turned their faces from any such prospect, and accepted the long, dark wait ahead of them.

* * *

When they first berthed in the bay in October, the shoreline of
Beechey Island was still visible.

It was a gray place, a beach of shattered limestone, crumbled to
shards and fragments, and whitened, near the edge, into something
like a silvery gravel. Beechey, and its greater sister, Devon, were the only
elevations to be seen in any direction. It was really the edge of the
world, where land disappeared and there was nothing for hundreds of
miles but flat and open vistas. Some of the men said that Adam saw
such a view when God turned him from Eden: no more color, no more
soil or flower, or the movement of leaves or grasses. Nothing but a
silent vacuum, so that Adam had nothing to look upon, or think about,
but his own self, and his shame.

But Gus wondered if Adam had been really so bereft at the edge of
paradise. He wondered if Adam might have felt as he felt now, that
ahead of him lay a white page, and that anything could be written
across it, and had felt his own small soul rising to the challenge.

He hid this from the other crew, because he suspected that such a
sentiment might not be Christian, and that, if it ever came to the attention of Sir John, it might offend him.

In sunlight Beechey—at the edge of Eden, or not—could be very
striking, arresting in its emptiness, arched over with a brilliant blue sky.
A spit of land connected the island to the greater mass of Devon Island,
a square block rising from the ocean. A few hundred yards back from
the shore, cliffs almost five hundred feet high dominated the bay, their
rock pitted and scarred by the freezing storms that beset them for most
of the year.

They set to work with a common will.

Very soon the crew had built an observatory, a carpenter's shop, a
forge, washing places, and a large storehouse on the shore, within easy
reach of the ships. They unloaded the provisions that they had taken
on in the Whalefish Islands into the storehouse, and Sir John allowed
the making of a shooting gallery at the eastern end of Beechey, to aid
the men in their hunting skills. To be able to shoot was an essential
thing, one that Augustus wanted to learn. He hoped that someone
would teach him, and Torrington, who had said that he would try,
walked out with Augustus on the very first Sunday after the gallery was

made and, leaning on the boy's shoulder, said that they would make fine marksmen, and shoot bears together by the light of the midnight sun next May.

But only two days later Torrington was confined to bed.

No one would say what the matter was, and Gus dared not ask when they sat down to eat. The temperatures fell rapidly outside, and the cold began to seep through the hull, so that ice could be seen in the hairline cracks of the timber. There was unnatural calm outside, as the light dropped and the ships stopped rising and falling with the waves. They were soon in the unbreakable embrace of ice, captured for months to come.

Painted ships on a painted ocean.

Gus tried to think where he had heard a phrase like that. It was in school, but had been about ships in the tropics, he was sure. Ships caught in a dead calm. The calm here was dead, too, though: nothing to see outside but the ghostly gray rise off Beechey and Devon and, a little way off, *Erebus*, a mirror image of themselves, stripped of her topgallant masts and topmasts so that ice would not weigh them down.

Even out on the island, where Gus was allowed to help the blacksmith build the forge, he couldn't find the words to ask about Torrington's absence. There was a conspiracy against the stoker's illness: like children afraid of the dark, they looked the other way, or shut their eyes, or made more favorable pictures in their mind.

But Gus could hear Torrington in the sick bay. They took food in to him and he refused it, and Gus could hear Torrington's raised voice, the very sound of which frightened him more than anything else, because it was not John's tone, but a stranger's.

Gus was standing outside the bay when Mr. MacDonald came out one evening, almost a week after Torrington was confined.

"Sir," he ventured.

MacDonald looked at him.

"Is Mr. Torrington well yet?"

MacDonald paused. Augustus dared to look him in the eye. He had summoned the courage to speak only because he knew that MacDonald, like him, had been in the Arctic on a whaling ship. He hoped the tenuous connection, a vague sort of camaraderie, might give him a little leeway: permission to talk where talk was not usually allowed.

"No," MacDonald said, at last. "He is no better."

The officer called the galley cook over and spoke softly to him. The cook went back and brought several of the lead-soldered Goldner tins from the stores. MacDonald selected two or three. "Meat," Gus heard him say. "And make sure he keeps it down."

Fear gave Gus courage. He stepped forward and called MacDonald's name.

The men around them fell silent.

MacDonald turned.

"Our neighbor at home had consumption," Gus said.

MacDonald glanced at the men, then back at Augustus. He frowned. Gus knew his calling out was insubordination—it could be called that, if MacDonald wished—but the boy was desperate to be told the truth. An idea had occurred to him, an idea so terrible that it made him nauseous. It was the memory of the curtains drawn at midday, and of a black handcart pulled up to the house, and a tired pony wreathed in crepe.

MacDonald gave the boy a long look, but eventually said nothing. As he left the deck, Gus turned to the nearest man.

"Is it the consumption?" he asked. The fear was knotted in his stomach now, squeezing the tight space under his ribs. "Is it?"

He read the answer in their faces.

Two weeks after coming to Beechey, Gus helped lay the road to the *Erebus*. The two ships were barely a hundred yards apart.

It had been marked with stones, but they took these up and drove rows of posts into the sea ice, so that anyone passing between the ships, even in the depths of a storm, would be able to see the way. On one side, the posts were strung with rope; on the other they left the lumps of limestone in a line. Gus would see the officers walking along the road, sometimes holding to the rope, and feel proud of the long hours he had spent sharpening the posts and holding them for the men as they were slammed into the ice with sledgehammers. After the road they made fire holes—hard, backbreaking work and one that, once finished, needed constant attention to stop the holes from freezing. Seawater must be available to put out fires, and the holes could not be allowed to close again.

The sun slowly went down.

The snow began.

Although he had seen plenty of snowstorms, Gus had never been on land for long to witness their smothering hold. Occasionally, at home, snow could envelop the fishing port; but it soon turned to slush and was kept swept from the doors of the houses. Here, they used snow on the decks, packing it down hard for insulation and scattering sand over the top to get a foothold. Snow, sometimes creeping in on them during the night without a sound, formed drifts right up to the ship's rails and over the top. The snow that fell in storms was almost horizontal, leaving blinding traces on the eye; but by far the most insidious and threatening were the silent snowstorms that dumped huge quantities on them in the darkness, stealthily, silently. Gus soon tired of running about in it as he passed, working, from ship to the island. He spent less than a day whooping up and down the shore, making balls to throw. It lost its glamour and became something to be mastered and fought, clogging his footsteps, crusting his clothes.

The surgeons were brought across from *Erebus* to look at John Torrington.

It was decided that Torrington should be walked on deck four times a day, to relieve the congestion of his chest, made worse by the stuffy conditions belowdeck. Gus was the first to volunteer to help him, and was pleased to see Torrington smile at him as he slowly negotiated the steps.

Torrington leaned on *Terror*'s rail and gazed at the island cliffs, now just white ghosts in the deep twilight.

"We are at the ends of the earth, Gus," Torrington said.

Gus tried to think of something to cheer him. But he couldn't. He wanted to ask about the shooting gallery, if John would walk there again with him, and at the same time, he knew that Torrington could probably not even descend from the ship.

John turned to look at him. "Aren't you afraid of me, Gus?" he asked.

"No," Gus said. "Why should I be?"

Torrington sighed, the sound tugged away at once by the wind. "Not afraid to be next to me?"

"No," Gus told him.

Torrington nodded. Gus thought there were tears in his eyes, but it was hard to see in the lowness of the light.

"I shall not breathe on you," John murmured.

Christmas came.

For the week before the season Augustus had been engaged in ferrying stores from storehouse to the ships, but on December 21 the captain, upon making for the shoreline observatory, asked Gus to go with him. Nothing was said between man and boy while they traversed the ice road; nothing was said on entering the house. Crozier simply indicated the stove, glimmering with its dwindling supply, and Gus set to, shoveling anthracite to feed the blaze.

There was barely light enough to see, although it was approaching noon. Crozier, clothed in sealskin pants and coat, and a dogskin cap, sat down on a box and prepared to take his readings; the thermometer read ten degrees below.

"We are warm in here, Augustus," Crozier murmured.

"Aye, sir," he said, watching the reading.

The magnetometer was perched on a pedestal of frozen gravel; stretching out from it was a telescope. Every six minutes Crozier made a note of the arc and recorded the reading in his memorandum.

After a while he glanced up. "You must move about a little, Gus," he said kindly. "Do not stand to attention. You will freeze to the floor."

Obediently, Gus marched on the spot.

"I have taken readings of the temperatures," Crozier said abstractedly, transferring his fox-fur mitten from one hand to another and shifting the chronometer. "There may be as much as thirty degrees difference between the point next to the stove, and the floor. Even our approach will alter the readings of the thermometer, for it picks up the heat of our bodies." He glanced at the stove. "At home they are filling the churches as well as the fires," he murmured.

He looked up at Gus. "What will your mother do, without you?"

Gus hadn't given it much thought. "I have a brother who can fetch and carry," he said. "He is six now."

Crozier smiled. "She will miss you in terms of labor?" he said. "More than that, I think."

Gus considered. He truly did not think that his mother would miss him at all. She had eight children; he had four brothers and three sisters. His two elder brothers were at sea, like him. His sisters, when not at the school, picked rags, sorting them for sale, and unraveling wool to remake and sell. Christmas in his house, since his father's death, was a hand-to-mouth nightmare, until his brothers came home with their wages. Then, perhaps, they would have a piece of beef, and their mother would have plenty of beer and porter, and more often than not they would sleep by the fire, so much warmer than their beds, and so much cleaner in the ashes than among the blankets. There were no lice in the ashes.

Gus blushed now, in Crozier's presence, to remember the house.

"They will think of us," he said. Because perhaps they would this time. Men in the alehouse would ask his mother about her son on Franklin's ships.

"Are you happy to have come here, Gus?" Crozier asked him.

It was a curious question.

Men did not ask each other, especially aboard ship, which was a job of work, if they were happy. Many complained, that was true; they complained of the lack of light, and of the oil being rationed so that sometimes they had light only from tapers of cork and cotton floated in saucers; they complained of the smell; they complained of the rats, which even ate their hair as they slept. They complained at strong proof whiskey freezing; they complained that the intensity of the cold made the snow hard to walk upon, rendering it like sand.

On the other hand, when in good temper, they sang, and had, in the last week, even sung carols; they had, when Crozier allowed it, races around the ship, with prizes for the fastest man; they aided each other in the worst jobs.

But they did not ask each other if they were happy.

Gus saw in Crozier's eye a kind of blindness. Just for a moment he glimpsed the black months, year after year.

It passed in a second.

"Yes, sir," he replied. "Very happy."

It was New Year's Day when John Torrington died.

Gus spent New Year's Eve with him.

Torrington had been quite jolly toward the end of the afternoon;

he played chess—or rather, half a game of chess—with Mr. MacDonald, and he asked for a Bible. They heard him singing for a few bars, then whispering to himself. Gus begged all day to be allowed to see him, and finally they relented, and let him forward in the evening, at eight o'clock.

Torrington was stretched out on a bed that had been made for him; a great concession, for only the officers had beds. Two oil lights burned next to him. The Bible was folded on his chest.

"Who is it?" he asked.

"It's me," Gus said. "Come to see the New Year with you, John."

There was silence while Torrington's hand stroked the Bible. "Eighteen forty-six, Gus," he said, finally, "and I shall be twenty-one."

Gus fought for something cheerful to say. "And then you shall run away to marry," he told him.

The man on the bed turned his head. Gus's heart dropped as he saw how desperately thin and wasted Torrington had become.

"Have you a sweetheart to marry, Gus?" Torrington asked.

"No, sir."

"What, never?"

"No, never."

Torrington gave a very faint smile. "What, not kissed a lass?"

Gus colored fiercely. "No, sir."

Torrington nodded. His mouth worked a little. "Nor I," he murmured. The light flickered in the nearest lamp, threatening to go out.

With an effort Torrington tried to rouse himself. "Is it snowing outside?" he asked.

"No," Gus said. "It is quiet."

"Any bears, Gus?"

"Not yet."

Torrington felt for Gus's hand.

John's fingers were long. Almost a gentleman's hand. Someone had scrubbed his skin so that you could hardly see the coal dust any longer. His first three fingers were almost the same length. Below the blue-striped shirt Gus could see every small bone. The knuckles looked huge and ungainly. The skin was parchmentlike, as if there were no blood at all beneath.

"Look under the bed," Torrington said.

Doing as he was told, Gus found a small tin box.

"Open it."

There was a letter there, and a key, and a little book of verse, and a leather purse.

"Take it," Torrington said. "You take it, Gus, and give it to my mother."

Gus didn't know what to say. This man, above any except perhaps the captain himself, had been kind to him, talking to him as if he were an equal and not the lowest of the crew. This man, in another time, might have been his teacher, using those fine-fingered hands to help him at his books. Torrington had something in him that was much more than his lowly rank; he deserved more than his hell's-gate task of tending the fires, working in the clouds of coal dust belowdecks. Gus could see it in his eyes: what might have been, in this fine nature, given other chances.

The boy started to cry.

He didn't want to. The tears came streaming out unbidden. He choked on them, and laid his head on Torrington's bed.

It wasn't for some seconds that he realized that there was a noise other than his own gasping, and in sudden horror he lifted his head to see Torrington, his gaze fixed on him, blood at his mouth.

Gus leapt to his feet. "Mr. MacDonald!" he cried. "Mr. MacDonald!"

For two days the ship's carpenters, Thomas Honey and his mate Alexander Wilson, constructed the coffin.

It was a fine mahogany, measuring three quarters of an inch thick by twelve inches wide, the lid and coffin bottom each made of three pieces: a long central portion, with two shaped sections, attached by dowels to each side. Gus went up on deck, under the canvas awning, and watched as Wilson kerfed the wood to make the shoulders, to bend it without breaking. The men worked in silence and secured the sections finally with square iron nails.

At midday on January 2 Torrington's body was brought on deck.

He had been washed, and dressed again in his cleaned shirt and trousers. His limbs had been bound to his body, with a length of cotton wrapped around above his elbows. Smaller strips tied his toes, ankles, and legs, and the long hands rested on his thighs. He was laid down carefully in a sweet-smelling bed of shavings that filled the coffin, his head resting on a larger mound of the same, to make a little pillow. A blue-and-white spotted handkerchief had been bound under his chin, and was tied discreetly at the back of his head, to hold the jaw together; but Gus saw, with a clench of dismay, how Torrington's mouth was still wide in that final grimace, and his eyes were open.

They put him in the coffin and nailed the lid, wrapping the whole in a navy-blue wool blanket, and draping the bier with a flag. Then, from below, they brought what Gus had helped to make in the last two days: a metal plaque, shaped like a raindrop, on which had been inscribed in white lettering,

JOHN TORRINGTON
DIED
JANUARY 1ST
1846
AGED 20 YEARS

They lowered him down the side of the ship and went out in a line across the ice, torches lighting their way. Halfway across they paused, waiting for a second line of torches through the midday gloom: Sir John Franklin himself, muffled, coated, and capped, his head bent against the first fine snow that was falling.

Captain Crozier fell in at his side, with Commander Fitzjames, and the two surgeons. Behind them came the men who would fill the grave, one of them carrying a headboard. The service was brief in the biting wind and the increasing flurries of snow that quickly settled on the coffin and obscured the inscription. No time was lost, when the funeral was finished, in filling the grave with the limestone shards. All Gus could think of, as he watched the shovels at work and the stones falling, was that one of the brass handles on the side of the coffin was still upright, and that he ought to have reached down and righted it before it was covered up.

For the following week a curious atmosphere fell over the ships.

The officers continually ferried between *Erebus* and *Terror;* there was much discussion—to which the men were not privy—in the officers' quarters and mess. Low voices long into the night.

To all the men's surprise, on the fifth day after Torrington was buried, Franklin ordered that the storehouse be unlocked and three boxes of Goldner's provisions opened. Gus did not know what passed afterward, other than it was rumored that a few from *Erebus* were ordered to take the boxes to the northeast slope of the island, and there open the entire stock of tins in each box. It was said that Sir John had the tins emptied, and the empty tins stacked neatly into rows, more than seven hundred tins in all, and the meat that had been in them was taken away farther still, and covered with snow.

Gus did not know what to make of it.

He had eaten from the tins himself, as everyone had. The officers, of course, more than most. Torrington had been given officer's rations, from the tins and the tins only, and hardly any biscuit at all. Vast quantities of their provisions were tinned, all painted red outside, and stamped with the words *Goldner Patent.*

How could there be anything the matter with the tins? Gus wondered. They were lead-soldered tight. The food in them could not decay. It looked all right when he had been given some for his Christmas feast.

When he asked one of the marines, the man shrugged his shoulders. "They found a bad box, I suppose," he said.

"But why did they open them after John died?" Gus asked him.

"How am I to know?"

"Did something in the tins kill him?" Gus persisted.

The man laughed in the boy's face. "Kill him?" he repeated. "Cold and consumption killed Torrington. He'd had it before, boy. Don't you know that? Enlisted on a sea voyage to cure himself, I don't wonder."

He'd put his face, grinning, unwashed, close to Gus's own. His breath was fetid. "Think I'd still be here if there was something in the tins?" His finger prodded Gus's shoulder. "Think *you* would?"

Gus turned away, went below. Took up the Bible that Torrington had left him. In an hour or two he had forgotten the leering face and prodding finger, and the tone of sarcasm.

But he didn't forget the seven hundred tins, taken away out of sight.

A bad box, he thought, afterward.

One bad box.

Ten

THREE weeks passed before Jo saw Doug Marshall again.

In that time April turned into May, and the two chestnut trees on Jo's street came into flower, and the aubretia that had somehow found its way into the wall next to her basement kitchen bloomed an improbable, almost fluorescent, lilac. One morning she found herself staring at it, coffee in hand, thinking what spring might look like in Cambridge.

She phoned him.

He took a long time to answer.

"Hi, it's Jo Harper."

"Hello, Jo."

"You sound out of breath."

There was a pause, then Doug laughed. "I'm lying on the floor."

"You are? Did you fall?"

"No," he said. "It's quicker to crawl."

"You're joking."

He didn't respond. She heard a huff of air. "Okay, I'm in a chair, upright," he told her. "I see you sold the story."

"I sold it everywhere," she said. "All over the world."

"Congratulations," he said.

"I wondered if . . ." She bit her lip. *God,* why was this hard? She felt sixteen, embarrassed. Tongue tied. "Look, I owe you lunch, at least."

"For what?"

"For selling my story."

"You did that."

"Okay, then. For being a national treasure. Everybody loves you."

He laughed again. "I'm beating them off with sticks."

"If I drove up, say, tomorrow?"

"Feel free."

They fixed a time; he told her his address. When she put the phone down, she grinned at the aubretia, brilliant in its dark corner. When she turned away, she caught sight of herself in the mirror in the hallway.

"It's just lunch," she told her reflection.

Early the next day she went straight to the Academy.

Mrs. Cropp was not on the visitors' desk; a student, sitting behind the counter and doing her utmost to be helpful, put the call through to Peter Bolton. Jo waited twenty minutes for him to come downstairs. When at last he appeared, she stood up and walked over to him, extending her hand.

"You're very persistent," he said.

"Could we start again?" she asked. "I promise not to harass Alicia. Cross my heart."

He smiled thinly. "I'm not sure you exactly harassed her," he said. "To be scrupulously accurate."

"Or get in her line of vision. Four-mile exclusion zone, whatever."

The smile became real. Bolton nodded down at the copy of *The Courier* that she was carrying. "You did a nice job."

"Oh, you saw it? I brought you a copy just in case."

"Yes, I saw it. Thanks for the publicity."

"Look, I . . ." She glanced over her shoulder, at the exhibit cases. "The last time I was here, I think you had Franklin pieces?"

"Yes, we do."

"Do you have any time? Five minutes?"

"What is it you need?"

"Would you explain them to me?"

"Are you doing another article?" he asked.

She blushed a little. "Maybe, I . . ."

"You got the bug."

"The paper had a lot of inquiries."

"Yes, so did we." He spread his hand. "This way."

The exhibit case was just as she remembered it; the sepia photographs, the silver spoon with the copper repair; the tiny piece of red tin.

"I know what happened in the first year," she said, resting her hand lightly above the relics, so carefully preserved and labeled on the green baize below the glass. "They spent their first winter in Lancaster Sound . . . ?"

"They wintered in Beechey Island in 1845–6," Bolton said. "They left in a hurry, leaving behind hundreds of artifacts."

"Why?"

"Why the hurry?"

"Yes."

Bolton shrugged. "The most popular theory is that the ice suddenly broke, and they had a favorable current. That's the way it went in those polar ships; you had to keep watch daily, wintering or sailing, for the change in the ice. If you didn't, you might lose your opportunity, at best. At worst, you could be dead."

"What kind of thing did they leave on Beechey?" she asked.

"The remains of excursions they had made, in that first winter, to the north of Erebus and Terror Bay, and to a place called Caswell's Tower, a rock mass a few miles away."

"To do what?"

"Mapping, primarily," Bolton said. "Collecting items for the botanists, recording wildlife migrations and sea currents, and the extent and depth of ice, the temperatures . . ."

"And these things were recovered from there?"

"No," he said. "A great deal of the relics on or near Beechey were things like rings of stones, to hold down tents, empty meat and soup tins, bottles. Bones of birds that they had killed. And two pieces of paper."

"Oh?" Jo asked. "What did they say?"

"They were just fragments. One had the name of the assistant surgeon to the *Terror*, Mr. MacDonald. Only that. The name. Then the other said, *To be called . . .*"

"But how did paper survive," Jo asked, "in conditions like that?"

"The Arctic is like no other landscape," Bolton told her. "An item left there, even paper if sufficiently protected, will simply stay put for hundreds of years. Skeletons of animals, or the very occasional Inuit bone, have been tested and found to be hundreds, even thousands, of years old, remaining where they fell. There's nothing to disturb them, you see. And the permafrost preserves them. Like Torrington."

Jo glanced up at him. "Torrington?" she asked.

"Petty Officer John Torrington, leading stoker on the *Terror*. His grave is on Beechey. His, and two others' from the expedition. John Hartnell—an able seaman on *Erebus*—died three days after Torrington. William Braine died three months later."

Jo remembered Doug's words on board HMS *Fox*. *Three died.*

"And the graves are still there," she murmured.

"Yes. They've even been exhumed and examined, by a team led by an anthropologist, Owen Beattie."

She was surprised. "Torrington, and these others?"

"Yes."

"But aren't they . . . decayed?"

"They're incredibly preserved," Bolton told her. "Their burials and bodies provided amazing information, not just about the expedition, but about medical science in the middle of the nineteenth century."

"Like . . ."

Bolton shrugged. "Hartnell had had an autopsy. No one had ever seen evidence of such a thing before."

"And the ship's surgeons would have done that?"

"Yes," Bolton said. "It was probably Harry Goodsir. He was trained in anatomy. He was the assistant surgeon on the *Erebus*. The *Erebus* was Hartnell's ship. Torrington was from the *Terror*."

"Goodsir," Jo repeated, almost to herself. Goodsir's name had been on the Internet printout, she remembered. Goodsir had studied at Edinburgh; he was the younger brother of Professor John Goodsir, an anatomist and morphologist. He had practiced medicine with his father at a place called Anstruther. He had been appointed to *Erebus* not for his medical ability, but because he was a talented and pioneering naturalist. And the character note alongside his name in the muster list had said that Commander Fitzjames had called him "a very well-informed man, who was a pleasant companion."

She recalled Goodsir's photograph too. Young, with a very pronounced, intense expression, he had seemed almost schoolboyish.

"Had Torrington had an autopsy?" she asked.

"No. Just Hartnell."

"Would that mean Hartnell's death was a surprise?"

"Yes, probably."

"Three days after Torrington. Unexpectedly," she said.

"Of course, quite a high proportion of the population had TB then," Bolton said. "Consumption, they called it."

"Wouldn't that frighten the crew?" she asked. "On a closed community like that, another young man dying?"

"It could have spread panic if it hadn't been properly managed," Bolton said, nodding. "Perhaps Goodsir was anxious to show the reason."

"And you said Hartnell's autopsy showed things we didn't know. . . ."

"That's right," Bolton told her. "The incision, what they call the Y incision, was upside-down, for instance. Nowadays a cut is made with the arms of the Y extending to each shoulder, and the straight line going down the front of the chest. Goodsir did it the other way around, with the Y arms coming from the point of each hip, and the straight line going up toward the throat."

"Was he interested in Hartnell's stomach, then?"

"Well, no," Bolton said. "Although it certainly suggested that from the shape of the incision. But when Roger Amy and Beattie—who unearthed these bodies—started the new autopsy on Hartnell, they found that Goodsir must have believed that the problem—the cause of Hartnell's death—was in the heart or lungs, because those were the organs that had been removed and examined."

Jo frowned. "And Goodsir found TB?"

"He must have done," Bolton said.

"And then he'd have told Franklin. . . ."

"Yes," Bolton nodded. "He'd have told Franklin and the captains, and then the job would have been to bury Hartnell as soon as possible."

Jo shivered. Her own grandmother had had a word for that sensation. *Someone just walked over my grave.*

"Tell me about Torrington," she said, trying to rid herself of the uncomfortable feeling in the pit of her stomach. "He was preserved, you said?"

"He certainly was," Bolton replied. "When they lifted Torrington from the grave in 1984, he was limp, and his head rolled onto Owen Beattie's shoulder. Beattie said that it was just as if he were unconscious, after they had thawed the grave."

Jo stared at him. "My God," she whispered.

"The exhumation was an expert job," Bolton said. "Beattie and his team really felt for these people. They showed them the utmost respect."

"I'm sure," Jo said. But still she shuddered.

"Torrington died of tuberculosis and pneumonia," Bolton said. "He was only twenty. Everything about him was as if he'd only been buried hours before. There was even a layer of snow on the coffin. It must have been starting to snow as they put him in the ground."

"You mean there was no decay?" Jo said.

"Basically, Torrington was intact. His eyes were a little open. His skin, fingernails, hair, flesh—his clothes—all intact. As for Hartnell, who died so soon after him, his preservation was nearly as good."

"And did he die of TB too?"

"Ah," Bolton said. "This is where it gets really interesting."

Jo eyed him warily. She wasn't at all sure what Bolton meant by *interesting*.

"Take William Braine," Bolton continued, really into his subject now. "He was a tough fellow. A royal marine. He'd seen action, earned his colors. He had a scar on his forehead, his teeth were in poor condition. So poor that the pulp in one of the front teeth was exposed. It'd been broken, and had no treatment. Must have caused him agonies. Now, here was a man used to privations, used to a hard life, used to the sea. He'd survived much worse than this. Yet he weighed only eighty-four pounds. He was really emaciated, a starvation victim."

"But . . ." Jo thought. "He died in April, right?"

"Right."

"Less than a year after they started out?"

"Yes."

"But they had all those provisions. Enough for years . . ."

"That's right."

"Thousands of cans . . ."

"Yes."

She stared at him. "So how could a man die of starvation, with all that food aboard?"

A bell rang down the corridor. The student behind the reception desk came out into the corridor, glancing up at the clock. It was ten o'clock; the doors were opening to the public.

Jo looked away, back to the framed exhibits under her hand. So very few fragments, from the huge bulk of those ships. Three graves, out of 129 men.

Bolton looked down, too, at the few remnants enclosed in glass.

"Both Braine and Hartnell had TB, like Torrington," he said, quietly. "Both probably succumbed to pneumonia. But it was the speed that it took hold. Because they were, in all probability, weakened already."

Jo looked back up to him, frowning.

"By what?" she asked.

"They were poisoned," Bolton replied.

Jo walked out into the fresh air, taking deep lungfuls as she walked alongside Midsummer Common. It was a lovely morning, the air very still, the sounds of the city muted, as if the world were standing still for a moment to appreciate the day.

Still, she couldn't rid herself of the image of the Y incision, of the examination in the candlelit dark of the ship, of the muted fear of the men. She said a little prayer to herself, to thank God for being born in the twentieth century, for being born female—anything, in fact, that had preserved her from having been born at the dawn of the nineteenth, and of serving on a ship like *Terror*.

She stopped at a florist's and bought an enormous bunch of pinks. She had no idea how Doug Marshall would react to being bought flowers, and she didn't really care. They were as much for her as for him. She had to have their scent and color in her arms for a few minutes, to banish the images of Torrington and Hartnell, which lingered in her head.

Doug answered the ring on the bell immediately.

"Come up," he said through the intercom. "The door's open. Four flights of stairs."

He was sitting on a couch with his leg propped on a stool in front of him.

"Well," she said, "you're looking fine."

"I feel okay," he said.

"Are you working?"

"Just messing."

She shifted from one foot to the other before she realized that she still had the flowers in her arms. "These are for you," she said.

"Thank you."

"I'll put them in water."

"Can you make tea while you're there?" he asked. "I'd do it myself, but . . ."

"No problem."

As she waited for the kettle to boil, she glanced around the room. It was obvious that Doug slept on the same couch that he was now sitting on; a pile of blankets and pillows was stacked alongside it. "This must be really difficult for you, with the leg," she said.

"Friends come in," he told her. "One of the secretaries has taken pity on me. She shops."

"And cooking?"

"I can cook. Anything quick."

She hesitated. "I was surprised when you gave me the address," she said. "I thought you'd be at Franklin House."

"Franklin House isn't my home," he said. "My wife lives there."

She turned to make the tea, feeling awkward. Behind her back, as she filled the mugs and set out the tray, Doug added, "We've been separated for five years."

"I'm sorry," she said. She omitted, tactfully, to tell him that she had already guessed.

Doug was sitting back. Glancing in his direction, she caught a fleeting look of pain. He shook his hand, as if swatting away an irritation.

Jo brought the tray over. "Is there a nurse coming in?" she asked.

"Yes, the district one."

She considered him. "Is there some medication you want now?" she asked.

He paused a minute, then made a submissive gesture, spreading his hands. "Shit, I thought I'd fool you," he said. "Top drawer. Just here, next to the couch."

She looked, took out the bottle, gave it to him. She went over to the sink and got him a glass of water. He swallowed the tablet. As he passed the glass back to her, his hand brushed hers. She felt herself blush. *Damn it*, she thought, *what's this? I haven't blushed since I was twelve.*

She busied herself with the glass and replacing the medicine bottle, hoping he hadn't noticed. "You should be in hospital, or some sort of convalescence," she said, over her shoulder.

He rested his head against the couch, then looked up at her. "Look, Jo," he said, "if we're to get on at all, don't fuss."

She said nothing. She sat down opposite him and drank her tea, smiling a little.

She wasn't at all offended: in fact, rather the opposite. Her father, while he had been alive, had been just this sort of man. Older than her mother by twenty-two years, and fifty when he had fathered Jo, he had been short on conversation and temper, and his turn of phrase could cut to the quick. But he had a soft heart that regularly brought tears to his eyes at the least expected times: watching the TV news, or reading an article in a newspaper. He had been six foot three, and heavily built, and wore a three-piece suit with the inevitable scattering of ash from his cigars. She could summon him at will, sitting in the front row of her school nativity play, looking like an elder statesman, and blotting his eyes with a handkerchief.

"What are you smiling at?" Doug said.

She jolted back to the room. "Nothing."

"Me?"

"Not you. My father."

"Great," he said. "I remind you of your father."

She grinned at him. Putting down her mug, she picked up the nearest book, which had fallen from the couch, and had been lying with its pages bent back against the spine. She looked at the title, *Field Anthropology*.

"I've just been hearing about an anthropologist," she told him. "Owen Beattie."

"Ah," Doug said. "Brilliant. Beechey Island."

"And this lead," she said. "The lead soldering on the tins from Goldner."

"Who's this from?"

"Peter Bolton. I've just been down to the Academy."

"Why?"

"To talk to Peter Bolton. . . ."

"But why? For an article?"

"No," she said. "I'm curious."

"Never met a woman curious about Franklin," he said.

"You told me that on the ship."

"Did I?"

"Yes," she replied. "You said that your wife had told you that Franklin bored women rigid. Something like that."

"Did I?" he repeated.

"I told you that I'd already met Alicia and she threw me off your property."

Doug nodded, as if this were to be expected from his wife. Then, "I'm sorry, Jo. I don't remember much of what we said on the ship."

"You were pretty well out of it, even the next day," she said. "But then, we didn't talk about Alicia then. Just Greenland and Crozier. But"—she leaned forward—"you didn't tell me about the cans. The provisions. This lead poisoning."

Doug nodded. He leaned back against the couch and slid a hand under the small of his back, pulling a face. "Good old Stephan Goldner," he muttered. "The Grim Reaper."

She nodded. "It reads like a murder mystery. He supplied all the tins to the expedition?"

"Every one."

"But he'd done this before, supplied Admiralty ships?"

"Yes, plenty," Doug said. "And always worked the same way. Delivered late, in all the wrong sizes. Basically to avoid having his work checked. When he was hired for Franklin, he had a good reputation. But he got much worse as time went on."

"But they kept on hiring him?"

"He did have the capacity to fill huge contracts. And he did have this . . . well, you and I would call it a death warrant. He called it his patented system for preserving foodstuffs." Doug shook his head. "More modern technology, you see?" he said. "They wanted the best, the newest patented this and that. . . ."

"And all the cans were contaminated. That's what you think too?"

"I don't think. I know. Getting worse and worse the longer they were left before they were opened. Beattie found lead in Torrington's bone and hair."

"Yes, Peter just told me."

"A huge quantity of lead," Doug said. "From four hundred thirteen to six hundred fifty-seven parts per million. In a culture that isn't exposed to lead—like the Inuits in the area, at the time, for instance—you might find, say, thirty parts per million."

"Jesus," Jo breathed.

"And Hartnell was anything up to three hundred thirteen per million."

"And Braine?"

"Two hundred eighty."

"And . . . all from the cans?"

Doug shifted again in his seat. "Well, Victorian society was lead saturated, compared to today," he conceded. "For instance, all their tea was wrapped in lead foil. And they had pewterware, and lead-glazed pottery. All those things could contaminate. Probably John Torrington's level was so high because of the lead in coal dust. Or perhaps because they'd fed him exclusively from the tins, for weeks, in an effort to improve his health. But"—Doug slapped his hand on the couch—"it was the tins, and Goldner's bloody greed. That's what did for them all."

"You think that Franklin's men opened the tins and found it bad?" Jo asked.

"In some cases, yes," Doug said. "In others, maybe the meat looked all right, but it was probably not only tainted with the lead solder that had been used to seal the tins in the first place, but with all kinds of toxic stuff. Botulism, for a start. Victorian slaughterhouses and food preparation left a lot to be desired. Okay if you ate the stuff straightaway, and cooked it thoroughly. But Goldner canned it and then cooked it, without any real proof that his heating method got through to the meat in the center of the can. So . . ."

"So whatever was on the meat in the center of the can, uncooked, or partially cooked . . ."

"Putrefied inside the can and infected everything in it." He grimaced. "Imagine opening that two years down the line."

"My God," Jo said, shocked.

He gave her a small smile, and hesitated. His gaze slipped over her, as if seeing her in a slightly new light. She saw the spark of interest, and her stomach did a lazy little flip. She crossed her arms. Defense.

Against herself? Him?

Well, what? she thought. She dug her nails into the inner flesh of her elbow, but a flush spread to her face in spite of herself. A phrase of Gina's sprang to her mind, something that Gina had said one night as they shared several bottles of Beck's, and put the world, and each other, to rights.

"You'll never get a man while you hold yourself back," Gina had said.

"What are you talking about?"

Gina smiled. "Keeping yourself behind glass."

"I do not," Jo had protested.

Gina had sat back, grinning at her. "Oh yeah? Name one man, then. Someone you really let yourself go with."

"Well, I . . ."

"Just *one.*"

"Simon."

Gina had hooted derision. "Name one within the last two years, I mean."

Jo had pulled a face. "I get along."

"Oh, yeah," Gina said. And she had leaned forward and touched Jo's arm. "Kid, I worry for you. I really do."

"No need."

"Right." Gina had nodded. "No need. But you'll fall. You'll fall, girl, and when you do"—she'd wagged her finger—"when you do, girl, you'll fall *hard.* You wait. Trust me. I know."

Jo had thought little of it at the time. She could get a man if she wanted, she always reasoned. She just didn't want. And there would be plenty of time and opportunity, when she was ready. And when she *was* ready, it would be on her terms, not his. Her time, not his. Her . . . She looked again at Doug.

Oh shit, she thought.

She suddenly leaned forward. "Do you mind me asking how old you are?" she said.

"I was forty last week," he told her. "Why? How old are you?"

"Twenty-six."

Doug nodded, a small smile on his face. "So . . ."

"Nothing," she told him. The blush came back with a vengeance. "Nothing."

She went back to a safer subject. "It seems like all sorts of things were wrong with this voyage from the start."

"Yes."

"Especially the lead."

"That's right. And to make matters worse, when they looked at William Braine's body," Doug said, "they found clostridium. In fact, they cultured it."

Jo did a double-take. "It's *alive*? The bacteria in his gut?"

"Yes."

"From a hundred and sixty years ago?"

"Yes."

"That's incredible."

"It is."

"And what is clostridium?" Jo asked.

Doug shifted again in his seat, easing the leg a little from its precarious balance. "Well, you find it in soil," he said. "It's the main thing that breaks down organic matter. It's the family of bacteria that causes tetanus and gangrene."

"If it's in soil, it must be very common," Jo said.

Doug considered. "You mean, common enough to be on items outside the tins, and not just in them?"

"Maybe. Didn't they have live cattle on the ships?"

"For a short time."

"And hygiene wasn't exactly pristine. . . ."

"It could have come from a variety of sources," Doug acknowledged. "But when you have thousands of tins belowdecks, there's a good primary source. And *Clostridium botulinum* flourishes in badly processed tinned food."

Jo sat back in her chair. She looked hard at him. "So, what do you fancy for lunch?" she asked.

His laughter was punctuated by the ringing of the doorbell. A few seconds later they heard one of the other tenants of the house go down the stairs, a muffled conversation on the threshold, and then a second set of footsteps—lighter and more measured—coming up to Doug's room.

"Expecting anyone?" Jo asked.

"No," Doug said.

Alicia appeared in the doorway.

The first thing that occurred to Jo was that Alicia looked even more composed, more glacial, than she had a month ago. She had also taken extreme care over her appearance, it seemed. Her hair was a shade or two lighter than Jo remembered, and a little softer, curling onto her shoulder. Her makeup was faultless. She wore a linen suit and carried a large portfolio leather case. On one arm was a little woven basket with a cloth tidily tucked over its contents. Her gaze traveled very slowly over her husband, then onto Jo.

"Hello," Jo said.

Alicia looked at her expressionlessly. She didn't reply. Instead she walked over to Doug. She leaned down and kissed his cheek.

"This is Jo Harper," Doug said.

"Yes, I know," Alicia replied. She perched herself on the edge of the couch. She looked into his eyes. "How are you?" she asked him.

"I'm fine. Alicia, this is Jo Harper."

"You don't look fine," she said. "In fact, you look utterly dreadful."

Jo wriggled a little in her chair. Doug did not look dreadful. Tired, maybe. Fussed with the nagging irritation of the ache. But not dreadful.

"I am fine," he repeated.

Alicia glanced down at the blankets. "Camping out," she said. "It's so unnecessary, darling."

Jo saw a slight flinch at the *darling*. "What are you doing here?" he asked.

Alicia smiled. If anything was dreadful, Jo considered silently, it was the sight of that tight, hard mouth. The older woman turned her head in Jo's direction. "More to the point, why are *you* here?" she asked Jo.

Doug visibly stiffened. "Alicia . . ."

"I read your piece," Alicia said.

"Did you? What did you think?" Jo asked.

"Unpleasantly sensationalist," Alicia told her.

"Really?" Jo said. "That's lucky."

"Lucky?" Alicia repeated.

"Lucky I don't really care one way or the other," Jo told her. "We're just going to lunch. Would you like to come?"

"Lunch?" Alicia said. "That will be interesting to see. He can't get down the stairs."

"I can," Doug said.

"I can help him," Jo added.

Alicia stood up. "It won't be necessary," she announced. "I brought lunch with me."

"I'm going out," Doug objected.

"No," Alicia said. "Not unless you're coming home. That would be different."

"For fuck's sake," Doug said.

Jo stood up. She picked up her bag. "I'll go, I think."

"No," Doug retorted, holding up his hand.

"Good-bye," Alicia said.

"Good-bye, Doug," Jo said. "Nice to talk."

"For Christ's sake, she's driven up from London," Doug told Alicia. "You might at least be civil. I invited her, not you."

"Let her drive back again," Alicia said.

"She's not bloody driving back again," Doug yelled. "I'm going out to lunch with her."

"I'll catch you some other time," Jo said.

"You will not catch me some other fucking time," Doug said. He was struggling to get up, casting about him for his walking stick.

"Don't be so absurd," Alicia said.

"Why don't you leave me alone," Doug told her. "Jo . . ."

"How do you think you'll get him downstairs?" Alicia demanded of Jo. "Do you realize that he hasn't been out of this room since he got back?"

Jo looked at Doug. "No," she said. "He didn't tell me."

"You see?" Alicia said to her husband.

"He has to go out sometime, I suppose," Jo observed.

"Damn right," Doug said.

Jo took a step forward. She put her hand on Doug's arm. He gave her a look that was almost plaintive, like a dog being left in the house when everyone else is going for a walk in the country. For a second she thought that he was actually going to say, *Don't leave me.*

"I'll be back another time," she said. "Really . . . it's probably impractical—"

"I'll show you out," Alicia said.

"Thanks," Jo told her, "but I can find my own way."

Eleven

THEY were under sail, heading south in the Arctic summer.

It was August 1846.

And Gus was ill.

He didn't know when it had started, or even that he was truly ill at all. But he knew that there was something different, especially in his dreams; dreams that invaded his waking hours. And he knew that he was thinner and lighter, and he didn't look at his wrists and hands anymore, hiding them, whenever he could, under the sleeve cuffs of his shirt or jacket. His hands did not belong to him. They belonged to John.

John, on New Year's Eve.

He was so ashamed of his conviction. How could he tell people that he had someone else's hands? It was so fanciful as to be funny. Perhaps it *was* funny. Perhaps he was living a joke that someone was playing on him. Perhaps someone had whispered, one night before he went to sleep, that they were not his own hands but Torrington's, and that thought had been sewn into his mind as if it were his own. Now he couldn't rid himself of it. Inside the coffin, far behind them now on Beechey, were his own fingers. The yellow-white hands that had been tied against Torrington's legs had been given to him.

He carried them like some terrible trophy.

He was so tired too; tired enough not to really follow where they were, even though they had left Beechey at a run one morning in July, scattering possessions, leaving behind even the stacks of tins that, lately, he had made into careful rows, and which some of the men intended to use for target practice. One of the mates left a pair of his best gloves, which he had pinned out to dry, weighed down by stones. Things of consequence and those of no consequence were scattered as they ran: empty coal bags; and pieces of canvas that they had been patching and ought to have been snatched up immediately, and not discarded.

Worst of all, to Gus's lasting horror and dismay, as he charged down the shore, he heard a faint metallic noise on the stones, stopped, and could not see what it had been. Only when he was on the ship did he realize that he had managed to drop the key from Torrington's little box, the key that he had promised to Torrington's mother. It was too late by then, of course; they were already under way. And with terrible shame at his carelessness Gus stared back at Beechey, and the three wood-headboarded graves, which looked so forlorn as they left the inlet, so very far from home.

As they sailed, he did not feel inclined to work, although work was the principal purpose of his being there, and he had formerly been so very proud of all he could do. On some days he was in good spirits, and only the curious obsession with Torrington's hands, and the shame of his own, stayed with him. On other days—the worst—a sensation of complete fatigue swept him under. Once his stomach cramped as he stood in line to climb the rigging, and he was excused, with a threat and the back of the hand. And he had hidden himself, trying to swallow down a strange, sweet taste like metal, longing for something from home . . . the milk from the cart. Plain milk with the top skimmed from it. He would have killed for a drink like that, for the feeling of it passing down his throat. For any taste at all that was not metal, or salt.

He thought, perhaps, that salt did not agree with him. But he did not say so. Everything that entered his mind was so entirely ludicrous. How could salt not agree with a sailor? But he truly seemed better when they did not eat the salted pork in the rations, and when they had feasted on the birds that had been shot on Beechey. He thought he would like to eat fresh meat every day. He even thought that, rather than cast off from the island, he would prefer to stay there and watch the skies fill with the thousands upon thousands of birds as they wheeled over from the south.

He liked the little dovekies best. They were small and stocky, with a black head and a clean white underbelly. Standing on Beechey's shore, keeping still and silent, he could sense the changes around him, as if the ocean were thrashing into life, and the skies filling. The solid ground of Beechey and the rising rock of Devon were nothing, mere lifeless strands. Out there—out there in the sea—was where all life congregated, in countless numbers of fish and whale and narwhal and walrus. For those first few weeks of summer he felt he was on some sort of carriageway, where invisible streams of giant foot and horse traffic brushed past him. He could sense their body weight pressing into the empty spaces. And he would glance back at the ships—that had looked so mighty against the Greenhithe dock—and think how very small they were in such a very large world.

The ice cracked on the last day of July.

They heard an explosion out to sea—just that, an explosion, as if God had mined his own white landscape and blown it to pieces. There had been a flurry of activity, with officers on deck, and signals passing between the ships.

"Ice moving!" he heard as he clambered on deck. It was Crozier's voice.

They came out into the Barrow Strait, into the very area where the ice had impeded them last year, and the wind rose, and *Erebus* and *Terror* plowed forward and picked up speed, racing like yachts. It was a brisk and blindingly bright day, and the roll of the water and the sound of the wind in the sails was heaven. Movement! Glorious movement! They rounded the northern shore of Somerset Island and entered Peel Sound, overjoyed to find this unknown strait going directly south.

"Now we're at it," the men said. "Now we're for the Pacific."

There were no icebergs to be seen. Only the sea, the beautiful sea with its many colors, so many wonderful colors. The relief from the gray and white of Beechey was like a drug. Blue, blue ocean—cobalt and aquamarine and dark green and deepest royal blue—rushed past them. They saw walrus and whale, of so many numbers that even Gus gasped at their quantity, their size. Enough whales to light the world with their oil, streaming past them. It was like passing through rooms of treasure, ignoring a lifetime of riches for the greater prize beyond.

On the second day after entering Peel, a message was passed from *Erebus*.

"What does it say?" Gus asked the nearest man.

"We are to keep sail," he told him.

"But why wouldn't we keep sail?" Gus asked, puzzled.

"Crozier wants to stop to build cairns," he was told. "On the shorelines, to post ships that might come after us, to say where we have been and when we were here."

Gus shrugged. It seemed stupid to halt when they were flying across the water with every hour. When they got to the Pacific, then there would be more than enough time to tell the world where they had come through and when.

" 'Tis orders," the men in the mess grumbled. But not for long. In truth, none of them wanted to halt the swift, sweet running of *Terror*.

They had been sailing out of Beechey for less than a week when they saw the ice again.

Bergs started to appear far to the south, and Thomas Blanky, the *Terror*'s ice master, was constantly on deck, as much listening for safe passage as looking for it. A man could hear the different voices in the ice as it passed—the gentle slow-stirring sound of melted ice granules in the water, the rasp of newly frozen pancake against the bows, the greater dull thump of pieces of isolated drift.

Men were posted to lookouts.

"Growlers," came the call, at midday on the third day.

High up on the masts the lookouts could see what the crew could not until the ships were almost upon them: large weighty chunks of ice that hit the hulls and whose reverberation shuddered through the entire ship. True to their name, they growled along *Terror*'s side.

"See that floe," Blanky said. "Old pack."

The words filtered through the ship's company. *Old floe* had a deeper significance even than the growlers. It meant a chunk of ice, perhaps as large as a house, with snow still stacked on top of it, and tide marks all around it. This was ice that had seen more than one winter. It did not appear in the ocean by chance; it came from deeper, faster ice behind it. Ice that had been there, packed tight, for perhaps many winters, and only the extraordinary warmth of the last weeks had freed it.

Still keeping a swift pace, despite the ice, *Erebus* and *Terror* covered almost 250 miles.

"Land!" came the cry.

All hands rushed to the side, following the direction of the lookout's outstretched arm.

Only just visible in the distance was a low, dim outline.

"What is it?" Gus asked.

"King William Land!" was the reply. "King William Land!"

Gus immediately looked to Blanky, and to Crozier, who were upon the bridge. He saw that Blanky was not looking south, but back, to the northwest, to the direction of the large, open stretch of sea guarded by Gateshead Island. They had passed the entry to it forty-eight hours before. As Gus followed Blanky's gaze, he saw how much white was piled in the sea in their wake—more white now than blue.

We're being closed in again, flashed through the boy's mind. *We shall be trapped.* And he shoved the idea away, pressed it out of his head. It didn't matter if the ice closed in behind them, as long as it kept open in front. King William Land, he knew, was not very far from the channel called Simpson Strait. If they passed King William, they would be in Simpson. And Simpson was past halfway, much closer to the Pacific than the Atlantic. The glimpse of King William was a glimpse of salvation.

Better not to look back at all.

At six in the evening the ships hove to. Clouds were gathering on the horizon, but the sea was calm. Crozier came on deck, with lieutenants Little and Hodgson, and with the captain's steward, Jopson. Jopson came down the gangway and grabbed Gus by his shoulder, hauling him to the rail.

Gus shrank under Crozier's inspection. The captain seemed smaller now than he had at Greenhithe the previous year. His gaze was stonier. His smile less ready.

"Augustus," Crozier said, "you're coming with me. I want you to see Mr. Goodsir."

Jopson pushed him in the back, between his shoulder blades.

"Aye, sir," Gus replied.

Crozier looked hard at him for a second or two. "Good lad," he murmured.

You would not have known that *Erebus* was the younger ship by some thirteen years. Bigger than *Terror* at 372 tons, she was 105 feet long, with a twenty-nine-foot beam. She looked darker, uglier; as if scarred by age. Boarding her at sea was a prolonged business, to get over the wood projecting two feet from the topside, built especially to prevent rising sea ice encroaching onto the decks.

As they neared her, Gus looked up at her slightly rotund, rolled shape. She was like a great floating dock. She moved in the swell of the ocean like a heavyweight boxer feeling his way around a dirt circle, his arms loose at his sides, eyeing the enemy. As he was brought up, Gus couldn't imagine that the growlers that still churned away to left and right could ever beset this almighty ship. It was almost as if she were staring them down. The fighter, ready for the fight.

They went down through the single hatch on an almost vertical seven-foot ladder to the lower deck. This was the only deck that was heated, and Gus could still smell the sooty residue of the winter; though brushed, the beams were dark, and the wood a little greasy to the touch. They went down a two-foot-wide companionway, a narrow tunnel with very little light. Gus realized where they were going. It was almost the same as *Terror;* they might even have been in the same ship. At the end was the officers' messroom. It was here that Jopson opened the door, and stood back to let Crozier, Little, Hodgson, and Blanky enter.

"Stay there," Crozier said to Jopson. "Wait until Mr. Goodsir comes to you."

Gus peered through the crack of the door.

The Preston patent illuminators, the circular glass skylights, let in pools of sunlight, scattering watery refraction across the cabin. Under one of these, his face rather ghostly in the bluish tone, sat Franklin himself.

Gus had not seen the great man in recent weeks. Not close like this.

The boy stared at the legend, a coat wrapped around him despite the risen temperatures. Franklin was looking down at maps spread on the center table; Gus noticed the roll of flesh at the collar, the drooping of the skin around the eyes. He looked far more than his sixty years.

The officers were already talking. As Gus watched, Franklin interrupted his men.

"There is no choice," he said, in a slow and surprisingly frail voice. "Poctes Bay may well provide ample wintering. But we are not looking for winter quarters."

They leaned forward over the map.

Franklin's finger was resting on the Admiralty North Polar chart given to him just before the ships had sailed. On it King William Land was clearly marked in their own vicinity; but the southern coast was not known. All that could be known for certain was that, from where they were anchored now, straits passed to either side of King William; to the east was James Ross Strait, to the west Victoria.

Crozier sat down at Franklin's side. He looked steadfastly for some time at Poctes Bay, a dotted line running from east to west, indicating that King William was fastened to the Boothia Peninsula and, as such, was part of the American continent.

"There is no way out down James Ross Strait," Franklin said.

Crozier looked up.

"This is my contention," Franklin said, seeing the expression on Crozier's face.

"I am not convinced, sir," Crozier murmured. "I am sorry."

It was his first utterance since entering the room. A small murmur went around the other officers.

"You don't agree?" Fitzjames asked.

"I am not convinced."

"No man can be convinced until he has seen with his own eyes, and the channel is traversed," Fitzjames agreed. "But fair guessing . . ."

"It is not my fair guess either," Crozier said.

A look passed between Crozier and Blanky, the ice master of the *Terror*. Franklin sat back in his seat. The reflection of the waves rippled over his folded hands. "Expand upon your theory," he said.

Crozier turned the sister chart, No. 261, toward him. "Here at the southernmost tip we assume the isthmus between King William and Boothia," he said, quietly. "Dease and Simpson and Ross have all assumed such a link."

"And the assumption is of sufficient strength to be mapped," Franklin said.

"But nevertheless it is an assumption," Crozier replied.

Franklin waved his hand. "And you think there is no isthmus, and the way is clear to Victoria, to the west? That King William is an island?"

"Yes, sir. It may well be so."

"And what relevance," Franklin asked, "is this to our discussion?"

"That if we went east, we find our way through as effectively as if we went west," Crozier said. "And we may not meet such heavy ice."

There was silence. Franklin considered Crozier for some time. At last he said, "There is no gamble in going west. There is a gamble—the gamble that we will meet the isthmus exactly as marked, and find ourselves in a bay, exactly as marked—in going east."

"But there *is* a gamble going west," Crozier said.

"Name it," Franklin retorted.

Crozier glanced up at Blanky. The Yorkshireman shifted a little, uncomfortably. He had sailed with the same Ross for whom this strait was named.

"I know nothing more than the next man," Blanky replied, "as to whether east is a dead end or not. But"—he glanced warily around the faces of the other officers—"with respect, Sir John, I do know the ice. And we have ice coming hard from Victoria. There is ice ahead, terrible fast. There may not be such ice on the other side."

"You cannot know it is fast," Franklin said.

"It is my opinion, sir."

"Based on what?"

"The condition of the passing bergs," Blanky said.

"We have steam to break through passing berg," Franklin commented.

"But not enough steam to break through fast pack and floe," Blanky answered.

Franklin smiled. "We have railway locomotives belowdeck, man."

"Not even they will break through what is to come," Blanky said.

There was complete silence. Franklin's expression was dead. Fitzjames made a little breathy sound and settled himself opposite Franklin, raising his eyebrows.

Franklin turned to James Reid. The *Erebus* ice master had his gaze fixed on Chart 261.

"What say you, Mr. Reid?" Franklin asked.

Reid colored. He did not always like to speak too loud; he was conscious of his North Country accent. He felt self-conscious belowdeck, even now, when the entire expedition rested on his and Blanky's skill.

"There is old ice coming past us," he said, finally. "But Victoria is the shortest and most direct route."

Franklin, for the first time, smiled. "Exactly," he said. "Exactly my point. We can outrace winter. Outpace the ice before it becomes solid."

Crozier visibly blanched. Blanky looked away.

"We have in our ships the most powerful methods of breaking

through even compacted floe," Franklin said. "We are armored. No ships are better equipped to break through. And we must seize our chance now. There may be less than two weeks before Mr. Blanky's predictions come true. I contend they are not true yet. But they might become so if we do not act quickly and make speed. Speed, down the shortest route."

There was a general murmur of consent.

Except for Crozier.

"Sir," Crozier said, "steam will not get us through Victoria Strait."

Franklin's face hardened for a second. Gus saw a flash of what he might have been as a younger man. Then it vanished. The older man, who saw himself as the father of his crew, reappeared.

"We know your opinion of steam, I think," he replied.

"Had I commanded this expedition, I should have refused to sail depending upon steam," Crozier said. "It is not the answer to our prayers. If we hope it will bring us through Victoria Strait, we are wrong. We shall be beset out of any safe harbor. The ice will close in upon us before we have passed King William. Before we sight Simpson. Long before."

It was almost insubordination. The officers froze, as if the slightest movement might cause offense. Crozier's voice had risen, and his Irish accent become profound. Gus saw a little spot of color on each of Franklin's cheeks—little round red farthings.

Franklin leaned forward. "But you are not commanding this expedition," he said.

Crozier colored.

"We shall not be beset in Victoria Strait," Franklin said, slowly. "We shall not sail to the east to find ourselves, as Ross himself predicted, in Poctes Bay, with no way out. We shall sail on through Victoria and reach Simpson before the week is out, and we shall blast our way, if necessary, through ice. And, with God's will, we shall see the Pacific before winter comes."

Crozier, at last, dropped his eyes.

"And that, Mr. Crozier," Franklin said, standing at last, "is my final word on the subject."

Twelve

IT was Friday night.

Jo was fast asleep on her couch, and the comedy tape she had rented from the video store was spooling away, entertaining thin air. She was lying on her side, dead to the world, when the doorbell rang.

She woke up and tried to think where she was. She squinted at her wristwatch. Nine-forty. She rubbed her eyes, wondering if the caller was Gina; earlier that day she had rung to invite Jo to her godson's birthday party.

"I can't," Jo had said. "I'm decorating."

There had been a moment of disbelieving silence. "No kidding."

"I *am*," Jo protested. "I've got paint and everything."

"What color?"

"Yellow."

"All over?"

"All over," Jo told her resolutely. "It's going to be bright."

"What brought this on?"

"Boredom," Jo told her.

"More like shame."

Jo laughed. "I emptied the moving boxes too."

"You did? Where did you put it all?"

"On the floor."

"Ah. Nice try," Gina said. "You're sure you won't come over?"

"Will there be jelly and ice cream?"

"Tons."

"Tempting," Jo said. "Look, if I get finished . . ."

"And if not?"

"Come around tomorrow morning. Bring food."

Gina laughed again. "See you."

The doorbell rang again.

Jo got up. "Okay," she yelled.

She looked down at herself. Her jeans were spattered with paint; her hair too. She had started off using a roller and, finding that she somehow managed to get more on herself than the walls, switched to a brush midafternoon. It had been slower, but more effective. Now her one large living room glowed. Even in the dark.

"I'm here, I'm here," she grumbled, as whoever it was on the other side began knocking. She turned off the TV. "Who is it?" she called.

"Doug," came the answer.

She stopped dead and stared, in surprise, at the door on her side. Then she rapidly undid the lock and chain.

He was leaning on the outside wall just by the steps. Even in the sulphur shadow of the streetlights he looked gray.

"My God," she said, "what on earth are you doing here?"

"I'm on a half marathon," he said.

"You what?"

"A joke."

"I thought you were Gina," she said.

"As you can see . . ."

"Yes."

"Jo," he said, "if you don't let me in, I can't guarantee I won't fall down."

She jolted. "Jesus, I'm sorry. You just gave me a shock . . . come in. Are you okay? Let me help you."

By a series of shuffles and stumbles she at last got him to the couch, Jo kicking the door shut with one foot as he leaned on her arm.

"Thank the Lord," he muttered, collapsing in the seat.

"You look awful," she said. "What possessed you?"

"Insanity," he told her. He looked around him. "You've been busy." She registered the powerfulness of the smell for the first time, since the fresh air of the doorway. "And yellow," he said. "Very yellow, isn't it?"

"What's wrong with yellow?"

"Nothing," he said. "It's a bit streaked, though."

"It is not," she said. She paused, hand on hip. "Where?"

"By that table."

"It's not a table, it's a box."

He smiled. "And to think that I was worried you'd be offended by *my* flat."

"I beg your pardon," she retorted. "This is not offensive. It's tidy." She looked back at him. "You really do look bloody awful," she said. "Do you want a drink?"

"I'm not allowed. Medication. What have you got?"

"I've got a bit of brandy. Tea and brandy."

"You persuaded me," he said.

She went to the kitchen and found the brandy bottle pushed to the back of a cupboard. "How long does brandy keep?" she shouted. "I got it at Christmas."

"Which year?"

She shook her head, laid a tray, took in the drinks, and a big teapot. She had rummaged in the biscuit tin and found two sad-looking wafers, slightly soggy.

"Look, this is embarrassing," she said, putting the tray on the carpet. "I could go and get takeout."

"Sit a minute," he said. He drank the brandy. Color gradually returned to his face.

"How did you get here?" she asked.

"A friend gave me a lift to Charing Cross. I got a hotel room. Taxi from the hotel."

"Just to see me?"

"Just to see you," he said.

"But why?"

"To apologize."

"Doug," she said. "I could have been out."

"I'd have tried again in the morning."

"But I could have been out all weekend."

"Then I'd try again on Monday."

"Come on."

"I have a meeting at the National Maritime then."

"Ah."

He shifted forward. "But that's not it, Jo. That's not as important. I came early to see you."

"To apologize for what, exactly?"

"Alicia."

"Oh," Jo said. She considered. "Well, maybe she should apologize."

"She should. I should have thrown *her* out, not you."

"You didn't throw me out," she reminded him. "I walked."

He fisted his hand around the stem of the glass. "She is just such a steamroller."

"It doesn't matter, Doug."

"It does," he said. "You took the flight out to the ship, you drove up to see me when I got back."

"None of which you asked me to do."

"Well, no. But I'm glad you did."

She smiled.

"So the least I could have done—"

"You can't throw your own wife out," she told him. "As far as she's concerned, *I'm* the interloper."

"If anyone's an interloper, it's her," he retorted. Jo could see she had struck a nerve. An old, ragged nerve that flared to life within seconds. "She won't take no for an answer," he said. "It's driving me mad. I've tried talking, I've tried shouting. I've tried breaking the furniture."

"You did?"

"A year or two back."

"She loves you," Jo said.

"She doesn't love me," he told her. "She's attached. It's parasitical."

"You're still her husband."

"Only just," he said. "I filed for divorce two months ago."

Jo drank her own brandy slowly. "Perhaps that's it," she said. "Losing you. Hanging on all the harder."

"I can't tell you," he said, "what the last five years have been like."

Jo paused, fiddling with the edge of the tray. It didn't feel quite right to sit condemning Alicia in the other woman's absence, even if Jo found it hard to cast Alicia in any kind of favorable light.

She found herself eating one of the biscuits, and tried not to pull a face. "How did you meet?" she asked.

He smiled. "Now you're asking ancient history," he said. "College. University."

"In Cambridge?"

"No. A place called Lancaster."

"I know it," she said.

"Do you?"

"One of my schoolfriends went there. I went up . . . God, three years ago? Near the sea."

"Lancashire coast," he confirmed. "Alicia took economics and politics."

"Fearsome."

"She always was."

"And you . . ."

"Alicia decided we would get married," he continued. "She was a very organized girl. She had this aura . . . you know, she would get things done. Moving. She was like no one else in that place. She was light-years ahead of the other girls. She had vision, a map of her life." He at last put the glass down, staring at it while remembering. "Where she would be by thirty. By forty. By fifty. She suggested the postgraduate degree. She seemed to think I had a bright future." He frowned. "I couldn't see it, but she did. We moved south, she got a job, she supported my studies . . ."

"And you got married."

"Only when John was on the way."

"I see."

Doug caught her expression. "Yes," he said. "I'm a selfish person."

"Oh, I don't know," she replied. "Plenty of people find themselves in situations—"

"I used her," he said. "She handled everything. She was a storm force. I think she even planned her pregnancy, although she denies it now."

"Didn't you discuss it?"

He hesitated. "I had someone else."

Jo looked at him in surprise. "You'd split up?"

"No," he said. "We'd been together for two years. I had met a girl, and was thinking of telling Alicia, break it off . . ."

"To be with this other girl?"

"Yes."

"And then Alicia told you she was pregnant?"

"Yes." Jo met his eye. "I know," he said. "But I couldn't let her down. She forgave me."

"Forgave you for loving this other girl?" Jo said. "That was good of her." She couldn't help the cynicism that had sprung to her voice. Seeing his reaction, she gave a little shrug. "I'm sorry," she said. "It just sounded a little like blackmail. Alicia's pregnancy. What did the other girl say?"

"She was"—he paused—"well, there isn't a good word for it, Jo. She was devastated. Really devastated. I was so torn, I didn't know what to do."

"Did you love her?"

To her surprise he blushed deeply. "Very much."

"More than Alicia," she said. It was not a question.

"I couldn't leave Alicia," he replied.

"So you did the right thing."

"John was born," he said. "We both worked hard. It faded. The girl got married to someone else."

"Do you still know her?"

"No. She moved away," he said.

"But with John around, things must have got better."

He looked up. He had been staring at the floor all this time. "Things never got better. I knew by then that I didn't love the woman I'd married. I knew she didn't share my interests. I just worked, and she worked, and she did the lion's share of bringing John up, which I was grateful for, because I was so often away. . . ."

He stopped. "I used her," he repeated. "She wanted a certain kind of life, home, career. Never wanted any other children. Never really interfered with what I wanted to do. We limped along." He scratched his forehead distractedly. "Like a lot of marriages by accident or habit, it's not a very attractive story."

Jo shifted. She was sitting on the floor, and she crossed her legs. As she passed her hand through her hair, she felt the hardened flecks of paint.

He glanced at her. "Jo," he said, "I didn't mean to tell you my life story. I just wanted you to know I was sorry." He started edging forward.

"What are you doing?" she asked.

"I ought to go."

"No, you oughtn't," she said. "I'm going for the takeout any minute."

"You're tired."

"I am not."

He smiled at her. "That's right," he said. I was forgetting. You're twenty-six. You don't get tired."

She gave him a wry grin. "I get shattered like any normal person."

"So . . ." He looked around for the walking stick that he had brought with him.

"But not tonight," she said.

He stopped and looked hard at her.

"I'm not tired tonight," she repeated.

A look coursed across his face: pure astonishment.

She knelt in front of him, and carefully avoiding the injured leg, she leaned forward and kissed him.

She thought that she had done with it all a very long time ago, the fantasy picture of the prince in the fairy tale. She had dispensed with it, just as she had dispensed with other toys, thrown away fiction for fact, made herself take on reality. She had made her way in the actual world, a world packed full of people who belonged in no one's fairy story. She talked to them every day, the egotists with feet of clay; the frightened and disenfranchised; the mundane, the stupid, the ambitious, the plain lucky.

And all this time she had had no idea that there was still a knight waiting in the wings, a fantasy still to be had. She didn't think that her heart had anything unprotected left in it, anything yielding, anything naïve.

She looked at him, and saw everything that had just passed through her own mind reflected in his face.

My God, she thought. *There are still miracles.*

He reached forward and hugged her to him, pressing his face into her shoulder. She felt his chest heave, his arms tighten around her.

"I didn't know," he murmured. "I didn't know."

She leaned back a little and looked him in the face.

"Neither did I," she told him. "But . . . I know now."

Thirteen

THROUGH the storm the great bear slept peacefully.

The temperature dropped rapidly, driving even the Inuit population of Bylot, Borden, and Brodeur into shelter. When the wind began here, there was no facing it: the animal migrants that had come to the fjords turned their backs to the wind, grouped together. Large bull caribou, waiting for the return of the females with calves, crowded in the lee of banked snow. They had crossed the ice from Bylot Island only two weeks before, and now could only endure the howling blast of the gale, bony and ragged already, their winter coats shedding.

The narwhal had already come, breaching the water from their winter in the polar ice fields. The bear sometimes heard the noise as she descended into the ocean. Ringed seal, her target, made barks and yelps like dogs; walrus were the bass and baritone; narwhal and beluga sounded in curious, alien harmonics, saturating the water with their signals.

She had closed her ears to it now, however; curling her huge front paw, she dropped her muzzle below it, covering the only part of her body that radiated heat. She was blissfully at ease. Cold couldn't touch her; only heat, or prolonged exercise out of water, could raise her body temperature. She was an ice machine. Now, as the wind picked up, she slumped slowly to one side, the snow piling on top of her. She was fat with seal, and craved sleep.

Her mate had lain down ten feet from her. For the past few days he had been shadowing her, mesmerized by the smell of estrus in her urine. On the first day of scenting her he had not been alone in his lust; three other males approached. Two had been far too young to bother him; crouching, they had merely observed him from a safe distance. But an eight-year-old male of nine hundred pounds crossed his track barely four hours later. The eight-year-old approached him, weaving a little, his head up to catch his opponent's scent. He raised himself up onto his hind legs, assessing the enemy, eyeing the female. He fell back down to the ice with a grunt from the arthritic pain in an old injury.

They walked toward each other with the characteristic ambling pattern; then the rush began. The heavier male was bigger, but he was also older and slower, and hungry. His bad temper erupted into slamming swipes of his paws, raking claws deflected over the younger male's shoulders. It was certain that they could injure, if not kill, each other, if it came to it. But after only a few minutes the older male retreated, rolling his head at the sound of the roar from his victor. In another continent, in other temperatures, it might have been taken for a lion's: a deep, rumbling, echoing boom.

He and the female mated that day. Over and over again they consummated their union on the ice. The long Arctic day was calm; they roamed the broken floes, stopping from time to time to assess the current. Toward evening they found the bearded seal.

Bearded were the best the male could bring her: bigger than ringed, adults could weigh up to five or six hundred pounds. Bearded seal were eating mechanisms, sucking up crustaceans, especially whelk, which they managed to rid of their shells. Between dives they rested on the ice floes, their stomachs stuffed, sleeping on their drifting white platforms.

The male lowered himself soundlessly into the sea, his huge body disappearing underwater. From time to time he surfaced, his eye on the seal's dark gray body a hundred yards ahead. The female dropped to the ice behind him and watched. He negotiated the ice channels underwater, and, from time to time, rose to the surface, with only his nose and eyes showing. His gaze was fixed: the seal turned its head, but did not see him, and flopped back again, turning her body with a lazy thump of blubber.

At fifty yards the male bear disappeared. For a moment the ocean was utterly still. Then the male exploded from the water, grabbing the seal by the head and following the impact of his claws with a huge blow from his snout. He didn't move like a heavy animal, but exactly like a cat, unbelievably fast and lethally accurate. Death was instant. The water reddened, the carcass was returned to the ice. Good hunting.

In his life the male would eat every available food source: seal, musk-ox, whale, narwhal, walrus, geese, carrion, seaweed, berries, eggs. He needed a lot to maintain his body weight, to keep the thick layers of fat. For most of his time far out on the ice, he would be followed, at a respectful distance, by his personal shadows—arctic foxes, who depended on his kills for their own survival.

The Inuit respected bear like no other creature. To them he was a religious object, a mythical being. In the early months of the year the appearance of the star Aldebaran, in the constellation of Taurus, was linked to the bear. Tracing its journey across the sky in the late afternoon, from northeast to northwest, it was called *nanurjuk*, the spirit of the polar bear, in Cumberland Sound, the sea known so well to the whaling ships; in Repulse Bay, to the west, at the southernmost tip of the Gulf of Boothia, it was *kajurzuk*, meaning a reddish color; in Coronation Gulf, far to the west above Great Bear Lake, the star was *agleoryuit*, the pursuers.

Aldebaran was a bear held at bay by Inuit hunting dogs, a low-shining great white star, with its scattered skirts of the Hyades. The three stars of Orion's belt were the human hunters, racing behind their dogs. The bear hung forever in the night sky, center stage in an eternal drama of light.

The ice storm lasted until the morning, when it stopped as suddenly as it had begun. For a while nothing stirred in the featureless landscape, where the newly sprung carpet of grasses and saxifrage had been swallowed up. Then the female began to move. She got to her feet slowly and shook her body free of its snow. She raised her head and scented the frozen air. The light blazed in the white-blue sky. In a few more hours the colors of the Arctic spring would begin to emerge again: the low, smoothed rocks where she had been lying would reveal their bright orange lichen. Everything would look as it had looked twenty-four hours earlier.

But the Swimmer, beginning to walk now, felt a change. During her sleep she knew that something had altered. The world had moved.

She did not look back at the sleeping giant behind her. Her mate was outlined in the blanket of snow, and he wouldn't wake for another hour.

And by then she would be far away.

It was unlikely that she would ever see him again.

Fourteen

ALICIA sat in the conservatory of Franklin House and looked down at the letter.

She turned it over, frowning.

"What do you think?" John asked.

He and Catherine were seated opposite his mother: the low table, with the neatly laid tea tray, was between them. It had begun to rain, and the drops made a soft pattern of sound on the roof.

"I honestly don't know what to think," Alicia said.

John leaned forward. "He's a good photographer," he said. "He has a great reputation."

Alicia laid the letter down, among the cups. "I don't doubt it."

"Well?"

She took off her reading glasses. For a second her gaze lingered on Catherine. "Let me get this absolutely right," Alicia murmured. "You want to go to Canada during the summer vacation. To work with this man."

"He's offered me a job."

She smiled at him. "Actually, he hasn't offered you a job as such," she observed, "as the position is unpaid."

John glanced at Catherine too. "Okay, then," he said. "As you put it, a position. For six weeks."

"I can't understand why he should want to do that," Alicia replied.

There was a silence; a silence during which John could be heard taking in a deep breath. "Because I've been writing to him."

Catherine laid her hand on John's arm. "Because you have been nagging him day and night," she said, smiling.

He smiled back at her; looked at his mother.

Alicia was not smiling. She inclined her head to the letter, then back at Catherine. "And you come from this part of the world?" she asked.

"No, Mrs. Marshall. But my father lives in Arctic Bay."

"This part of the world."

"It's a long way from Churchill. Churchill is on Hudson Bay."

Alicia pursed her lips.

"Mother," John said, "it's an experience."

"But why there?"

"A huge number of bears congregate in that area."

Alicia got to her feet suddenly. Tension was spelled out in her rigid shoulders. She gazed at the garden beyond the windows. "Only last week you were offered a summer at the Spitalfields excavation," she said.

"Everyone's been there."

She looked at him. "I asked for that place for you. To help with your coursework."

"I know," he said. "But I didn't ask for it, did I?"

"John," Catherine murmured, a warning.

"You may not have asked for it, but I've arranged it for you. You might thank me."

"I want to go to Churchill," John reiterated. The tone of his voice was rising. "I spent last summer at a bloody excavation. How many chances like this come along? None."

"It isn't as if your course has anything at all to do with Arctic civilizations."

Now John got to his feet too. "It isn't about coursework," he said. "It's just something different."

Alicia met his gaze with a stony expression. "I know exactly what it's about," she told him. "Following some pointless crusade, the same as your father. And you come here asking me to finance it."

Catherine now got to her feet. She walked to John's side. "It's really nowhere near the Franklin sites," she said.

Alicia's expression hardened. "Would you mind very much not continuing your lesson in geography?" she said. "John is only interested in this particular place and this particular job because the man is chasing

a bear *that has been seen on Franklin sites.*" She folded her arms in a gesture of triumph. "Oh, you think I don't understand," she said. "Perhaps
you think I'm unable to call up an Internet site, when you tell me a person's name. I know full well who Richard Sibley is, and his connection
with Franklin, and his obsession with this particular bear. Which," she
added, "if you ask me, is nothing more or less than eyewash."

"But nobody did ask you," John fumed. He snatched the letter up
and stuffed it into his pocket. "I knew you wouldn't get it," he said.

"And to think," Alicia said, "that I haven't heard enough of Franklin
in my lifetime." She stepped closer to her son, in an attitude that was half
cajoling, half threatening. Looking at her, Catherine felt a chill run down
her spine. The attachment, on Alicia's part, was plain to see, hard to witness: it was almost as if John was her partner. She looked at Alicia's hand
on John's. She was gripping him tightly. "What has your father ever
achieved in searching for them?" she asked, softly, insinuatingly. "One
small copper canister. Why do you want to compete with your father?"

"I'm not fucking competing with him," John retorted, coloring suddenly and pulling violently away.

Alicia stared at him.

He turned on his heel and slammed out of the room, leaving
Catherine behind.

The two women looked at each other.

"You had better go with him," Alicia said.

"I've not influenced him, Mrs. Marshall," Catherine said quietly.

"Haven't you?" Alicia asked.

She walked to the conservatory door and pushed it open. The scent
of the garden flooded in. Catherine glanced at the severely manicured
lawn, clipped back hard, the blades of grass packed tight, like a bowling
green. It was not a place to lie in the sun. Even to walk. Only to admire.

Catherine picked up her shoulder bag and followed John.

He was out in the hallway, dialing a cab.

"Don't leave her like this," Catherine said.

"I'm only asking for airfare," he said.

"She doesn't like to lose you."

The cab firm answered. He gave them the address, replaced the receiver. "This bloody stifling house," he muttered.

"She adores you," Catherine told him.

She was struggling with the idea that Alicia was actually right. John might dress the Sibley offer up as being a new venture, but it was really the old venture, the old obsession. And in one thing John's mother had hit the nail absolutely on the head. Catherine knew how much John wanted to outdo his father.

"Ask my father," John was muttering, repeating what Alicia had said earlier, before the second discussion of the letter had begun.

"Well," Catherine observed, "you could try."

John laughed. "Oh, yeah, and like, he'd be willing to listen. *He'd* give me the fare, just like that."

"I'm sure he'd listen, yes."

John crammed a hand to his forehead, totally exasperated. "Did he ever listen to anything I've wanted?" he demanded. "Do you think there's a hope in hell of his listening now, now that this woman is monopolizing him?"

Catherine eyed him warily. "You mean Jo Harper?"

"Who else?"

Catherine bit her lip for a second before replying. "For what it's worth, I think she's nice. And she's making your father very happy."

"Oh, yeah," John replied viciously. "Yeah. Happy. Great."

He wrenched open the door and went out onto the drive. The rain was still pattering through the magnolia, whose petals littered the ground.

Following him, Catherine stepped ahead and barred his path. Her eyes ranged over his face. "You are jealous," she said, wonderingly.

He said nothing. He pushed her aside and began to walk. She ran after him.

"You are surely not jealous of your father's happiness?" she demanded.

He stopped. Stared at the ground. "What do you think I am?" he said. "If he's happy, fine. Why should I care?"

She looked at him intently. The rain was wetting her hair, her face; forming distinct droplets on the leather jacket that John wore.

"I think you do care very much," she said.

"Who asked you to be an amateur psychiatrist?" he muttered. "Especially such a bloody bad one."

"I don't think I'm wrong," Catherine said. "You think it is Franklin, or some goddamned thing about a dead man and a dead crew and dead ships. Or now, this wildlife photographer. This bear. When that is not it at all. You don't want to get to Peel Sound, Beechey Island. You want to get to *him*. That is what it is."

He had still not looked up at her.

But when he finally began to reply, it was low, almost guttural.

"And you know all the answers," he said. "And just because I want to take up a bloody perfectly good offer, a fucking good opportunity. I don't want to go to Canada for six weeks. It can't be that simple, can it? It's not that I just want to get away from this claustrophobic bloody place." He pointed a finger at her accusingly. "You're going to Arctic Bay, aren't you?" he said.

"I always go, every summer," she replied, frowning.

"Why?"

She shook her head. "Why?" she said, confused. "To see my father. I've seen him every year, every August for ten years."

"But you wouldn't take me, would you?"

She stared at him, astonished. "John, you never asked me."

"But would you?" he demanded.

"I don't know. . . ."

He started to walk. "Well, that's fine, then."

"John," she called. She tried to pull on his arm. "You never asked me. . . ."

"Look," he said, stopping for a second. "That's all right. You go and see him. It's a traditional thing, I understand, I know that. Awkward to take me, I realize. But, like"—he pressed his fist, closed, against his forehead, for a moment—"but when I want to go to Canada, just don't tell me what my bloody motives are, all right? Don't be like her." And he jerked his finger back to the house.

"It's because we love you," she said simply. "Just as your father loves Jo Harper. Just as you love him."

He stared at her.

There was a silence, a very long silence, while the soft green landscape wept.

Then he walked away, toward the gate to the road.

Fifteen

PANIC set in as they entered the strait.

The first thing that Franklin ordered was steam: the locomotive engines below roared, and the ships at first broke through the gathering ice, cracking it like gunshots. The sun was high, the wind strong; the ships plunged through ice and waves alike. A high white light began to beat down on them, as if there were more than one sun in the sky. Gus stood slackjawed, bumped by the men who brushed past him, trying to see where the new light was coming from.

Terror sailed in *Erebus*'s wake, and barely had *Erebus* found her way through, when they saw the ice re-forming behind her. They plunged into it, each man with a single hope in his heart.

Just through these miles. Just through this strait. There will be free water on the other side.

The ice did not surrender silently to them. Far from it. It whistled and whined and thundered; sometimes it sounded like animals baying, or like birds screeching. Sometimes it grumbled low, as if there were something under the waves, some sea monster, beating the underside of the ship. It was as if the ice were alive. It snaked and snapped and fell away from them, and as they pushed on from the front, it tugged at the stern, huge cold hands swatting the timber.

As noon passed, Gus realized what the new light was: it was the reflection from ice ahead. There was electric-blue water, and streams of floating pack, but beyond that, far ahead, the whole world was white, and the light was pouring from it and filling the sky, and the decks looked white themselves, bleached almost clean of their color. *Terror* shook like a man in a fever, and rolled as she was pushed. The more she rolled, and the more *Erebus* rolled ahead of them, the more steam was called for, and the belching from the funnel cut a black channel through the light.

At one o'clock Augustus was sent below. They needed more men with the stoking, and he was fly and small, and could dodge quicker and rake harder, pushing the coal forward. It was like Hades down there, in the harsh glow, and so hot that they worked naked to the waist, coal dust and sweat running down them. Gus ran as fast as he was ordered, feeling the dust coating his throat and making his lungs tight.

The man nearest him never stopped swearing. He cursed the heat, the ice, the ship, the captain.

"Never wanted to see no Pacific," he ranted, as he shoveled. "Never want to see no more ocean. Never no more ocean, never more ocean, ocean. . . ."

It rolled like a song. They worked relentlessly, until sweat ran into their eyes, and they had to be replaced by others, because they couldn't breathe anymore in the blazing pit.

As Gus staggered out, he felt the ship wrench.

"Mother of God," said one man. They froze where they were, feeling the shift under their feet. "She's going over."

Terror lifted up. An enormous boulder of ice had pressed her suddenly and hard. They felt her lose contact with the water and dance along a little. For minutes *Terror* skirted along the ice. No one looked at each other. Instead, they looked up, at the low beams of the deck above, waiting. Then, just as suddenly, the pressure eased, and *Terror* dropped back down. Augustus looked around, searching for the sailor who had told him, not so long ago, about ice relaxations. Although he knew full well that this had not been like the others they had felt. The blow from the ice had felt like the strike of Olympus: massive, implacable.

"Don't let us be killed," Gus whispered.

A call went up on deck. Two men came down the ladder.

"He's sending out a boat crew," they said.

Six men from each ship were sent down onto the floes ahead. Here, for two hours, they hacked at the ice. It was a deadly business. At any moment each man risked being thrown into the water, for no one could tell whether the grinding ice was inches or feet thick—it changed with every moment. The men slithered and slipped at their task, working like black demons under the very prow of each ship with axes. From time to time both *Erebus* and *Terror* backed up and rammed, backed up and rammed.

Gus sat in misery below, while the *Terror* groaned and jolted.

They were going to be stuck. They were going to be here another winter. They would surely starve.

He had heard it said that if they were stopped here, the rations would be reduced. A winter in the strait would bring them into the third year, and in truth, after expending so much coal already, and not having shot as much game as they had anticipated on Beechey, they did not have enough food to see them through safely for another twelve months. And not enough coal to cook it. The rations would be cut to four-upon-six. That meant that every six men were issued with the allowance for four, and it would be a case of tightening their belts and putting up with it, right through the worst of the coming weather. And they would depend, from now on, entirely upon the tins and hard tack, and salt pork.

Gus hated the tins. They never saw meat, but they had plenty of the soups—parsnip, carrot, potato. He had never much liked vegetables, and he had to hold his breath to swallow it. He had grown to hate the Goldner name too. Every single pack had the familiar scripted letters upon it, and Gus wished he could meet the supplier, to force his own sickly, bland bouilli down the man's throat. The idea that he would probably have to eat most of his reduced meals cold, to save on heat, made him want to vomit.

But of all their rations the situation with the coal was probably worst of all. When he had been at the fires, Gus saw that there was not much left. Steaming, especially the ramming, took vast quantities, guzzling up far more than they were able to shovel. Today they had gone through over three tons. He knew that they needed that coal. They needed it in the winter, for heating the lower deck, so that they did not freeze in their beds. They needed it for heating up the food and for melting ice for water. If they tried to break through the ice at this same pace for very much longer, the coal would be exhausted entirely, and such a prospect was unthinkable. It would be a signed death warrant.

He put his head in his hands, covering his eyes.

They would be without color again. They would be in the dark.

He tried to summon up the colors he remembered. He tried to think of what London had been like on the day he was brought down to the ship. He thought of the red-and-green awnings over the stores; he thought of the trees coming into leaf, the bright acid-green of new leaves in sunshine. He thought of the acres and acres of apple blossom in Kent, where his mother had lodged for three days with her sister before taking him to Greenhithe. All those hundreds of trees, their branches waving like frothy petticoats.

He thought of the colors of clothes—not sealskin or fur or moleskin leggings, but soft, thin clothes: pale cream breeches, tan jackets, blue coats. He thought of the blazing scarlet of a woman's dress as she had stepped down from a carriage: such brilliant, gently folding fabric. He could visualize it exactly now: exactly how it fell to the ground. Exactly how the petals of flowers drifted quickly under the dress and reappeared as she turned on the pavement. He saw the polished brass of the door knockers on the houses. He saw the lemon-sprigged muslin across the window in his aunt's little house. The sunlight in the kitchen.

"Franklin is out," a man said.

Gus opened his eyes. "On deck?"

"You can hear him shouting."

Gus crept up the long ladder. Skittering around the starboard side, he saw the officers, Blanky among them. *Erebus* was perilously close. So close that half a dozen men, hands linked and legs astride, could have bridged the gap between them. The ice was screaming, grinding, keening. And it was true: Franklin himself was on the deck of *Erebus*, and he was shouting, his voice as wild as the ice, high pitched. Gus froze in shock: Franklin had never raised his voice, never shown any prolonged temper. The noise coming from his throat now did not belong to him. It was the voice of a man defying the elements. Pitting himself against an impossible foe. It was the kind of noise a man would make in the throes of a last despair, and the blood rushed to Gus's face and his heart squeezed.

There was a sudden flurry on the *Terror*.

"He is down," Blanky called.

Who was down? One of the men on the ice?

Who was down?

Terror lurched. Ice sheered upward between the two ships, a great white solid fountain. Particles showered the deck, landed on Gus's shoulders and face. He was so close to *Erebus*, he could hear the squeaking of the ropes as they strained. He could see the flakes of paint coming from her keel.

Then came the giant.

As Gus listened to the mixture of shouting voices from *Erebus*, he heard another cry go up from his own ship.

"Dear Mother of God and all the angels!"

He turned to look.

They all did.

About a quarter of a mile to stern they saw the pack behind them suddenly pile up, as if the enormous weight of the ice was nothing more than paper cards. It crumbled and fell, rose up again and fell, reached upward and fell, and with every falling and climbing, greater layers of floe lay tumbled in huge blocks at the feet of the newly forming berg, pushing it ever higher after each temporary destruction. Something massive was pushing it from behind, something grotesque. It was as if God himself had come down into Victoria Strait on invisible ships and, with an energy that made the mountains and seas and continents, was making a new sea now, a new vast plate of tumbled ice. It was Genesis in the making, the creation of a world.

And it was coming straight for them.

"Our Father," Gus stammered, "who art in heaven . . ."

He was not in heaven, though. He was here. He was charging them down with His great white hands. He was stampeding His oceans, whipping them into frenzy, freezing them where they once boiled and flew. And the result—the house-high, thousand-ton wedges of berg—were ramming their way forward, as if everything in their way were nothing at all, carried no weight, occupied no space. *Terror* was merely a shadow, a breath that would soon be snuffed out.

It was two hundred yards away.

It was one hundred yards away.

It was taller than the ship, a white rock wall, a fortress, flying.

"Thy Kingdom come, Thy . . ."

Gus stopped. Was this His will, to extinguish them? Was he to pray for that, for the end? To be blasted away, to be drowned? The thought flashed with utmost clarity in his head: he did not want to be drowned. He did not want to go into that sea. He did not want to feel the heel of God on his neck.

He closed his eyes. "Thy will be done," he breathed.

He gave himself up to his Maker, wished for a quick death.

Waited.

"Dear Jesus," a man said at his side.

Gus opened his eyes. The grinding, crashing, whining, of the approaching ice wall had abruptly stopped. There was, again, the unearthly silence of pressure meeting pressure. Between *Erebus* and *Terror* a broken landscape of ice had appeared, and both ships, tilting in opposite directions, lay skewered on its surface. And overhanging them both was the mountain that had done the impossible, and found its feet, and run: it towered eighty feet high in their wake, not more than fifty yards away. It had stopped.

"Captain, sir!"

The voice broke the silence. Every living soul on both ships could be heard to breathe suddenly out, a gasp of relief and disbelief. They were still alive.

"Captain Crozier, sir!"

Crozier was at the rail.

The first mate of *Erebus* was barely twenty feet away.

"What is it?" Crozier shouted.

"Mr. Franklin, sir! Sir John, sir!" the man babbled.

"What is the matter?" Crozier demanded.

There was no reply. Gus could still hear the steam engine whining belowdeck. Crozier turned. "Shut off the steam, for God's sake," he yelled.

The moments that followed were eerie. The ice hung above and between them. The ships did not make a sound.

"God save our souls," someone murmured.

"What is the matter?" Crozier repeated.

"Sir John is taken," came the reply.

They waited aboard *Terror* for a half hour.

"He is dead," the crew muttered, "and so are we."

It was six in the evening before Crozier at last called the crew together. The wind had risen a little by then, but the ice seemed to have stopped. They could feel that they were being carried very slowly by fits and starts. The bergs were blue in the glowering sky.

"Sir John has suffered an apoplexy," Crozier said, raising his voice against the wind. "He is recovered. There is nothing at all to worry about."

They heard him, and they heard the difference in him. They looked at each other, and back at the captain ahead of them, who had predicted this day: that they would meet the huge ice currents flowing down the strait—that there would be no getting through them. That they would not have the strength, with all the damned engines sitting impotently now under their feet, to take more than a few hours' grace from the deadly pressure of the freezing sea.

Crozier stood before them for some time, but he did not give the speech that they had expected. He did not say that, tomorrow, they would try to break the ice again. He did not say that it was only temporary, or that a distant way might yet be seen and attempted. He did not say that they would be here another year, or that, come the summer in twelve months time, there would be no ice to impede them anymore. In short, he neither encouraged them, nor said that it was just as he had feared, and that he had been right, and that Franklin had been wrong.

He said nothing at all, other than issue a double portion of rum and tobacco.

And went below, to his quarters.

Sixteen

THE snow was falling in Cambridge.

It began during the night, a thick and softly moving curtain drifting across the country. By the time Jo woke at seven, it had covered the city streets and lined the roofs, and when she went to the window and looked out, it was onto a different landscape from the one she had left the night before. The snow had smothered sound. It was as if the whole world was asleep.

She went to the bathroom, and coming back onto the stairs, she saw that the roof light was almost covered. She could only see a small letter-box shape of the view across the city; far across the fields, the few poplars were frozen, a black network against the growing light, isolated in a white sea. She reached up, holding the banister rail for support, and touched the sloping windowpane, tracing the pattern of the packed snow. Then, wrapping the blanket tightly around her—the cold, out here on the landing, was nipping at her feet—she went back into the bedroom.

It was six months now since she had been living with Doug.

She got back into bed and pressed the length of her body to his, resting her face in the warm depression between his shoulder blades, and wrapping her arms around his body. He murmured in his sleep and stroked her hands.

Six months.

It was almost Christmas now; today was the twenty-second of December. It hardly seemed possible that so much time had passed, or that so much had changed. Six months ago she had been alone in the flat in Fulham that now stood empty, testimony to her indecision. She didn't know if she should sell or wait; she hardly trusted what had happened to her. She sometimes thought that her whole life with Doug would disintegrate—vaporize and vanish overnight. It would disappear, just as the city had disappeared under the snow. She would find herself back alone, in a single bed.

She shook herself free of the thought and turned onto her back, crossing her fingers in superstition for a second, like a child. She gazed up at the ceiling.

The house was very narrow and very old, a four-story Regency building, with a cellar, a cramped back kitchen, a luxuriously broad sitting room on the first floor, and this bedroom on the top, tucked under the roof. Doug had brought her to it only last month.

"Do you like it?" he'd asked, as they stood in front of it. The pavement outside was barely wide enough to take two people. A post-office van edged down the narrow entry, squeezing along between the double-yellow-lined curbs, almost brushing their sides.

She'd gazed up at the tiny frontage. It was squeezed in a haphazard, uneven row of others, black timber against white plasterwork, with a red brick hem. Looking up farther, Jo noticed that the tiny leaded panes of the top windows caught the various tones of sky, and were speckled white and blue.

"Whose is it?" she'd asked.

"Would you like to live here?"

She'd turned to look at him. "Is it likely?" she'd said.

"I want to buy it," he'd told her. "For us."

"You can't buy it," she'd countered.

"Why not?"

"Because . . . if we live anywhere, buy anywhere, I want to put in half." He'd laughed. "Come on."

"I'm serious," she said. "You don't have to support me. It's only fair."

He'd sighed. "Look, you haven't even got the Fulham flat on the market yet. And why shouldn't I support you? I *want* to support you."

"Thank you," Jo had said, "but I don't want to be a princess."

He'd stared at her, truly perplexed. "A what?"

She'd waved her hand. "Bought things for. A kept woman."

"Kept woman?" he'd repeated. "What year is this, 1902?"

"Quite. There you go."

He'd shaken his head. "Look," he'd replied, "it's a place to live, better than my flat. That's all. I saw it in Flaxter's window, I thought you'd like it. These places *never* come on the market. Don't you like it? Look at it. It's Gothic."

"I love it," she said.

"There's a garden at the back. A walled garden, Jo."

"I'm sure there is."

"Then . . ."

She'd screwed up her face, shuffled her feet. "Don't let's change," she said.

He'd turned her to face him. "Don't move house?"

"No."

The Post Office van was back, this time reversing down the alleyway. The driver gave an apologetic grin as they did a quick dance to avoid him.

"Give me a decent reason," Doug said.

She'd shrugged. "There isn't one. I don't want to move. That's it."

"The world won't fall down if we cart our belongings four streets across town."

She'd looked at him. "And I don't want to be bought things," she reminded him.

"I'm not buying it for you, you silly tart," he'd replied equably. "I'm fed up living in three rooms and falling over your shoes, and I want a study. And there's the other thing. We need more space."

She'd bitten her lip, then smiled at what had become their softly spoken catchphrase recently. "Yes, the other thing," she'd murmured.

He'd looked into her face, considering her. "We won't break," he said quietly. "We're not that fragile."

Aren't we, she'd thought. *I fell in love with you, and you with me, and you don't call that fragile, breakable? Move house. Break the spell. No, thanks.*

But they had. Doug had put down the deposit, but the house was in both their names. She'd almost changed her mind in the solicitor's office, felt that creeping sense of alteration. Some mirror shattering. Some distant echo.

Her hand had paused over the contract. Doug had leaned over to whisper in her ear. "Sign," he'd said. "If it makes you feel better, when the Fulham flat's sold, I promise I'll take you for every penny you've got."

Since that first night at her flat in May, they had barely been apart. Jo couldn't actually remember, now, what it was like to be without him; they had fitted together seamlessly, without any of the half-expected strains of adjustment. For the first month he had lived with her in Fulham, during the absence from work imposed by his leg. When it was healed, he went back to Cambridge, and she went with him. There was barely any discussion about it. She worked as well in Cambridge as in London, going down to Gina and her other contacts by train a couple of times a week. She grew to love coming back in the evenings, watching London disappear and be slowly replaced by fields and low hills, and eventually by the open spaces and red earth of her second home.

Doug never made any demands on her. He never said that she should alter her life. He never insisted on her being there, or looking after him, in any way. There were no relaxations in the tidy and austere way that he looked after himself; he was a practiced housekeeper and made no fuss about it. He even kept quiet about Jo's habitual mess, which tended to trail after her like the train on a wedding dress. Though she sensed that he bit his tongue more than once.

In everyday things they were not alike at all. It was at some deeper level where they were molded from the same material. They were wanderers both; and they tended to bend rules. There were years between them; they were of different generations. They looked nothing like each other. They inhabited different worlds. And yet they were the same. The same at heart.

Jo smiled now at herself, at her thoughts and superstitions about this house. She gently stroked the center of Doug's back. He woke up. "You're cold," he mumbled.

"It's snowing," she said.

He rolled onto his side and looked at her. "Is it? Much?"

"Like a Christmas card," she told him. "Full-on drifts. I bet there's a robin sitting on a spade in the garden right now. Not to mention people in Victorian costume on stagecoaches, chestnuts roasting on an open fire, Tiny Tim, et cetera."

"Tiny Tim roasting on an open fire," he mumbled. "There's an idea."

"There *is* an idea," she agreed.

He smiled. "And how are you?" he said.

"Fine."

He sighed, rubbing his eyes. He glanced at the bedside table. "What time is it?"

"Almost eight."

They looped arms, lying in the bed. He gently ran his thumb over her wrist, and smoothed a little circle in the palm of her hand. "They'll all make an excuse not to get here, if it's snowing," he said.

"Not Gina," she said. "Gina will single-handedly shovel her way up the M-Eleven. You'll see. And John will come. Catherine will make him."

They smiled, but Doug's mood suddenly faded. "I still think we should have told Alicia," he said. "I've got a bad feeling."

Doug had seen his wife only twice since May. In July, a couple of days after Jo had moved into his Cambridge flat, he had taken himself off to Franklin House one morning, without telling Jo where he was going. She only realized where he had been when he turned up again at lunchtime, flushed in the face, looking almost ill.

"What's the matter?" she'd asked him. "What've you been doing?"

"I've been to see Alicia," he said. He held a letter out to her. "This came today."

It was his decree nisi. There were a mere six weeks left between it and the end of his marriage.

"I knew she would have got hers today," he continued. "And I thought"—he'd grimaced; frowned—"I thought, even now, that she wouldn't accept it, so . . ."

They'd sat down on the couch, side by side, sunlight filling the room. There was a scent of the flowers that Jo had bought the day before: old English roses, their color filling the table by the window.

"What did she say?" she'd asked.

"The usual rubbish," he told her. Distracted, he ran his hand through his hair.

"Let me guess," she had murmured. "She blamed me."

"I filed this before I'd even met you," he said. "We've been apart for five years. There's nothing she can do."

"She'll never let go of you," Jo replied.

"She'll have to," he said. "I want us to get married."

There had been a moment of silence, while Jo stared at the hand in hers. "You don't want to get married so soon after the last," she'd murmured.

"I do," he'd answered. "It's the only thing I want. Marry me as soon as this becomes legal."

"No," she said. "I'd be expecting Alicia around every corner, waiting for me with an ax."

"Marry me next month."

"No."

"Christmas, then."

She'd smiled at him. "Saddled with a second wife," she said. "A second wife years younger than you."

"Christmas."

"The same generation as your son, who hates me."

"John doesn't hate you," he said. "He's just mixed up."

She'd narrowed her eyes. "He's jealous, Doug," she said. "Of you and your time. Now you're going to tell him this."

Doug had looked away from her temporarily. He shook his head slightly. "I lost a lot of years with him," he said. "I'm not going to lose them with you as well."

"Oh, Doug . . ."

"I'll get him back," he countered. "I promise you that, Jo. I'll do my damnedest to make up what I've lost with him. But I'm not losing you. I want you to marry me. Say you will. Say you will, at Christmas."

The scent of the roses flooded the room.

She remembered that, above anything else.

It was eleven o'clock that morning when they got to the Preston Arms.

It was the closest pub to Shire Hall, and the place where they had arranged to meet Gina and John and Catherine, before the ceremony. They'd been forced to walk from Lincoln Street, heads down against the still-blowing snow, fine and grainy now, more ice sleet than flakes, and settling on the already transformed roads. Traffic ground through Cambridge as if in slow motion. The sky looked low and gray and full.

They were out of breath when they arrived, and stood in the doorway, shaking the snow from their coats.

They looked up and saw Gina bearing down on them, her arms outstretched.

"My God," Jo said, hugging her. "How in hell did you get here?"

"Hell is right," Gina said. She looked Jo up and down. "Nice dress. Goes with the wellies."

Jo laughed. "What can I do? Doug likes rubber."

"Oh, yeah?" Gina rolled her eyes. She turned her attention to Doug, enveloping him in the same strong embrace, until he grimaced at Jo over Gina's shoulder. Eventually, they parted. "Don't tell me you drove up today," he said.

Gina smoothed her hair, smiling. She was perfectly turned out in a red suit, and red shoes with killer heels. "I read the weather forecast yesterday afternoon and drove up last night. I got here about midnight. It was just starting."

"You should have rung us," Jo said.

"At midnight? No way," Gina replied. "Come and have some champagne."

They went into the next room. An ice bucket and five glasses were already on the table. "I thought, wait until after the ceremony," Gina said, sitting down. "Then I thought, nah. Before *and* after is better."

Doug glanced down at the glasses. "Shall we wait for John?"

Jo looked at her watch.

"Have we time?" Doug asked.

"It's five minutes' walk to Shire Hall. Ceremony eleven-thirty. . . ." She looked back up at him. "He should be here any minute. You could open it."

He hesitated. "Maybe I'll just wait until he gets here."

Jo shot Doug a sympathetic look. She knew that he didn't want John to come in and find them drinking without having waited for him. He was making an effort to do it right: not offend John, not get under his skin.

Ever since they had told John that they were getting married, Doug's son had been strange. He had been very formal and rigid with them. Conversations with him were conducted as if in the presence of a total stranger.

"He makes me feel like a scientific specimen," Jo had said to Doug. "He acts like—like he's preparing a paper on us or something. It's so strange."

Doug had shaken his head. "I don't understand any more than you do," he'd replied.

She'd taken his hand. "You two have got to get around this," she said. "I don't mean us, the wedding. I mean you and John have got to find a place together. Not this. Not like this. It's excruciating to watch you both, Doug. It's painful."

"I know," he said. "He freezes me out."

"Well, don't let him."

"I've tried."

"You think it's Alicia?"

"Easy to blame Alicia."

"Then try some more, Doug."

He'd given her a crooked smile. He just didn't know where to start, how to begin, what to say. And John wasn't about to help him. His expression when he looked at his father—when he looked at them both—was utterly implacable, like ice.

"Well," Gina said now. "You look good. Both of you."

"We are," Jo said.

"An hour from now, Mr. and Mrs. "

"Yes," Jo said. She couldn't help a grin.

"Aha," Gina smiled. "Broke your cool."

"I'm not cool," Jo admitted. "I feel really nervous."

"About what?" Doug said.

"Oh"—she shrugged—"I don't know. Nothing."

Gina leaned forward, touched Jo's knee. "Have you told John?" she said.

At the same moment the door opened. They looked up. John and Catherine stood in the doorway, Catherine dazzling in a white sheepskin jacket. John a little less so, in jeans and a Barbour.

Doug got up. He walked forward, hand extended.

"Told John what?" John said.

Doug let his hand slip from John's weaker grip. He kissed Catherine. "Come and sit down. Let me open this bottle."

"Great," Catherine said. She gave John a look, a marked warning look. Then she came over and kissed Jo's cheek.

"Let me introduce you two," Jo said. "Catherine, this is Gina, my editor at *The Courier*. Gina, this is John's partner, Catherine."

The two shook hands. "Hello Gina," Catherine said. "Some weather for a wedding."

John had walked over to the table. He hadn't kissed Jo. He watched

Doug peel off the foil on the champagne. "Is there news?" he asked, very level. Very pointed.

Doug's eyes flickered, just once, to Gina. Then he uncorked the Bollinger and filled the glasses. "Good luck," he said.

"Every happiness," Gina added.

John looked at his glass while they drank.

Doug set his back down on the table. "We're . . . well, starting a new venture," he said. "In every way."

Jo had been looking hard at John. There was a hitch of silence.

"I'm getting another series of *Far Back*," Doug said.

John's gaze turned to him. "They aren't doing another series," he said. "You told me that."

Doug smiled. "They told me that, too, last year," he said. "But the Greenland episode . . . It's with the Academy too. . . ."

"They offered you another series because of the Greenland fiasco?"

Doug flinched a little at his choice of words. "To cut a long story short. I suppose."

"We're doing it together," Jo said. "He hired me to carry bags."

The weak little joke fell flat.

"I see," John said. "That's a good angle." He put his glass down. "The reporter who got her man because of Greenland, flying out to meet him . . ."

"That was all hype," Jo countered quickly. "I never said all that about moving heaven and earth to meet him. The paper put that in. I told them it was a family flight and that I hitched a ride."

"But that isn't true, is it?" John asked softly. "You did move heaven and earth to meet him. Big romance. It was me who hitched a ride."

"Well, it doesn't matter," Doug said.

"I think you should know," Gina murmured. "It's eleven-fifteen."

Catherine stood up.

"So," John said, "you'll be traveling."

"Yes," Doug said. "There is traveling involved."

"To where?" John asked. "Greenland?"

"Yes, Greenland . . ."

"And Victoria Strait?"

Doug's face betrayed him. He jolted a little, as if John had hit a nerve.

"You're chasing Franklin," John said.

"It's never been done before," Doug said. "Franklin. In detail."

"You're right," John agreed. "It hasn't."

"Look John," Jo said. "We want you in on it. Of course we do. We know it's your passion."

John's gaze flickered over her. "My passion," he said.

"So . . ."

John's chin suddenly tilted upward. He seemed to brace his shoulders. "It's always someone else," he said, slowly, to Doug. "Someone else going with you."

"John . . ." Doug interjected.

"No, fine," his son continued. "That's okay. I'll show you." He turned on his heel and walked out of the room. Jo stared after him, aghast.

"John!" Catherine called.

"Doug, go after him," Jo said.

"I will not," Doug told her.

Jo pulled on his arm. "Go after him right now," she said.

"To say what?" Doug demanded.

"Bring him back."

"What for?"

Jo's mouth dropped open. "What *for*?" she repeated.

"Okay, okay . . ."

"Call him back, Doug. Quickly." She glanced at Gina. "I just knew it," she said to her. "I just knew he'd blow a fuse."

"It's what he's dreamed of," Catherine said.

Jo looked at her. "I know. We both know that. Doug told the TV people he wanted John in on this. Right from the beginning. We made so sure of it. His name's on the project."

Catherine frowned briefly. "Maybe . . ."

They all waited. "Maybe what?" Doug prompted.

Catherine shook her head. "Maybe he wants to do it alone, you know."

"How can you look for Franklin alone?" Doug demanded. "You need backup and crews. . . ."

"Yes, it's"—Catherine paused—"it's a big barrier," she murmured. "He can't let go of it."

"He *can* do it with me," Doug said.

Catherine could not meet Doug's eyes. Her gaze dropped to the floor.

"He doesn't want to do it with me," Doug said. "Is that it? He wants to best me in some way."

Jo stepped up close to him. She put her hand on his arm, then touched his face with her fingertips. "Doug," she said, "go find him. We need to sort this out. Now. Please."

Doug tore his eyes from Catherine's averted face. He looked shaken, hurt. He patted Jo's shoulder, almost absentmindedly. "Let's get married," he said.

"I mean it, Doug," Jo insisted. "Go after him."

"No," Doug said. His tone was altered. Firm. "If he can't swallow down this bloody envy for one morning, that's his problem." He picked up his coat and put it on. "We're getting married. It's more important."

Gina watched Jo's face. Jo's expression had hardened. Looking at her, Gina felt that she had seen that determined look a thousand times. It was the same expression that Jo wore when she got close to a story and was brushed off with an excuse.

Doug reached for Jo's hand. But she neatly stepped out of his reach. "We are not getting married without your son as your witness," she said firmly. "That's what we planned. That's what will happen."

He stared at her. "You must be joking."

"I am not joking."

"What do you want me to do, run?"

"Yes," she said.

"But we'll be late," he objected, throwing his arms out in a gesture of exasperation. "Bloody late for our own wedding!"

"Fine," she told him. "So you'd better start now. Go to it."

He opened his mouth to object, then looked at Gina. She raised her eyebrows at him. He looked back at Jo. She kissed him, slowly and softly, on the mouth.

"God, you are the most awkward woman on the planet," he said.

"Time's wasting," she replied.

He went out the door, with a single backward glance in Jo's direction.

They followed him, out into the snowy street. John was not to be seen anywhere. Doug jogged to the end of the pavement, slipping a little on the icy slush under his feet. He got to the road junction and looked up and down Castle Street and Huntingdon Road. The traffic lights were changing, and the line of cars was edging forward.

"I can't see him," Doug called back. The three women made their way in his direction.

"Maybe he's gone up onto Castle Mound," Jo said. They looked that way, but it was impossible to know. Castle Mound could only be approached via a little passageway between houses.

"God damn him," Jo said. She looked at Catherine. "I'm sorry," she said. "But you know, this means a lot to Doug."

"And to John," Catherine said.

"I know that," Jo retorted. "I—"

"There he is," Gina said.

Doug had already seen John on the other side of the street. It looked as if John had started to make his way up Chesterton Lane and thought better of it, maybe because the incline was just too slippery. Doug ran across the road, dodging a van that had just started to pick up speed. There was a blare of horns. They saw Doug reach his son.

They talked a moment. Doug caught hold of John's arm. John looked hard at his father, listened, and then wrenched away. Doug turned him back, pulling his sleeve. They heard their voices raised, although not the words. Then John ducked his head and seemed to say something, something soft, something brief, close to Doug's face. There was a split second where the two men froze, looking directly into each other's eyes, and then, to Jo's horror, she saw Doug raise a fist.

"No!" she cried.

John stepped backward; Doug stopped, looked at his own raised hand, and dropped it. John took a pace back, over the pavement, into the road.

"John," Catherine breathed.

Doug tried to grasp his son's hand. Misinterpreting the gesture, John pulled away, seemingly oblivious to the fact that he was standing in the road at all. Doug was urgently speaking, shouting. John put up his hands. Doug's fingers glanced off his son's arms, trying to draw him back out of harm's way.

"Doug!" Jo shouted.

Doug turned to look at her.

The truck was coming down the hill quite soundlessly, the driver just visible through the snow-smeared windshield, pulling at the wheel. Just for a moment Jo registered the massive tires turning without purchase over the ice, and the back wheels moving out, pulling the vehicle sideways on. There was a screech of brakes from the other side of the road, where the incoming vehicles saw the obstacle rushing toward them—fourteen tons of container, now bouncing against the curb and jumping the load so that it shook, the metal-screened sides of the load shivering like fabric rattled in a breeze. The truck mounted the pavement and smashed against the lights, tearing them from their position.

For a second it was impossible to say which way the impact would take the load.

It won't hit them, Jo thought.

She saw that quite clearly. Some still, small, objective voice in her head decided that they were too far away. The road surface was not that bad where they were standing. Other traffic had come to a halt. There was space, there was time, for them to get back.

The load was at an angle, an almost perfect forty-five-degree angle to the road. It seemed to hover there for impossible minutes. They saw the panic on the driver's face.

Doug suddenly began to move, holding John, pulling him toward the pavement where the women were standing. Relief was in his look. He had judged that distance, too, Jo thought.

But none of them saw the car.

It had been driven too fast all morning. Coming full pelt along Chesterton Road, it was driven by a boy who had only passed his test five months before. The lad had never driven in snow; he was late in the delivery he was making by more than an hour; his assessment of the scene ahead of him was way misjudged. Way too arrogant. Way too quick.

He actually put his foot down to overtake the stalled car in the center of the road. He only saw the truck—saw the load crash over—as he rounded the car.

And he didn't see Doug and John at all, until it was too late.

Seventeen

GINA stood by the door and watched the afternoon light fade.

It was three o'clock. The snow had stopped at midday, and the temperatures fallen below freezing. From the stultifying heat of the hospital corridor, it was strange to look out on what seemed to be a monochrome landscape. The streetlights were just coming on. Their first faded violet would add another single color, just before the dark.

She closed her eyes. A tear ran down her face, and she brushed it away with the heel of her hand. "Oh, Christ," she murmured.

Hearing a noise behind her, she opened her eyes and turned around, to see Jo standing opposite her. The door to the rest room was closing behind her. She looked ashen. "Are they ready?" Jo asked.

"Yes," Gina said. She took her friend's arm.

It was only a few yards away, but the door to the chapel seemed a very long distance to cover. The floor was mirrorlike with polish; the walls blue.

"Is it cold in here?" Jo asked.

"Yes," Gina lied.

The doctor was waiting for them; there was staff nurse by his side. It seemed to Gina that she had to manhandle Jo forward; the other woman hung on her like a deadweight. There was a terrible moment, as they passed through the doors, when, between them, they almost carried Jo into the silence of the room beyond.

Jo stopped a few feet inside the chapel.

Doug's body lay on a white-sheeted gurney by a small altar. Even from where she stood, Gina could see there was no mark at all on his face. On either side of him were two great bouquets of flowers—left over, Gina supposed, from some other person's misery—and she saw Jo look at them, look at the apricot-colored roses.

"I can't," Jo said.

John was sitting with Catherine on the second row of seats. He had his back to them. Hearing Jo's voice, he stood up and faced her.

The bruise over his right eye was already turning black, closing the lid. A deep scratch ran the length of his face from forehead to neck; his skin was pitted by the dirt of the road. He had been flung by the force of the impact on his father, whose arm he had been holding. In the very last moment Doug had spun him out of the direct line of the speeding car. John had been unconscious for more than five minutes, waking to hear the sound of the ambulance siren, and to see Jo on her knees in the center of the road, trying to wake his father.

Jo stared at the boy in front of her. Beside John, Catherine was pale, her eyes reddened, her arms crossed tightly over her chest.

Jo walked toward him.

She saw Doug in his son's face. In the set of his mouth. In the color of his eyes. She hesitated in front of him.

"I'm sorry," John said.

She felt the roses reach out and touch her, their lingering scent resting on her like soft hands, and she closed her eyes, and saw sunlight, and Doug's room, and an open window, and the faded pattern of alpine flowers on the carpet.

She opened her eyes.

"You killed him," she said.

John reeled back.

"You killed him, you took him away from me," she said.

"Jo," someone said. A woman. Someone close.

"I'll never forgive you," Jo said. "Do you understand? Can you hear me? I'll never forgive you."

"Jo," the voice repeated.

John had almost backed into his father's body. He stopped, feeling the wheels of the gurney against his foot. What little color there was in his face drained from it. He glanced back at Doug.

"That's right," Jo said. "Look at him. You did that. You see him? You did that with your jealousy."

Gina caught her hands. She turned Jo away, pulled her into her own body, wound her arms around her, held her.

John walked away, down the short and echoing aisle. Catherine ran after him. As they got to the door, she put her hand on his, on the handle.

"Leave me alone," he said.

"Let me come with you," she said. "You need someone with you."

He stared at her. Tears were threatening in his eyes; as they stood, face to face, the first drops spilled.

"I don't need anyone," he said.

"John . . ."

"She's right!" he cried.

Catherine stood stock still, open mouthed with horror. "No, John . . . she didn't mean it. . . ."

He pulled savagely away from her. "Well, I do," he whispered. "Keep away from me."

He opened the door and they heard his footsteps: walking, stumbling, running.

Jo began to shudder in Gina's embrace. Catherine, shocked, turned to stare at the two women.

Jo slumped against Gina's shoulder, and they edged together toward the chairs, where Gina sat her friend down. She reached in her pocket to find a tissue, but then saw that Jo's face was dry. The other woman was staring at Doug.

"It's all right," Gina said. "It's okay."

Jo looked at her slowly. "It's not all right," Jo murmured.

"No," Gina said. "I didn't mean . . . God, Jo. I don't know what I mean." She shook her head in desperation. "I'm so sorry."

Jo's gaze trailed away, over the flowers, out to the snow beyond the glass. "It's the other thing," she said quietly. A ghostly smile came to her face.

"What other thing?" Gina asked.

"We called it that," Jo said plaintively. She looked up. Catherine was standing at her side, white faced.

Jo suddenly stood up and went to Doug. She put her hand on his chest and ran it up his shoulder. To the other womens' dismay she gave him a little push, as she would do to wake him.

"Come back and sit down a minute," Gina whispered.

Jo turned, to look at them both.

"It's not all right," she said. "Because I'm going to have his baby."

PART
TWO

Two Years Later

Eighteen

THE bear had spent a long time trying to find the right place.

She was looking for fine and hard-packed snow. It was the same consistency that the Inuit looked for when building igloos. She needed it for much the same purpose.

When she finally came upon a bowl-shaped slope, she began to dig, progressing quickly through the drift with her massive, raking claws, until she had made a narrow doorway. As she worked, the snow she had pushed aside formed behind her and plugged the entrance. She worked upward, finally making a rounded chamber about eight feet long and six feet wide.

This would be her home through the winter, the place where she would give birth. She made a small air vent in the roof, but from outside it was impossible to see that anything was alive in there, even that any animal had passed that way. Her pawprints soon vanished in the snowstorms. Inside, the temperature was pleasant, forty degrees warmer than the tundra outside. She scuffed the den floor for a while until she was comfortable, and then lay down to sleep.

The faultless machinery of her body ticked slowly as, for week after week, she lay isolated from the world. Her temperature and heartbeat were lower than normal, and she passed into the suspended animation of hibernation, neither eating nor drinking, while her fat was metabolized to provide her food and water.

In this dreamlike state her cub grew inside her.

He was born early in the year, a tiny scrap of life. His future as a male polar bear would dictate that his body weight ought to rise to something between twelve and fifteen hundred pounds. His breed was the largest carnivore on earth. And yet, when his mother produced him in the blue twilight of the den, he was just over a pound in weight. He was blind and deaf, his body barely covered in thin wool. Following instinct, he suckled his mother's milk, luxuriously rich at thirty-one percent butterfat and twelve percent protein.

Outside and above them the sky flickered with the specters of the aurora borealis. But the mother and cub saw nothing of the flames and mists that billowed across the heavens. The mother bear wrapped her cub in her embrace, surrendering to sleep.

Only when four months had gone by did the mother rouse herself to dig a tunnel to the world.

By then it was March, and she had lost over four hundred pounds during her self-imposed exile. Her cub had grown to the size of a small dog and was lively and inquisitive. He was no longer satisfied with the confines of his winter nursery and was anxious to push past his mother.

At first the light blinded him. There were no storms. The sun was a swimming disc, steely gray, emerging through yellow clouds. He waited at the entrance, uncertainly eyeing the new light, while his mother, still drowsy and moving in slow motion, walked away from the den and began to scrape the snow from the ground. When she found the frozen mosses and algae, she ate them ravenously, mixing them with snow.

But for a while food was not her priority. She remained near the den, watching her cub's tentative explorations. She lay at the den entrance on her back. Her cub played for a while in the newly found expanse stretching out in front of him; from time to time he would stop and stare ahead of him, as if considering the vastness of his empire.

But eventually he returned to his mother's side.

She was his only protection under the ice-white sky.

Nineteen

THE sun was shining into Jo's bedroom.

Jo woke suddenly and stared at the barred pattern of light on the opposite wall. If it was a dream that had propelled her so quickly into the day, she couldn't remember it.

She looked at the clock. Six A.M. And then at Doug's picture on the bedside table. The photograph had been taken on the day that they had moved into this house. He was on the doorstep, half turned toward her, laughing. As always, she looked at him for a while, then touched his face with the tip of her finger.

She got up and sat for some time on the edge of the bed, letting the familiar regret wash and recede. Then, running her hands through her hair, she rose from her bed and pulled on her dressing gown. She went out along the landing and into what had once been the storeroom, and which now belonged to her son.

She walked softly to the side of Sam's bed: he was fast asleep, the blankets in a heap around him, his face almost buried in the pillow. She reached out and gently stroked his forehead and hair. He was snoring slightly, with the leg of his blue teddy bear clutched in his fist.

After a moment or two Jo went downstairs, padding along the hallway to the kitchen, where she made herself tea. With the hot cup in her hands she opened the door and stepped outside into the garden, bare feet on the worn terracotta brick of the path.

As always, in these first few silent moments of the day, she stood still, closing her eyes. Letting herself drift.

When she and Doug had first moved here, the garden had been the bleakest square of untended gray grass. In December it had disappeared under the snow that froze England for more than six weeks. But she recalled vividly the very first day that she had walked out into it, a March morning.

She had never even opened the door until then, because there was no way out from it; everything came and went through the front, along the narrow little street. Glancing at it sometimes from the bedroom, she had thought it looked like a prison yard, and so she habitually turned her face from it. She already had a yard like that inside her head, a dark square where only her thoughts raced; an exercise yard for demons. She didn't want to put her body into a spot that matched her mood.

But that March morning had taken her by surprise. The snow had long gone, and the grass was growing. She had suddenly realized that the malnourished-looking tree in the corner was actually a lilac. She had seen that the twisted net of vines on the wall was a clematis, in desperate need of pruning before its spring growth. And there had been celandines all along the flagstone path. She had stared at their color, and thought how unlikely they were, how surprising. They were alive, blazing like small suns right along the path, right to the back wall.

She came back to life with the garden.

It was a long, slow journey.

When Sam was born in June of that year, she had taken him out onto the lawn when she came home, and sat with him in the shade of the lilac. By then the clematis had already flowered, and was a sheaf of green leaves, racing, it seemed, full pelt along the top of the wall and diving down the other side. The whole left-hand side of the garden, under the high walls, had given her a dramatic flush of bluebells in April. She had cut the grass—huffing over it while she was eight months pregnant—and it was now a neat green page, springy, as if it were downland turf and not a city patch.

The very last thing that she had done, just before Sam's birth—as it turned out—was to buy a patio rose. Just one little container. One miniature rose. An apricot. By then she could just about bear the sight of roses.

She had sat with Sam in her arms, oblivious to Gina's anxious fussing—rearranging of chairs and the sun parasol—and she had lowered her face into Sam's body, inhaling the newly bathed scent of him, and feeling the sunlight on her neck and back, its almost tender warmth. She had felt suddenly flooded with feeling—a feeling that there was some sort of connection, some sort of thread that passed out from them both, mother and child, through the leaves, out into the greater world. She felt a touch on it, a communication down the wire. She had raised her head, eyes widening momentarily. It had been like a hand brushing her hair, a name whispered in her ear. She had looked at Sam, and seen her son gazing, eyes fixed somewhere past her face, as if he had heard it, and was listening too.

When she thought about it afterward, she had changed her mind about that moment. She had decided that, contrary to how she had felt at the time, there had actually been nothing surreal in it. There had been no touch, no wire, and no whisper. Nothing at all but the lilac leaves moving in the afternoon breeze above her head. Besides, she had decided months ago never to believe in phantoms. Never again to trust in miracles.

Sam was real. Very real, in the sleepless nights that once again accentuated her loneliness. He was real, with his inquisitive, searching looks, and the tight grip on her fingers. He was real in her embrace, his naked little body against her own breast. Real when he cried. Real when she leaned over the cot to catch the passing of each breath. But other things were not real at all.

Dreams, for one.

She opened her eyes now to the ever-brightening day. She finished her tea, and walked back into the house, and walked upstairs, to draw the curtains in the sitting room.

The same sunlight that streamed into Jo's bedroom was filling the open space. Doug would hardly have recognized the way Jo lived now. Not only was she organized—he would have been amazed to see her desk, rigorously in order—but she was also now almost pathologically neat and tidy, as if she had taken on part of his character.

She looked about herself, pleased at the room. How it always seemed to be flooded with light and space. It had been another job before Sam was born: to take down the old red brocade curtains that they had inherited from the last owner, pull back the carpet to expose the oak floorboards. She had bought a secondhand couch that filled one side of the room, a pale, well-worn cream linen that she had filled with yellow cushions. Opposite the couch, books lined one wall. And the final touch was the deep bowl of flowers, filling the low table by the window. There were always flowers by the window. It was Jo's one and only house rule.

She heard a noise from Sam's bedroom and went back to him.

He was lying awake now, staring into space. He hardly ever cried when he woke up; sometimes it seemed to her that he was far away, traveling. Until he saw her, and truly woke up.

She knelt down. "Hey, soldier," she murmured, and stroked his face. "We've got your party to organize. Wake up."

A smile transformed his face. His birthday had been several days before, but the party was organized for today, Sunday. Reaching to pick him up, Jo caught her knee on something by the bed. She picked it up. It was a piece of Lego.

Sam immediately snatched it. "Fix," he said.

She considered the distorted piece of green plastic. "I can't fix that," she objected. "You ran over it with something."

"Fix."

"It's all squashed. What did you do, put it under a tractor?" she asked. "It's destroyed, you vandal."

Sam's eyes lit up. "Tractor," he said.

"Tractor's in the shed, Sam."

"Tractor, now!" he pulled heavily on her arm.

"No, Sam," she chided gently. "Breakfast now, tractor later."

He pulled a face and slumped back to a lying position on his side.

"Come on, Sam," she said. She held out her arms. "Come on, jump up."

He turned his face away from her, shoving the end of the Lego into his mouth.

She pulled on his T-shirt.

And stopped. "Hey," she murmured, "what's this?"

The bruise at the base of his spine was large, and odd looking.

"What did you do?" she asked him. She lifted the T-shirt and inspected him quickly, running her hand down his chest and over his legs.

"Fix," Sam mumbled.

She couldn't make out if he meant the toy or the bruise.

"Does it hurt?" she asked.

He wriggled away.

Still frowning a little, she managed to grab and lift him, taking his well-padded weight against her as she stood up. She pressed her lips to his neck and blew a raspberry. Squealing with delight, he threw his head back and looked at her. Doug's smile. Doug's eyes.

"Hungry?" she asked him.

"Yea," he told her.

She grinned, hoisting him onto one hip. "Nothing much wrong with you, is there?" she said.

By eleven o'clock she was standing in the kitchen, which was completely cluttered with pans, dishes, and mixing bowls. When the doorbell rang, she ran along the hall, licking chocolate mixture from her fingers.

Catherine was on the doorstep.

"You came," Jo said, hugging her. "Oh, thank you."

Catherine stepped in, closing the door behind her. "Crisis?"

"Just two dozen jellies that won't set." Jo grinned.

"Perfect," Catherine commented. "Sloppy jelly is more messy to throw. No other kind for kids' birthdays."

As Catherine took off her coat, Jo poured her a coffee from the stove.

"Where's Sam?" Catherine asked.

"Asleep," Jo told her. "He just slumped on the couch a quarter of an hour ago." She sat down opposite Catherine, and smiled at her over the rim of her cup.

After Doug had died, Jo hadn't seen John's girlfriend for over six months. The first two, Jo had spent with Gina in London. She had been afraid to go home, afraid to go back to the Lincoln Street house after the funeral. She had spent precisely two days alone, before packing a bag and turning up at Gina's London house, trembling with panic on Gina's doorstep.

Jo had thrown herself into work with a feverishness that had really worried her friend, who constantly pleaded with her to relax. Gina

knew very well that Jo barely slept, and so it had been hardly any surprise when she had woken up one morning—about a month after
Doug's death—to find Jo crouched on the floor of her room, weeping
helplessly. Having tried to run herself into the ground to avoid her
grief, she had finally given in to it.

There had followed a week of utter despair. Gina, taking a week off
work, had nursed her through it. Jo barely ate, but she slept hour after
hour—ten, twelve, fourteen hours a day. And at the end of the ten days
she had emerged looking like a battle survivor—pale, fragile, and
painfully thin. But with a cold clarity back in her face.

It had been sometime then—early in the spring—that Jo had tried
to contact both John and Catherine.

She met a dead end in both cases. John—so a stranger's voice told
her over the phone—had moved from his flat, leaving no forwarding
address. Catherine, too, had moved from the student hall of residence.
Frustrated, Jo had finally written to John care of Franklin House. She
wanted to start to repair the gulf between them. She was haunted by
the thought that she had pushed him away, as Doug had admitted to
doing. But her letter had been returned to her.

It was February, the real dead heart of the year—short days, long
nights—when Jo went back to Cambridge.

And it was May before she saw Catherine Takkiruq again.

Jo had spent the morning researching a political piece. She was
due to travel to Manchester the next day, and she had been thinking of
that as she climbed the stairs of a bookshop in the city center. Reaching
the coffee shop, she had turned gratefully toward an area of over-
stuffed chairs and country-house couches, coffee cup in hand.

Catherine was sitting there.

Jo was transfixed for a second. Her first thought was that Catherine
was as lovely as ever, her thick black hair pulled upward in an untidy
pleat, loose strands escaping it. She had a book open in her lap, and
a pile of others stacked by her feet. Then, as Catherine glanced up
and recognized her, Jo saw something different in Catherine's face,
and the breath caught suddenly in Jo's throat. There was a trace of grief
on Catherine's expression. Not dramatic enough, perhaps, to be immediately noticeable. Except to someone who knew that feeling only
too well.

"Hello," Jo said.

"Hello," Catherine responded.

The two women stared at each other. For a moment Jo thought that Catherine was going to look away, back to her book. Then, the girl's eyes strayed to Jo's stomach. "Do you need a hand?" Catherine asked.

"No. Thanks. I'm fine," Jo told her. "Am I disturbing you?"

Catherine shook her head. She cleared the pile of books out of Jo's way.

"You're taking your finals," Jo said, once she had got herself seated.

"Yes," Catherine replied. "I come here to get out of the way. For some peace."

Jo had stirred her coffee embarrassedly. She didn't quite know what to say. "I tried to contact you," she said, finally. "They told me you had moved."

"I got a cheaper room, with a girlfriend," Catherine said. "I tried to phone you. Someone said you'd gone to London."

"I did," Jo told her. "For a while."

They gazed at each other, over the wreckage of those grieving months. All the time Jo wondered how to frame the question in her mind.

"Do you know where John is?" she asked.

At once it seemed that she had hit the nail on the head. Catherine's eyes suddenly filled with tears.

"Oh," Jo said. "I'm so sorry. If only you knew how sorry I am. I've tried to reach him."

Catherine waved her hand, a gesture to stop the flow of words. She closed her eyes a moment; then, opening them, "It's not your fault."

"Where is he?" Jo repeated. "Is he at home? Alicia returned my letter."

"He's not there," Catherine told her.

Jo's eyes ranged over her face. "Not with Alicia?"

"He's not in Cambridge," Catherine said. "He disappeared."

Jo stared at her aghast. She simply couldn't speak.

"He stayed with his mother after the funeral," Catherine said. "But in the new year, he left."

Jo leaned back in her seat. "Oh, my God," she said. "I've done this. I've done this with what I said to him. I had no idea."

Catherine leaned forward, reaching for Jo's hand. "No," she said adamantly. "I really don't think that, Jo. Alicia . . ." She stopped herself.

Jo gazed at her. "Alicia thinks it," she murmured. "She blames me."

"Alicia is very bitter," Catherine said. "It's no use pretending otherwise. She is the kind of person . . . you know? She looks for someone to blame."

"And she's found me," Jo said. "Not just for John. But for Doug's death, because he was with me. Marrying me." Catherine reddened slightly. Jo squeezed her hand. "I can imagine," she said. "It's okay."

Catherine bit her lip. "John wouldn't talk to us," she continued slowly. "Of course, Alicia, when I saw her, she would be the opposite. She would never *stop* talking." She shook her head. "I sometimes think she drove John away," she murmured. "Then I think, it's not just Alicia . . . it's not just what you said. . . ."

Jo frowned. "Then what?" she asked.

Catherine shook her head. "He is just lost," she said. "Lost."

"But he's written to you?" Jo prompted.

"No," Catherine said. "I've heard nothing at all."

They sat together side by side for some time.

"I'm so sorry," Jo said.

At last Catherine raised her head.

"I thought you must still be in London. Maybe with Gina?"

"Yes, I was," Jo told her. "But I always intended to come back. I wanted Doug's child to be born here, in the place he had chosen. To be brought up here, as he wanted."

Catherine nodded, understanding. "There is some happiness to come for you, Jo."

Jo looked down at herself, biting her lip. "I don't know what kind of mother I'll make," she admitted, voicing a small but persistent fear. "Sometimes I feel it'll be okay. Then . . . well, I don't know much about babies."

She looked up to see Catherine gazing back at her with what she would come to know, ever afterward, as her smile of infinite patience. Of a truly sweet nature.

"I don't know much about babies either," Catherine replied. "But I can help you, Jo. If you would like."

"I couldn't ask that," Jo said. "You'll have a job to go to. . . ."

Catherine had shaken her head. "I have a research post," she said. "Two years, here in Cambridge."

"Well," Jo wondered, not liking to impose on her. "Maybe, baby-sitting sometimes . . . ?"

Catherine placed her hand, very gently and fleetingly, on Jo's stomach. "I mean *help*," she said, seriously. "For Doug."

Their alliance was forged in that moment.

The party began at three; but long before that Gina arrived.

She held out her arms to Jo at the door and hugged her.

"You're looking fantastic," Jo said.

"And you're looking thin," Gina said. "What's the matter, child? They don't feed you here?"

"Sam steals my sausages," Jo told her.

She stepped inside and turned. Her husband, Mike, was standing on the pavement.

The sight of Mike always made Jo want to laugh. It was just because of his size. At six foot six and 240 pounds, and most of that muscle, Mike was your archetypal rugby player still, even though he had given up the game four years ago, and was now *The Courier* sports correspondent. Which was how he and Gina had met. In fact, Gina, with an eye to her own future, had almost wrestled the managing editor to the ground to get him to hire Mike before anyone else.

"I just saw his picture and I thought, yes," Gina had explained to Jo a year ago.

"Just, 'yes'?" Jo had asked.

Gina had laughed. "Just *Yesssss!*"

However, it had been months before Gina had actually told Jo what was going on. Gina had driven up to Cambridge one Sunday afternoon—almost to the day, now, it had been Sam's first birthday—and confessed.

"What are you looking like that for?" Jo had demanded.

"Like what?" Gina had said.

"Like you're ashamed of him."

"I'm not ashamed," Gina had replied. Then paused. "It's just . . . well . . ."

"Doug," Jo had murmured.

"Yes, Doug."

Jo had sat down with her friend and taken her hand in hers. "Look, Gina," she'd said. "Do you think that means you aren't allowed a life?"

"No . . ."

"You just don't want me involved in it."

"That's not true!"

"You've known this man—whoever he is—for six months and never said a word."

"I didn't know what to say," Gina had confessed.

"Do you think I begrudge you being happy?" Jo had demanded. "For God's sake, Gina!"

"It's not that," Gina had said. "It's just that I can't bear seeing you *un*happy."

Jo had shaken her head. "Tell me his name."

"Mike Shorecroft."

"Not the rugby player?"

"Yes."

"He played for England!"

"You know him?"

Jo had raised her eyes to heaven. "I do have *some* red blood left in my veins. Mike Shorecroft!"

Gina had actually blushed.

"You're in love," Jo said.

"We're getting married in September," Gina had told her.

And so it had been. A wonderful, joyful celebration, where the bride smiled fit to burst through the whole ceremony, and the groom stumbled over his words, and shed several tears, and, at the reception, Jo found herself mobbed by what seemed like dozens of Gina's relations, who all seemed intent on hugging and kissing anything that moved. Or, indeed, anything that didn't move. When Jo had come home that night, she found that a little of Gina's bliss had rubbed off on her; she went to bed smiling, remembering only with pleasure what love could be like.

She watched Mike now as he stepped over the threshold. He almost filled the narrow hallway. He kissed Jo's cheek enthusiastically. "How are you?" he asked.

"I'm good." She stopped. "What in heaven's name is *that*?"

He was pulling a parcel behind him, an enormous odd triangle shape, wrapped up in bright yellow paper. Before he could reply, Sam appeared at the back door. "Sam!" Gina called. "Come and rip something up!"

She swept Sam up in her arms and kissed him, releasing him and putting him on the floor as he pulled a disgusted face.

"Take it in the garden," Jo suggested.

Mike and Sam went out together. Catherine and Jo had spent most of the morning blowing up balloons and hanging them from the fence and trees. Jo's arms were aching from the effort.

"Jesus," Gina said, accepting the glass of wine that Jo offered. "Tell me there aren't three thousand balloons out there."

"There aren't. There are precisely two hundred and twenty-six," Jo said.

"Only two hundred and twenty-six? What happened? Lungs collapse?"

"Balloon pump broke. Have a Rice Krispie cake."

Gina devoured it in one go. "My next party, everyone's coming in school uniform and we're playing musical chairs," she said. "I decided. It's more fun."

They went out onto the lawn. Sam had torn the paper from the present. It was a trailer for his beloved tractor, with a giant pivoting arm.

"You can hook stuff up and it's a kind of crane as well," Mike said.

"Mike, it's great."

Sam was concentrating on piling his toy cars into the back.

"It's maybe a bit technical right now," Mike wondered.

"He'll get the drift," Jo said. "Thanks so much."

The doorbell rang.

"I'll get it," Catherine said.

The garden filled as the other guests arrived. Jo had invited the mothers who had been in hospital at the same time as she, and who had been with her on prenatal classes. Even Sam's visiting nurse, Eve, was there, who had seen Jo through the last stages of her pregnancy, and helped bring Sam home. Soon the grass was packed with little bodies, strewn toys, and mothers gratefully sitting in the shade, devouring whatever chocolate cake the kids had left in their wake.

"How are you doing?" Gina asked Jo, in a quieter moment. They leaned against the house wall and watched Sam balancing bricks on his tractor seat.

"Can't complain," Jo told her.

It was their usual coded conversation about money. Gina worried that Jo had none. Jo constantly reassured her that work was flowing. Of course, Gina knew that that meant Jo worked all hours, fitting it around Sam's play school and baby-sitters. But it was useless to suggest that Jo might have been in a better financial position if Alicia had not muscled her way into Doug's estate.

It was a particularly thorny subject, one that made Gina's blood boil, and that Jo always claimed that she would rather forget.

After Doug's death they found that his financial affairs were in a mess. The worst kind of mess. In the hassle of buying the house and moving home only six weeks before, the solicitor told Jo that he had advised Doug to redraw his will, which was ten years old and left everything to Alicia. Doug had promised to do so—in fact, he had written out a draft document at home—it was among his letters. The draft made it clear that Jo was the new beneficiary. But it had never been signed, never witnessed.

Jo had been left with half of the Lincoln Street house, and her flat in London. That was it.

Alicia laid claim to the other half of the house—the half in Doug's name—and all his savings, which amounted to some fifteen thousand pounds, and a set of shares that had been, in turn, left to him by his father. Jo was astonished to find that these were worth almost forty thousand.

It was a lot of money. Enough to ignite Alicia's temper. Not two weeks after the funeral Jo had received a letter setting out Alicia's rights under the existing will. It ought to have been a blow—perhaps an unbearable blow, one too many. But Jo had been just too shocked to take it in. It was Gina who waded in on her behalf, hiring a firm of solicitors who acted for *The Courier*.

"They're shit hot," she had explained to Jo. "They'll see Alicia off."

But Alicia had not been ready to be seen off. She had dug in her heels, citing John's precedence over any offspring that Jo may or may not produce.

That phrase had almost given Gina a seizure. "May or *may not!*"

she'd ranted to her own mother. "Does she think Jo's making her pregnancy up? Is she hoping she'll miscarry?" She had knotted her fists in a gesture of intense, impotent fury. "That's what she's hoping for, the jealous bitch, I bet. I'll see her burn in hell," she'd vowed.

But Alicia had not burned in hell. She had remained alive and kicking hard, and at the end of the summer—eleven months, from start to finish—Alicia had graciously accepted Franklin House and the forty thousand in shares and the contents of Doug's bank accounts. Jo kept the Lincoln Street house. Finito.

Gina looked at Jo now; her friend was leaning her head on the wall, rolling the wineglass stem in her fingers. She had her back to the lawn, shading her eyes against the sun, listening, with an absentminded expression, to Catherine and Mike's conversation alongside her.

Then there was a sudden scream behind them.

Jo dropped her wineglass. It shattered on the stone path without her even registering it. Sam, who had, unseen by her, been balancing for a few seconds in the back of the new trailer, had toppled out of it. He had landed on the tractor.

"Oh, my God," Jo breathed. "Sam!"

She dashed across the grass. Sam was lying crookedly, one leg still on the trailer side, the rest of him on the grass. He looked up at Jo with an expression of surprise; then he began to cry.

One of the mothers who had sitting close by had run up too. "It was just a second," she said. "I was watching him. . . ."

I wasn't, Jo thought guiltily.

"He hit his head on the tractor," the mother said.

"Sam," Jo cried. She knelt down next to him and picked him up. "It's okay," she murmured. "It's all right now." She pushed his hair back from his forehead and saw a small cut above his eyebrow. It seemed to hit her in the solar plexus, the thought that he was bleeding. She glanced up to see Eve at her side.

"Bring him inside," Eve said.

A little procession of people went back into the house: Sam and Jo, Catherine, Eve, Gina, and Mike. They sat down on the couch and Catherine brought a box of antiseptic wipes. Jo tore one open and wiped Sam's forehead.

Eve, meanwhile, was looking him over. "No broken bones," she said. "It was such a bump," Catherine murmured.

Gina glanced at Mike, the unspoken thought passing between them that it had been their trailer, their present.

Eve smiled as she rubbed Sam's leg. "He's fine," she said. "Let him rest just a second, get his breath back."

Gina brought a feeder cup of orange juice. Very aware of the eyes on him, Sam played up for a second, turning his head away from the drink until Jo made a move to put it down, when he grabbed it and drank greedily.

"Maybe a little sleep," Eve said. "Five minutes' peace." She glanced up pointedly at the group in the room.

Gina took the hint. "I'll make some coffee," she said. She pulled on Mike's arm.

When the door was closed, Jo sat back. Sam wriggled a little in her lap, throwing his arms over his head. Then, bored, he turned over on his stomach and slipped down onto the floor, dragging his feeder with him. Catherine sat down on the chair opposite, her eyes glued to Sam's progress. Then she glanced up and gave Jo an apologetic grimace, as if to say that she should have been looking out for the boy. But Jo returned the look with a barely perceptible shake of the head.

Sam, meanwhile, was bumping his way, on his bottom, over to the window, where he stood himself up to get a look from the window.

Jo looked over at Eve, smiling.

The other woman's expression halted her in her tracks.

"Jo," Eve said quietly, "how long has Sam had those bruises?"

Twenty

IT was almost two years since the ships had left Beechey Island.

It was no use saying anymore that they were the pride of Her Majesty's Navy; it was months, in fact, since Augustus had thought of them as ships at all.

They had ceased to be the giants that had set out from Greenhithe in 1845; they did not race, or keel over in the strong salt spray. Their rigging did not ring anymore; it had been taken down fourteen months ago and never put back again. They were no longer, even, floating objects that might be described, by some flight of the imagination, as a boat or a vessel. Because they did not float in water. They would never float in water again. They were ice, part of an endless white landscape.

Erebus and *Terror*.

He had asked one of the royal marines, Mr. Daly, what the name *Erebus* meant. Daly said that it was strange that he had come so far without knowing what the title of the sister ship signified. Gus had always supposed that it was a god's name. One of those Roman gods, or Greek. That was what it sounded like to his untutored ear: he thought it might have been the name of one of those angels, half men, half spirit, who could fly. It had a lilt of flight, after all. It was a fast ship. It had a kind of wings.

"It's a name for our predicament, to be sure," Daly said. "A name and a half, Gus."

"Is it good?" Gus had persisted.

"Good?" Daly had shaken his head. "No, Gus. *Erebus* means darkness, boy. It's the place between heaven and hell."

So, Gus had thought, half of them were in terror, and half in darkness.

It was March now, 1848.

This was the year that Augustus Peterman would be fifteen.

He had grown out of his clothes. For a while he wore a pair of trousers that one of the sailmakers had made for him: too long and too wide, he had been a figure of fun, but he did not really mind. He pulled the waist in with a belt and let the legs hang over his boots. They were warm breeches, if not fitted. And he was grateful for that.

No, it was not the trousers that bothered him, but the jacket. It seemed to him that his arms were so much longer, in proportion, to the rest of his body. And, as he grew, the sensation that his limbs were not rightfully his only got worse. Sometimes, in the dark, he would still think he had Torrington's fine-boned hands. Sometimes he would think he was taller than it was possible to be . . . curious, a thing he could not explain. He felt monstrous—so large that he would never get out of the hatchways, never get back on deck. The feeling would wash and recede, wash and recede, like waves on a shoreline. His map of himself, the map of the body that was stored in his head, felt as if it had been tampered with. His fingers were broad and flattened; his knees ached and felt huge; his feet were splayed, like the snowshoes they took on journeys. And sometimes he couldn't feel the edge of things. Tables, pencils, the brass corner of a swinging lamp. The rim of his plate. Sometimes he couldn't even feel the fur that lined their outer coats. And that hurt him, because—he would not have told this to anyone—he got comfort from the fur, stroking it.

There were other things wrong, of course. Everyone had something wrong. Some of the men had had the first signs of scurvy—bleeds under the skin, and their teeth affected. Most bore it with nonchalance; a few had even lost teeth, on previous voyages, to the illness. Others became breathless before they even had the swellings of the skin and the bruises. To any man who showed a sign, the surgeons prescribed two ounces of lemon juice, sweetened with sugar and diluted with an equal amount of water. On the *Terror* Crozier insisted that every man affected swallow the lemon within his sight, to make sure that it was taken.

With a few of the men the problem was not physical illness so much as it was the dark, the winter. It had shocked Gus to see that the prospect of another winter really disturbed a handful of the sailors. He hadn't been able to understand it. They were handpicked; used to the sharp decline of the light, the sound of the wind, the long weeks of twilight. Yet, in November and December of 1846, two of the men on *Terror* had broken out of their confinement belowdecks during a storm. They had gone out in the earliest hours of the morning—no one knew quite when—and let themselves down the side of the ship, and run away from the ship, into the howling blizzard. It was fantastical, he thought, even now: unbelievable. To do such a thing was certain death, even within a hundred yards of the ship. The temperatures were thirty degrees below zero. They took no special precautions other than their usual workwear. Worst of all, what they had done could not have been predicted.

They had not even been rebellious, mutinous. They were both quiet men, both enlisted at Woolwich. They did not know each other, especially, however, and could not have been described as friends. That they had both been seized by the same demon—and demon it was decided upon to have been—was chilling, astounding.

"In the Americas they call it cabin fever," one of the mates had told the crew. "When the winter's in, and no one moves out of the forts, and the log cabin gets too small for a man to bear."

"Now I am cabin'd, crib'd, confin'd," murmured Mr. Helpman, the clerk-in-charge. But he would not say what poet had written it, or from what play it might be.

"Never known it before," muttered Wilks and Hammond and Aitken, who had also come on at Woolwich.

"Fever of the mind," the mate decided.

And so it was. Mind fever.

They found them two days later. They were together, about a half mile from the ship, in the direction of King William Land, as if they had been making for the shore. One lay on his front, curled, defending his face with his hand. The other lay, curiously, on his back, his arms raised in the air, his knees drawn up. They were frozen solid; and they buried them where they lay, cutting a great hole in the ice and lowering the bodies into it.

Nothing more was said of them.

It was in May of last year that Sir John had ordered a search party to go out to King William itself. He named Lieutenant Gore and Mr. DesVoeux, from *Erebus*. The party's orders had been to leave messages in cairns, but by far the most important part of the job was to go south, as much as twenty miles south, to see where the ice leads might be that could set them free. It was high summer coming; they had perpetual light. Mr. Gore, the search team leader, was to find the passage that would take them home.

Home.

Every man's heart rested with that team. Mr. Gore's task was to find a little channel—it did not have to be a very big channel. Somewhere out there in the endless white monotony, he was instructed to find a small stretch of clear water. He was to find it, that's all they wanted. Just find it. A little blue water. A little fresh current. A chance. A chance.

They all dreamed of that open water. They all hoped for that breaking of the way. Stuck, alone, isolated, seemingly forgotten, they were so close, they felt. So close to a breaching of the ice pack. The summer would bring it; and, even if it did not bring it right to the ships, by melting the grip of the winter floe, it would bring a lessening of the pressure, a scent of salt, a warm draft of air. It would bring possibilities. And Mr. Gore had just that one simple task: to find that scent, to see the way it lay. To haul them back, with the overladen sledges, a dream of freedom. A dream of human companionship.

Gus knew, of course, that they were not really alone in the world. Somewhere, far past this place, the world went on just as before. There were cities; there were fields and trees. There were roads and railway tracks and houses. There were churches and farms.

But it was hard to remember them. Gus felt as if they had been cast away. The fate of the seagoing man for centuries. Castaways, the only living creatures left on earth. Sometimes that feeling would be briefly broken—they had bears within sight of them, sometimes—and, very occasionally, they even glimpsed men. Natives. Faint figures who could be seen a distance away, eastward. Their dogs could be heard, the sound of barking drifting across the intervening sea. Sometimes there were hares or ice foxes, and a few were trapped. And once there were falcons, and once deer.

Just once.

The team left the ships on Monday, May 24, 1847.

Lieutenant Gore. Mr. DesVoeux, and six other men from *Erebus*.

Gus watched them go. He was angry that all the men were from Sir John's ship—angry that no one on *Terror* had even been given the choice. He would have liked to be with them, the handpicked few who were loaded down with two sledges packed with provisions. The natives had dog teams, but the ships had no dogs, and so the men pulled.

Of course, Sir John had chosen the toughest of the crew, the biggest. Gus had to bear the disappointment. The humiliation. He was five feet eight inches tall—taller than some—but he was thin. He knew that. Too thin to pull a sledge for long. Too thin, really, to walk a great distance. He had clenched his fists and watched them walking away, the men's bodies seeming further thickset by their clothing—cloth trousers, wool, shirts and jackets, wool coats, and their cleated shoes topped with fishermen's boots of waterproof canvas.

The runners of the sledges had been burnished to make them slide better. On board they carried calico tents and poles, blanket sleeping bags, food, cans of spirit fuel, rum, cooking utensils, axes, shotguns, and powder and shot. And Goldner's cans. On search parties and treks each man was assigned much more than the shipboard ration. They needed it. Walking in such conditions drained the muscles, thinned the blood, sapped the strength, drenched, and froze, and pounded them. And it was not only walking, but climbing too: breaching the rubble ice, piled haphazardly in all possible directions, like tumbled toy blocks that could be twenty or thirty feet high. In less than ten minutes the crew on *Terror* saw the men make the first climb of many: slithering back as often as they lurched forward, the little black dots that were their comrades ascended an ice wall. It took more than an hour before they vanished over the other side.

They waited for them as patiently as they could.

"They'll not cover more than two miles a day," it was said. "If they are lucky." Gus reckoned on his fingers that that meant they would be gone twenty days. Perhaps thirty. A month.

A month would bring them to June. Surely in June there would be some little sign of the ice cracking. Gore would come back, perhaps to say that there was a wider severing of the ice hold just a little farther south. Maybe it would only be a mile from where they were now. Maybe two. And if there was a thaw this year, as there had not been last year, then with a little luck they might be able to break through.

It was a persistent theme, a kind of permanent hymn in Gus's mind. It was surely such an ironic fate, to be lashed to an unyielding, barely moving floe here, when only a few miles north or few miles south there could be clear water. Crozier, talking to the men one evening, had smiled when they had asked him the same question—where the ice would be yielding—for the fiftieth time.

"No man knows the answer to that," he said, affecting an almost cheerful countenance. "But I can tell you this, lads. There had never been known to be ice like this here. Never, in all the conversations I have had with the natives."

"No natives have come close to the ship," one man piped up. "Don't you think that's peculiar, Captain?"

Crozier had nodded slowly. "It is strange," he said. "But if the Es-quimaux cannot fish—and the ice is too thick to fish, and there are no seal—then they won't come here."

"But we've heard them passing, across the strait. Heard their dogs."

"Yes," Crozier agreed. "And take heart from that. For they must be passing to some hunting ground that is within a walking distance. We may not have found it yet, with all our treks to north and south," he added, naming their anxious expeditions from the ships over the last year, which had been so fruitless—"but it is only a matter of time. It is a bad season, a bad year. That is all."

"Why don't they come to us, as they come to the whalefish ports?" another demanded.

Crozier had shaken his head. "They are not used to seeing ships here," he said.

"They think we are dead men," a third muttered, so low that Crozier did not hear. "They daren't come. We are bad luck. They're afraid of us."

There was silence after that speech.

Each man wondered at the strength of the Esquimaux. They seemed like ghosts themselves, in the way that they could survive in this place. Inhabitants from some other, immaterial sphere, who materialized and vanished at will. Whenever some of the crew went out from the ships, the effort of the walk alone taxed them beyond measure, drove them to their knees by nightfall. If it were not the wind that so decimated and exhausted them, then it was the snow, whose color, in fine weather, blinded them, despite the mesh goggles they were given. And even in sun or bright light the cold was still agonizing, piercing the lungs as a man drew breath. And the struggles to set up camp were so slow, and the thirst so terrible. How did these people survive, these hunters in their animal skins, with their tattooed faces? How could they survive, when an Englishman, with all his wealth and idealism, could not?

After that night Gus wondered a lot what the Esquimaux thought when they saw the great ships marooned here. Over on low far stretches of the ice, where they traveled with their dogs, how did they regard the masts and hulls? What did they think they were? They must know, surely, that they were ships. And, if they were ships, then there were men on those ships. But, he thought, curling into a ball in his sleeping canvas at night, perhaps the Esquimaux didn't believe they were men like them. Perhaps, just as he was tempted to believe that the Esquimaux were ghosts, they, in their turn, thought that he was a bad spirit, come to haunt them.

Dead men.

He tried not to think of it. Instead, he fixed his mind on Lieutenant Gore, and imagined what mountains he might be climbing, and put himself in the officer's shoes, and willed him on.

On June 8—Gore had been gone fifteen days—word came from *Erebus* that Franklin was not well. The men were not too concerned, because ever since the attack when they ground to a halt in the strait, Franklin had rarely been seen on deck. He would come up for the religious services, wrapped in his great fur coat and full uniform, attended by his stewards and officers, and he would read out the lessons. But he was not the man that he had been eighteen months before. He had shrunk a little, Gus thought, as if the apoplexy had taken a part of him away, and actually shortened him. One hand would tremble sometimes; once Franklin took a long time ascending the steps.

His stewards rallied around him like housemaids. Nothing was too much trouble. They served him his four-course meals twice a day; they laid the cloths and shined the cutlery, and gave him hot water and soap to wash, and brushed down his clothes, and kept his cabin warm. And so, when he first fell ill, everyone thought it was a passing infection that would be cleared.

If Gus, or any of the crew, could have seen what was happening in Franklin's quarters, they would have been less confident.

The captain had dined as usual on the night of June 7. He had been served soup, pickles, and meat with vegetables, raisins, and a little cheese. Of course, the meat was tremendously salty, and the potatoes bland, and there was an unpleasant taste of grit—which some of the officers privately believed must come from the vegetables' not having been washed properly before being canned—and the cheese was terribly poor and hard, but it was a full meal. Franklin had consumed everything, had a glass of Scotch ale, and retired to his bed.

It was early in the morning, before the usual hour of rising for him, that Franklin called the surgeons. He told Stephen Hanley and Harry Goodsir that he had stomach cramps, and they administered dogwood bitters. Half an hour later Franklin took brandy, and all was quiet for the morning.

Yet that night Franklin did not take dinner at all. He complained to Stanley that he could not feel one side of his face. Opium was given, to help the captain sleep, and he took a little Goldner soup and tinned tapioca.

Then, all hell broke loose during the night. On *Terror* the first that was known of it was that Crozier, and Lieutenant Little, and Lieutenant Hodgson, and John Peddie, were called to *Erebus*. It was three in the morning. Torches were lit to guide the small party across the ice, under skies that fluctuated with an opal green light and trails of luminous high cloud. At four Mr. MacDonald was sent for, and John Diggle, the ship's cook. Diggle went across to *Erebus* with a face paler than the snow, not understanding why he had been called, and afraid of the silence on *Erebus*, and the tense line of men who met him there when he had climbed to the deck.

It was said that Mr. Stanley had prescribed both calomel and tincture of lobelia, and Rochelle salts and Peruvian wine of coca, which some men called cocaine. But nothing had the least effect.

Then, at five in the morning, Sir John sat upright in his bunk, with one hand fisted against his chest. And he died like that, without any sound, without a murmur of complaint. It was over in a matter of seconds. His personal steward, Edmund Hoar, fell to his knees and began to weep, and had to be half lifted, and half dragged, from the room.

At first no one knew what to do.

No senior officer had ever died on an Arctic expedition. No officer was ever expected to. Their lives were so different from those of the men—they were so protected from the ravages of temperature and diet that the crew underwent as a matter of course—that, while an officer or a captain might suffer, he would not be exposed to the infections and exhaustions of his men. The deaths of Torrington and the others, while a blow, had not been a shock. To the officers the Torringtons of this world, while acknowledged as good men and true—gallant even, in their way—were fodder to the great machine. They came from backgrounds utterly different from those of the officers; they lived in a perpetual state of uncleanness, and many did not even know what it was to bathe. Occasionally, when some seaman was enlisted in port, the other men would have to teach him to shave and cut his fingernails. They came from cities where regular waves of typhoid or cholera routinely wiped out thousands, and where sewage floated in the streets and rivers, and they lived in stinking tenements where there might be a hundred in four or five stories of rough-planked, bare-bricked holes in the wall that could not be called living spaces. More often they were dying spaces—the children dying quicker—much quicker—than the parents.

That the ships had only lost three men from disease so far was a testimony to the way that the *Erebus* and *Terror* were kept clean. Even with their cramped, smoky, and tar-smelling quarters, most of the crew were far better off than they had ever been on shore.

But for officers it was an entirely different matter. These were men raised in comfort and kept apart from their working class fellows. That pattern was repeated on the ships. No crewman—or very few—had ever seen an officer's cabin. The closest they came to officers was to see them on deck, on the bridge. The fact that Augustus had even spoken to officers—MacDonald and Crozier—was considered a fine rarity, condescension to the boy's age. It was not normal to, not even welcomed by, officer or man.

And so, when Franklin died, there was, for several hours on end, a vacuum on the ships. No routine was in place for storage of the body, for instance. It was plain that Sir John could not be stowed below, as had happened to Braine for a while. The rats would eat him. Yet the surgeons, fearing what had killed him, did not want him kept in the cabin. Eventually it was decided to bury their commander that day, at midday, out on the ice.

But worse still than the helplessness of not knowing what to do with a commander's body was the fear of what had killed him.

As the officers gathered in the great cabin of *Erebus*, surrounded by the lockers filled with a library of over a thousand books, the controversy raged.

"It is not the cans," Lieutenant Fairholme insisted. "How may it be Goldner's provisions? We have been eating them for months. We are all alive."

"It is something in the cans," Crozier said softly.

"We took two cases out onto Beechey," Fitzjames pointed out. "But for the few soup that had putrefied, none of the others had a concave appearance. We wasted a whole stock there, piercing and emptying them on your suggestion."

"There is something wrong with the cans," Crozier repeated.

"But what?"

Crozier sat staring at his feet. He was terribly aware of Franklin, laid out for burial, in the next cabin, only a few inches away through the thin partition.

"Sir John died of heart failure," Fitzjames continued. And he looked at Stephen Stanley.

Stanley, the senior surgeon of *Erebus*, was a London man born and bred. He had known all the illnesses contingent upon so large a city— all those epidemics that the crew knew so well. He had trained at the Royal College of Surgeons and obtained their diploma in 1838, and there was little he had not seen, either in the primitive operating theaters of the city, or on ship. He had served in the Chinese war on HMS *Cornwallis*, and he had even specialized, and published an account of a rare spinal condition, a case where a complete dislocation of the fifth and sixth vertebrae was observed without any accompanying fracture.

But for all his experience Stanley had not seen a case like Sir John's.

He had dimly heard of something like it, however.

"Sir John did die of heart failure," he agreed, slowly. "Of a congestion of the heart already present from his first attack last year. . . ."

"But?" Crozier prompted. They had all heard the hesitation in Stanley's voice.

"But the intestinal cramping which went before," he said. "And the paralysis . . ."

"Botulism," Goodsir said. It was such a quiet remark that it might have been missed, if Stanley had not nodded his agreement.

"Botulism?" Crozier repeated. "What is that?"

"We don't know the cause," Stanley said. "But it is a fast-acting poison, and they say it is caused by eating preserved meat."

For a moment all their thoughts flashed to the cooking galleys. To the pots and utensils, the knives, the plates. Their eyes strayed to the glasses of port before them all.

"No one knows what causes it," Stanley said, "or how it can be prevented."

"But all the food is boiled," Fitzjames commented.

Crozier opened his eyes and leaned forward. "What did Sir John last eat?" he asked.

The officers' cook, Richard Wall, was brought in. Wall had been sitting morosely outside, aware that Stanley thought the food was somehow to blame for Franklin's death, and whispering his fears to John Diggle, from the *Terror*. When called, he felt that he was testifying in a court—perhaps his own court-martial. He was already flushed as he stood in front of them.

"I washed everything," he said, when questioned. "My stoves are clean, sir. My cooking pots too. You may see them, sir. Please, sir, examine them. I am a clean cook."

"What did Sir John eat two nights ago?" Crozier prompted.

Wall pressed one set of fingertips into the knuckles of the other hand, to stop himself from obviously wringing them. "The officers ate roasted beef."

"From the tins."

"Aye, sir. But Sir John ate pork."

Crozier looked at Fitzjames. "He ate a different meat from the rest?" he asked.

"Yes, sir. He expressed a wish for pork."

"It's true," Fitzjames said. "I remember."

"And the pork was boiled, the same as the beef?" Crozier said.

"Yes, sir . . ."

Crozier frowned. "And?"

Wall had blushed deeply. "I put the pork in last of all," he said. "But it boiled the same, sir."

"For the same amount of time?"

"Yes, sir."

"All right, Wall," Crozier said.The man was dismissed.

Inside the great cabin, Crozier rested back on the seat and rubbed his eyes with one hand. "Is it your opinion, Mr. Stanley," he asked, "that this disease could be present in the tins of pork? Perhaps is some illness that was introduced during the canning, and is not here on the ship, but inside the tins? And has been there since we took them on board?"

Stanley glanced at Fitzjames. He did not want to contradict a senior officer. "I don't know, sir," he said, finally. "In all truth I do not know."

"We have eaten pork before," Goodsir said.

"Yes," Crozier agreed. "We have."

Abruptly, he stood up.

Every man there looked at him: an Irishman who had worked his way through to his rank, whose bearing was not that of an officer such as Fitzjames, but who now was promoted to lead them all. When Francis Crozier had been given the second-in-command in England, no one believed that he would ever succeed to such a position. He bore his newfound responsibility poorly, Fitzjames thought. His eyes were red rimmed. Crozier had been weeping—Fitzjames had seen him weep at Franklin's bedside. He disapproved of such behavior, but he did not say so. He merely looked away from Crozier's face.

"No man is to eat anything more of the pork, until every tin has been examined for leakage or damage," Crozier said. "We will continue to eat the beef." He drew his coat around him.

The officers withdrew.

Crozier watched them go; then, left alone in the cabin, he paced the lockers.

He could not rid himself of one other thought, a thought so terrible that to mention it again—he had hinted at something like it on Beechey, to Sir John—would only cause greater alarm. He could not rid himself of the idea that there was something else wrong with the tins. When he looked around himself daily at the crew, especially at boys like

Augustus Peterman, he could not help thinking that they seemed worse than might be expected. Even accounting for the winters and the lessening of rations, and the scurvy, there was something else wrong. They were too pallid, too irritable, too easily tired.

What obsessed him most of all was that, when a man fell very ill, as Torrington had done, and they gave him officer's rations from Goldner's tins, he seemed to get worse, and not better. He ought to have rallied, at least for a while, eating the richer food. But he had not.

He had noticed something else. Men like himself, who did not always relish meat and preferred the pickled fish or vegetable, or even the caramelized fruit, seemed to him to be much better in spirit than their colleagues. Men who—here he bit his lip and smiled wryly—men who liked their drink, as he did, and who perhaps occasionally drank in favor of eating . . . men like him seemed fitter.

Why should that be? he wondered. It did not make sense. If it was something in the tins, something besides this filthy botulism, would it not have made itself manifest by now? They had checked and rechecked on Beechey. They would check again now, for leaking, for decay. They would boil the food. But if it were something else . . .

He frowned, frustrated. He could not shake the fear that there was some invisible enemy among them, weakening them by degrees.

But he had no idea what.

His fingertips trailed along the books. *The Vicar of Wakefield* . . . Shakespeare's sonnets. Spenser's *Faerie Queene.* Tennyson and Wordsworth. He had been thinking of Sophia all day. He had been thinking of that canister, and his message. *And the stately ships go on.* What had possessed him to do such a thing? It was not a pretty poem. It was full of despair. He had not felt particular despair on the morning he had written it. He had only felt what he had felt all along . . . unhappiness at losing her, and dismay at Franklin's reliance upon certain courses of action. But he had not had a broken heart . . . or, more precisely, he had a heart that had now mended.

It was perhaps an ungentlemanly thing to do, to write that message. If the canister was picked up, and it were returned to Lady Jane Franklin, and her niece read the inscription, then Sophia would know. She would realize that he was speaking of her. He had said the same line to her, half in humor, the smile fading on his face, on the day that she had refused him. "Well," he had said, "my stately ship shall go on, Sophia. I shall be a lone sailor."

She had not replied. She had looked up at him sorrowfully.

He had pressed his case too fast, he knew. Forced her to react too swiftly. If he had waited, perhaps another year, she might have accepted him, no matter what the pressure from Franklin and his wife to refuse him still.

He should not have written the line.

She would be angry with him for that, when he returned.

As he held the volume of Tennyson in his hand, there was a knock at the door. Surprised, he turned around. It was Stanley.

"What is it?" he asked.

Stanley came in and closed the door behind him. "I am thinking of Lieutenant Gore," he said.

"Gore?" Crozier asked. "In what respect?"

Stanley's face was grim. "What, of Goldner's provision," he asked, "did Lieutenant Gore take with him?"

It was June 22 when Gore's party returned to the *Erebus* and *Terror*.

They saw them coming across the ice, and Crozier himself went out to meet them.

Gore had marched to the coast of King William Land, a distance of four miles from the ships. It had taken him four days. There he had left a note in a stone cairn, on May 28. He had put it in a canister and secured the tin case with solder. The note had given the position of the ships, and continued,

> . . . *having wintered in 1846–7 at Beechey Island in Lat. 74.43.28 N., Long. 91.39.15 W., after having ascended Wellington Channel to Lat. 77, and returned by the West side of Cornwallis Island.*
> *Sir John Franklin commanding the Expedition.*
> *All well.*
> *Party consisting of 2 officers and 6 men left the Ships on Monday 24th May, 1847.*
> *Gm. Gore, Lieut.*
> *Chas. F. Des Voeux. Mate.*

The note had been written on the *Erebus* before Gore had left. He and Des Voeux signed their names. Franklin, too, attached his signature, although in an unfamiliar handwriting. No one noticed that the years quoted at Beechey were wrong.

After leaving the note at the cairn, Gore had marched south for twelve miles and reached the south side of Back Bay, where he had built another stone cairn and left a duplicate of the first message.

He and his men saw that Victoria Strait did indeed continue to the west, as Franklin had always said, and that, if the ice melted, there was a wide way forward.

On June 11, the very day that Franklin had died, the party turned back for the ships, and by way of celebration at the enormous effort of their mission, and having done all that was demanded of them, they cooked themselves a meal, opening the second case of Goldner's tins.

Lieutenant Gore died three days later, on June 14.

When Crozier met them out on the ice, Gore's body, and that of two others of the men, were being pulled behind them on the second sledge.

Twenty-one

IT was early on Tuesday morning that Jo saw her doctor.

She had been there only the day before, at Eve's insistence, for a blood sample to be taken from Sam.

"I'm not worrying about this," Eve had told her then, "and neither should you. It's a precaution, that's all."

All last night, bathing her son and putting him to bed, Jo had repeated this information to herself, even after the receptionist had telephoned late in the afternoon to tell her that an appointment was fixed for eight forty-five the following morning. *Eve is not worried.* It was the last thing she thought of before finally falling asleep. *There is nothing to worry about.*

"Has the blood test come back?" she had asked the receptionist over the phone. "Is that why I have to come in?"

There had been a rustling of paper. "I think so" was the reply.

"What was the result?"

"I think that the doctor would like to discuss that with you."

She drove into the parking lot now, narrowly missing another car that was trying to reverse out. The driver scowled at her; she barely noticed him. Behind her Sam was fretting. He had already thrown his toys—kept in a hanging affair on the back of the driver's seat—onto the floor of the car.

"We're here," she told him. She got out of the car, and retrieved his Beanie Baby, and gave it to him while unlocking him from his baby seat. She hoisted him onto her shoulder. "Be good now," she whispered. "Show Dr. Jowett what a good boy you can be."

They were waiting for her when she got in. Looking over her shoulder at the patients waiting, she realized that she had been given an appointment before regular doctor's hours. The little gnawing ache in the pit of her stomach grew suddenly.

Dr. Jowett stood up as she came into his office. He came around the side of his desk. "Hello, Sam," he said.

Sam hid his face in Jo's shoulder. "He's in a bad mood," Jo said. "I wouldn't get out of the driver's seat in traffic to get Beanie back from the floor."

Jowett smiled. He indicated the chair to one side of the desk. Jo sat down, with Sam cradled in her lap.

"How has Sam been?" Jowett asked.

"Fine," Jo said. It was a reflex action, a defense. Against what, she didn't know. "Well," she relented, "not exactly fine. All the usual baby things."

Jowett glanced at his notes. "We had a chest infection a couple of months ago," he said. "An ear infection . . ."

"The usual baby things," she repeated. "I mean, it was winter. A lot of kids had that cold that wouldn't go away."

"Yes," he agreed. "And his mouth ulcers . . ."

"He hasn't had one for ages. It was when I weaned him. He was allergic."

"Did you find out what to?"

"Very milky stuff," she replied. "Some yogurt . . . cream desserts . . ."

"Right," he said.

"He was a bit sick."

"Right," he repeated.

She stared at his profiled face. Quite suddenly she saw a pulse beating in Jowett's throat, at the side. *He's afraid,* she thought, quite objectively. *He's afraid to tell me.*

"What is it?" she asked.

He looked up. "Jo," he said, "I'm afraid that Sam is a sick little boy."

All she could think of, at that moment, was that she had been right. Jowett *had* been afraid. He'd just said so.

"Is it the blood test?" she said.

"Yes."

"Why? What did it say?"

Jowett shuffled the slip of paper and Sam's notes before replying. "He had a deficiency in his blood," he told her. "A low platelet count. Low red count too."

Instinctively, she tightened her grip on Sam. He objected to the pressure, turning his face up to hers. She stared at Jowett. "What does that mean?" she said.

"Well," Jowett said, "many conditions lead to a reduced blood count. It means that the body is fighting something. It might be a viral infection."

"Like a chest infection?"

"It might be a viral infection," he continued, as if she hadn't spoken. "A disorder of the immune system, or a result of drug treatment, a dozen things. Whenever we have a serious illness, our body fights back. It has to produce the right kind of blood. At the moment Sam's blood isn't doing that. It's laboring, if you like. Trying to keep up, but not achieving it."

"And did that cause the bruising?" she asked.

"Perhaps."

"But"—she hesitated—"don't you get that with meningitis? Bruises that don't go away? That's septicemia, isn't it?"

"It isn't that kind of bruise," Jowett said.

She laughed. "How many kinds of bruise are there?" she said. "A bruise is a bruise."

"We need to do more tests, a full blood count, and a blood film report, and possibly something called a chromosome analysis."

She shook her head. "Just for a bruise . . ." Suddenly her face was on fire. Her skin seemed to hurt all over. "He fell on his tractor," she whispered, as if, in some distorted way, this was where Sam's problem had come from.

"You need to take Sam to the hospital," Jowett was saying. "I've made an arrangement for you this morning."

She tried to concentrate. "Now?" she asked.

"Yes. Straightaway."

"I have to go to the hospital right now?"

"You go to the hematology department." He was already writing the form.

"Just a minute," she said.

He glanced up at her. "I'm sorry," he said, "but it is urgent."

He handed her a piece of paper. On it he had written the address of the department, and the road and gate number she should use. "Don't bother with the main parking lot," he said. "Just take him direct to that gate, go through, a hundred yards. Park on the left. There's six spaces there."

She looked at the paper, then back at him. "Straight through," she repeated.

"Yes."

She got up in a daze. She had almost got to the door, and Sam had insisted on being put down, and was pulling on her hand, and trying to reach the door handle, when she turned back to Jowett. It was as if all the information had only just hit her. "Low blood count," she said. "That's what you have when you get leukemia."

Jowett got up and walked toward her. He put his hand on her shoulder. "It might be one of several things, not necessarily that," he said.

It was as if the ground had just dropped out from under her. She felt it go. One minute it was solid—the green carpet of the room, the concrete below—then there was nothing. She was dropping—free-falling.

"He's not that sick," she said. "He's okay, really."

"Good," he replied. "Then we'll prove it today."

She looked down at Sam. He had stopped pulling and was looking first at her, and then at the doctor.

"Are you okay to drive?" Jowett asked her.

"Yes . . . yes."

"Let one of the girls make you some tea. Rest for a second outside."

She pulled away from his hand and opened the door.

"I can tell you something for nothing, Dr. Jowett," she said. Her voice felt like someone else's—thin, reedy, aggressive. "My son hasn't got leukemia."

She grabbed Sam, and walked from the room.

* * *

It was some time before she arrived at the ward that Dr. Jowett had described. She drove as far as the hospital, and then pulled up outside it, the engine running, staring at the buildings ahead of her.

She had the feeling that, if she went in, she would set in train some awful chain of events, something over which she had no control at all. If she didn't go in—if she just disappeared—then those things would never happen. She heard the breath snag and catch in her throat as her hands tightened on the steering wheel. Whatever was waiting for her behind those hospital walls could never materialize if she didn't go in, she told herself. She could hold back time; she could freeze time itself. Everyone around her would remain in the same unchanging moment, but she could carry on. With Sam. Take him somewhere. Somewhere safe. Somewhere warm. Someplace far away. The Seychelles. Mauritius. Grenada . . . She pictured him on a hot beach, letting the sand run through his fingers, grinning. The last time they had been on a beach, she had made an octopus out of sand. He'd loved it. She would do that again . . . take him there. Away.

Whatever he had in his blood—whatever the *hell* it was—would simply stay the same. Never change. Never grow. Never affect them. They would be someplace else, out of reach.

She'd pressed both palms to both temples. The nursery-rhyme tape that she'd put on for Sam came to the end with a click. She looked around and saw that he had fallen asleep.

Tiredness. Lethargy. Bruising.

No, it wasn't possible. Not leukemia. They had had their share of bad luck. The nightmare had already happened to them. They weren't due any more. Jo had lost her lover, her husband in all but name. Sam had lost a father he had never known, never would know, except by photographs. Lately she had begun to think that they had turned a corner, and she could see clear water. So leukemia could not happen to them. It had to happen to somebody else, somebody who hadn't had any misery yet.

She didn't deserve it. Sam didn't deserve it. Sam, most of all.

"Oh, God," she whispered. She fought down the incredible urge to run, and the irrationality of her own thoughts.

If only Doug were here, she thought.

Even now she sometimes forgot his death. Actually forgot that he had gone. It was a safety mechanism, she supposed, against the loss. Giving yourself, subconsciously, a break from the experience. That it was some kind of dream. Then, waking from that delusion, she would read something in the paper, and turn to tell him . . . or the phone would ring. She would be two beats into the ringing, moving toward it, before she would remember that it could not be him.

But there was no way to forget now.

She had to go into the hospital.

She had to do this alone.

Eventually a van pulled up behind her. It was some sort of delivery truck. The driver got out and tapped on her window.

"If you don't move from here, love," he mouthed at her through the glass, "you'll be towed."

She wound down the window. "What?"

"Ticket, at least. Just warning you, like. You're on double yellows."

She'd blinked. "Oh . . . thanks. Thanks."

He nodded at her. As he walked away, he glanced back, once, with a frown. She looked in the rearview mirror and glimpsed her own white face.

Slowly she put the car into gear, and indicated right.

Twenty-two

THE evening went on forever.

It was one of those days in June when the light seems reluctant to leave. Even though the streets looked dim—the lights were just coming on—the sky was a light, improbable turquoise, and as Jo leaned her head against the glass of the hospital window and looked out, she saw people going down the street, arms linked, talking, passing under the trees.

She wondered if the day would ever really end. It had lasted centuries already.

As soon as she had come into the ward with Sam—almost immediately—he had been hooked up to a drip and given a blood transfusion. Someone had stood by her side, the head nurse, and told her why it was necessary. She heard the words, but they fell through her. She couldn't seem to make any sense of them. She had held on to Sam's hand and soothed him. Talking. Talking about anything. Her heart had pounded until she felt sick. She didn't look at the bag of blood hanging over him. She didn't look where they had put a tube in his arm. She played round-and-round-the-garden a couple of times, but had to stop because it made him move too much. She told him about Dumbo, who was painted on the wall, and the crows who couldn't believe he could fly. The nurses brought her tea, but she didn't touch it. Sam cried, and scratched at the needle in his arm, and flung his head from side to side.

Halfway through the morning she suddenly remembered Gina and Catherine, but after she got out her mobile phone, the staff told her that she couldn't use it in the hospital. They brought her a pay phone, but she picked up the receiver and then just stared into space. What on earth was she proposing to say to them both? How could Gina drive up here again? She'd only gone back thirty-six hours ago. She'd be busy. And Jo realized that Catherine, working now on an anthropology thesis, usually turned her mobile phone off.

And what would be the net result of ringing either of them, anyway, Gina or Catherine? Jo thought. They could do nothing. She would only be spreading her terror around.

She'd put the phone back.

They had sedated Sam a little, and he had slept, a frown on his face.

"Mr. Elliott will see you this afternoon," the head nurse told her, at about one o'clock.

"Who is Mr. Elliott?" she asked.

"He's the consultant," the woman said, and patted her shoulder. "He's very good with the children."

I hope he's very good with the parents, Jo thought. She wanted to shake this anonymous man. She wanted to hit something. She felt like saying, *This is a mistake, you've got me mixed up with someone else.*

They took Sam's details. His date of birth; what kind of birth it was; what illnesses he had had; his height, weight. They took more blood. Jo watched the vials fill up. She thought, objectively, that was all they really were. She and Sam. Everyone. Blood and bones. Tissue. Chemicals.

Her thoughts had bounced around haphazardly. By midafternoon she was exhausted listening to the random firing of her own mind, the tangents and irrelevancies it was engaged in. Her brain was playing a sort of weird mental tennis. Back and forth. Back and forth. That morning, before going to the doctor's office—sitting at home over breakfast, Sam at his chair, reaching awkwardly up for his cereal, a skill he had just mastered, and she writing a shopping list—*God! It had only been this morning*—she had planned what she would buy after leaving the doctor's. And now, along with the nameless nightmares stalking through her head, she kept thinking that she needed orange juice, and Pampers. Somehow this particular thought—that Sam wasn't even toilet trained yet, that he was lying here in his diaper—seemed the most outrageous of all. How could a child in a trainer pant be attached to a blood drip? It was a farce. A sick joke of the worst kind. She screwed her eyes shut, willing tears away. He wouldn't wake and see her crying. Her fingers smoothed through his thick, dry hair.

The consultant arrived two hours later, at five.

He came to the bed, where Sam was, by now, awake, and eating ice cream.

"Hi, Sam," he said. "That looks good."

Sam stared at the stranger, not sure, spoon poised halfway to his mouth. The man smiled and held out his hand to Jo.

"My name is Bill Elliott," he said.

"Jo Harper."

"Nurse Stevens would like to sit with Sam, if I could talk to you?"

Jo glanced at her son. "Can't we talk here?"

"We won't be long." He stood back, indicating the way to a room across the corridor.

Jo leaned down and kissed Sam's forehead. "Back in a minute," she said.

"We'll keep the door open," Bill Elliott told her. "We'll put your chair by the door. He'll be able to see you."

That evening light was just beginning. The room, facing west along the line of trees in the road, was bathed in a rosy light. Jo glanced at Elliott's desk, and a framed photo standing there, a picture of Elliott with his wife. They had three children, it seemed. Two girls and a little boy of about Sam's age. All through the interview that followed, she kept looking back at them.

"We have the results of some of the tests," Elliott said.

Jo couldn't reply. It was hard to breathe, let alone talk.

Elliott didn't look at his notes, or the file on his desk. He leaned forward, elbows on his knees, hands clasped.

"Have you any idea what is wrong with Sam?" he asked.

"Just tell me," she said. "Please."

How many times have you done this? she wondered.

Someone outside in the street shouted, calling a name. Laughing.

"Sam has a problem with his blood," Elliott said. "Let me try to explain a bit." He stared down at his clasped hands for a moment. "Blood is made in the bone marrow, the spongy tissue in the middle of bones. Our bodies control the growth of marrow." He glanced up at her. "It's hard work," he continued. "About three million red cells and about a hundred twenty thousand white cells are produced every single second."

"I see," she murmured. She, too, unconsciously, knotted her fingers together.

"We have several kinds of blood cell in our bodies," Elliott told her. "Lymphocyte T-cells—they control immunity, kill viruses. Lymphocyte B-cells—they make antibodies. Granulocytes—mainly neutrophils—they fight infection and kill bacteria." He smiled a little at her. "Too complicated?" he asked.

"No, no," she said, frowning. "Go on."

He nodded. "Then there's monocytes," he continued. "They work at antibody production, among other things. The red cells carry oxygen, and the platelets help clotting, prevent bleeding."

"Yes," she said. But she had probably only retained twenty percent of what he had said, holding on to the thought that whatever the words meant, they were irrevocably connected to Sam, and the bruises.

"All these different cells have different lifespans," Elliott said. "Red cells live for about four months after they leave the marrow. Neutrophils for a few hours. Platelets for a few days. Because white cells and platelets go so quickly, they can't easily be replaced by transfusion."

She looked away from him, to the picture, and back again.

She took a long, deep breath. "Has Sam got leukemia?" she asked.

Elliott sat back. He waited a beat, as if thinking how to phrase his next sentence. "We need to do more tests," he said. "I would like to do a bone marrow biopsy tomorrow."

"But has he got leukemia?"

"No," Elliott told her. "I don't think that Sam has got leukemia."

She stared at him a second, then gave an almighty sigh. Until that moment she hadn't realized she'd been holding her breath. "Oh, thank God," she said. "Thank God." She put her head in her hands, covered her face. She felt Elliott's hand on her knee. He was giving her a tissue.

She wiped her eyes and face. "You just don't know how relieved I am," she said. "Oh . . . all day today, I thought . . ." She shook her head. "Thank you," she repeated.

"I think that Sam has got aplastic anemia," Elliott said.

She blew her nose. She was half laughing. "Anemia," she said. "Just anemia. That's okay, then, isn't it? You can cure that, can't you?"

A spasm crossed Bill Elliott's face: a reflex of real pain. Jo stopped, the tissue pressed to her mouth for a second. Then her hand slowly dropped into her lap. "You can cure that, can't you?" she repeated.

"Mrs. Harper . . ."

"Jo," she said.

He nodded. "Jo. Look, we need to talk again tomorrow. Maybe the next day. These tests have to be done several times. We have to make sure."

"But you're sure he hasn't got leukemia," she pointed out.

Elliott frowned. He rubbed his face with one hand. "It's been a long day," he said. "Much longer for you than for me, and believe me, it's been a long day for me. So"—he rose to his feet—"you go home and get some rest. Let Sam get some rest. We need you back here in the morning."

She remained where she was, staring up at him. "Aplastic anemia," she said.

He frowned, shook his head. "I'm getting ahead of myself," he told her. "We need to do the tests—"

"What is aplastic anemia?" she insisted. "What made you say that?"

He looked at her for a moment, saw that she wasn't about to be moved. "When you look at aplastic anemia on a blood film, it looks like nothing else," he said.

"And that's why you said—"

"I want to be a hundred percent, Jo," he told her.

She did, at last, get to her feet. She heard her own voice shake for a second as she began. She gulped down air; restarted the sentence. "Suppose . . . It's a hypothesis, right?" she said. "At this moment . . . at this minute?"

"Yes," he said.

"Okay," she answered. "This hypothesis, aplastic anemia. Tell me about it. It's not anemia. It's not what I thought, is it? Not something simple?"

"I don't—"

She really tried hard to stop herself screaming at him. "Will you please give me a straight answer," she said, "for Christ's sake."

His eyes ranged over her. "Sit down," he said.

She did so; he followed her, moving his chair so that it directly faced her.

My God, here it comes, she thought. *What is it, what the hell is it?*

"Aplastic anemia, if this is what Sam has," he said slowly, "is a serious illness, as serious as leukemia. It's a life-threatening illness," he said. "If the . . . hypothesis is correct in Sam's case."

Jo took a long, slow draft of air. Screwed the tissue to a ball in her fist. Her heart began thudding again, but slower and heavier. Each beat a blow in her chest, as if it were struggling to do its job. Each beat a needle of pain.

"I'm very sorry," Elliott said. He got up and went to the door of the room. Jo glanced up and saw Sam. Her son was sitting with his legs dangling down the side of the bed. He was twisting the arms of a teddy bear this way and that. The nurse was holding a reel of bandage, and he was winding it around the bear's arm.

"Could we have some tea?" she heard Elliott say.

"Yes, of course," someone replied.

Elliott came back in, and sat down again. "Are you all right?" he asked.

"No," she murmured. "Aplastic anemia. I never heard of it."

"It's a rare disease," he was saying. "We get maybe a hundred, a hundred and twenty, cases a year in the UK. The number is rising. Most of the people who get it are between fifteen and twenty-four, and over sixty."

She gasped. "Then Sam can't have it," she said. "He's only two years old."

"There have been cases of children born with it, I'm afraid," he told her gently.

"*You're* afraid," she snapped. Immediately regretted it. "I'm sorry," she said. "The GP said that this morning, that he was afraid."

"I'm sorry," Elliott said. "It's a turn of phrase. We know we aren't as afraid as you. We know we never will be. We *hope* we never will be."

The nurse came in, carrying a tray of tea. She put the tray down on the desk and, as she left, propped the door farther back to ensure Jo's view of Sam.

"People with aplastic anemia don't produce good blood cells,"

Elliot continued slowly. "When we look at the bone marrow under a microscope, we see a large number of fat cells instead."

"But how would he have got it?" she said. "Would he have caught it from somebody?"

"No," Elliott told her, "it isn't catching. But we might find that Sam also has an immune-system problem. Sometimes they go hand in hand."

"Could I have given it to him when I was pregnant?"

"No."

She thought. Then, "When I was three months pregnant, his father died," she whispered. "Could the shock have done something to him? Hurt him, before he was born?"

"It's impossible to say. But it's unlikely. Don't think that way. It's not your fault."

"But it must have come from *somewhere*."

Elliott spread his hands. "We're just guessing," he said. "We suspect things like radiation, or benzene, or hepatitis, or antibiotics—"

"Antibiotics?" she repeated, aghast. "Sam's had several, for his chest infections."

"We just don't know. It might be the cause. Equally, it might not. It just suddenly starts. The patient gets tired and pale; they run out of steam; they bruise easily. Sam's bruises are very characteristic. They're caused by a low platelet count."

She put her hands to her face briefly. "I don't understand it," she said. "I can see he's tired. I can see he's bruised. But he runs about. He plays."

Elliott nodded. "I know," he said. "But the blood-film report is really clear. Aplastic anemia looks very distinctive on a blood film. It's like nothing else. In fact, the blood film shows a *lack* of abnormalities—that, combined with the other tests, would be classic AA."

"But you'll double-check," Jo said. "You'll do something else?"

"Of course," he told her. "That's what I've been trying to explain to you. Look, I'm sorry this conversation got this far. That's my fault. It's worrying you needlessly."

"I asked you," she reminded him. "I insisted."

He put his hand briefly on hers. "We'll do an aspiration. Sam will need just five minutes' anesthetic in the morning. We take a little marrow from his hip."

Jo shuddered involuntarily.

"The good news," Elliott added, "is that, ten years ago, seventy percent of people with this died. Now, the same percentages live. We're breaking new ground all the time. New drug protocols—"

"Is that what you would do for Sam?" Jo asked. "Give him drugs?"

"Sam would be started on what we call immunosuppressive therapy," Elliott said. "He would have ALG—antilymphocyte globulin. That knocks out T cells. And cyclosporin. That inhibits T cells."

"And these T cells could be doing the damage?"

"T cells will attack the marrow. The body turns on itself. We try to stop it."

Jo glanced back to Sam. She tried desperately to get her head around the idea that something inside him, his own blood, was attacking him.

"What if it didn't work?" Jo said. "What else can you do?"

"We try to give it a chance to work," Elliott said. "Occasionally the marrow regenerates and starts working again of its own accord. Or rather, with a kick up the rear. We take blood weekly to see how Sam's doing. We give him blood and platelets. . . . We always try to think positive. . . ."

"But what if that doesn't work?" Jo said. She tore her attention from Sam and looked Elliott in the eye.

"Think positive," he repeated kindly.

"Worst case," she murmured. "Please, tell me the worst case."

Twenty-three

IN August a camp was established on Cape Felix, on the shore of King William Land, four miles from *Terror*. The shore party was made busy, on Captain Crozier's instructions. Establishing the camp itself; setting traps; collecting the magnetic observations; cutting the deep fishing holes in the ice, which as soon froze over unless there were six men to each, hacking at the ice to keep it free, and a canvas cover tented over them.

Gus had begged to be brought here, even though it was less than a week since he had been bled on board the ship. The men had told him that bleeding would do him good, but he did not know if they were right. He hated to see the thick, viscous fluid come out of his arm: it made him feel mortal, human. It made him feel that he might die, because all he was was just a collection of bones, and this red blood that trickled into a bowl.

He hadn't slept, let alone dreamed, for two nights afterward. He felt that something had really been taken from him, and that if he closed his eyes, he would cease to exist. Finally, he had fallen asleep at the very foot of the deck ladder, and been carried inside, and put in the sick bay. He dreamed then, and no mistake. Fish leaping from the ice and into his bed. Arms wreathed in winding sheets. His own blood dancing in a rivulet and the same fish thrashing in it and choking, and dying. Dreamed of other fish too. Fish in the canals of home. Wood boxes of sea fish on the quayside. The knee-deep viscera of the great fishes, the whales on board his uncle's boat.

He tried to draw himself now from the same kind of reeling sleep.

Early that morning half the shore party had left the tents and trekked for a mile or more following the trail of reindeer. Gus was desperate to be with the men who carried the rifles: he wanted to be allowed to fire, as he had learned on Beechey. Heavy with their coats and furs, however, they had not got far before a fog came down, obscuring everything.

"God blast this weather," one of the mates said. "I never saw the like. Where is the damned summer?"

They had turned back; but the fog got worse, and Gus, bringing up the rear, had lost his bearings. He could hear the voices of the men ahead—and several times they turned back for him—but he had fallen, and, while getting up, he had lost them. For a while their voices seemed to come from all directions, and he stumbled in their tracks. The ground was a little higher: scree and broken shale showed through the hummocks of snow. He floundered around before having the sense to scoop out a hollow in the snow, piling it, as best he could, around him, in a slight depression of the land.

For a while he slept.

And once, thinking he woke, he thought that a pair of hands had pressed something between his own palms. He had looked up, through the mist, and thought he saw a face—pretty, female. Even with the tattoos that ran from the corners of her mouth to the corners of her eyes, she was lovely. But looking down at himself afterward, he could see nothing except a few dry flakes, iridescent scales, on his gloves.

They found him again at midday.

"Augustus!" cried a man's voice.

He screwed his eyes against the distant glare of the horizon. Deeply asleep for the last few minutes, he had imagined himself in a beautiful polar night, the night of summer that never grew truly dark; the shoreline thick with ice, the frozen sea beyond, and the orange of the sky reflected, in long trails of light, over the blue ice and sea and shore. Just on the horizon there was a brilliant gold line, almost too bright to look at. He imagined it would be like that when you reached heaven: a thread of gold blazing into day. But now, opening his eyes, he saw the mist draining away, and the long sloping landscape in front of him.

"He's here, sir! Here!"

Four men were approaching. He squinted to see the faces.

The first was John Handford, one of the able seamen. He dropped to his knees and began chafing Gus's face.

"Where have you been, boy?" he shouted. "God look at you, frost-bit. Where did you go?"

Gus couldn't tell him. A second face loomed out of the grayness. "Is it he?"

"Aye, Sir. Frozen."

"Get him up. Walk him."

Gus could not resist. He looked at Irving, one of the lieutenants. They hauled him to his feet. His legs refused to bend.

"Carry him," Irving said.

Handford stared at Irving but a moment; then he hauled Gus onto his back.

"There are tracks," Irving said. He was peering at the ground.

"Animal," Handford offered.

"Not animal," said the third man, now coming alongside, heaving for breath, and looking sick at the effort. "That's a human print. Not a boot."

Irving turned Gus's face toward him. "Has there been someone here?" he demanded. "Peterman . . . was there anyone here?"

"A girl," Gus breathed.

There were twelve officers and some forty men on Cape Felix.

Taken both from *Erebus* and the *Terror*, they had set up three tents. Boarding poles were used as tent poles, and bearskins and blankets lined the interiors. Fireplaces were made near each tent. Here they cooked and smoked. They had a copper cooking pot that had been made on board ship, and they used what timber they had brought from both vessels for fuel.

Crozier had ordered that Cape Felix should be self-sufficient and use no tinned goods at all. He organized the fishing parties and took the hardiest men farther onto land, where they had trapped foxes, and found ptarmigan. Some of the men complained at the constant diet of fish, almost raw because the small amounts of timber would not let a fire go for long. But Crozier had insisted upon it.

"You'll be better for it," he had told them all. "The native Indians eat their food entirely raw. They do not have scurvy. We shall live entirely as they do while we are in camp. We shall copy them. We shall find how they survive."

It had been an unwelcome gospel.

Most of the men did not want to live as the Esquimaux lived. They were English; they were not savages. It was said in England that those men who came to the Arctic and lived as the Esquimaux lived did not deserve the same status as those that survived, and lived, as Europeans. To do so was a descent from grace; to do so would forfeit their heritage. They would allow themselves to fall back to what man had been millennia ago.

They had been taught since childhood that Christian man, the white man, had a duty to convert the unknowing tribes of the earth to their ways, their knowledge, and their advancement. To live as a native was to rescind that understanding; it was to allow the native to have superiority over the European. It was an admission of failure and weakness.

But they could not disobey Crozier, who was their most senior officer. They were obliged to follow his orders.

His constant preaching, though, irritated them beyond measure.

"When the Esquimaux, who some call Inuit, eat, they do not bother, necessarily, with fire," he had told them, as the fireplaces were built on which they were to try to boil their lukewarm tea. "On other voyages I have purchased sealskin bags," Crozier went on, "and found great quantities of venison and salmon, and the paws of walrus. And this they eat raw, most happily, even though the meat may be over a year old."

"Sweet heaven," Handford had grumbled.

Crozier had continued determinedly. "And they enjoy a delicacy," he told them, "of the raw liver of caribou, cut in pieces of an inch square, and mixed with the contents of the animal's stomach."

They had huddled around the brief fire. It had been made from a pike pole, the metal tip having been sawn away.

"It is no shame to live as the Indians live," he had insisted. "It is an education. We shall see how we thrive."

They had not believed him; they longed for their bouilli; they hated the messes of lichen and the few stalks of greenery they had dug from the snow. They reasoned that they would only suffer more, and die out on the land here. Surely Crozier was mad, or becoming mad, they said; there was nothing to be gained from this barren place, where the seasons of the year had ceased to exist.

And yet the diet did make a change in them. Those men that had been suffering scurvy began to improve; they had no more pain in their gums and teeth; they had no more lesions on their skin.

"You must eat the fish," Crozier had told Gus. "Even the entrails and guts and gills, and the heads. You must eat it all, Gus."

He spat out the bones, though.

He couldn't stomach that.

Crozier watched the boy carefully, and purposely did not tell him the worst, the part that, privately, he thought they might yet be reduced to. The Coppermine Indian thought the greatest delicacy of all was lice, and set their wives to cleaning their caribou-skin clothes to find the greatest quantities of them, and would scoop them into their hands and devour them with enormous relish. He had thought about that often, and wondered if they should not follow their example. After all, there were more lice on board than rats. Such crawling things were nourishment to the Indian, and the Indian was a man, as they were men. He had never known an Indian to suffer from combing out the vermin. Rather, he flourished.

Crozier thought of such things when the others slept. He considered it his duty to think the unthinkable, knowing that any one of these ideas might be the route through to life, a triumph over the barrenness that faced them.

He thought of the way that the Coppermine dressed the skins of the animals that they had killed, by lathering the animal's brain with the softest of the bone marrow, and soaking the hides by the heat of a seal-oil lamp, and hanging them up in the smoke of the same fires for days. He had once worn such skins, and felt their soft and luxurious texture, and marveled at how everything worn by these people came from the animals that roamed around them, or the contents of the seas beneath them. Not one factory belched smoke to provide their needs; not a child labored fourteen hours a day. No streets teemed with dung and sewage as result of their habitation. They threw nothing away. Their needs were simple, not complex. They took only what they needed, no more. They were, by comparison with the European, clean and re-sourceful and long lived.

But such thoughts were unacceptable. And so the captain kept them privately, when he was awake and others slept.

Gus was brought back to camp by one o'clock. They lit a fire and sat him in front of it, and kept turning him so that all sides of his body were close to the warmth for a few moments. They wrapped him in bearskins.

Crozier came to see him.

"Now, Augustus," he said, "are you mounting an expedition of your own?"

"I fell down," Gus said. "I'm sorry, sir. I fell asleep."

Crozier nodded. "When you are exhausted, and fall," he said, "you should resist the urge to sleep. You are lucky to be alive."

"I saw a woman," Gus said. "I dreamed her. She had a tattooed face."

Crozier paused, frowned. "When?" he asked.

"This morning, sir."

"What kind of tattoo?"

"In lines like the lines when we smile," Gus said.

Crozier glanced at the men around them. "And was she real?"

"I don't know, sir."

"Did she speak?"

"No, sir. But I thought she gave me something to eat."

Crozier bent down and looked into Gus's face. "You are to keep your face in the furs." He touched Gus's cheek and forehead. "Can you feel my hand?" Gus nodded. "Does it feel as normal?"

"Yes, sir."

Crozier remained looking intently at him. "How tall was she, Gus?"

"Not very tall."

"An Esquimaux woman."

"Yes, sir."

"Like those you have seen before."

"Yes, sir."

Crozier nodded. He got to his feet and stayed looking down at the boy for a moment, before walking away.

They raised a cairn that morning.

It was set on a small hill, the highest point, Crozier thought, for many miles. It took some time to haul the stones from the surrounding, ice-cracked land, especially the largest slabs that formed the base. Crozier sat upon this base to write the record that would be put inside it. He had no Admiralty forms with him, and so tore a sheet from his notebook.

HM Ships Erebus *and* Terror, *25 June 1847.*

Party consisting of 12 Officers and 40 men journey from here 26 June south in continuation of the exploration made by Lieutenant Gore.

Sir John Franklin died on 11th June 1847 and Lieutenant G. Gore on 14th June 1847, the total loss to date two Officers and seven men.

Ships beset in unseasonably heavy ice at latitude 70/05N, longitude 98/23 W.

They built up the cairn with stone five feet high, and on the top they placed two bottles, into which Crozier sealed the note. The bottles were covered, then, with further stones. When they had finished, they stood back and looked at their monument.

"Will it stand?" asked one of the ratings.

"For years," Crozier said. He had shrugged himself deeper into the coat he wore. "I have seen places where the depressions in the earth made by Parry's sledges are still visible. Bones you see scattered on the shore, of seal, or bear, may have been there for centuries." He ventured a smile. "Nothing moves here," he said. "There is nothing to move it."

They turned away and went down the hill, and it was only as they drew closer to the tents that they saw their first Esquimaux.

Crozier heard the raised voices before he breached the slight rise between the cairn and the camp.

He saw Augustus, still sitting by the fire, humped over with the skins, his small face peering out at the group who were walking toward him. One of the seamen rushed out of a tent, carrying a rifle.

"Stop!" Crozier called.

They ran down the hill. Or, rather, they attempted an approximation of running.

The silence of the camp was profound: Crozier was suddenly acutely aware of the miles, the hundreds and thousands of miles, that stretched in every direction, with this little band of Englishmen at its center, stranded and blistered and cold and ill, with their little cache of skinned fox and plucked birds. The band that faced them now were, by contrast, well fed and well clothed, and entirely at ease. And curious. Very curious.

Three men came up to Crozier. They stopped a few yards from him. At their back their team of dogs watched, alongside the women and children. Crozier looked into the men's faces. They had cropped dark hair, with a single lock hanging down at each side of the face.

Crozier repeated the few words he knew. "*Kammik-toomee*. We are friends."

The Esquimaux grinned. They advanced on him, all talking at once.

Several men at Crozier's back raised, and cocked, their guns.

"Don't fire," Crozier said.

The first man reached out and, with a dark brown finger, tapped Crozier on the chest. He was grinning from ear to ear. He turned around and called out to those behind him. Men, women, and children all ran forward.

"Mr. Irving," Crozier said, "go and get the chest in the tent. The small wooden chest with an iron latch."

The children circled Gus. They pinched at the furs, giggling.

"Don't be afraid, Gus," Crozier said. "Don't shout, or move."

A woman to Crozier's right walked straight past him and into the nearest tent. Two of the crew went after her. Not fifteen seconds later she emerged, carrying tobacco pouches and some of the timber stored for fuel.

"Watch them," Crozier said. "Stand by the tent doors. Don't let them in. Stand fast. Don't touch them. Don't touch the women."

He opened the box that was brought to him. The Inuit peered down into it, still grinning, still talking.

"Needles and knives," Crozier said. He showed the needles in the flat of his palm.

The men ignored the needles. They touched the knife blade.

Irving's hand hovered over the rifle trigger.

"Don't shoot," Crozier said.

"Sir," Irving replied, "I shall shoot a man who raises a knife to you."

"No one will raise the knife," Crozier said. "Wait. Be patient."

Gus sat stock still. His legs were tingling now. It was agony as they came back to life. He needed to move, to stretch the affected limbs, but dared not. He looked from the strange, weather-beaten faces of the Inuit to Crozier's, which was so light and had a tinge of redness, showing his Celtic ancestry. The captain's eyes were raw and inflamed. Looking from one face to the other, Gus suddenly saw, for the first time, how sick the Europeans looked next these seemingly indestructible natives, whose skin was faintly oiled looking. The whites of their eyes were brilliantly clear and white, uncannily so. He noticed now that everyone from the ship, even the captain, had the same bloodshot look to their eyes. He felt suddenly feeble.

A package brought from the Esquimaux sleds was displayed. The men directly behind Crozier stepped back, away from it, but Crozier did not move.

"Blubber and seal meat," he said at last. "Frozen salmon."

The men pushed Crozier on the shoulder. A great hubbub of talking broke out among the natives. They were laughing. They pointed back at the dogs.

"We have no dogs," Crozier said.

The children were running round the camp, pulling up stores and turning them over. One of the marines caught one and lifted him up. It was boy of not more than four or five. He squealed as he was turned head-over-heels and dangled above the snow.

"They have no fear," Irving said.

"They have nothing to be afraid of," Crozier said. "Your rifle there is no more than a stick. They have no idea why you should stand there clutching it so, or pointing it at them. They have never seen a gun before."

Irving glanced at him. He found it hard to tear his eyes from the sledges, where the men were now working, pulling more from their packs. "That's not so, sir," Irving said. "In Greenland they use guns always."

"We are not in Greenland," Crozier said. "We are in the region of other tribes, other family groups. These people work this strait, not Lancaster Sound or anywhere near it. They may not have seen a white man before."

As if to demonstrate that he was right, the women had gathered around Gus. They poked their fingers into the fur and stroked his face, prodding the area of frostbite on his cheek.

"It's her," Gus called.

Crozier stepped forward.

"Let her look at you," he said. "It's all that she wants to do."

But he needn't have given this instruction. Gus was already enthralled.

He had never seen such eyes, almost ink-black. A face framed with sumptuously thick, oily dark hair. The girl was his own age, and she wore a caribou-skin jerkin and trousers, like a man, with a white fur edging that had been combed into fringed strands at the hem of the jerkin. The hood almost covered her face at first, but she pushed it back to show the tattoos that Gus remembered: extraordinary henna-brown lines in arcs on her cheeks, and radiating along her chin.

Another woman squatted down by her side. This one was older: he wondered if she were the girl's mother. The older woman had the tattoo, but in addition her face was positively crisscrossed with deep folds of skin, a mimicking of extreme age, that had been hatched by the extremes of weather. It was impossible to say exactly how old she was, but when she smiled Gus saw that the teeth in her mouth were ground very low.

The packages from the sledges had been hauled to Crozier's feet. There was plenty of meat, all raw. The man who had tapped Crozier's chest deftly took the knife and pushed it into his sleeve. The women were called: they took the needle and wood, and the iron tips of the pikestaffs; and the old woman would have taken the copper cooking pot had not one of the crew wrested it from her grasp.

"Offer them food," Crozier said.

They showed the Esquimaux their stock of rock ptarmigan, but the birds were refused. None of the men were surprised, for the flesh of ptarmigan was hard and bitter and dark, but it was all they could shoot with any ease.

They opened a box of raisins, and of figs, and sugar.

The Esquimaux dipped their fingertips in the sugar, rubbing between thumb and forefinger before tasting it. The sugar had solidified to something like molasses, and the Esquimaux spat it out. Similarly, they chewed for only a few seconds on the figs and raisins before hawking them into the snow.

The girl had not left Gus's side. After suffering her stroking and prodding his face, he finally got to his feet, relieving the agonizing prickling. He stumbled a little. She gripped his arm and spoke to him, pointing at the sleds, laughing.

"Aye," Gus said, "but they're not like ours."

He was right.

The Esquimaux sleds were neat and slim. They were over twenty feet in length, Gus estimated; and less than two feet wide. Sealskin line was threaded through holes in the runners and passed over the ends of wooden crossbows, each one not more than three or four inches apart. They looked long and lithe and flexible, and there was not a nail to be seen. By contrast the sledges that they had hauled from the ships were two refurbished lifeboats, with runners attached to them, wooden and broad and heavy. Gus saw at once how the Esquimaux sledges would glide, if pulled by dogs at any speed, over even large humped ridges, whereas the *Terror* sledges balked at every ridge, and got stuck, and took minutes of maneuvering and effort to free them. Just looking so briefly at them, he wondered why men like Franklin, who knew the Esquimaux, didn't order sledges like theirs, whippet-thin and graceful.

The girl ran away from him. She went down to the sleds, looking over her shoulder. There was a lot of gesturing and talking: something was lifted from the first sled, cradled in the girl's arms, and brought back to Gus's side. Two other girls on either side of the first were screaming with delight, pointing at what she had brought him.

He looked.

They were dogs. Puppies. Two barely weaned huskies, with their knowing, vixenlike faces, stared back at him. The girl bundled them out of her arms and into his.

"Captain!" he called.

But before Crozier could reply, there was an explosion.

The Esquimaux froze: a tableau of surprise. One of the marines closest to the first tent was standing with his gun raised in the air, the barrel slightly smoking. In front of him stood an Esquimaux woman, her hand still outstretched. She stood, dumbfounded and stock still. The report of the gun seemed to go on forever, rolling away across the tundra. The Esquimaux dogs began to bark wildly.

Irving was first at the marine's side.

"She tried to take it off me," the man said.

The woman raised the outstretched hand to her head. The hood of her jerkin was marked with a scorched brown line: she took her hand down and looked at it. Blood seeped from her palm and fell on the snow.

"She's wounded," Irving called. He tried to approach her: with a cry, she sprang backward.

"Let me see," Irving said. "Where is the wound?"

"Has it touched her?" Crozier shouted.

"She is bleeding," Irving replied.

The women were crowding around. They took down the woman's hood and explored the crown of her head, her face, her neck.

Crozier began to run.

Abruptly the man who had touched him blocked his way, gesticulating. Others came up behind him and pulled on his arms. There was a flurry of talk; the crowd eased back, across the snow, across the rutted ice.

The girl who had been standing next to Gus turned to look at him, eyes wide with fear. Then, turning on her heel, she made full pelt across the ground, flinging herself to the sleds. The women followed.

"Is she hurt badly?" Crozier demanded.

"It's impossible to see," Irving said.

"I told you not to shoot," Crozier shouted to the marine, furious. "You had an order not to fire!"

"I didn't shoot, sir. She pulled the gun."

"For God's sake!" Crozier stormed.

They watched, helpless, as the sledges were manned. The dogs bounded forward, lead dog biting its neighbor on each team under the cut of the whip. The snow made a slurring, whining sound. From the rear of the last sled Gus saw the girl stare back at him. He shielded his eyes to follow them; dropped his hand to the place on his face where she had touched him. Behind him, on the snow, the puppies yapped and squirmed in the open crate where he had stowed them.

Crozier threw the chest that he had still been carrying, to the snow. "God damn it!" he cried. "God damn!"

Not a man moved. No one had heard him utter an oath in his life.

They stared at him, while the full significance of the gun and the shot dawned on them. It had been the first time in over two years that the crews had seen other living human beings. It was the first time that they had been given fresh meat for which they had not had to fight with every ounce of their strength. More terrible still, much more of a loss, was the knowledge that the first sweet human kindness had been shown to them, a portion of the pity that any of their families at home might feel for them, and wish could be extended to them. And they had frightened it away.

They stared at the ground, while the first few flakes of gathering snow fell on them.

Finally, rousing himself, Irving edged the nearest sealskin bag—lying on the snow before him—with his boot. "We shall eat now, at least," he murmured.

Handforth glanced over at the dogs. "Aye," he agreed. "There is that."

Twenty-four

CATHERINE rang the doorbell of the house in Lincoln Street that night.

She had tried phoning Jo several times that day to see what the doctor had said about Sam; and although not overly worried, she made a detour on the way home.

No lights were on at all downstairs; she glanced at the upper windows, frowning. Then the hall light came on. Jo opened the door.

Whatever Catherine had been about to say froze in her throat at the sight of Sam's mother. Jo looked drained, white. Behind her in the house Catherine could see Jo's shoes lying at the foot of the stairs; and, all the way up, Sam's clothes littering the steps—his socks, dungarees, T-shirt.

"Jo," she said, "what on earth's the matter?"

Jo said nothing. She left the door open and, without a word, went upstairs. Catherine closed the door behind her and followed her.

"What is it?" she asked. "Jo . . ."

The bathroom and bedrooms were on the third floor. As she reached this landing, she at last saw a light in Sam's room. Jo had sat back down on the floor opposite his bed. Sam was asleep, only his head showing above the coverlet.

There was a glass of red wine, almost drunk, sitting on the top of Sam's toy box alongside Jo. Catherine came over and sat down beside her. Softly she stroked Jo's arm.

"What is it?" she repeated. "What happened?"

Jo's lip trembled. "Do you know where he is?" she asked.

"Who?"

"John."

Catherine stared at her. "John? No."

To her surprise Jo suddenly grabbed her arm. "Because if you do, you have to tell me," she said.

Catherine looked from Jo's hand and back to her face, truly disturbed now. "I haven't heard from him at all," she said. "And that's the truth."

Jo put her head in her hands. "I've got to find him," she murmured.

Catherine glanced across at Sam, worried that the obvious panic in Jo's voice would wake her son.

"You must hate me," Jo said. "Why don't you hate me? You have a perfect right. I drove him away in the first place."

And to Catherine's utter surprise Jo suddenly dissolved into tears. Catherine reached forward and took her in her arms. They stayed there in the awkward embrace, on the floor littered with Sam's plastic soldiers and Pokemon mascots and pieces of wooden jigsaw.

"For God's sake," Catherine said, "I don't hate you."

"You should," Jo said. She pulled away, and sat, wiping her face with the sleeve of her sweatshirt.

"What the hell happened today?" Catherine asked.

Jo didn't reply. She merely shook her head repeatedly. "It's ironic," she said. "That's what it is. A bloody irony."

Worse than the outburst of sobs were the tears that now coursed silently down Jo's face. Catherine's heart wrenched to see them. Jo hardly ever cried. She would curse her fair share on occasion; she had seen her kick a door or two if truly frustrated. And she didn't suffer fools gladly, Catherine supposed. But this . . . not this total abandonment to grief.

The last time Catherine had seen her in this state was at Doug's funeral. Standing then at John's side—and God knew, that had been difficult enough, with John barely speaking, and as rigid as stone—Catherine had felt seriously divided loyalties when she had seen Jo. It was hard to get through to John, who had withdrawn into himself and seemed intent on rebuffing and excluding her; but Jo's feelings were evident for all to see. Catherine had wanted to rush up to her then and hold her. She had been prostrate with grief.

Now, it seemed, she would have her chance.

Something as bad as the loss of Doug seemed to be etched on Jo's face. "Come out," she whispered, tugging gently on Jo's arm. "Come downstairs. Talk to me."

Jo resisted. "I can't," she said. "I can't leave him."

Her eyes were fixed on Sam's sleeping form.

"Can't leave Sam?" Catherine said. "Why? Just for a minute."

"Not even for a minute."

"But, Jo . . ."

"You don't understand," Jo said. She picked up the wineglass next to her, drained it, and put it down. She cast about her as if looking for something, and then picked up one of the jigsaw pieces. It was the face of a magpie, black-and-white, with a patch of green behind it. She made a sad little huffing sound. "One for sorrow," she mumbled. She turned it around in the palm of her hand, over and over.

"He has to be watched," she said eventually. "We have to watch him all the time. He can't be allowed to cry or have a nightmare, or have a tantrum, or fall down, anymore. He can't throw himself off the couch downstairs. He can't be allowed to cycle down the path. We can't let him try to climb. . . ."

Catherine was totally confused by now. "We can't?" she echoed. "But why not?" She looked at the glass, then back at Jo. "What did the doctor say?"

"He sent me to the hospital."

"Hospital?" Catherine echoed. "Why?"

Jo put her head in her hands.

"Jo," Catherine said. She put both hands on Jo's shoulders and shook her gently. "What has John got to do with this?"

Jo finally raised her head.

"Have you ever heard of aplastic anemia?" she asked.

"Aplastic what?" Catherine echoed. "No."

Jo gave a ghost of a smile. "No, neither had I," she replied. She put down the jigsaw piece. "It can't be seen." She shook her head again. "That's what I can't understand," she said. "You can't see it. It's inside . . . it's not like a broken leg. It's not like a cut. I mean, even if you took an X-ray . . . you couldn't see it. . . ."

She bit her lip.

"Aplastic anemia," Catherine guessed. A nightmarish feeling had just shot through her, a kind of terror. "The blood."

"The bone," Jo said. "The bone marrow."

Catherine swallowed hard. "And Sam's got this? A failure of the bone marrow?"

"Yes," Jo said. She flung the jigsaw piece away. It clattered behind Sam's bed. They watched him turn over, arms flung out.

"When I got him inside," Jo said, "when I got him home today . . . I had to wash him. I had to bathe him. I had to get the smell off him. . . ." She squeezed her eyes shut. "He has to go back again in the morning," she continued. "Oh, Christ. . . ."

Catherine looked at Sam helplessly, then back at Jo.

"We have to find John," Jo whispered. "We must."

"Jo," Catherine said, guessing, but not daring to voice her suspicions, "why?"

Jo suddenly and unsteadily stood up, her hand to her throat. Catherine got up too. In a few short steps Jo went to the bed. Her hand hovered over Sam—over his face, his chest, as if she needed to touch him but was afraid to hurt him. "There's things that can be done," she said. She turned to look at Catherine. "To stop it, temporarily . . . if we're lucky. There's blood, and steroids . . . a thing called cyclosporine. But he's so sick. He's so very sick, Catherine."

Catherine couldn't speak at all now. She bit her lip, anguished.

But Jo had meanwhile lifted her chin, and for the first time since she had come in, Catherine saw a faint glimmer of hope in Jo's expression. "There's something called stem cells," she said. "You can donate stem cells, your own, as his mother. . . . They take them out of me, out of my bloodstream. They give me a drug to make me produce more of them, so much more that they spill out of the marrow and into my bloodstream. They harvest the overproduction, then they freeze those cells." She was ticking the stages off on her fingers, although her hands were trembling.

"They take them away and they freeze them," she continued. "To use if there was nothing else left to do, nothing that had worked. . . ." Her face had gone very pale, so pale that it looked to Catherine more like a mask than Jo's real, living flesh.

"And you know what's so awful," she whispered, "is that I would only be a half match for him. Even if I did all that, the chances of it working are small. . . ."

"Oh, Jo," Catherine whispered.

Jo took a step toward her. This time it was Jo that gripped Catherine's arm. "But there's something else," she said. "If we got that far, if he didn't respond. There's a bone-marrow transplant. And the closest matches are siblings. Brothers."

Jo's eyes searched Catherine's face.

"But, Jo," Catherine whispered, "John isn't a brother. He's a *half-brother*."

"It lowers the chances of a match," Jo said. "But—"

"There are bone-marrow registers," Catherine said suddenly. "I've seen them on television. There was that baby on the news. . . ."

"The registers can search the world over and never find a match at all," Jo said. She clenched her fist and put it to her mouth. There was a moment of silence, as she tried to calm herself. Sort the words, the explanation, out in her head. "Okay," she whispered. "There might be a better match than John. It's a long shot, because—God, this is so complicated, the doctor wrote it on a notepad, he drew me a diagram, for Christ's sake, I tried to concentrate. . . ."

"It doesn't matter right now," Catherine said. "Come downstairs—"

"No," Jo snapped. "It does matter. I have to get this straight." She frowned hard. "John and his father and Sam might share the same tissue type. A haplotype. If it were rare, and if Alicia and I had the same *common* haplotype . . . then we'd match. We'd all match, and John would match Sam, and he'd be close enough. You see? He'd be close enough to save Sam."

The silence seemed to balloon around them.

Catherine felt a tightening in the pit of her stomach, a dread. "Jo," she said slowly, "that is an awful lots of *ifs*."

"Yes," Jo said, "I know."

"How likely is it that John and Doug and Sam share the same tissue type, this—"

"Haplotype."

"Haplotype," Catherine repeated. "You're saying that all three would have a *rare* haplotype."

"Yes. They might. It's possible."

"Okay," Catherine said slowly, "so father and sons share the same rare type. But then, you and Alicia—"

"That's possible too," Jo said. "Ten percent of the population have the same haplotype, and if I and Alicia had the same—"

"John would be a match for Sam."

"Yes."

Catherine put her head to her forehead. "Oh, God Almighty, dear God," she whispered.

"But it's *possible*," Jo insisted. "It's probably more possible than finding an unrelated match."

"Then John would be Sam's best hope," Catherine said.

"Yes," Jo told her. "Yes."

And she held Catherine's gaze for a second, before her shoulders dropped. All at once she seemed to cave inward, her back bending, as though she'd been punched in the stomach. She crossed her hands over herself and bent forward over the hands. Quickly Catherine put her arms around her, holding her tightly.

"I'm here now," Catherine said. "I'll help you, Jo."

The other woman shuddered in her embrace. "I know it's a long shot," Jo whispered. "But if it turns out that we don't have a choice . . . If there isn't another donor . . . then, you see, don't you, Cath? You understand? John would be the only hope that Sam had left."

It took another hour, but Catherine managed to get Jo downstairs eventually, after they had found the baby alarm that Jo hadn't used in six months, and plugged it back on in Sam's room.

Catherine made Jo sit in the kitchen while she made soup, and watched over her to make sure that Jo ate it to the very last drop.

Then she sat down next to her and held her hand.

"Maybe Alicia knows," Catherine said.

Jo stared at her. "Would he write to her and not you?" she asked.

"I don't know," Catherine said.

Jo was sitting very straight, staring at her. "Do you think he might be working his way across to the Franklin sites, in Nunavut?"

Catherine shook her head. "Alone?" she murmured. "How?"

"Wasn't there a photographer?" Jo asked.

"I can't even remember his name," Catherine said. "That was three years ago, and I think this man worked all over the world. Where would he be now?" she said, thinking aloud. "Maybe Alicia . . ."

Jo bit her thumbnail, thinking. "Would John ask Alicia for money?" she asked.

"I don't know," Catherine admitted.

"How is he financing himself?"

"Working, I suppose," Catherine said. "On excavations, or wherever he can."

"He *must* have got in touch with Alicia."

"Don't count on it, Jo."

Jo suddenly stood up and went over to the phone. "I'll ring her," she said.

Catherine swiftly got up and stopped her. "She won't speak to you," she told Jo. "She'll hang up. Let me try." She took a diary from her handbag. "I think I kept her number."

The phone rang for some time before Alicia answered.

"Mrs. Marshall?"

"Yes?"

"It's Catherine Takkiruq."

There was a pause.

"Mrs. Marshall, I am trying to find John."

"John," the other woman repeated. Catherine could hear a slow intake of breath. "Why?"

"I'm sorry?"

"Why ask now?" Alicia demanded.

Catherine paused, acutely aware of treading carefully. To mention Jo's name would be a red rag to a bull. "I wondered how he was," she said.

"If he hasn't written to you, I shouldn't think he wants you to know," Alicia replied.

Catherine frowned. "Has he written to you?" she guessed.

"I can't see it's any of your business," Alicia said.

"But—"

"I haven't seen you in more than a year, and suddenly—"

"But I thought you didn't want me to come and see you," Catherine objected.

"I didn't say that."

Catherine colored. Beside her Jo winced. She laid a hand on Catherine's arm.

"When I last came to see you," Catherine replied slowly, "you told me that you couldn't see any purpose in my coming to Franklin House. You made it plain that I wasn't welcome."

"Together with that Harper woman," Alicia replied, "you drove him away."

"But that's not true!"

"You hung around him when it was quite plain he didn't want to see you."

"That's not right—"

"You never gave him a moment's peace," Alicia said.

This was so desperately, distortedly wrong that Catherine took a shocked breath, momentarily silenced. If anyone had driven John away, it was Alicia with her endless self-pity. Catherine had never once heard Alicia voice any appreciation of John's despair. When John had told her of Jo's words at the chapel, Alicia had been incandescent for days, interpreting it solely as an attack on herself through her son, a slight to her family. Jo had wounded *her*, stolen *her* husband, accused *her* son. It was as if John were a sideshow at Alicia's personal drama.

"I have nothing more to say to you," Alicia said now.

Catherine forced herself to keep calm. "Please, Mrs. Marshall. It's very important . . . do you know where John is?"

But she was listening to a dead line.

Alicia had hung up.

Catherine handed the phone to Jo, to let her hear the disconnection, then hung up herself.

"Oh, God." Jo groaned. She walked back to the table and slumped into the chair next to it. "That woman. Oh, God," she repeated, wiping her eyes. "How are we going to get through to her? Do you think she knows where John is?"

Catherine shook her head slowly. "If she does," she murmured, "she's never going to tell us."

They looked at the dark squares of the windows, at the night.

Upstairs, Sam began to cry.

Twenty-five

SHE wanted to teach him what was closest to her heart.

The unseasonal storm in the strait had swept east, and the bear was walking on the fringe of the sea ice now. Occasionally she would look back, sometimes seeing the cub stumble, sometimes standing still, looking away from her. It was this that confused her most of all, for cubs shadowed their mothers, watching and learning.

It was as if he were traveling away from her, focused on some distant object that was invisible to her.

She followed her instinct south.

Once, in the encroaching winter, she had been at Devon Island on Lancaster Sound, and she felt the echo of that winter feeding in her head, a winter that she wanted to give back to her son. If he had been strong she would have taken him there again, drawn toward the inlets where the beluga sometimes became trapped in moving pack ice.

The beluga had become trapped at an ever-diminishing breathing hole, and she had been with other bears who waited as the sea choked off the whales' escape, and presented the catch to the bears as readily as a fisherman might haul in his nets.

The bears simply pulled the beluga from the sea and slaughtered them on the ice. Forty beluga, young animals, still gray in color. She could remember the smell now, the scattered blood patterning the frozen landscape.

She wanted to teach him to swim, the freedom of her soul.

But it was not good here. Not good halfway down the great, swift-running gulf of water. She hated the tremor from under the sea, the old imprint of fear. Its invisible mark might be here for centuries yet—the terrible echo from under the water, the trail of some dark memory on the edge of ice and land.

She grunted now as she came to the top of the pressure rise, and then stopped dead in her tracks.

An adult male bear was staring back at her: a mass of thin fur drawn over bones. She glared at him, lowering her head in her shock and surprise. She had had no warning that he was hidden there, half covered with the thinly blowing granules of ice. He looked back at her with a dead, exhausted eye.

Stock still, she assessed him. He was lying with his head on a raised hummock; he had come, it was evident, into the lee of the sea wind, to die. This was the end for any bear. He might be fifteen, twenty—perhaps even thirty—years old. His time was over, and she turned away.

As she did so, she saw the strips of darker color on the ridge. They were attached to even older bones than the male stretched out below her. There was no flesh left on them, but the stuff that blew about them was dark: strips of wet cloth. She tasted them before throwing them to one side. Not seal. She pushed the material aside and nosed at the motionless objects next to the skeleton.

Red-painted tins.

Nothing at all, less than nothing, to her.

She sat up on her hindquarters and gave a braying call.

The cub came slowly after her, picking his way over the long-dead human debris.

Twenty-six

ALICIA left Cambridge early the next day.

It was a beautiful summer morning; but she drove almost without registering the sun. By six forty-five, she was on the outskirts of London, negotiating the M25, and was on the M3, heading south, by half past seven.

She put her foot down, and the towns of outer London and the southeast disappeared behind her. By nine she had left the highway and taken the long road across the tops of the Wiltshire Downs, passing south of Salisbury Plain and through Cranborne Chase, and emerging into the Blackmore Vale.

England had nothing more beautiful to show on that morning. The country of Thomas Hardy—the Vale of the Great Dairies, where Tess had searched for wild garlic in the pastures under the eye of Angel Clare—was spread in front of Alicia in a checkered green carpet. But Alicia simply frowned at it as she negotiated one narrowing lane after another. At one point, furious with herself for mistaking yet another turning, she stopped the car and sat with the map in front of her, and realized that she was trembling. She took several deep breaths, trying to unknot the tightness in her chest, the fluttering of nerves in the pit of her stomach.

The letter lay beside her on the seat. She looked down at the note she had written and taped to the page of the map. *Hermitage Farm, Cerne Magna.*

It was almost midday by the time she found it, tucked under a chalk ridge and a piece of woodland, with no sign to point the way, and only a huddle of decaying outbuildings betraying its working past. Four-wheel drives and a couple of old Ford vans were parked on the rutted lane and shoulder.

No one seemed to be about. Alicia walked through the yard and out onto the field, and, following the faint sound of voices, walked through the clumps of nettle and thistles and grass to a stone wall.

"Good morning," she said.

The girl who was sitting on the other side almost dropped the cigarette she was holding. She looked over her shoulder. "Hello."

"I'm looking for John Marshall."

"John?" she said.

"Yes. Is he here?"

The girl glanced back. Somewhere in the trees above them the excavation of the Anglo-Saxon settlement was in its fourth week. As far as the girl knew, they had never had a visitor.

"Well, he's somewhere about, I suppose." She looked Alicia up and down, and, finally, stood up. "Are you from the university?"

"Not this one," Alicia said. "I'm nothing to do with the excavation. I'm John's mother."

The girl's mouth dropped open. But she said nothing. She merely looked Alicia over again from head to foot, then ground out the cigarette. "This way," she said.

They went up the hill. Just before the top the ground leveled out, and on a flat piece of grass under the shade of the trees, half a dozen people were working in a series of shallow pits.

"Mike," the girl said. "Someone for John Marshall."

The man nearest her looked up. His clothes were coated in chalk from the ground. He hauled himself out, and wiping his hands on his jeans, he offered Alicia his hand.

"Mike Bryant."

"Hello," Alicia said. "I spoke to Charles Edge yesterday."

Bryant nodded. "Yes, he rang me last night," he said.

He hesitated. Alicia frowned. "John *is* here?"

"Yes . . ."

"Did you hire him?"

"Word of mouth. A friend in Bristol recommended him."

"Do you know he's been missing?" she said.

She hadn't meant it to sound like an accusation, but nevertheless, it came out that way.

"No," Bryant said.

"He's been gone for nearly two years," she told him.

He looked hard at her. "We don't ask for life histories when they arrive. I'm sorry."

"He has a place at Cambridge," she said. "He shouldn't be here."

"Look, Mrs. Marshall," Bryant said, "I didn't kidnap him."

She bit her lip. "No," she admitted. She felt a tic begin at the corner of her mouth: a tremor of anxiety. "No," she repeated. "I'm sorry. It's not your fault."

Bryant frowned. He glanced at the crew behind him, some of whom had stopped work to listen. He touched Alicia's arm. "Would you like to sit down over here?" he said.

"I'd like to see John. Where is he?"

"Maybe if I just talked to you first," he said quietly.

He walked her over to a table and chairs. Brushing the dust from their canvas seats, he settled one on level ground and waited until Alicia was comfortable.

"I can see you're a bit impatient," he told her.

"Put yourself in my place," she said.

He sat down next to her. "Yes," he murmured. He picked at a loose thread on his shirtsleeve. "You see, John has . . . well, to say he worried me . . ."

"What's the matter?" she asked. "Is he ill?"

"No, no," Bryant responded. "Not as such."

"What, then?" she said. "What do you mean, *as such?*"

Bryant made an embarrassed face. "You know, we see a lot of different folks in this job," he said. "Students, enthusiasts. Old bastards like me." He grinned. Alicia stared at him. "That is—"

"I really don't have all day," Alicia said.

Bryant looked rebuffed. He sat back. "Did John ask you to come here?" he asked.

Alicia colored. "You know that he didn't," she said. "Otherwise I wouldn't have had to ring half the country to find out who was carrying out an excavation in Dorset." She pushed a strand of hair behind her ear. "But he will be glad to see me. I'm sure when he *does* see me—"

Bryant rocked back in the chair, hands crossed over his stomach. "John never wants to see anyone," he commented.

Alicia stared at him. "What do you mean?"

Bryant's face softened. He gave her a sympathetic look. "Mrs. Marshall," he said, "I don't interfere in students' lives, I don't tell them how to act," he said. "But I worry about John. I really do."

Alicia stared at him. Very slowly, Bryant brushed dirt from between his fingers. "John lives up here, on site," he said. "He arrived with a tent, and he lives here. Camps here."

"Don't you all?" she asked.

"Some do," he replied. "But John took himself off, out of their sight. Doesn't come down at night. He"—Bryant gazed at her—"he just doesn't talk, Mrs. Marshall," he said. "And . . ."

He stopped, and then, slowly, stood up. He had evidently decided to say nothing more. He pointed up the slope, in the direction that she might find him. "Well," he said, "you'll see for yourself."

John was lying on his back.

He was past the trees, and up in the open, on the stretch of downland above the wood. The sun was hot, now, on his face, and he stared into the sky, arms folded over his chest, feet crossed at the ankle.

He liked to come up here. It was quiet. He would often come up alone, at night. He had got used to it, and even if he lay here for hours, he no longer felt the hardness of the ground. It was a better bed than the one he had had in Bodrum, at least. There he had slept in the back of a van for nine weeks.

It wasn't far enough away, of course. Not here.

But then, nowhere was far enough away.

Still, the Bodrum work had suited him. The site had been off a jetty that had been constructed between two sheer cliff walls to accommodate the divers, the dive gear, the weights, and lifting apparatus. It had been an enormously complicated operation, the retrieval of four hundred amphorae from a vessel that had sunk in the twelfth century.

He worked up to the team of six, learning from scratch—the decompression stops, the regulators, the location of the backup sources of the breathing gases, the technical work of gridding the site, the air-lifts to remove sediment. He had loved it, and most of all he had loved the utter silence of the dives. It could be desperately mind-numbing work, especially if the current got up and the visibility dropped, but that was exactly what he wanted from it: to be in the silence of the underwater dig, even almost invisible in the wreaths of silt, with only his own breath for company, the staccato intake of oxygen. He liked to go down when others were reluctant to. He liked his world compressed to these few obscure feet of sea floor. He liked, too, the cold of the water, welcoming the sensation when the coldness got to you—and it did, even in those seas. He relished the anesthetic of cold.

More than all the rest, however, was the realization that he didn't have to think down there, and that he was reduced to the few square yards in front of him. More often than not he had to be reminded to stop work, because his dive time was expired.

He even enjoyed—if enjoyment was the true description of any-thing that went on in his head—the suspension of the decompression stops. The other divers complained of the occasional boredom of wait-ing. But he looked forward to it. He wanted the complete necessity of doing nothing, and thinking nothing. If he hated anything at all, it was actually returning to the surface—the explosion into light, the rushing inward of sound and color, the voices of the other divers.

Four hundred amphorae. He would have preferred to bring each one up himself, singly. He would like to be doing it now, floating in si-lence. Listening to his air thinning. Hanging at decompression level, eyes closed, tugged gently backward and forward by the sea.

But the job had only lasted six months. That was the nature of the work, and its great drawback. He could never lose himself for long.

"John," said a voice.

He looked up, shading his eyes.

"Hello," Alicia said.

He stared a second, then scrambled to his feet.

"Aren't you going to give me a hug?" she asked.

He hung back at first, but then walked over to her and opened his arms. She returned his embrace, resting her head temporarily on his shoulder. "Oh, John," she whispered.

He stepped back. She held him at arm's length and stared at him. "Look at you," she murmured.

"What's the matter?" he said.

"Well, John . . ." She waved her hand to encompass him; then stopped.

He was filthy, as if he hadn't washed in days. Alicia tried not to show her utter dismay. She tried to smile, biting the inside of her cheek to stop her eyes filling with tears.

Words were rushing into her mouth. She wanted to take his hand and pull him away, get him in the car, take him home immediately. She forced herself to stay calm. "Shall I sit down?" she said.

She perched on the grass. He sat down alongside her.

"What a lovely spot," she said. Though, in truth, she saw nothing. Her eyes were ranging over his face. John didn't return the glance: he picked at a piece of grass alongside him. "How are you?" she asked.

"Fine."

"You don't look fine at all."

He shrugged.

She swallowed hard. "Are you glad to see me, John?" she asked.

He smiled a little.

"I had to come," she said.

"Okay," he murmured.

"Your letter," she said. "I can't . . ." She stopped. She took a handkerchief out of her bag and pointedly wiped her eyes. But looking up at him again, she was shocked to see that it had had no effect on him. He was gazing away from her, across the fields.

"You've broken my heart," she whispered.

There was no response.

"John," she said. "Two years. Two whole years . . . what did I do to deserve that?"

"I'm sorry," he mumbled.

"If you knew how worried I was. Worried absolutely sick, John. How could you do that?"

"I'm sorry," he repeated.

"And only to write twice, with no addresses . . ."

He turned toward her. "Look," he said. "I am going, so if you've come here to stop me, it's been a wasted journey."

She gave an affronted little gasp. "Is that all you have to say?" she asked.

"What do you want?" he asked. "If you want to stop me—"

"Who am I to stop you?" she said. "As if I could. I'm only your mother. I'm only the person who cares most for you in the world."

He plunged his face, momentarily, into his hands. "Oh, please, not that," he muttered. "Don't start all that." He dropped his hands. "If you care that much, you'd be glad I was doing what I wanted," he said. "Finally what I wanted, Mother. You stopped me before. But he's made the offer again, and I'm going." He threw the twisted stem of grass that he had been holding onto the ground. "I'm going to Canada to work with Richard Sibley," he said. "He's going to Gjoa Haven this summer, all right? I told you."

"It's ridiculous. Going off like this. Like some sort of hippie, John. That's what you look like."

"Fine," he said, bitterly. "That's fine with me."

"As if you hadn't a home, or a penny to your name."

"I'm doing it," he said. "I'm going."

"And what are you doing for money?" she asked.

"I've got the airfare. I've saved it."

"If you came back home, and went next year, next summer," she told him, "I would pay the airfare then."

He stared at her. "Why would I want to do that?" he said.

"Because I would like to see you, have you home for a while. Look after you," she said.

"No, Mother."

"Look at you," she said. "You're obviously wretched. Come home."

"No," he said.

"I don't know why you went away," she continued. "But whatever it was—"

"I had to," he said. He rubbed his hands over his face, then wiped his eyes with the sleeve of his sweatshirt. "I kept thinking about it," he mumbled, almost to himself. "If I weren't there in Cambridge, I wouldn't think about it."

"Think about what?" she asked.

"The accident," he said. He got to his feet. He looked for a moment as if he were going to walk away.

"I don't understand," she said.

He shook his head, half laughing, half grimacing. "No," he muttered. "You don't understand because you don't listen, do you? I tried to tell you. You just wouldn't listen to me."

"But—"

"It was my fault."

Alicia stared at him. "The accident?"

"Yes."

"It was not!"

"You weren't there," he said. "He wouldn't have been in the road at all if it weren't for me."

"And you wouldn't have been there at all if it weren't for her," she said. "Jo Harper. Have you thought of that?"

He looked up. "Where is she?" he asked. "Do you know?"

"I haven't the faintest idea," she lied.

"Is she still in Cambridge? How is she?"

"Who?" Alicia asked, confused.

"Catherine."

Alicia at last realized who he was talking about. "John," she said, "it's in the past. Everything."

He turned his head away, stared out over the slope of the hill.

"Come home," she said.

"How many more bloody times."

"There's no need to punish me." Alicia wept. "I did nothing."

"God," John muttered, "I'm not punishing you."

"What else would you call it?" she said.

"It's not like that."

"Have you any idea what it's been like for me?" she asked.

"Mum—"

"You don't, do you?" she said. "The suffering you've caused me . . ."

He started to walk.

"What are you doing?" she said, surprised.

"I've got to work," he said. "This was my lunch break."

"I haven't finished," she said.

She ran after him, almost tripping over the tussocky grass. "John," she called. She grabbed his arm. He stopped, but didn't look at her. "Listen . . ." she said.

He lifted his head. "You don't understand," he said. "You never will." Slowly, his entire face flushed. She realized that he was shaking. "Always you," he said. "This isn't about me, or Dad. You don't give a toss for either of us."

"That's not true! How can you say that!"

"All you think of is yourself. You don't care about Catherine."

"Catherine?" she echoed.

"I left her too," he said. "Did you ever think about that? I loved her. I still love her."

"Then"—Alicia wavered—"come home. I'm sure we could find her."

"I can't do that!" he shouted. "Don't you understand? Can't you see what I'm fucking well telling you? Can't you?"

She stared at him open mouthed. Shocked by the desperation, the violence, in his voice.

"I killed him!" he shouted. "Do you understand *that*! Jo was right. I killed him. I saw it in Catherine's face when we went to that chapel."

"No," Alicia whispered, "no, you're wrong."

"I'm not wrong," he said. He was ashen, gasping for breath.

"John, darling—"

He tore himself out of her grasp. "Look"—he stumbled over his words—"I've tried to escape it for two years. Get away, and not think about it. Go to some of the places *he* went to. But he wasn't there. There's only one place on earth that he can be."

Alicia was aghast. Faced with the true and living breakdown of her son, instead of her own dramas of embittered grief, she was helpless. She saw the depth of his pain for the first time, and it frightened her as nothing had ever frightened her before.

"You're ill," she told him, realizing that it was true. "You need to be with people who love you," she said. "Who can help you. If you like, you can see Catherine, and—"

He wheeled around. "Do you think I can look her in the face before I've sorted this out?" he cried.

"Oh, John . . . darling—"

"Don't *darling* me!" he shouted. He clenched his fists and pressed them to either side of his head. "I can't go back. I can't walk where he used to walk. I can't go into that college. I can't see the people he taught. I can't see people like Peter, or Catherine, or anybody. I don't want to see it in their faces."

"But you won't," she objected. "They don't think that you killed anyone, John."

He stared at her. "They do," he said. "And even if, by some bloody miracle, they didn't, *I* would know. *I would have it in here*," he said. Tears came to his eyes: they began to fall. With terrible poignancy Alicia saw the first few drops make tracks in the dirt of his face. She tried to wipe them away, but her son pushed her off.

"I've got it inside," he told her, weeping. Distraught, he covered his face with his arm.

"John," Alicia murmured, "please, we'll see someone. We'll see a counselor. A grief counselor. They're awfully good. They would help, I know they would." She was wringing her hands. "He was your father, it's right to feel terrible, you wouldn't be human if you didn't . . ."

He laughed suddenly. Dropped his hand. A crooked, mirthless grin was on his face. "Human?" he said. "Christ! I'm not human."

She gazed at him, horrified. "What do you mean?" she said.

He waved her away. "I left the human race," he told her. "I'm out in the cold."

She felt, then, an awful wrench in her chest. The pain was so sudden and so crushing that she was forced to take shallow, rapid breaths. It ground on for half a minute. Flecks danced in front of her eyes. Then it eased. Never in her life had she felt an emotion like it.

"John, dear," she said, "that's not true. You're my son, my only son. Please come home with me. Please."

He turned, finally, and looked at her.

Somewhere below them, disconnected sounds floated up. Far beyond the farm a dog was barking. She heard the rusty-gate call of pheasant; a car was passing along the lane that she had driven up that morning: she saw the sunlight flash on its windshield and roof, heard the note of the engine die away as it disappeared through the trees. Soon, all she could see was its color as it turned a corner by a house half a mile away in the valley. Then, even the color was lost.

She met John's eyes and saw that she had lost him too.

"I have something to do," he said. "Something to finish."

He started to walk quickly down the slope.

"Go home, Mother," he told her. "Go home."

Twenty-seven

JO dreamed the same thing, over and over again.

She was in a car on a roller-coaster ride. The metal shoulder harness was down: the breeze, as the car made its slow ascent, was cool on her face. She could hear the noise as the chain below turned over its tracks—a regular, heavyweight sound that shook through the car and set her teeth on edge. Gradually, as the car rose up the steep incline, she could see the tops of trees. Water reflecting on the lake below. Crowds passing by, their faces occasionally turned up to look. Distant music.

The seat below her was hard. There was no one else in the car, no one else on the ride. All the other cars were empty, and as the car stopped on the very peak of the rise, there was a moment of absolute silence and stillness, the breeze stronger now, bearing ice-cold scents of water, salt, decay.

The decay would always surprise her. Its fierce, pungent, and unexpected assault on the senses. She would turn her head to avoid it, and then she would see Sam, her Sam, passing on a parallel track, helplessly ascending another ride, the cars of that ride slipping past her, just out of her reach.

At that very second she would go plunging down, a scream ripped from her throat, air forced from her chest. Falling, she would see the world flash past in a riot of color. Glimpse those upturned faces, just for the briefest of seconds. And then, suddenly, everything would disappear—the ride, the car, the securing harness. She would be thrown forward, out of her seat, into a vast space, dropping with increasing speed, until she knew with absolute certainty that she would never stop falling, and that the ride, the drop, would go on forever.

It was always at this point that she would wake, gasping. Sit upright in bed, her heart thudding so hard that she thought it would tear right out of her chest. Sometimes she heard the scream pinched in her throat—heard herself gulp it backward, try to contain it. Sometimes the scream itself woke her. Whichever way, she would sit on the side of the bed, gasping for air, bathed in sweat.

The conscious ride was almost the same.

She had no control anymore in her waking world. She wanted so badly to get off this roller coaster. Wanted to stand at the side of the road and look up, as the people in her dreams looked, at someone else strapped into the ascending car. She wanted to be the observer. She wanted to have a day, an hour, to think. To choose.

But there was no time.

And there were no choices.

She had come to London, and was staying with Gina. Sam had just finished a course of ALG—antilymphocyte globulin, cyclosporine, and methylprednisolone, drugs designed to knock out the lymphocytes in his system, and the T cells attacking his bone marrow.

"We're learning all the time with AA," Elliott had told her. "Twenty years ago, faced with an illness like this, we were mostly at a loss. It had been known to medicine for nearly a hundred years, but trying to track it, to chase it down, was like running through a shifting maze. We know that ALG works in a lot of cases, but we don't know really how it works. We assume through immunosuppression, but there's actually a poor correlation when we try to replicate ALG in vitro acting on AA."

They had been standing by Sam's bed. He had been moved to an isolation unit, a small single-bed ward. He had been crying on the first day; his tears wore him out. He was staring at Jo with a blotched, miserable face, his expression full of condemnation.

Why are you doing this to me?

She wished she could lie on the bed and take it for him. Hook herself up to the machines, the drips. She'd switched on the overhead television, but his gaze had skated past the picture, to the window.

She'd hesitated, holding the hand he didn't want her to hold, his grip slackening on her.

"Soon be better," she'd reassured him.

She had hated herself for the lie. How could she know that? How could she know he'd get better? How could she possibly even begin to find a way through this maze for a child of two, find words that could explain it to him, when she didn't understand it herself, and was terrified every time he was laid down to be treated? She didn't know if he would get better, and that was the truth of it. The truth she kept locked away in her head, and clamped down hard whenever she was close to him.

When it had been explained to her—the treatment, the drugs— she'd had a real problem taking the information in. It was as if her brain had shut itself off. *No more, no more.* Going home at night, she'd stay up into the early hours, culling Web sites and downloading their versions of the same drug therapy. In the morning, looking at those printed sheets over breakfast, she invariably found it hard to read. Actually hard to make sense of simple sentences. And she had always used to pride herself on how much information she could retain about all sorts of subjects. She hardly ever needed notes, for instance, when interviewing. She remembered. She just remembered. Always.

Except now.

"I feel as if my brain is dead," she'd confessed to Elliott. "I hear what you're telling me, and I think I get it. Then, two hours later, I can't remember."

Elliott had only nodded. "It's normal," he'd said. "Don't worry about it. We can tell you twenty times. We don't mind. It's no problem."

No problem. No worries.

Normal.

What the hell was normal, anyway, in this crazy, house-of-mirrors world? She no longer knew. She tried to think back to what normal had meant only a couple of weeks ago. Maybe walking through town trying to get Sam not to touch displays, or run off through the crowds, or pick up others kids' toys. That would have been a normal day. Or sitting alongside him as he splattered a milkshake down himself and her, wresting it off a table and straight into his lap. That would be normal.

Trying to stuff a dozen jelly beans into his mouth at once. Normal. Normal Sam. Sitting on her lap looking interestedly at the laptop screen, seeing Gina's name come up on e-mail. He knew the letter *G;* he knew that, more often than not, whatever followed the letter *G* would make his mummy laugh, and now it was a kind of trick with him, seeing *G* everywhere, and grinning, party to a secret joke. Normality, Sam. Normality. Remember that? Or lying in her arms at night, thumb stuck in his mouth, eyes drooping, purposefully keeping himself awake. *That* was normal. *That* was her son.

Used to be her son. Used to be.

Now she was in some other place, where none of the usual rules applied. And she glimpsed other people—other mothers, walking along in town, trying to keep their kids close while they shopped, casually wiping their faces while they sat at café tables . . . God, it was unbearable. She wouldn't have thought that she could be like this, so angry, so anxious, and still be herself. Still be Jo.

Every day when she looked at herself in the mirror, she would feel faintly surprised to see the same old face staring back at her. She found it hard to believe that the new world, the house-of-mirrors world, wouldn't show in her flesh, her expression. That the pain wouldn't be obvious, like a scar, or a birthmark. A distortion, a warp, a piece of the fairground glass. She almost expected to see something horrible, terrible . . . blood in her eyes, maybe. Skin that peeled back to show the vein. Black mouth, pooling bruise . . .

She always had to shut off that recurrent thought, the horror movie playing for an audience of one. It was a fact that nothing at all in her was either changing or falling apart. She was the same.

It was not her. It was Sam. It was Sam who was changing.

He had to be kept as free as possible from sources of infection. He couldn't go to play school anymore. They couldn't take public transport anywhere. No trains, no buses, no planes. No crowds. No parties. No swimming pool. Not even his paddling pool in the garden, whose water had always used to fill with leaves and soil as he rushed in and out. No more of that. No garden, if she could help it. The heaven-sent patch she had tended for him had become fraught with danger.

His diet had altered dramatically too. He couldn't eat uncooked fruit or vegetables. His meals had to be boiled, to reduce even ordinary bacteria. No fresh milk. No soft cheese. Only variety boxes of cereal, that could be opened and consumed in one day. Packaged, boiled, canned. It was like being on some long voyage, where they couldn't get hold of fresh food. A journey into space. A long walk through an empty land. Tasteless, frozen. Bland. Sealed off from the world, turned in on their private anguish, obsessed with their private fight for survival.

The ALG had taken a week.

The worst of all was the fitting of the Hickman line. Because Sam needed so much injected, the Hickman line was designed to make things easier for him, by fitting a permanent line through his chest. Easier . . . well, yes, she conceded that first night. It *was* easier for Sam. The innocuous-looking plastic adaptor plug hanging from his chest wall was well done; if you looked briefly, and then looked away, you might see little more than the plaster tape holding it in place. But it was, of course, far more than that.

Seeing it as he was brought back from the operating room, something washed over Jo. It wasn't fright, or revulsion. It was the knowledge that this was unalterable, that the world had heaved and turned, and could never turn back again. Sam, with the line entering his body and threading through his artery, was smack in the closed fist of this storm. She could see him, she could hear him, even touch him—but she couldn't get him out.

They had put him back, gently, into bed, his eyes opening.

"Hi Sam," she'd said. "How're you doing?"

He had gazed at her, his bottom lip trembling. Then he suddenly became aware of the line. His fingers fluttered toward it, at the entry point under his arm. Then, almost in slow motion, his eyes widened, and his hand, outstretched, hovered above his neck.

It must feel as if he's been invaded, Jo had thought. *Something has got inside him. Something I've allowed to happen.*

"It's okay," she'd tried to reassure him. "It makes you a special boy. Special, Sam."

He'd stared at her.

She saw utter trust in his face.

"Fix," he'd whispered. "Mummy, fix."

Somehow she'd managed to smile at him. Fuss the bedclothes over him, smooth his forehead until he mercifully dozed.

And then she walked to the loo, shut herself in, and wept in agony.

The Hickman line went farther, deeper, than she had ever gone. All the times that she'd bathed him and cuddled him and fed him, all the times she'd lain with him on her bed and marveled at him—his skin, his fingers, the extraordinary softness of him, the perfection of him . . . she had never even got close, she realized. She had never got as close as this drug they were pumping into him. She had never got as close as this plastic line that wove its way to his heart. She had never, would never, get as close as this damned illness, that lived right in the center of him, deep in his bone.

The ALG had started with a test dose for an hour. The nurse had given her a leaflet about the drugs—like any medication it listed the side effects as well as its benefits—and she'd screwed it up and shoved it out of sight, because the list of side effects was so long. She didn't want to know that it could result in cardiac arrest, liver failure, or renal failure. All she wanted, all she could focus on, was that it would do the other thing. It would make him well. It would bring him back.

Two hours later, at four o'clock in the afternoon, he'd started receiving the main dose. Eighteen hours a day for five days, and, when the eighteen hours were finished, platelets and blood and antibiotic.

She'd stopped crying around the third night or so. The tears were someone else's, anyway. They belonged to some nameless stranger: some gutless crying woman. A woman who had a tissue permanently fastened in her hand. God, how she hated that woman, that mother who wept when the drugs went into the Hickman. What the nurses thought of her, she couldn't imagine.

If truth were told, she didn't care.

Her heart hurt inside her, as if she'd taken a blow right over it. Her ribs ached because she often held her breath without knowing it. She just sat, watching him. She didn't even feel hungry.

But the worst was to come. Worse than the crying and complaining. Sam became silent, acquiescent, accepting.

His eyes followed the nurses, and then he would watch his mother, his gaze switching between the two faces. And when Jo turned back to him, he would look at her with a complete faith that she could protect him.

And that was the worst of all.

* * *

At the end of the week Elliott had told her that she needed to go to London for her stem-cell donation. Though she had been expecting it, it's coming so soon after the first ALG had been a blow.

"It's a form of insurance," he'd explained to her. They had been sitting in his office again, after Sam had finished on the fifth day. Jo had found herself staring at the same notepad where he drew her his diagrams. Elliott had spoken slowly and carefully, glancing at her to see if she understood. Looking hard at her, he was worried by Jo's flatness, her dull expression.

"Here's what will happen," he'd told her. "We give you a chemical that makes you overproduce stem cells. We harvest them. We can freeze them. They'll be there if we need them. If the worse comes to the worst. Then it would be worth a try."

"How?" Jo asked. "How do you do it?"

"We put you on a machine," Elliott said. "The process is called apheresis. It just means separating the blood, your blood, into different components."

"Under anesthetic?" she asked.

"No, just sitting in a chair, with a tube in both arms. It takes about four hours."

"Oh," she murmured. "Okay." Her stomach had turned over.

"Five days beforehand we give you a drug called G-CSF. It's a growth factor. It's administered by injection, just a little under the skin surface. You have five doses over five consecutive days, at the same time each day. Say halfway through the afternoon."

"And what happens?" Jo asked. "How will I feel?"

Elliott spread his hands. "Every person reacts differently," he said. "What we're doing is making your body mirror the effect of fighting off a virus. So you'll maybe get flulike symptoms. Muscle aches. Tiredness. Headaches. You might get bone pain, and there's a good reason for that. It's a good sign."

"Why?" Jo asked.

"The bone marrow's expanding, making more. Making too much. It spills over into the blood. Lots of stem cells, the building blocks of marrow. Good. Now's the time to catch those cells while they're circulating round in you."

"Right," Jo said. *Christ,* she thought.

"Then, after the harvest, they freeze down your cells. Cryopreservation. They put them in liquid nitrogen, slowly, so as not to form ice crystals. Then they can keep them for a long time. Years, if necessary."

Jo considered. From feeling nauseous at the idea of having needles in her arms for four hours at a time, she had suddenly begun to see the skill of it all. It was audacious, like taking God on at a game. A little light was turned on inside her. For a couple of days she would be like Sam. She would partner him in his role, in his battle against the anemia. She'd be his running mate.

That gave her first flush of satisfaction. Then, thinking about it, she realized how simple and brilliant it was. Taking her own cells out of her, wiping them free of the blood, putting it back. It was so clever, and it was something she could do—she who had felt so helpless and ineffective standing at Sam's side.

Elliott had smiled at her, trying to read her thoughts. She'd leaned one elbow on his desk and put a hand over her face.

She could beat God—the implacable, unsmiling God in her head—at this game. She smiled at last and looked up. Elliott relaxed back into his chair.

"Well, hello," he said.

She raised an eyebrow. "What?"

"A smile," he said. "The first I've seen."

"I used to do it a lot." She shrugged. "Used to be pretty good at it." She got up to leave. He walked her to the door.

"Do it some more," he told her. "You'll need that skill again."

She was sitting now in University College Hospital, London.

Beside her was Gina. It was the day of the first stem-cell donation. Next to them stood one of the *Courier*'s photographers.

When Jo had first asked for this favor, there hadn't been a moment of hesitation on Gina's part.

Could *The Courier* run an article—any article, it didn't matter how small—on what Jo was doing? Jo had asked her, over the phone two days ago. Could it print a photograph? Could it mention Sam, or Doug, or both—could it say how important it was that Sam find a donor?

"Of course," Gina had said.

"I hate to ask, Gina."

"Why?" Gina had replied. "It's news, isn't it? I do news."

Jo had laughed down the phone. Gina had frowned at the thinness of the sound. "Maybe they'll remember Doug being airlifted," Jo said.

Gina was already seeing the page. The shout line. *The most desperate rescue of all.* A picture of Jo wired up to apheresis. "Doug was a brave man, Jo," she replied softly. "You got a family tradition to keep up."

"Thanks," Jo said.

"You'll stay with us when you come," Gina had said.

"It can only be overnight," Jo told her. "Cath is with Sam. I have to get back."

Gina tried not to think of the days when Jo had visited before, brought Sam, and they had sneaked off to Regent's Park or the Dome with him, taking time off that neither of them could really afford. Gina tried not to think of the other Sam, whom she chased up and down her Victorian hallway in Holland Park, playing Power Rangers.

"Gina," Jo had said, before she put down the phone, "do you mind me asking, do you have a cold, anything like that?"

"No," Gina said.

"Or a tummy bug?"

"No, it's okay. We're fit."

"Sorry to cross-examine you."

"No problem. See you soon."

Yet the phone calls hadn't prepared Gina for Jo's appearance when she stepped off the train. Always trim, her friend was now lighter to the point of being thin. Her jacket hung off her shoulders. Her skin was pale. Only the hug was the same: wiry defiance in every pore.

"Down to fighting weight, I see," Gina had observed, holding her at arm's length.

Jo had raised a clenched fist. "You'd better believe it," she'd told her.

Twenty-eight

THE phone call came through at eight-thirty the next morning.

The Courier had been on the newsstands for less than three hours. Gina and Jo were in Gina's office, looking out over the view of the river, watching the morning ferries, the tour boats. The Thames was lower than usual, they thought. Already the morning was heavy with heat.

Gina picked up the phone. "Features." There was a pause. "Yes, that's me."

Jo glanced at her. Gina had raised an eyebrow, then sat down at her desk. "I see," she murmured. "Yes."

Jo watched her draw concentric circles on her memo pad, a sign of deep concentration. "Hang on a moment," Gina said. She put her hand over the receiver. "Do you know an Anthony Hargreaves?" she asked. "From HMS *Fox*?"

Jo thought. "The principal medical officer who treated Doug," she said. "Yes, of course."

"Jo Harper is right here with me," Gina said into the phone. "Would you like to speak to her?"

She smiled. Wordlessly, she handed Jo the receiver. Jo put it to her ear.

"Jo Harper."

"Miss Harper. Anthony Hargreaves."

"Hello," she said. "How are you?"

There was a fractional pause. "More to the point, how are you?" he asked. "I read your piece."

"I'm okay," she said.

"I'm so sorry about your son."

"Thank you."

"I just wanted to say . . ." He paused. "It's none of my business, I'm probably telling you what you already know. But you said in your article about donors. Bone-marrow donors. How Sam needed one."

"Yes," she said.

"Well . . . you have talked to the James Norberry Trust?"

"James Norberry?" she repeated.

"The James Norberry Bone Marrow Trust. It's there in London. They keep a register of people who've offered to donate."

"No," she said. "Should I?"

"Doug and John went on their register," he said.

The room seemed to flex in and out of focus for a second. Jo sat down on the nearest chair. "They what?"

"Didn't you know?" he asked. "When they were on the ship, we had just had a whole ship screening. The Trust had come to the ship when we were in Portsmouth. It was a recruitment drive for donors. One of the men on the ship—"

"The little girl," Jo breathed. "There was a picture of a little girl on your notice board."

"That's right," he said. "Chrissie Wainwright. She was nine years old. She was our warrant officer's niece. She had leukemia."

"I remember," Jo murmured. But she dared not ask if the little girl had survived. She was afraid of what the answer might be.

"Well, both Doug and his son took a blood test," he told her. "We managed to get the bloods out with the next flight. They went to the Trust."

"He never told me," Jo said.

"He would have got a card," Hargreaves continued. "A donor ID card."

Jo tried to cast her mind back to the time after Doug's death. His solicitor handling the will, the fuss that was made, the difficulties with Alicia. She had sorted through a lot of correspondence then, but she couldn't remember if there had been such a card or not.

"He had a medical card with his medical number on it," she murmured. "His National Insurance card, I think. . . ."

"This is a cream card like a small folder," Hargreaves said. "Anyway, if you can't find it, the Trust would have the records."

"I'll get in touch with them," Jo said.

There was a pause. "Well," Hargreaves responded, "I don't think they would tell you the names of their donors, but I just thought, for your own peace of mind, John would be on their list already."

"But no one knows where he is," Jo said. "I said in the article—"

"Yes," Hargreaves said, "but John might be in touch with the Trust. He might have told them where he is now. I just wanted to say that to you. You might not know where John is, but the Trust might. They might have contacted him already, be talking to him."

"And they would know," Jo said. "They would know now if John is a match."

"Probably," Hargreaves said.

"Oh, God," Jo breathed.

When she had thanked him and said her good-byes, she put the phone down and stared at Gina.

"Is it good news?" Gina asked. "What did he say? What is it about John?"

Jo remained where she was. Her hand strayed to her mouth.

"What?" Gina said. "What?"

"Have you got a phone directory?" Jo asked, after a second or two.

"Of course," Gina said. She promptly fished it out of her desk drawer. "Who do you want to find?"

"The James Norberry Trust."

Gina flicked through the pages. "Here it is," she said. "SW-One."

"What's the address?" Jo asked.

"Tarrangore Street."

Jo nodded. "I've got to go and see them," she said. She reached for her handbag from the floor.

Gina sprang up from her desk and came around to her. "Whoa," she said, "hold on. You can't go across London. Not now."

"Why not?"

"You've got to be at University College at three."

"So?" Jo said. "I've got hours."

"You're supposed to be resting," Gina said. "It was only four days ago when you told me you were feeling like shit because of the GCSF, remember? I saw you take those aspirin this morning."

"I'm fine," Jo said.

"What are you going there for?" Gina said. "What is it, a bone marrow register? Those people don't talk to the public."

"I'm not the public," Jo said. "I'm a patient's mother. I'm a relation to one of their donors. I want to know where John is. Hargreaves says they could know."

"If they know, then it's between John and them," Gina pointed out. "They're not going to tell you what one of their donors has said to them."

"Yes, they will," Jo said.

"Jo, they won't. Think about it."

"They'll tell me," Jo said defiantly. "They have to."

"Jo . . ."

"Don't you see?" Jo said. "If they're talking to him, and he refuses to cooperate, what then?"

Gina frowned. "I don't know. I guess they can't force him."

"Exactly," Jo said. "If they've found him, and he says no, what can they do? Nothing. But *I* can do something."

"What?" Gina said.

"I can go and see him, wherever he is. I can persuade him. I can apologize for calling him a killer, for a start."

"You didn't mean it," Gina said.

Jo eyed her sadly. "That's the whole point," she said. "I did mean it. I meant it from the bottom of my heart. I believed it. But I don't believe it now. I thought that he would come back to Catherine, and when he did, I was going to tell him that I was sorry. But he never came back."

"And you think, if he knew about Sam, he wouldn't come back?" Gina said. "Sure he would. He'd have to be inhuman not to come back. He'll come."

"He doesn't have to be inhuman not to come," Jo said. "He just has to be messed up and guilty and lonely and afraid. And if he is, maybe I helped him to be that way."

Gina held her arm gently. "Why don't you wait?" she said. "Elliott will tell you soon enough if a donor's been found."

Jo pulled away from her. "I can't wait, Gina," she said. "If there's a fraction of a chance that I could alter something, speed this up, I have to do it."

"But he might not even be a match!"

Jo was already halfway out the door. "I just have to do it," Jo repeated. "That's all."

The James Norberry Trust was nearly invisible.

Jo got out of the taxi to find herself in a busy street. There was public housing on one side, in a great gray block; a news dealer, liquor store, hardware store, a row of terraced houses. Traffic lights on a busy junction. A pub on the corner. A betting shop. A florist. She could have been in any street in any town, and the Trust was nowhere to be seen.

She walked down the row of shops, looking for the numbers. Twenty-three . . . 34. She stopped, and looked down at the address she had scribbled on the scrap of paper. The Trust was numbers 26–30. But where was it? She had missed it somehow. She retraced her steps, and found it at last, a single doorway sandwiched between a video store and a launderette. She pressed the keypad on the wall.

"James Norberry," said a voice.

"My name is Harper," Jo replied. "I need to talk to someone about a donor."

There was a pause before the door unlocked.

She made her way up a flight of stairs. At the top the way ahead surprised her: it was much bigger than it looked from the outside, with a pair of glass doors leading to a reception desk. There was another lock on the door: the receptionist looked up, then pressed the door release. Jo walked in.

"Mrs. Harper."

"Miss," Jo said. "Look, I need to speak to someone."

The girl behind the desk smiled. "I recognize you from the paper," she said.

"Is there anyone I can talk to?"

The girl nodded. "I've buzzed Mrs. Lord," she said. "Here she is now."

Jo turned to see a woman who had come from another office off the reception landing. Small, slight, and dark, she held out her hand to Jo.

"Hello. I'm Christine Lord."

"Jo Harper."

Christine Lord glanced at the receptionist. "Sarah," she said, "we're in the interview room. Could you bring us some coffee?"

Impatient, Jo followed the woman. The interview room turned out to be tiny, airless, gray, and crowded out with boxes.

"I'm sorry," Christine said. "We have nowhere to put deliveries but here. Space is at such a premium."

"I appreciate you seeing me," Jo said. "I want to talk to you about a donor on your books."

"Okay," Christine said.

"His name is John Marshall. He and his father, Douglas Marshall, came onto the register about three years ago."

"I see," Christine said.

Jo looked hard at her. "They're here? On the list?"

"I can't tell you that."

Jo tried to take a breath. "They gave blood on a ship called HMS *Fox.*"

"We saw people from the ship, yes," Christine said.

"And you got John and Doug's blood."

"I can't say. I'm sorry."

Jo took a deep breath. "Douglas Marshall died," she said. "He moved house, and then, two months later, he died in a road accident. So maybe you've tried writing to him to update your records, and can't find him? Well—"

"I know that Douglas Marshall died," Christine Lord said. "I remember reading about it at the time."

Jo nodded. "Well, after his death, his son John moved," she said. "He moved out of his flat. Sixteen-A Wilding Crescent, Cambridge."

There was no reply.

"Do you know where he is?" Jo said.

"If matches come up in response to searches, then we write to the last known address," Christine said.

"Have you written to John Marshall at that address?" Jo said. "Okay . . . you can't tell me. All right." She tried a different approach. "If you do, there won't be a reply. Did he give you another address? Has he contacted you with some other address?"

Christine Lord was listening, hands clasped on the tabletop. She shook her head. "Everything we do there is between us, the donor, and the transplant surgeon," she said. "We have to protect identities. It's crucial."

"This isn't a normal case," Jo objected.

"With the greatest respect, every case we have is abnormal. Every single one is an emergency, a crisis."

Jo had to literally bite her tongue. She felt like screaming that Sam wasn't like anyone else, but, just in time, saw how illogical that was. In this room, in these offices, Sam was exactly like everyone else. They were all looking death in the face.

Christine was watching her. "We value every bit of information about donors' whereabouts," she said. "People register with every good intention, but they can forget to tell us when they move."

"John would have done that, I'm sure," Jo said. She told herself to keep this calm, straightforward tone in her voice. It would do no good at all to get angry, excited. "He left suddenly. He was—he was distressed at the time."

"If a match comes up, we have contact officers. These are people whose job it is to try and find missing names."

Jo leaned forward. "Is your contact officer looking for John Marshall?" she said. "Have they found him?"

"I'm sorry, but—"

"Oh, please don't tell me that you can't tell me that!" Jo cried. "You *can* tell me. I'm the mother of his half-brother. His half-brother is dying. You *can* tell me!"

Christine Lord shook her head. "I can't tell you, Miss Harper," she said softly. "Not because I don't want to, but because I'm legally constrained not to."

Jo put her head in her hands.

"Donors must be protected," Christine Lord went on. "They must be sure that no one will ever come knocking at their door demanding they give bone marrow. We must encourage people to go on the register, and to do that, we must guarantee that they'll be under no pressure, either from parents or relations, or doctors, or ourselves, to make decisions for them or pressure them in any way."

"You don't understand," Jo said. "I'm not going to pressure him. I have something to tell him, something personal, for his own good. Something from before all this happened." She blushed. "I have to apologize to him," she said.

"It doesn't matter what the nature of the contact will be, we can't allow it," Christine replied, as gently as she could. "Imagine what could happen if we gave that information out. Imagine a child is dying, and the family doesn't care what lengths they go to. Imagine someone calling on a donor, offering them money. Or worse still, threatening them or their families."

"I'm not going to threaten him," Jo said.

"I know that," Christine answered. "But this is the donor's decision alone, and they must have privacy. We counsel donors, we support them, we do all we can to make it easy for them to donate. We book them into private hospitals, for instance. We pay their expenses. We have people standing by at any hour of the day or night to talk to them, dispel their anxieties, give them information. We act as go-betweens, if necessary, between the donor and medical staff. We provide translators; we contact religious leaders of their faith, if they need one. We make sure their diet and personal preferences are all catered to. But by far the most important thing we do for them, more important than all that put together, is to keep their anonymity and respect their decisions, no matter what they are."

Jo stared at her. "You mean, if John refused to help Sam, you'd just accept it?" she whispered. "Even if he turned out to be a match?"

Christine spread her hands. "Naturally we'd do all we could to find out what it was that bothered him. Sometimes it's just the thought of actually giving marrow," she said. "We'd try to explain all we could. But we don't press hard. We don't use emotional blackmail. We don't even tell them who the patient is. Yes . . . to answer your question. If anyone refused to donate, we can't insist. Even if they say yes, even if the patient is prepared for the transplant through chemotherapy, even if the doors of the operating room are open, and the donor is on the gurney, if that donor suddenly says no . . . well, that's it. No transplant. No donor."

"Surely nobody does that," Jo whispered.

"Personally," Christine said, "I know of no one who's withdrawn at such a late stage. But that's not to say that it won't, or can't, happen. People do withdraw."

"But why would they do that? Surely they know there's a life at stake."

"That's right," Christine said. "But bear in mind the reasons why they registered. Seven times out of ten they'll have put their name down because someone they knew was ill and needed a transplant. They gave their blood then to get registered and see if they were a match." She shrugged. "But times change. Maybe that person they knew died. Maybe they gave bone marrow before, and *that* person still died. Maybe the whole process is so tied up with pain, with terrible memories, with feelings of guilt, that they just can't go through with it." She sat back in her chair. "We deal with human beings," she said. "There are no guarantees, and there are no perfect people with perfect responses. We speak to people under stress all the time. We're under stress here too. We try to tread carefully, as carefully as we dare."

"Even knowing a child might be dying at that very moment," Jo said.

"Yes," Christine replied. "Even knowing that."

There was a soft knock at the door. The receptionist came in with a tray of coffee and put it down on the table in front of them. "Would you like anything else?" she asked Jo. "A glass of water? Fruit juice?"

Jo stared at the tray for a second, miles away. Then she looked up. "A glass of water," she said. "Thank you."

Christine Lord turned, reached behind her to a small desk, and took out a piece of paper. "There is something I can offer," she said. She pushed the paper across the table to Jo. "If ever John Marshall contacted this office," she said, "I could forward a letter to him, under certain conditions."

Jo gazed at the paper. "You'd do that?"

"I can't guarantee anything," Christine said. "But I could keep your letter here. If we ever did get in touch with John Marshall, for whatever reason—*if* we did—I could tell him that there was a letter here from you. But I would only pass it on if he specifically asked me to do so."

"Thank you," Jo said.

She took half an hour to sit, alone, in the interview room, and compose what she wanted to say to John.

It wasn't easy. Her first draft was an outpouring of panic: how ill

Sam was, how desperate she was, how he had to come back. Even that it was his duty. Rereading it, she realized that it was a demand, a piece of emotional blackmail. She tore the page from the pad, crumpled it, and tried again.

This time she found all she wanted to say in four short sentences.

John, please forgive me for the terrible thing I said to you.
    I'm so very sorry. We badly need your help now. If you can come home, or need help to do so, please get in touch.

She wrote her telephone and e-mail address on the bottom, sealed the envelope, and went back to reception, where Christine Lord was waiting.

"If you ever hear," she said.

"We'll do our best." Christine took the letter and put it in her pocket.

Jo paused one last time, biting her lip. "I don't suppose you'll tell me if there are any matches, even if it isn't John?"

Christine Lord put a hand on Jo's shoulder. "As soon as there are matches, or a single match, we tell the transplant surgeon," she said. "We do recommend that he tell you only if he makes the decision to go ahead with that donor. Even then the surgeon will only know the donor's identity number, not his name. But I can assure you, whenever we have a positive result, none of us here waste a moment's time. Not a second."

Jo searched her face. She saw sympathy, but nothing else.

"Okay," she murmured. "Thanks."

She glanced once more past the reception, to a corridor with other security and pass-only locks on them. She tried to visualize what lay behind them. Somewhere in those rooms, she knew, John's name was waiting, a link in a chain that could not afford to be broken. Maybe there were other names there too. People she had never met, whose blood miraculously matched Sam's. Maybe some of them were close, but not close enough. Maybe some were perfect, but they would refuse to donate.

She would never know.

She looked back at Christine Lord. "Well . . . good-bye," she murmured.

"Good-bye, Miss Harper. Good luck."

Christine Lord listened to Jo's footstep on the stairs and to the sound of the outer door to the street closing. She went back into her office, and watched again through the window as Jo Harper hailed a taxi and got into it.

Then she walked through to her office and sat down at the computer.

She glanced around herself, at the banks of computers, at the overhead fluorescent lights that strained the eyes; at the huge in-trays of application and update forms, promotional leaflets and appeals, and the precious letters from people asking about donorship.

She caught a glimpse of herself in the mirror on the windowsill: a very tired woman who was always meaning to take a vacation, and never quite found the right time. Past the mirror the spider plants drooped, unwatered, and the wastebaskets overflowed. Since joining the Trust, Christine thought, smiling wryly to herself, there was never enough time for anything. Time was the one element that ran through their fingers. It was the thing they raced against every day. And despite their best efforts both time and money were always running out on them.

She turned to the introductory contact on the top of the pile.

That very morning, barely twenty minutes before Jo Harper had knocked on the door, the James Norberry Trust had received a request for a match for a two-year-old boy. He lived in Cambridge, and he was not responding to ALG treatment.

Christine Lord ran through the patient details. On the top of the search request form a box asked if the search was urgent. *Yes,* the doctor had said.

Date of birth: June 11, 2000.
Sex: Male.
Race: Caucasian.
Diagnosis: Severe aplastic anemia.
Name: Samuel Douglas Marshall.

With practiced speed Christine transferred the details onto the search procedure. Class 1 Serology typing, Class 1 DNA typing, Class 11 Serology typing, Class 11 DNA typing, CMV status, referring physician, transplant center, date of diagnosis.

When the information was complete and a profile record had been constructed of Sam's blood, she switched the computer to search mode.

It was always at this point that everyone working here crossed their fingers and said a prayer. It didn't matter how long they had been working there, or how many searches they had initiated. When search was instructed, there was this same moment of suspense, while fate unceremoniously shuffled the cards.

It was a massive, awe-inspiring process.

There were over two million donors to search worldwide. Each search was focused on exactly the same components; the HLA antigens in the blood. There were three main sites—HLA-A, HLA-B, and HLA-DR. Twenty-four different possible antigens had been identified, to date, at the HLA-A site, fifty-two at the HLA-B site, and twenty at the HLA-DR site. With each antigen the possible combinations of crossmatching multiplied out of sight. Since every person had at least two antigens at each site, more than six hundred million combinations of HLA antigens were theoretically possible. And through those six hundred million the search engines went roaring away, chasing the matches and mismatches down ever-narrowing tunnels of probability, presenting, examining, and rejecting many times a second.

And the odds lengthened even more at tissue-antigen sites other than HLA sites, whose very roles in transplantation were unclear, undiscovered, or unknown. It was thought that these shadowy sites and levels might be eventually found to be responsible for the failures in transplant, where graft-versus-host disease tore the apparent matches apart, made the body rebel against the incoming marrow, and caused the transplant to fail. DNA testing was already revealing that antigens that were once thought to be identical had, in fact, as many as ten different variations or microvariants within them.

Christine Lord often wondered what they would think of their methods of matching in the future, when the delicate and as yet unknown components of blood and the body were discovered. She wondered if, as an old woman, she would be able to look back and see what an enormous gamble any transplant had been in the year 2000, throwing antigens together, pouring drugs in to combat rejection, messing a whole body's building blocks of life, shunting together two different people to try to overcome an illness. It was a miracle, when you thought about it, that any transplant at all worked, such were the gigantic odds stacked against it. And yet they did work. And, when they did, they transformed very sick people into well people, and very sick families— grieving families—into places of joy.

Miracles, dancing down the phone lines, the letters, the computer data banks. Miracles coursing through a baby's bloodstream. Miracles set out in ten-page detail on a drug protocol form in any transplant surgeon's office. Miracles in the faith and endurance of the parents and friends, who never stopped hoping.

Christine Lord watched the flickering image on the screen in front of her, the only clue to the activity hurtling around the world.

She rested her head on her hand and waited.

Six hundred million combinations. Two million donors. One little boy in an isolation unit in Cambridge. It didn't bear thinking about, and yet she did think about it. She watched the screen as if it were her own son's life on the line.

Samuel Douglas Marshall needed to share his father's rare haplotype with his half-brother. Jo Harper needed to share a different haplotype with John Marshall's mother.

Christine put both hands to her face and covered her eyes, resting her head in her hands, shutting out the image in front of her.

She put the chances at twenty million to one.

Give or take a million or two.

Twenty-nine

APRIL 27, 1848. Maundy Thursday.

Crozier stood alone on the ice.

A hundred yards from the ships he looked at them with a full heart. They said that sailors were married to the sea, and their ships, and it was true for him. Whether that made him more of a sailor or less of a man, he could not guess. But his whole soul was welded to his vessel, whose back had still not been broken by the hurricanes that winter.

His fate had been tied to the *Terror* for nine years. He had seen two ice continents in her. He had crossed thousands of miles in her. He had sailed to the Antarctic in her under the command of Sir James Clark Ross. He knew her better than any man alive. Her shape and sound, her abilities and strengths. The rock-hard, stubborn feel of her. She was his, his partner, his pride.

And despite the assault on her by the storms, she was still a fine girl. Standing at a slight angle in the ice, she had keeled over only a little, and closing his eyes, he might imagine that she was tilted in some seagoing breeze, rounding a shoreline, making out of harbor for an open sea. And she had traveled, even in the last winter. By his own calculations both *Erebus* and *Terror* had, in fact, traveled nineteen miles south, carried by the ice drift. A little progress, but not enough. Not enough by a hundred miles.

He wondered how long the ships would stand.

They might be broken up tomorrow by the weather or the ice. Or they might drift for years, if the ice did not break up. At nine and a half miles a year it was conceivable that, in ten years or more, these two extraordinary giants might even break free and be washed out into the straits that flowed westward. Crozier wondered if that would happen. He wondered how *Terror* would fare, unmanned, unmasted. A ghost ship riding the unmapped ocean. He wondered if she would find the Northwest Passage alone, without him.

Without any of them.

Because, no matter how much she meant to him, and how much married he was to her, he had to leave *Terror* now.

He looked down at his hands. It was a mild day, only ten degrees below freezing, and he had ventured to remove his gloves. Out here in the bright light of the day he could see more clearly. He lifted his hands closer to his face and turned them over, palm upward. The bruises had even begun on the fleshy mounds of his palm and around the fingernail of his thumb. His skin was ochre pale, splattered with pigment like an old man's. On his wrist, thread veins. On his knuckles, lesions. Cuts that were neither cold sores nor injuries, but a curious, creeping disintegration.

He put the gloves back on, carefully, slowly, allowing the truth of their situation to come to the front of his mind. He had pushed it away for months. He had pushed it away even in the last few weeks, when he had ordered stores to be ferried from the ships to the shore, because he was afraid that the terrible storms might break up the vessels. Even in the last few hours, after he had given orders for the men to pack their belongings, he had actually pushed the real facts away.

And the truth was that they were dying. Even the best of them. Even the marines. Even the ice masters. Even him.

The worst of the scurvy had started last year. He didn't know—no one knew, not even the doctors—exactly what it was that caused it to appear. That it was something to do with diet they knew, and that fresh meat and the daily ration of lemon juice could keep it at bay. But what exactly—what chemical, what deficiency—was the culprit, they had no idea.

Scurvy was feared, but expected. When a man became tired, and he bled under the skin, and his gums became swollen, and his teeth became loose, sailors recognized it for what it was. The sufferers would become breathless on the slightest exertion; they could not concentrate even on routine tasks. Mental work—the writing of a journal, the making of calculations—became mountains to climb, whose impossible gradients sharpened by the day. Crozier knew that his own mind wandered. Often he could hardly form words to complete sentences; he found himself clumsy, even about clothing himself, or washing. He could not finish a chapter in the books he loved. He was irritable with everyone. And whatever he suffered, it was multiplied a hundredfold around him, in every face.

There was one surefire way to combat scurvy, and that was to provide antiscorbutics. Lemon juice. Both *Erebus* and *Terror* had come equipped with plenty, packed into kegs, measured by pounds. There had been over four and a half thousand pounds of lemon juice on both ships, and they still had three months' supply left. But Crozier was sure that it had lost whatever qualities it once had to prevent the disease. They still issued the lemon—four days' lemon juice and three days' vinegar—but its effect wasn't as it should be. It had been frozen and unfrozen perhaps a dozen times. Maybe that was it. Maybe the freezing did something to it. He didn't know.

He looked up and saw Fitzjames coming toward him across the ice.

He looked hard at the slow progress of his second-in-command. Fitzjames had once been called the handsomest man in the navy. Once tall, dark, striking, he seemed to have shrunk a little now. His shoulders were hunched, his steps sluggish. And as he drew close to Crozier, no man alive could describe his face as handsome.

Fitzjames had suffered in the last few weeks. He had had pneumonia. The surgeons claimed that they had eradicated it, but Crozier was not so sure. You could hear Fitzjames breathing from yards away—rattling ominously.

"What are the results?" Crozier asked.

He had that morning asked Fitzjames and William Rhodes, one of the quartermasters, to check the remaining supplies.

"Not good," Fitzjames told him. He coughed, frowned. "We have ten days of coal."

"For steam."

"Yes."

"And for cooking?"

"It might last the summer."

Crozier beat his fist impotently against his hip.

Today was the first calm day in four weeks. For the last month they had been in the grip of one relentless storm after the other. The sun that they so longed for had hardly been seen. No one had got out to fix traps. Only a handful of men had managed—and then at a cost of one man's life—to cut holes in the ice to get fish. The fury of the gales had been demonic, unbelievable. And so, at the very season when they ought to have used less fuel and less canned food, they had run through their supplies at double rate.

They had only ever been equipped for three years. And the three years were finished on May 19.

Scurvy had arrived in earnest in January. Since then twenty-three men had died of it. Their deaths were prolonged, their battles heroic. But finally they lay down and gave in to an inexhaustible foe. Two succumbed in their sleep, four of consumption, eight others of pneumonia. And the rest—nine men, shadows of their former selves—died hallucinating, weeping, and rigid with seizure.

In their deaths Crozier was haunted by the same recurrent idea. There was something else on the ships. Something besides the deadly botulin, whose very name he loathed. There *was* something else, he knew. Something to do with the tins. The deaths were harder and quicker than on any other ship he had known; the cases of tuberculosis were quicker too. The pallid look of the men, even those not reported sick, was unnerving. And the arguments, and imagined slights, and the stories they told each other—it was not the same. It was just not the same as other ships.

Trying to shake himself free of what he constantly feared was delusion—another sign of the sickness—he knew that there was no time to lose. They could not stay on board the ships. No fuel and little food. Their only hope was the fresh meat that lay to the south of them. They would leave, and outrun the ghosts. They would turn their backs on their only security before it became their tomb.

"That's not all," Fitzjames said. "It's not the worst."

Crozier glanced up at him. "Not all?" he repeated. "What do you mean?"

"We inspected every last carton," Fitzjames said. "We have taken out the very bottom shipment, the first of Goldner's that came in."

"And?"

"There are blown cans in every case," Fitzjames said. "Meat."

They stared at each other.

"How many?" Crozier asked.

"Ninety-one six-pound tins."

"Dear God," Crozier muttered. "How many have we left?"

"Eighty-two tins of meat and a hundred soup."

Crozier stared back at the ships. At half rations that meant they had barely enough food for seven weeks. Seven weeks took them to the end of June. Last year nothing had moved here in June. Not a single fracture of the ice. They could not afford to take that gamble again.

He had to take his men to wherever the ice might thaw. Not north, not west; there would be hundreds of miles to traverse before they reached open water. South. It was the only direction. They would go where the ships could not go, toward the passage that Gore claimed to have seen, or guessed at, in his final journey.

He looked at Fitzjames. "I am sorry, James," he said.

Fitzjames gazed back at him. There was no need to spell it out. He knew what Crozier knew. The waiting was over, and the march must begin. But not a flicker of emotion passed over the younger man's face. He had had difficulty even negotiating the hundred yards between them and the ships. His face was livid with sores, especially at his mouth. The ulceration spread to his lips: it was visible on his tongue. Fitzjames was not fit to walk a mile.

Crozier touched his arm.

"There is no choice," Fitzjames said.

Together they walked back across the ice.

Gathered on the deck of *Erebus* were 104 men. In the past three years they had lost twenty-five of their number, including Franklin. For a moment Crozier remembered not only his commander, but a man from the lowest of the ranks, poor Torrington. Then, in the crowd, he searched out the face of Augustus Peterman. Gus was tall now, wiry. A little more than skin and bone, but not by much. His mother wouldn't recognize him now, Crozier thought. The boy was a man.

He let his gaze run over the others. Felt their apprehension.

"When we began this journey," he told them, "we did so with every hope of success. That we had floundered in the ice I need not tell you; it is you who have known and lived what no other man had ever done, no sailor before you."

They waited, listening. Not a man moving. He supposed they knew what he had to tell them. Above them the sky was perfectly clear, and the light cast on the deck was opalescent, bringing up every detail. If he looked closely, he could see on others the very bruises that he dared not look at for too long on his own body. He caught a man's glance, a dogged look of determination. Another looked away, bringing his fist to his eyes.

"I could not have asked more from you, and you could not have given me more," Crozier said. "And for that I salute you, as your country salutes you, for your fortitude."

Silence. Not even the ice pack shifted. No murmur even from the ship, pinched in its intolerable embrace.

"We set out from Greenhithe equipped for three years," Crozier continued. "And by good judgment and care we have provisions still for three months." There was a groan somewhere below him. The crew had already guessed the result of Fitzjames and Rhodes's frenzied counting and recounting that morning. Yet he still had paused, unwilling to declaim their fate.

"We will abandon both ships in the morning," he said. "We will load three boats. We will make for the Backs Fish River."

Then, there was a real murmur. Having expected it, he let it flow over the crowd, reach a crescendo of doubt, even of dissent, before fading away.

Backs Fish River was 210 miles south. They could not haul boats more than a mile or two a day. Even if every man had been healthy, fit, and strong, they would not have made the river for at least 150 days. And from the mouth of the river to the first Hudson's Bay outpost at Great Slave Lake was 900 miles. Every man there knew that they were not likely to make Great Slave Lake. Many of them would not even make the river.

"I have maps of the area," Crozier told them. "Maps in detail, which I do not possess for the area to the east, across land. Backs Fish River is a tortuous route, I know. But when we reach it, it will still be summer.

There will be no ice on the river, which is at a more southerly latitude. And I am confident that we will be met on the river by scouts from the Hudson's Bay Company, who will be sure to set out for us if there is no news of us by this spring."

The murmurs continued. Not all of them placed so much faith in Hudson's Bay.

"Sir George Back recorded that there were large numbers of deer, musk-ox, and birds at the river mouth," Crozier said. "There we can eat our fill. We can stock for an entire winter, if need be."

He did not tell them what else Back had said: that the river was a never-ending series of rapids and waterfalls, running through a landscape of frost-shattered rock.

The voices had become louder at the back of the crowd. Crozier looked down toward them. "Speak up," he said "Speak up if you have any doubts."

The men looked at each other.

"Fury Beach," a voice called.

"What of it?"

"There is food there," came the reply. "Ross left a cache there."

Fury Beach was hundreds of miles north, on the east coast of Somerset island. It was almost back at Lancaster Sound. It was named for HMS *Fury*, which had been wrecked here in 1825 while commanded by Sir Edward Parry, and all *Fury*'s stores had been dumped on the shore.

Crozier shook his head. "The provisions on *Fury* are over twenty years old," he said. "What we need is fresh meat and game. There is no fresh food on *Fury*, and there is no game. Sir John Ross said as much ten years ago." He turned to his ice master. "Mr. Blanky served under Sir John at that time," he said. "He has told me that Fury and Somerset are barren. There is no game, barely any foxes or hares. Nothing to sustain even five men, let alone a hundred."

The crews looked at Blanky, and back at the captain.

"I'll not lie to you," Crozier said, leaning forward. "We are in desperate straits. We cannot stay, and we cannot go west, or east overland, or north. Our only hope is south, and to go south is certain death for some. Yet to stay here is certain death, in my judgment, for us all. The ships have survived this far, but there is nothing to say that the next storm could not break them up. We must assume the worst. If this summer is the same as last, there will be no food here, and no breaking of the ice."

There was no more calling. Silence returned.

"We take three boats," Crozier said, "each weighing eight hundred pounds and mounted on oak sledges. We take awnings and sail and weather cloth and paddles, and food and clothing, gunpowder, guns, and fuel." He paused, a sudden emotion flooding him, threatening to break the steadiness of his tone.

In his hesitation each man's thoughts fled from where they stood. Some thought of home; of streets, or farms, or other islands. They thought of wives or parents, or children. They thought of Easter; in three days time both the churches and the alehouses would be full. They thought of spring, turning to summer, in England.

One or two of them bowed their heads. Easter . . . Christ's temptation, betrayal, and suffering. They would leave on Good Friday, the day of the crucifixion. Religious men among them shuddered.

It was not a good omen.

Crozier stared southward, into the ice-blue day.

He deliberately did not look at Fitzjames, or Little, or Irving, or any of the officers standing at his side.

"We leave the finest vessels in the world to God's mercy," he said softly, "and we commend ourselves to His care."

Thirty

AT eight-thirty the next morning Catherine was waiting.

She stood in the hallway of the Exploration Academy, gazing down the path through the glass doors. When Alicia arrived, she stepped forward.

"Mrs. Marshall . . ."

Alicia came through into the main body of the hallway, then stopped. "You" was all she said.

The doors behind them opened. Other people came in, people who evidently recognized Alicia and stopped to wait for her.

"Excuse me," Alicia said. "I have a trustees meeting to attend." She began to walk away.

Catherine ran after her. "Is he still in this country?" she asked.

Alicia had got to the foot of the stairs. "Who gave you permission to be in here?" she said.

"John," Catherine said. "I must know. Please."

A man walked up behind them. "Is everything all right?" he asked Alicia.

"I don't know how this person got in here," Alicia told him. "The doors are supposed to be closed to the public until nine-thirty."

"Please," Catherine said. She searched through her shoulder bag, took out a little wallet, and opened it. There was a photograph of Sam inside. She pulled it from the plastic casing and held it out.

Alicia froze. "Who sent you?" she said.

"I came by myself," Catherine said. "Do you know this little boy?"

"The Harper woman," Alicia said. "That's who."

"His name is Samuel Douglas Marshall," Catherine said. "He's only two."

"Shall I call security?" the man asked.

"He's very sick," Catherine said. "Did you know he was very sick? He has an illness called aplastic anemia."

Alicia seemed to flinch, just for a moment.

"He was in the newspapers," Catherine said. "Did you see his mother? She was in *The Courier*, an article—"

Alicia's face drained of color. She snatched at Catherine's elbow, dragging her to one side. "What makes you think," she hissed, "that I would want to see this child's mother?"

"He's very sick," Catherine repeated.

Alicia's grip tightened. "I have a son too," she said. "And I had a husband. Perhaps you've forgotten that, like everyone else."

Catherine tried to pull her arm away.

"I supported my husband, and I stood by him," Alicia continued, barely above a whisper. "I brought up his son. I helped his career. I sacrificed myself to him and what he needed. And when he at last succeeded, and began to enjoy some success, what happened?" She flicked at the photograph of Sam with her fingernail. "This child's mother took him away," she said.

Catherine blanched. She pressed Sam's photo to her chest.

"And that isn't all," Alicia said. "Not content with taking him away, she accused my son of murdering him." She stared at Catherine, looking her slowly up and down. "And she took John away from you," she added. "But evidently that didn't mean as much to you as it did to me."

Catherine returned the stare. She took a long moment to reply. "People say a lot of things when they are hurt," she murmured at last. "Perhaps you are the same."

Alicia bridled at this. She straightened and started to turn away. Catherine stepped up next to her on the stairs. "They regret it afterward," she said. "Just as Jo has regretted it."

"I am not interested," Alicia said.

"John didn't leave just because of what Jo said," Catherine told her. "He stayed here after the funeral, didn't he? But in the end he couldn't bear it. And that has nothing to do with you, or me, or Jo. It's to do with John and his father. That's why he went and that's what keeps him away, and all our love can't bring him back until that is resolved, Mrs. Marshall."

For a second Catherine saw that her words had hit home. Just for the briefest flash she glimpsed a realization in Alicia's face.

"Won't you forgive her?" Catherine asked. "What John carries in his heart is not Jo's fault." She paused and then added, "And she is very sorry."

Alicia raised her eyebrows. "Oh, is she?" she said sarcastically. "Oh, well. That makes everything perfectly all right, then."

Catherine blushed. "I don't know about your husband very much," she admitted. "But I know about your son, Mrs. Marshall. I know how much he loved his father."

Alicia stared at her.

"He needed to be with him," Catherine continued. "He wanted that more than anything."

"You know nothing at all," Alicia said.

Catherine's face flushed. It took a great deal to make her angry, but she still felt the dismissive, insulting flick on Sam's photo. "Did you read the newspaper article?" she asked.

"No."

Catherine shook her head. She looked at Alicia closely, as if she could read her mind. "I don't believe you," she responded. "I think you read every word."

Alicia turned. "James, would you mind?" she called to the man still standing close by. "This person really shouldn't be here."

"I think you read it," Catherine repeated, in a low voice strung with tension. "But you still don't understand. Sam is very sick." She held up the photograph. "I think he looks like his father," she said. "Is that why you won't look at it? He looks just like Doug."

Alicia's mouth trembled slightly.

"He's a very sweet little boy, isn't he?" Catherine said. "His father's eyes." She pushed the photo under Alicia's nose. "Except you can't really see his eyes very well just now," she told her. "He's taking drugs to try to cut infection. His eyes are swollen," she said. "And he cries a lot, but we try not to let him cry too much, because a child with aplastic anemia mustn't cry."

This time it was she who grabbed Alicia's arm. "Do you know why that is?" she said. "Because his system's breaking down. He mustn't raise his blood pressure. He has nothing to fight injuries to himself. Nothing to combat bleeding."

She tried to shake Alicia, as if she needed to wake her.

"He was fit and well," she said, "and he looked like his father, and now he's sick, and he looks like death. Like the walking dead. You understand what I'm saying?" Her voice shook with emotion. "He's dying. He's dying right now, your husband's son. And his mother—this person you call the Harper woman—she's at home right now. You know what she's doing?" she demanded. "She's sitting with her son. He won't eat. He likes ice cream, but she's not allowed to give him ice cream. She's trying to make him drink milk. He can only drink one kind of milk, and he doesn't like it, and she's been sitting with him since five o'clock this morning, and he's been sick, vomiting, and the doctor has been to him, and he has had an injection, and now . . ."

Catherine gasped for breath. She steadied herself against the wall.

"This . . . *Harper woman*," she whispered. "She is trying to keep her son alive, and she doesn't know how to do it, or what else she can do."

There was a silence for a moment.

"You think I don't understand that," Alicia murmured.

Catherine looked up at her. "I am sorry," she said. "But"—she pushed the hair back from her face, and looked down again at Sam's photograph—"Sam is the only brother that John will ever have," she said.

The two women stood face to face. A small knot of people had gathered at the foot of the stairs. The other trustees of the Academy glanced at each other, unsure as to whether they ought to intervene.

"This little boy needs his brother," Catherine said. "He needs him right now."

"I don't know where he is," Alicia said.

Catherine almost screamed in frustration. "You don't lie to me, Mrs. Marshall," she said. "You don't do that!"

"I don't know where he is," Alicia repeated, her voice rising in response.

Catherine looked away, down into the body of the hall. There, in the cabinets, she could see the Franklin artifacts. The fragments that

McClintock and Kane had brought back from King William Island. So many people had gone looking for Franklin. So many boats, so many men. All searching, just as they were searching now for John. And all that had ever been found of Franklin's ships were a few tattered remains. She could see the sepia image of Crozier from here.

She looked back at Alicia. "Has he gone to Gjoa Haven?" she asked. "Did you give him the money to go there? Is that where we should look?"

Alicia did not respond.

"Gjoa Haven," Catherine repeated. "It's a small town on a place called King William Island, in the Arctic."

Alicia dropped her eyes to the floor, her mouth tightened in a thin line.

"Don't you see," Catherine whispered, "we are all afraid. We have all lost someone. Please, Mrs. Marshall," she added softly, "don't let us lose anyone else."

Alicia turned her back and walked on up the stairs.

Catherine watched her until she was out of sight, slow tears running down her face. She glanced back then at the hall, where the other trustees were still standing, eyeing her uncertainly.

She picked up her bag and put the photograph back inside it. Then she walked past them to the display cabinets, pausing for a moment by the images of Franklin and his first officer, and the heart-wrenching evidence of their decline.

She put her palm on the cold glass.

"Where are you?" she whispered. "Where are you all?"

Thirty-one

THE city was heavy with heat. It was Sunday morning, barely eight o'clock. As Bill Elliott walked down Senate House Passage, he thought that he had never known Cambridge this warm in August. Any August. It might have been midafternoon; you could feel the humidity, and the pressure in the air. He looked up as he came out opposite King's; thunderclouds building out on the Fens, big rollers. Eerie to see their distant towers rising already over the sun-barred trees.

Jo had said to come early. But he thought that he had probably been too early, because when he got to the house, the curtains were still drawn on the floors above. He didn't like to knock; he knew what kind of night they might have had, and how precious sleep was. He had turned away and started to walk instead, to kill an hour in the quietest part of the day.

He had seen her last week, at the hospital.

Jo Harper looked much older now. She was not the twenty-something who had paced the wards that first day, fretting at her child being tested and hooked up to blood, and demanding to know what the problem was. She was not the same young woman who had wept into a handkerchief with relief at it only being anemia. She was weary now, and the attitude had gone.

She had lines around her eyes now. She had cut her hair short. The style didn't really suit her.

"You needn't say that I look bloody awful," she had said, smiling a little as she had seen his eyes stray to the new style. She'd run her hand over the boyish crop. "But I haven't time for anything else."

It wasn't exactly awful. It was a little cruel, hard on her, revealing the nakedness of her eyes, the high cheekbones.

"You must eat," he'd told her.

"I do," she'd told him. He didn't believe her.

It was too early for King's College Chapel to be open to the public. He skirted the entrance, glancing up at its ethereal face. Beautiful simplicity, a triumph of grace. He wished Jo Harper were alongside him now, so that he could stop and show her the product of man's faith.

He went to the river down Garrett Hostel Lane. The river was low; the drought had taken its toll here, as everywhere. It had been eighty degrees in the east of England in the last month. He looked down at the Cam from the bridge and saw the muddy bottom of the water. He thought of Sam, mesmerized by the electric fan they had brought in alongside his bed during the last transfusion. Small things could distract the child now; his world had contracted to tunnel vision. He no longer fretted to run about. He wanted his mother, and his Beanie Baby toy, and the flexi-straws on feeding cups.

The boy reminded Elliott of the pictures of children discovered in Romanian orphanages years ago, fascinated and abstracted only by the pattern of their fingers against the cot bars. They had had no world beyond the bars, and Sam was now uninterested in anything but immediate detail: the straw, the toy, the hands of the person next to the bed. Illness and isolation were tiring, draining, confining. Colors shifted away. Causes diminished. Games faded.

Elliott bunched fists on the bridge parapet.

Last month Jo had brought a photograph album into the hospital. She had been trying to distract Sam with it, and when Bill came in, she had shown it to him.

"This is Sam and John's father," she had said, and smiled shyly. "The owner of the rare haplotype, the awkward cuss."

She'd handed him the pictures with pride. Douglas Marshall smiled back at her. Douglas Marshall on a beach somewhere. Douglas Marshall on an icy shoreline.

"He had a fixation," Jo had said. "He passed that to his son too. Franklin."

The name had been in the news so much recently, as a result of Jo's *Courier* article, that Elliott felt that he knew the story backward. Jo and Catherine Takkiruq were so sure that John had gone to the Arctic, to a place called King William Island, that Canadian and Nunavut newspapers had carried Sam's story. Appeals had been made to every organization that ran any kind of transport out there. John's picture had been posted in Canadian airports.

"I forgot about Franklin," Jo had told him. "Can you imagine that? Franklin got Doug and me together. We were going to do a program on him at one time. And yet, since Sam was born, I hadn't given those ships a single thought."

She'd been in quite high spirits that day. "He'll come back," she had said confidently. "He's a good kid. He'll come."

But John hadn't come.

Four weeks. No one had heard of him, either in England, or Nunavut, or Canada. Even Catherine's father, in Arctic Bay, had not heard any news of him. John Marshall had simply not turned up to follow Franklin's footsteps.

Elliott had witnessed Jo Harper's savage disappointment.

He longed to tell her what he knew. What professional guidelines told him was more politic to keep private. He had been wrestling with this problem, witnessing Jo's hesitation.

She knew he was not supposed, ethically, to disclose if a donor had been found, let alone if John were a match. She was pursuing John with metaphorical fingers crossed, placing all her hopes in the belief that he could match Sam.

But she didn't know for sure.

No one did, except the Norberry Trust, and himself.

And that knowledge weighed very heavy.

Elliott turned away from the river, and went back to St. Bene't Street.

In the hushed road the church was already open, and Holy Eucharist had begun. He hesitated before opening the door, anxious not to disturb the service. Going in quietly, he took a place at the back and closed his eyes.

St. Bene't was the oldest building in the city, built in the reign of King Canute. Elliott had used to come here regularly when he was a student, to hear the bells. The earliest bell was dated 1588. The altar in the south aisle was medieval. The widely splayed windows were thirteenth century. Men had worshiped and prayed here for centuries.

He leaned forward now, elbows on knees, and prayed too.

He got back to the house at ten minutes to nine.

He found that the TV crew had now arrived; their van, and a couple of four-wheel drives, were parked on the double yellow lines. As he looked in the open door, he could see Jo down the hall, Sam on her hip, his head on her shoulder. She glanced around as she heard his footstep on the flagstone floor.

"Hello, Bill," she said, smiling. "You nearly missed our big moment." She handed him a cup of coffee. "We decided on the garden," she said, and nodded toward the back of the house.

The chairs were set on the lawn, under the lilac tree.

"Looks very professional," he said.

"Yes," she murmured. "Hope I don't fluff it." She gave him a helpless look. He touched her arm as he looked at Sam. The child stared at him silently. He touched the boy's cheek, ran his finger down the fine downy skin. Jo looked at Elliott. Her expression was unreadable as she turned and walked into the garden.

"We're ready for you," the director said.

Jo sat down on the chair facing the camera, rearranging her skirt, and making sure that Sam was comfortable. They took a light reading.

"Hey, Sam," the director said, taking something from his pocket, "want to hold this?" He held out a Beanie Baby.

Sam took one look at it and began to cry.

There was a murmur of concern.

"Hey," Jo said, turning her son to face her, "what's up?"

Sam arched his back.

"He's tired," Jo said. "I'm sorry."

"No matter." The director reached instead to the grass behind him and handed Jo a clapper board. Sam looked at it out of the corner of his eye, and his hitched sobs petered out.

"Ready?"

"Yes," Jo said.

Bill Elliott found a lump coming to his throat.

"Turning," someone called.

Jo lifted her face to the camera.

"This is my son," she said, smiling. "His name is Sam. Just under three months ago we found out that Sam was ill."

Sam, intrigued by the clapper board, had turned his head away.

Elliott closed his eyes, seeing the negative imprint of the tree, the woman, the child.

"Like any two-year-old," Jo was continuing, "Sam likes to get into all sorts of trouble." She stroked his shoulder. "And like any mother, I'm used to getting him out." She gently pulled Sam around so that he was facing the camera.

There was an awful silence in the garden, as Sam at last looked directly into the lens.

He had been a handsome, mischievous little boy with a thick head of straw-colored hair and startlingly blue eyes, not so long ago. But the face that would reach into every home on every TV screen the following weekend was not handsome or mischievous anymore.

He had lost a great deal of hair. His skin was yellow.

Worst of all, Elliott thought, was that look in Sam's eyes. He had seen it a thousand times before. It was filled with a knowledge of pain. Elliott had often thought before that there came a point—to some early, to others later—when a child, and the parents of that child, inherited an expression that was not quite of this world. They went to places of the spirit that were so cold, so frightening, that it changed them forever, and the evidence appeared in the expression of their eyes. They were different inside. Not just because of the illness, but because of the peculiar and particular journey that they had made in their hearts. They were travelers, all. And in countries where no human soul could survive for long.

Tears filled Bill's eyes. He looked down at the ground, frowning. Hoping no one had seen him, as he quickly rubbed them away.

"But this time I can't get Sam out of trouble," Jo was softly saying. "He's got something called aplastic anemia, and if you're like me, you'll think . . . well, that doesn't sound so bad." She smiled. "But unfortunately, it is bad. Sam needs a bone-marrow transplant."

She paused. She, too, seemed to be struggling with her emotions.

The crew looked at each other. The director, watching her, held up a restraining hand. *Wait for her.*

Jo finally raised her head. "That's a pretty bad position to be in," she said. "And Sam needs a donor. A bone-marrow donor."

She glanced, very briefly, at the director. She was making a picture sign at her, to demonstrate that she should carry on, and that images would be overlaid at this point.

"This is John Marshall," she said. "He's Sam's half-brother. It's just possible that John could be a bone-marrow match for Sam. It's a kind of straw that we're clutching at right now." She gave a hesitant smile, took a deep breath. "The problem—and it's a big problem—is that we don't know where John is, and we wonder if you could help us. John is an archaeological student. He used to live in Cambridge."

The director's hand made a slicing motion. The image was back with Jo.

"Sam and I would like to ask you today if you have seen John Marshall," Jo said. "He might be in this country, or abroad. Perhaps you've traveled recently, and you've seen him. At an airport, or in another country. He's tall, and fair haired, and he . . . well, he looks quite a bit like his father, Douglas Marshall."

Bill Elliott quietly moved closer, across the grass.

"The James Norberry Trust is an organization that matches up bone marrow donors to patients like Sam," Jo said. "There are millions of people all over the world who offer to donate their bone marrow," Jo said. "And it can make all the difference. It can save a life. Right now. This minute. Today. John Marshall was registered with the Trust."

Sam leaned back in her arms and, as if on cue, gazed up at his mother.

"So, if you think that you could be a donor, or if you think you have seen John Marshall," she said, "please contact the number at the bottom of the screen today. And"—she bit her lip—"thanks very much," she murmured. "Thanks."

They were all finished by half past nine. Bill Elliott had made his thirty-second shot with Jo. Between the beginning and the end of her appeal, there would be other shots of him sitting with case files in his office, and talking to nurses on the ward. Cut in through both Jo and

Bill and the images of John would be the work of the Trust. The item, originally sponsored by the Trust, was due to be screened the following Sunday, in the traditional appeal slot just before the late-afternoon news.

In terms of publicity it wasn't a huge amount. But it certainly was better than nothing.

"You did well," Jo said, as they sat together after the crew had left.

"Not if you saw the stuff they took yesterday," Bill said. "They showed me the rough cut in that Handycam they carry. . . . I walk like a duck." Jo began to laugh.

"Imagine living to my advanced age and never knowing you walk like a duck," he said. "It's appalling. I've got to balance books on my head or go to classes, or something."

"You do not walk like a duck," she said.

"It was folding my arms behind my back. That put the cap on it."

Jo laughed. He saw her eyes trail up to the bedroom window above them, where Sam could be heard fretting.

"His temperature is all to hell," she murmured.

"I ought to go," he said.

She glanced at her watch. "Are you late?"

"No," he said, "but I like to be early. I get one Sunday a fortnight with the kids, and I don't like to make them wait."

She stood up. "It must be tough for you," she said.

He shrugged. "It's amazing what you can get used to."

"To go to their new house and everything," Jo said.

"See someone else in your place, yes," he agreed.

She moved to the door of the house, which led through to the kitchen.

"Jo," he said, "you know that, if they find a match, you must go to Great Ormond Street for the transplant."

She looked back at him. "I'm glad you believe in a match," she said.

"You have to believe it," he said. "Plan for it."

"Excuse me if my faith is a little thin," she said.

"You know what my head nurse tells me?" he offered. "You go in flesh, and you come out steel."

"What?" she said, frowning suddenly.

"When you face a crisis," he said, "it's like a furnace. You go in flesh and you come out steel."

She paused. The color had flooded to her face. He hesitated, wondering what the matter was. What he had said.

"I hate that stuff," she muttered.

"I'm sorry? What stuff?"

"God makes burdens for the broadest backs," she muttered. "All that stifling ridiculous sanctimonious crap."

He halted, shocked.

She was looking away from him, into the shadows of the house. "I had a priest here yesterday," she said. "Apparently he's the local vicar." She sighed. "I wouldn't know, because I don't go to church. I don't even know how he knew who I was." She picked up a tea cloth from the nearest chair, folded it abstractedly. "Do you know what he said to me?" she asked.

"No. Tell me."

"He asked me if I could give my sorrow to God." She threw the cloth down and turned to him, hand on hip.

"And can you?" he asked.

She threw up her hands. "Oh, don't *you* start," she exclaimed.

"You don't believe in God," he said.

"Have you looked at Sam? Do you blame me?" She glared at him. "You know, Catherine has a faith," she said. "And it looks like you have."

"Yes," he said.

She shook her head angrily. "Well, tell me," she said, "how do you do that? I don't get it. Catherine watches Sam as much as I do. He's almost like her brother or son. And she just—she just doesn't get angry."

"And you're angry," he said.

She advanced on him, eyes blazing. "Bloody right I'm angry," she said. "You want me to think there's some logic or reason behind all this? Some omnipotent being? You want me to pray? Ask Him for help?" Her mouth trembled. "I can't ask Him. Do you understand that?" she said. "I can't pray anymore."

They stood, face to face.

Bill Elliott had the intelligence to say nothing at all.

He tried to touch her, but she didn't see him. Instead she caught sight of the coffee cups, waiting to be washed, on the drainboard.

She snatched up the nearest and threw it at the wall.

"Jo," he said, flinching as the pieces scattered over the floor.

"Nothing will happen." She sobbed. "John won't be a match, he will never come back. Sam is going to die."

"You mustn't believe that," he said.

"Don't start telling me what to believe again!"

"I'm not," he said. "I'm telling you that you must hold on."

"I can't," she cried. "I can't bear another day of watching him go from me. I can't do it anymore."

"You must," he said. "If you don't believe, Sam will sense it."

"I can't help it," she said. He saw the utter devastation in her face. "I'm nowhere. I am actually nowhere. I don't have any compass points." She gasped. "I don't know where to go or what to do. I can't see a way out. And all this talk of John, it's what I said for the TV just now, it's just a straw, isn't it? I'm clutching at straws." She sat heavily down in the nearest chair and plunged her head into her hands. "He isn't a match." She groaned. "He isn't a match. Nobody is."

"He is," Elliott said.

There was a pause. Then she lifted a tear-streaked face to his. "What?"

"John *is* a match," he repeated.

She got slowly to her feet.

"Christine Lord told me last week," he said.

She stared at him, open mouthed. "She isn't allowed to say," she murmured. "Neither are you."

"No, not really," he agreed. "But pressure gets to all of us. And I wanted to know."

"He's a match," she echoed, hardly daring to believe him. "How good a match?"

"Almost perfect."

"Perfect . . ." she breathed.

He took a scrap of paper out of his pocket. He had written a number on it. *AZMA 552314.* He pressed it now into Jo's hands. He had a desperate, really desperate, urge to take her in his arms, to hold her, to give her strength, to take the pain from her. But he stopped himself, fearing to take advantage of her and of the moment.

"This is the donor number of the match," he said. He closed Jo's fingers over the piece of paper. "Among John's things will be a donor card. On the card will be written that number. If you ever wanted to double-check, that would be your proof."

"A match," she repeated. She closed her fist over the paper and brought it to her lips, still looking at him. "Oh . . . thank you so very much," she whispered.

Thirty-two

THE snow was falling softly, drifting without wind. It had traveled for days down the empty stretches of Victoria Strait, silent, phantomlike, heavy with thick, palm-sized flakes. A thousand-mile curtain being drawn across the sea.

In such weather the whales in Lancaster Sound broke the surface in huge numbers, raising themselves out of the life-rich water and into the fantastic silence of the air. There was no sky anymore, only a compressed white world. There were no stars at night. There was not a breath of wind.

It was very rare to have such a prolonged snowfall. In any one year the falls in the Arctic might not be more than four or five inches, at most. But 1848 was not a year like any other year. This was the year that the Eskimo, for decades to come, would call *tupilak*. The ghost.

Nothing lived in it.

Or, at least, nothing lived in it for long.

Three months before, the men of *Erebus* and *Terror* had found four miles of ice ridges between them and the King William coast. They set out at eleven o'clock on April 21, and had only gone for an hour before they reached the first ridge. One of the officers, Fairholme, had climbed to the top of it, to assess the route forward. The jagged fold of ice was forty feet high, and when he got to the top, he saw the ridge extending at least a mile in each direction, and, directly ahead the ice lay scattered about in acres of rubble. Sometimes, between the blocks, the frozen floe showed through, looking like a flat sand beach rippled by retreating waves. He had turned and called down to the first sledge party.

"There's no other way," he shouted.

They ascended the ridge.

Four men went first, trying to flatten the ice with spades and picks, to make a channel through which to haul the boats. Once done, a dozen men were attached to the front of the boat with harnesses and ropes; the remaining eighteen were stationed on either side and at the back. They were already cold, but the effort of simply standing their ground on the racked ice shelves made their feet colder still, as they jammed their boots into the ledges to get purchase.

As they leaned on the ropes, those at the front felt the weight dig into their shoulders, arms, and backs, almost cutting the blood circulation from their chests and throats, such was the load. Those hauling at the sides slipped and fell, slipped and fell, the ropes slipping through their gloves. Each loosening of the ropes dropped them into the snow; they took hold again of cables coated with snow and ice. Eventually, even before they got to the top of the first ridge, their gloves were soaked through, their boots caked with ice, their coats and trousers wet.

The boats on their wooden runners were hell on earth to pull, let alone lift. The contents, wrapped in tarpaulins and secured with rope, might as well have been blocks of marble. The sweat broke out on their skin and froze. Their hair, slick with sweat, froze on their scalps. The sun goggles cut into their faces.

It took an hour and a half to negotiate the very first ridge. By the time that they stood on the summit, it was one in the afternoon. And as each man labored to the top, he fell silent. For there was nothing else to see when he got there but another ridge, and another, and another.

Not a man said a word. They descended the ridge, heaving and leaning backward on the ropes to prevent the boat from careering to the bottom on its own. And as soon as they reached the bottom themselves, they walked hardly ten paces before they started to climb again.

It was six o'clock before they stopped for the night.

They put up the tents, muscles aching, lungs scorched with the effort. Everything that they touched froze and stuck to their fingers; within minutes the canvas tents were rigid, their material cold enough by morning to have snapped in pieces had the breath of the occupants not kept a tiny current of warm air. As the men camped, the cooks melted down ice, and brewed tea from a fire that took an age to take light. They ate lukewarm bouilli from the tins, and raisins that they had to keep in their mouths before the fruit thawed. Crozier recorded a temperature of minus thirty-two that night.

It was four days before they reached King William.

It was almost as if Fitzjames had waited to get there.

The second-in-command had been carried in the boat for the last mile, wrapped in bearskins, and when the surgeon came to look at him once they had erected the first tent, the man looked peaceful.

"James," Goodsir said, "can you hear me?"

Fitzjames barely opened his eyes.

"James . . ."

"I am tired," Fitzjames said.

Unpacking the boat for the cooking utensils, they found that even the whiskey that had been under Fitzjames's feet was frozen solid.

"Don't sleep," Goodsir said. With his own hands numbed beyond feeling, the surgeon chafed Fitzjames hands, chest, and arms. He leaned him against his own body and rubbed his back through the thick wool coat and sealskin wrap.

Fitzjames's gaze flickered to the tent flap and came back to the surgeon. He whispered something.

"What is it?" Goodsir asked.

"Apple blossom now," he murmured. "In England."

Goodsir held his hand. "We shall all be in England before long," he told him.

Fitzjames shook his head. Goodsir listened to his shallow, scratchy breathing. Outside, the wind picked up. The last party was having trouble pitching their tent. Goodsir could see two men sitting on their sledge, heads drooping. He dreaded that bodily look. *Sleepy comfort,* the men called it. The desire to sleep when you did not feel the cold any longer.

He looked back at Fitzjames.

In the short interval of his looking away the man had died.

They buried him in the morning, using precious energy to cut

down through nine inches of ice to lower him into the scant water of
the shoreline, the ground behind them being far too hard to dig.

Finding the cairn left by Gore the previous year, they had unearthed his message and added their own.

Fitzjames had insisted upon writing the account; it had taken him
almost an hour. Crozier had indulged him the time, and was glad now
that he had. For James had fretted at his own invalidity. He had sat
painfully upright inside the first pitched tent, composing the message
while one of the able seamen had held a light for him.

25th April 1848.

H.M.Ships Terror *and* Erebus *were deserted on the 22nd April, 5
leagues NNW of this, having been beset since 12 September 1846. The
Officers and Crews consisting of 105 souls—under the command of
Captain F.R.M. Crozier here—in Lat 69 37' 42", Long 98 41'. This
paper was found by Lt. Irving under the cairn supposed to have been
built by Sir James Ross in 1831, 4 miles to the northward—where it had
been deposited by the late Commander Gore in June 1847. Sir James
Ross' pillar had not however been found, and the paper has been transferred to this position, which is that in which Sir J. Ross' pillar was
erected—Sir John Franklin died on 11th June 1847 and the total loss by
deaths in the expedition has been to this date 9 Officers and 15 Men.*

James Fitzjames, Captain H.M.S. Erebus.

The message had been shown to Crozier when Fitzjames had
finished.

Crozier had looked at it for some moments, regretting that so long
had been spent describing the location of the cairn pillars. There was
no room left for him to note their proposed direction, other than to
squeeze a few words at the very bottom of the page.

F.R.M. Crozier, Captain and Senior Officer
And start on to-morrow 26th for Backs Fish River.

They lightened the sledges here. If they were to encounter any
more ridges, they needed less weight.

They threw aside clothes and cooking stoves, pickaxes, tin cups, a medicine chest with all its contents, a sextant, a gun case, canteens, and books.

Crozier almost screamed in frustration. He looked at the pile left behind—stacked neatly in rows—and saw the stoves and axes and shovels, but felt sick at heart and crushed. He walked over and kicked at the stoves with his boot.

"We have four more, sir," Fairholme told him. "They are all duplicates."

Crozier stared at him. "We're overloaded."

"There's nothing else. Sir."

"Show me your pack."

Fairholme was shocked. "*My* pack?"

"Show me your pack!"

Fairholme turned out his things from the sledge. Crozier unwrapped a brass curtain rod and a piece of lightning conductor, and a brass handle and plate. "What are these for?" he demanded.

"To deflect lightning," Fairholme said. "It was your own instruction, sir. Lightning conductors on the tents."

Crozier paused a second. He couldn't remember what his orders had been only the day before, let alone when they had left the ships. "Leave them," Crozier ordered. "Brass handle, brass plate . . ."

"For barter," Fairholme told him. "Metal . . . your order, sir."

Crozier flushed scarlet. "Don't recount my own orders to me!" he shouted. "Leave them!" He hauled the package from the sledge himself and threw it onto the pile. Incensed, he walked up and down the waiting rows of men. "If there is anything of weight in these packs, dump them," he yelled. "Everything of weight except weapons and cooking apparatus. Everything!"

The men did not move.

"Everything!" Crozier yelled.

No man stirred.

Crozier stared at them, seeing the exhaustion. He knew that they couldn't think what was in their packs, most of them. Let alone decide what to jettison. He felt morbidly, dangerously angry. Acid rose in his throat. Their implacable, dogged expressions stared back at him:

dumb, loyal beasts to the slaughter. Ice flurries, vicious little ripples blowing off the packed snow, cut at their faces.

"Move on," he ordered.

He caught a look of the deepest disappointment and injustice from Fairholme, but he couldn't bring himself to say a word to the man.

They walked.

The journey along the King William coastline was a little better; they made an average of two miles a day, and the temperatures were up, almost ten below.

For a whole day they walked through snow gullies. The ridges of ice were not as bad as those by the ships, but they were bad enough for all three sledge parties to find it easier to follow the troughs between the ridges, which were fortunately lying northwest to southeast. The wind was less in the lee of the ridges, but the snow was worse, thick and cloying.

Augustus Peterman had been the lead man on the first sledge, and only relinquished his place at midday. He handed over his rue raddie— the line arranged to draw as near as possible to the line of the center of gravity—to one of the ship's stokers, a fierce little Liverpudlian, whose hands still bore the grimy marks of his trade.

"You did well," Crozier told the boy.

Gus looked at him with empty eyes.

The team, having changed men, tried to get the sledge started again, but it was terribly hard. The snow was knee deep, and the weight of the load drove the runners into it, so that there was only any real forward movement when a little speed had been achieved. Both Gus and Crozier joined the team at the back, pushing and heaving until the forward runners lifted slightly, and the men leaned hard on the traces, hauling with their bodies at a thirty-degree angle to the ground.

No one commented anymore at an officer doing the men's work. A pair of hands standing idly by could not be tolerated.

Once they were moving, Gus stood up. He passed his hands over his eyes.

"What is it?" Crozier asked him

"Nothing, sir."

Crozier looked hard at him. The lad's eyes were running with water, smarting at the snow. It wasn't sunny, but nevertheless the color and cold made the eyes stream, the head pound.

"Where are your goggles?"

"I can't wear them, sir."

"Why not?"

Gus looked at his feet, his arms hanging by his sides. "Imaginings," he said.

"Imaginings?" Crozier repeated. He glanced around. The sled and its team were ahead by thirty yards. "You must wear the glasses," he said.

"When I get warm, the sweat makes my eyes sting," Gus told him. "And then, when I'm not pulling, the sweat ices."

"If you walk without them, you will get snow blindness, and then someone will have to lead you," Crozier pointed out.

"I don't care," Gus whispered.

"Put them on," Crozier ordered.

Gus did so with exaggerated slowness. When he had finished, he looked at the crews ahead. "How many are there?" he asked.

Crozier frowned at him. "How many what?"

"Men, sir."

"On this team? Thirty-one, Gus."

"Thirty-one," Gus muttered. "Thirty-one."

Crozier took his arm, worried by the question and by the dead note in Gus's voice. "Walk with me," he said.

Gus did as he was told.

"Wipe your face of sweat, and cover it," Crozier told him.

"I am cold inside," Gus said.

"Wrap the scarf tighter."

"Inside my skin," Gus murmured.

Crozier pushed the boy in front of him and began to talk, as their boots sank into the drifts.

"It's not so hard to survive here," Crozier said. He watched Gus's swaying, veering gait. "Think forward. Think what you'll do when you get home."

The boy was silent.

"Men have lived through worse than this," Crozier said. "Three hundred and fifty men walked over the ice off Greenland in 1777, Gus.

They were off a whaler that was shipwrecked. They reached the Danish villages on the west coast."

There was no reply, but Gus stumbled and went forward on his hands, righting himself only with difficulty.

"Ten years ago British ships were beset in Baffin Bay," Crozier continued. He reasoned to himself that his continual voice could keep Augustus upright and moving. "The ice held them just as it held us."

Gus was brushing snow from himself. His movements were slow, as lethargic as an old man's.

Crozier touched his shoulder. "Every single ship of that group reached England," he said. "Three years before that the *Shannon* out of Hull—"

Gus looked at him wearily. "I knew the mate of the *Shannon*," he said.

"There you are. You see? It is possible to survive."

"Sixteen men and three boys were swept away," Gus said. "And when the two Danish brigs found the rest, there was no water and no food." He stared into Crozier's face. "I knew that man, in the public houses," he said. "He never went out on the boats again. He drank. He said it was his thirst. He had . . . a thirst."

Crozier pulled Gus's drooping head back up. "But he lived," he insisted.

"Aye," Gus muttered. "There was a life."

Crozier shook him hard. "What a man does with his life is his own affair," he said. "God returned his life to him. We all have choices, then, what we do. Whether we live out our days drowning the memory. Whether we stand up to fight again. That is God's gift to us. The choices in our lives. Our freedom to chose."

He turned Gus to look at the struggling crew ahead of them.

"Look hard at those men, Gus," he said. "God will not give life back to every one of them. Perhaps He will not give life at all again. But we must live out that life to its last breath. We don't let it go, Gus. We don't despair of a gift like that."

Gus's mouth trembled. He was struggling not to cry.

Crozier lowered his voice. "Are you very cold?" he asked gently.

"Not so very cold," Gus mumbled. "Not now."

"Can you walk on?"

"Yes," Gus said.

"We'll walk on to Backs River," Crozier told him. "All the way."

"Yes," Gus whispered. "The way that . . ." The lad paused and frowned, as if puzzled. "Thirty-one," he said softly to himself. "There are thirty-one men in my team."

Crozier patted his back. "That's right, Gus," he said. "That's right. Good lad."

During that night, the tenth away from the ships, there was no snow and no storm. A perfect silence fell upon the camp.

Gus lay with the sick. He closed his eyes, and put his hands to his ears so he couldn't hear their keening breaths. Goodsir had put him here, at Crozier's instruction, but he tried not to think that he could be as bad as those men around him. His teeth ached, and his mouth was sore, but he was not like Kinningthwaite, who had been laid on his side and stared at Gus's face. Kinningthwaite could not breathe. His chest rattled. A bruise blackened one side of his face. The man lay with his eyes open, glassily staring. He looked like a puppet with a waxy face, splashed with dye. His eyebrows and beard were full of crystallized ice, adding to the effect that he was not real, but painted.

"Kinningthwaite," Gus whispered, "can you hear me?"

The man's gaze flickered.

"Are they back?" Gus asked.

Kinningthwaite had told him, when Gus had been given the task of feeding him, that there were people at Gus's shoulder.

"What people?" Gus had asked.

"Dead," Kinningthwaite said. He had given a horrible smile.

Gus had weaved back from him, spoon and cup hovering in his astonished grasp.

"There," Kinningthwaite said. "Count them."

Gus's reply had been immediate. "Thirty-one," he told Kinningthwaite. "They're not dead, Michael," he said. "They are us. We are alive. We'll be fifty miles south of Point Victory tomorrow," he added, regaining his grip on the cup and clutching it to his chest. "We have come sixty-five miles, Michael."

"Count them," Kinningthwaite said.

Gus couldn't look at him anymore. He turned away, heart pinching a painful little thread in his throat. He counted too. He counted all day.

Was it a sign of this sickness? he wondered. He couldn't help the numbering. Faces merged in front of his face. Sometimes the team looked like five men, and sometimes they looked like fifty, and sometimes one man had more than one face. He had been thinking all day of the mate from the *Shannon*. He used to count too.

He had counted the dead and the living.

Even if they didn't count out loud, their brain counted for them, over and over again.

How many were left?

How many were walking with them?

He knew what Kinningthwaite meant. After you stopped being pierced by the cold, wrung through to the bone, you began dreaming while you walked. Watching your feet as they plunged into snow, slithered over ice, slipped on ridges, you often thought that there were other feet walking alongside you. You heard voices. Women, sometimes. He heard the voices of the women that his mother knew, as they hung washing on lines between houses, or cleaned their doorsteps, or sat outside, gossiping, cursing, calling.

He heard his mother singing. Country songs from when she was a girl. He heard her singing his name. She became his mother again, and he became her child again, with all the long-forgotten softness of her at night, in the last flames of the fire, cradled in her arm in the fireside chair. He would remember being two or three years old, and warm in his mother's lap, while heat or rain or sleet hammered in the Hull street, and the wind or the summer evening brought the noise of the sea straight up from the docks and beaches.

And he would count all the people gathered beyond her chair, and look down, and find he was counting his own footprints in the snow.

He lay down in the tent in the dark now, and put his face into the blanket, and cried. Thirty-one. One hundred and three. Eight. Eighteen. One.

But it didn't really matter about the numbers now.

They were all alone, each man cast adrift, each man singly pursuing his Maker.

They reached Terror Bay by June.

In the six weeks that it had taken them to get there, they had lost twenty-eight of the original 104. Of the officers, John Irving—the man who had rescued Gus on the day they met the Eskimos—died six days after James Fitzjames.

As Crozier buried Irving, he wondered why Irving had left the navy eight years ago and emigrated to New South Wales, only to return six years later. He had always meant to ask him what had caused that particular about-face. Whatever quirk of fate it had been, it had now brought him here, a thirty-year-old man who had never really had the sea in his blood. Before committing him to the ice, Crozier took a medal from his coat to send home with his belongings: the second mathematical prize, awarded to John Irving by the Royal Naval College in 1830.

Richard Aylmore, the gun-room steward, was the next. He fell while pulling the last sledge, and had lain on the ice for some minutes before he could be made to stand. He never recovered, seemingly, from the fall, dying in less than twenty-four hours. Thomas Work and Josephus Geator and William Mark, all able seamen from the *Erebus*, were next; John Weekes, the carpenter who had made the oak runners for the sledges; Solomon Tozer, the sergeant of the royal marines for the *Terror*.

William Hedges, his corporal, and the cook John Diggle, who had been so afraid at Franklin's death, died in the very tracks of the boats they were following. Magnus Manson and William Shanks and David Sims, and John Handford, and Alexander Berry and Samuel Crispe, all seamen from the *Terror*, passed within three days of each other.

As they neared the southwest corner of King William, they could not bury the last that died. A fierce northwesterly wind was blowing. Those that remained had no strength. Instead, they wrapped poor Berry and Handford and Crispe in blankets, and scraped snow and stones over them. It was horrible, but it was not so bad as they had imagined. The bodies were already frozen as they said the last words over them, and so thin from disease and starvation that they were as light as tinderwood.

Crozier had almost lost sense of where they were, even of what they were doing, by the time they pitched camp fifty miles south of Point Victory. Ten more had died where they fell—in one morning, four within the space of an hour. Turning over one of the bodies, Crozier had seen the bloated, blackened mask of the scurvy. Exertion brought the blood to the face, hands, chest, and legs. And there it coagulated and filled the flesh. There was nowhere for it to go, it seemed. The circulation simply broke down within minutes. Sometimes—it was too awful, Crozier thought afterward, it was shameful—they were too tired to care about the dead. Cold and lethargy had atrophied their emotions; they had no grief left. Nothing to mourn with. Nothing to cry with. Nothing to feel.

They would look back and realize a man was down. They would stop and watch. Someone might go back to him, slipping and stumbling over the ice. But it was hopeless. Once down, they were dead. Crippled, asphyxiated. Empty hulks.

At Point Victory, Crozier felt more than tired; a huge sense of weariness had invaded him, seeping into his bones. His whole body felt enormously heavy.

Around him he could see that the rest of the men were fading. Of the sixty-six remaining, only perhaps three or four did not move with the same clumsy slow motion that he felt in himself. Their efforts at pitching tents, securing lines, and setting up sleeping quarters was terrible to witness. It took twice the time that it had when they had set off from the ships. It was now at least an hour and a half before the whole party could move off every morning; it was twice that, in the evening, to set up camp.

He sat down and tried to calculate how many days it would take to get to Backs Fish.

He could hardly figure in his head. Thirty days, perhaps. Forty, fifty. At one and a half miles a day, now that they were so slow.

The ridges of the open sea had gone, but the whole landscape was still one long sheet of ice. Hard to conceive it, but it was summer. The gneiss and limestone of the land should not only be showing through the ice, but in full view. He ought to have been able to distinguish the pockets of water, pools and rivulets, that Ross had claimed made up the body of King William. He ought to have been able to feed the men on the lichens that were supposed to cover most of the ground. They should have had hunting parties bringing down the deer that were reputed to move across this peninsula.

But there was nothing.

No ground, no lichen, no deer. No thaw at all, though this was the kindliest of all the Arctic months.

God had forgotten the summer above the Barren Grounds.

He brought out his charts and had them laid, with difficulty, on the single narrow chest that he had brought with him.

At a mile or so a day, they might reach Backs Fish in a month. August. He plunged his head into his hands at the very thought. Sir John had told him that, when he made his expedition in the 1820s, he, too, had reached the northern coast near the Coppermine in August, and that, contrary to what weather had been anticipated, ice drove in by the end of the month, and by September the Coppermine was choked with snow.

He stared at the map. No man knew what lay to the west of the Backs Fish, except that it was a strait of some kind. If they were lucky, the strait might lead directly to the point where Franklin had stood more than twenty years before. It could be hundreds of miles west, but that in itself was not a problem. If they were still able to launch boats, they might take advantage of what sea currents there were and sail directly toward the Pacific.

It might be a better option than trying to get up the endless rapids of Backs Fish.

With a little luck—and God surely owed them that, just a small fraction of the ordinary luck that any expedition leader before him had counted as normal—they would find enough fresh fish and game at the mouth of the river to sustain them. Enough to sail west or, perhaps a small party of them, to ascend the river.

A small party of them.

He stared out of the tent and considered.

Finally he called in Goodsir. Standing in the half-light of the evening, he thought that, of any of them, Harry Goodsir was the worst. He shuffled with a broken gait, bent over at the waist.

"How many are sick?" he asked him. "How many can travel on?"

Goodsir didn't reply for some time. "How many can walk to Backs Fish?" he asked eventually.

"Yes."

"None."

Crozier leaned forward. "Harry . . ." he said gently, "we must go on. An estimate."

Goodsir shrugged. "Twenty."

"How many are we now?"

"As of this evening, sixty-four."

They contemplated each other. Forty-four sick. Goodsir raised a hand to his face, to rub ice from his beard. His hand trembled too much to achieve the task. He fumbled at it for a few seconds, like a small child trying to master his coordination. Through the beard his mouth showed blue. His tongue rested on the swollen bottom lip.

"I've never seen scurvy like this before," Crozier murmured.

"Nor I," Goodsir said. He paused, trying to force coherence into his words.

Goodsir wanted to explain something of importance, something that had been occupying him all day. It was a stroke of insight, an answer to a puzzle that had bothered him for weeks. So many men fell dead as they worked, and the bruising . . .

The bruising under the skin meant a breakdown of the blood vessels, he realized. Perhaps the sudden deaths during exertion meant that the scurvy was in the heart. If vessels under the skin were failing, then the heart itself . . .

But the train of logic eluded him. He sat with his hands hanging between his knees, the perception swiftly fading.

Meanwhile Crozier had got to his feet. "I want you to make a hospital tent," he told Goodsir. "We will leave you with as much as we dare. I want you to stay here with MacDonald. Stanley and Peddie will come with me."

Crozier looked down at the man whose interests had so fascinated him before he was enlisted—the pathologist with a passion for natural science, who had so enthused at the prospect of Arctic exploration.

Goodsir's expression was almost blank.

"Mr. Stanley is too sick to walk, sir," Goodsir told him.

Thirty-three

THERE was no night now.

From May to July, twenty-four hours of sunshine was the great bear's world. She stood now on the edge of Simpson Strait, her head hung low with exhaustion. It was raining, the steady forty-mile-an-hour wind blowing the rain horizontally toward her. The sea ice was breaking up.

She had no idea if the cub were alive or dead. She had not been able to feed him. The seal were far out in the water, and she had had no luck in pursuing them. She had walked one hundred and eight miles, and she no longer knew the purpose of her movement. The cub lay on the rocky shoreline, curled slackly in upon itself. She regarded it with dull perplexity, until a movement in the water distracted her.

Offshore an adult male bear was still-hunting.

The water was relatively shallow, and a seal was feeding and diving, resurfacing in almost the same spot every time that it needed to breathe. The female bear onshore could not see the prey, but she could see the predator, lying motionless in the water every time the seal came back to the surface. He lay absolutely still, in imitation of floating pack ice, until he was only a few yards from his victim. Then, abruptly, he lunged, snapping his jaws together over its back. There was a flurry of water and blood, until the seal's body was flipped out onto the nearest ice, wriggling helplessly in its death throes.

The female had slumped to the ground, after scenting the kill. She had no wish to cross the male's path or interrupt his feeding. She lay inert, her cub at her back, waiting for the male to pass up the strait and leave her alone.

It was midnight when he came ashore.

She was lying with her back to the wind, in a pit dug from the gravel ridge of the beach, the cub pulled to her side. The smell awoke her. She lifted her head and saw a second fresh kill drawn up on the rocks, and the male walking, with a deceptive, careless, shambling gait, toward them.

In a moment she was on her feet.

The male skirted her, scenting the cub, interested in its immobility. He would have no compunction in killing it, if he could get close enough, and as he suddenly increased his speed, the female charged him.

She had one, and only one, advantage over him. He was heavier, well insulated, and slower than her undernourished bulk. She took him in the shoulder, fastening her teeth close to the bone, tearing his flesh and drawing blood. Surprised, but not deterred, he backed up, head still low, signaling his aggression.

She stood her ground.

If he could not get to the cub, it was highly likely that the male would kill her, feeding on her body before her offspring's. All that he needed was that the kill should be short, so that his thickly covered body would not overheat. If she held him off for half an hour or so, he would give up, intolerably hot, his temperature close to danger point.

She did not reason that her life should be given up for her son. She did not even register him anymore. This was a battle of instinct and not emotion, a determination for the survival of her own line. She would fight to the death for him.

Her second charge was harder than the first, expending most of her energy. She pounded his shoulder with her forelegs, as he snapped at her head, trying to find the softer spot below the jaw. This was not the ritual posturing of his early adult life, between himself and other young males, characterized by open-mouthed threats and the wrestle to pin the opponent off-balance on the ground. She was a greater challenge than he had anticipated, and he only managed to hold on to her for seconds. He backed away, grunting, his eyes on the body of the cub.

Then his pain registered.

He assessed her, as the blood colored his pristine coat.

Then, as quickly as he had come, he walked away.

She watched him, eyes narrowed, head raised, until his shape merged with the slate-gray-on-white coloring. He eased back into the ocean, swimming slowly, ignoring the seal, heading out to the harder ice floes.

She stood for almost an hour before catching the faint message on the air. It took her almost as long to rouse the cub, before they walked on. As she made the first few steps, she was aware of the new sensation at the base of her throat.

But she ignored it.

It was of no importance.

Thirty-four

SINCE Jo's Sunday-evening broadcast, all hell had been let loose.

The TV appeal had begun at six-twenty. It was just a five-minute slot. The first two minutes outlined the James Norberry Trust; then pictures of Doug Marshall came onto the screen. Excerpts from his series reminded viewers of the personality that had earned the series high ratings. They had chosen one program in particular, the broadcast from the Severn Estuary, where a Neolithic woodhenge had appeared from the sea at low water, and where Doug had insisted that the henge stay in situ.

Superimposed over that same shot came Sam's face. This was Sam at his first birthday, hands plunged into lime-green Jell-O and face transformed with delight.

And then Sam was shown as he was now, face swollen, arms bruised. Pasty colored, listless. Helpless.

The phones began ringing at the James Norberry Trust after the first of Doug's pictures went up. Every single phone was occupied as Sam's birthday photo appeared. And the switchboard was jammed by the time that the camera rested on him as he lay in Jo's arms under the lilac tree.

The trust had received forty-eight hundred calls from potential donors by Sunday midnight.

By Wednesday the figure had become twenty-six thousand.

The Courier, too, was swamped.

It had run a front-page picture of John on the Friday, and by the following week their post was full of letters, each claiming to have seen Doug's son. Unfortunately, it appeared that he was in several hundred places at once. In Thailand, on holiday. In New Zealand. In the south of France, or Ireland. And all over England.

"And so it goes on," Gina muttered.

She had done her share of the letter opening, staying late with Mike, painstakingly reading each one.

"If only the insane ones would leave us alone," she'd muttered, just last night. She'd flung a piece of closely written paper at Mike. "See that?" she demanded. "Some middle-aged woman in Cleveleys reckons she's got John tied up in her sitting room."

They'd exchanged reluctant smiles. Other letters stocked up on the Cleveleys pile. At the end of the day they dare not trash them, however. They locked them in a filing cabinet.

Just in case.

This morning, drumming her fingers on her desk, Gina thought awhile. She had heard all about John's passions and preoccupations from Jo long before; they had discussed him a countless number of times lately. Ignoring the fact that she had a meeting scheduled for five minutes ago, she logged on to the Internet and searched *polar bear.*

Alta Vista came up with dozens of sites. Choosing one at random, she spent ten minutes gazing at the explanation of the polar bear's plight. How global warming was shrinking their habitat, increasing the summers, shortening the periods of ice.

"Jesus," she muttered, scrolling down the page. "Fifteen thousand bears in the Canadian Arctic. Fifteen thousand distractions."

She pinched the bridge of her nose, trying to ward off a threatening headache.

She scanned through the net for the Canadian Hydrographic Service. Found it. Brought up the cloud/snow/ice conditions from the Service's satellites that showed the weather conditions in the area that fascinated John: King William Island and Lancaster Sound. They showed a Landsat data graph, with ice breaking up in Cambridge Bay in July. Sea ice in Victoria Strait in August. Impossibly complicated shallow- and deep-water images, and networks of tiny islands.

She rested her chin in the palm of her hand and stared at the screen. If John ever tried to get there, he would put himself completely out of reach, she thought. Victoria Strait was about as isolated as any place on earth could be, frozen in for eleven months of the year—in a good year. It was unnavigable by any normal shipping, littered as it was with gravel shoals and sandbanks that made it dangerous. When it wasn't frozen, the shoreline was flooded with ice runoff, and there were no landmarks to be seen on the flat, barren island. Gina shivered suddenly.

She closed off the site and pursued a different route.

After five minutes she came up with *The Franklin Trail*, several expeditions that had been made in the area in the 1990s, specifically to gather Franklin data. Every day the team's activities had been submitted by satellite phone to their Web master, and Gina watched as the screen loaded up a whole raft of images. An arctic poppy and yellow lichen; ice drifting off King William Island; a commemorative plaque. A femur with deep knife marks.

Surprised by the last photograph, Gina leaned forward on her desk, brow furrowed with concentration.

Purpose:
To excavate, analyze, and interpret a Franklin site discovered on King William Island in the summer of 1992 by Barry Ranford and Mike Yarascavich. To do some further exploration of the Terror Bay area.

Summary of the trip:
The team of seven worked at the primary site from July 15, 1993, to July 29, 1993. Three hundred bones, including 5 skulls and 7 mandibles, were collected and shipped back. . . . Barry Ranford, Derek Smith, and John Harrington searched for the "hospital tent" of the Franklin expedition. . . .

Results:

As Gina's eye traveled down the page, she caught her breath.

A minimum of eleven individuals were represented. . . .
92 bones had postmortem cut marks. . . .
Lead content of bones 82 and 83 parts per million. . . .

She sat back. "Postmortem cut marks," she muttered to herself.

Interpreted as evidence of possible cannibalism. . . .

She looked away, feeling sick.

She tried to think of something else.

Over the river beyond her window, somewhere in that city land-scape, Jo was, at this very minute, seeing Great Ormond Street Children's Hospital for the first time. Sam had been transferred there. Right now, she would be walking into the wards.

"Come back," she whispered, to the empty office. "For God's sake, John. Come back."

She went straight to Great Ormond Street when she left work.

It was a terrible journey on a packed tube train. The smell of over-heated, overcrowded Londoners jammed into the carriage was not in-spiring, and to add insult to injury the escalators were broken down. By the time Gina emerged in Russell Square, she was gasping for air, and the walk up to the hospital seemed to take forever.

She eventually found Catherine and Jo in the corridor outside Sam's ward, both leaning against the wall, a polystyrene cup in each of their hands. The coffee in them, Gina noticed, as she kissed both women, was stone cold.

"How is he?" she asked.

"Sleeping," Catherine said.

"He just had another platelet transfusion," Jo said. She looked at Gina with a new expression: one tinged with something more than fear. If Gina had had to put words to it, she might have settled for *fixated horror*. Jo looked like an accident victim. Walking shock. Gina's own weariness suddenly evaporated, to be replaced with fear.

"What is it?" Gina said. "There's something else. What?"

Catherine put her hand on Jo's shoulder. "It's the latest tests," she said. "His neutrophils are zero point one. WBC five point four. Platelets eleven."

The three of them had got used to this spoken shorthand. Sam had a blue sheet that was filled in daily. It was a record of his blood results and treatment. On the left-hand side was the date, then his weight, then the various levels, followed by the treatment given. Even Gina had dreamed of this form. It obsessed them all. They waited at the ward stations for the results to come back, and one of them filled in the figures herself.

Sam's hemoglobin today was 102. The normal count was between 120 and 140.

His white blood count was 5.4. Not too bad. Normal was between 4 and 10.

Gina looked around for a chair. There was a bank of half a dozen farther along. "Sit with me," she said, gently tugging Jo's arm.

They crowded together on the chairs. Huddling for comfort.

"Neutrophils zero point one," Gina repeated slowly. She knew the score only too well. The neutrophils were part of the white blood count. They were the cells that responded to antibiotics. They fought infection in the body. A normal level was anything between 1.5 and 8.5 per cubic millimeter.

"It can go to zero," Jo murmured. "They record zero all the time. The head nurse told me." She raised her eyes to Gina's. The light in them was pleading.

"The platelets," Gina whispered. "What happened to the platelets?"

She saw that Catherine's eyes were filled with tears, and the girl was struggling not to let Jo see. No one said a word. They all knew that the normal level for platelets was between 150 and 400.

Sam's was 11.

Oh, sweet Lord, Gina thought. Eleven thousand per cubic millimeter.

Less than ten percent of what he needed, minimum.

Sam's transfer here to Great Ormond had been a vote of confidence by the medical community, they had all thought. Taking Sam to the transplant center so that he would be ready at a moment's notice, as soon as John was found. Now Gina wondered if Sam's transfer had also had another motive. To bring him here now, because he would be too weak to survive a journey if his condition continued to deteriorate.

Would they still do the transplant if he got worse? Gina wondered. Surely he wasn't strong enough to survive the preparatory chemotherapy if this carried on. He'd die in the isolation ward while he waited for the bone marrow.

He's going to die anyway, a voice said inside her head.

A wave of horror washed over her. She glanced at Jo, terrified in case the murmur inside her head had actually been real. Heard.

Jo was already looking at her. "Somebody from the *Echo* rang me," she murmured.

Gina wrenched her train of thought back to Jo. "The *Echo?*" she said. It was the UK's largest tabloid.

"They said there's a eighty-five-percent match for Sam. Someone else. Not John."

Catherine looked at Jo sympathetically, and then glared at Gina. "Can you believe this?" she asked. "They ring us up, here. The call came through to the ward."

"When?" Gina demanded.

"Half an hour ago."

"And said what?"

"That they have an eighty-five-percent match. Someone in the USA who registered last month."

"But John is ninety-five-percent," Gina said—then realized that she was stating the obvious: the unwelcome, desperate fact that the near-perfect solution was out of their reach. She shook her head. "But how the hell did the *Echo* find that out?"

"We don't know," Catherine said.

"The Trust isn't supposed to tell anyone," Jo murmured, as if to herself. "But they found out anyway."

"The *Echo* hasn't any bloody business telling you," Gina fumed. "And to ring you here . . ." She clenched her fists. "Who was it? Bradley? Marsh? Who?"

Catherine interjected. "The Trust says the information didn't come from them. And it was some woman. I didn't hear the name. Just what she said."

"The fucking bitch," Gina retorted.

She caught a small flash of a smile from Jo—an achingly thin parody of humor.

"I'm sorry," Gina told her. "But it makes my blood boil. They've sent someone out to get this information, they get half a story, they have the sodding audacity to ring you while Sam is being treated—"

She stopped, struck by a thought. "But would it be any good anyway, an eighty-five-percent?" she asked.

"We don't know," Jo said. "We're waiting for somebody to tell us."

"Oh, God in heaven," Gina whispered. She clasped Jo's hands, lost the battle not to shed tears, and to her shame, started to cry. She rubbed at the tears. It was not her business to start weeping, she told herself. She was supposed to be stoic. Jo's support. Catherine's helper. But still . . . "Oh, Lord," she said. "Lord, please."

She felt Jo stiffen beside her. Suddenly Sam's mother got up, wrenching her hands from their grasp. Remaining in the seats, both Catherine and Gina stared up at her. Jo swayed slightly. "It doesn't matter if it's eighty-five-percent, or ninety-percent, or a hundred-percent," she said. "It doesn't matter if John gets here. They'll be too late."

"No, they won't," Catherine said, getting to her feet.

"He won't make it," Jo said. "He's too sick."

Gina sprang up too. "Don't say that," she told Jo. "Don't even think it. He'll make it."

"Why don't you both stop lying to me!" Jo cried. "You only have to look at him. He's not responding to anything. The ALG did nothing at all." She turned away from them, raised her arms, pressed both hands to the window glass, and stayed there, in a totally unconscious attitude of crucifixion. "They'll be too late," she murmured. "His body's given up already."

Catherine reached out a hand, hesitated. Dropped it to her side.

Jo pressed one cheek to the pane. They stared at her white profile.

"He's gone through to some other place," she whispered. "He's fighting his dragons all alone in there, and he hasn't anything to fight them with, and I can't get through to him. I can't get through." Her mouth trembled. She took in a great gasp of air, a grieving sob.

Gina promptly turned her around, both hands on her shoulders.

"Listen to me," she said. "He's not going to die, Jo. He's not dead already. He'll get the bone marrow. We'll pull him through that door, we'll get him back. You can be sure of that. He'll come back to you."

Jo looked at her friend, then dropped her head. "Oh, Gina," she murmured.

Gina pulled her close and held her.

And despite what she'd said, all Gina knew for sure at that moment was that she wanted to rush into the ward, get Sam, and run.

Not with any purpose in her head.

Not to achieve a single thing.

Just run.

Thirty-five

As Alicia walked out onto King's Parade, she saw John.

She stopped dead in the hurrying crowd.

She had only just come down Lensfield Road and along St. Andrew's, passing the Museum of Archaeology. It was somewhere that John used to love when he first took a place at Cambridge. He had always talked about the Pacific collections, the accumulated trophies of British expeditions in the Franklin mode. Cook's first and third voyages. Haddon's Torres Strait holdings. Going in here was like touring the world in half an hour, he once told her. Jericho to the North American Plains; Kechipauan to Fiji-Vanuatu.

Coming out of the museum and into the clinging heat, she had paused on the steps, thinking that John was just like his father. John had wanted to leave, and she had kept him. Tried to keep him. Finally, failed.

When she saw him opposite King's, she actually believed it was him, standing head and shoulders over the crowd. Then, with a double thud of her heart that almost choked her, she realized that someone had got hold of a college picture of him and enlarged it to actual size, and pinned it in a café window. Getting closer, she saw a red banner stuck across the lower half.

HAVE YOU SEEN JOHN MARSHALL?

He was everywhere. In newspapers particularly. She no longer took *The Courier* because of the relentless campaign they had been running.

She had thought of ringing them up to complain. She was John's mother, and yet no one had ever consulted her. It was as if Sam and Jo Harper were the only mother and child in the world. Simply leafing through the same newspaper, one could see ample evidence of other misery, but none of that seemed to count.

She turned away from the shop, hand pressed to her face.

She drove home in a daze. The car smelled dirty in the heat: she wound the windows down, and the red dust flew in, and the chaff from the fields. She sat behind a farm tractor towing a load of grain. The harvest was good this year; even at ten o'clock at night she could hear combines out in the fields. She would lie alone, the windows and curtains open, gazing out at the endless skies that the tourist industry so raved about here. *Artist's skies.* What did they know? Emptiness. That's what they meant. The skies over East Anglia were vast and empty.

She turned into the drive. She saw that the evening paper was waiting in the mailbox. She pulled it out and sat, with the car engine idling, as she stared at the front page. A small paragraph at the bottom had caught her eye.

> Sam Marshall, the local boy who continues to make headline news over his fight with a life-threatening illness, was yesterday transferred to Great Ormond Street Hospital in London to prepare him for a bone-marrow transplant from his half-brother.

Blood rushed to Alicia's face. She gunned the accelerator and swung the car around in front of the house in a cloud of dust. Wrenching the keys from the ignition, she rushed indoors and grabbed the phone from the table in the hallway.

She dialed the paper's number.

"Evening Clarion."

"I want the editor," she said.

"Who shall I say is calling?"

"Mrs. Marshall."

She waited impatiently, stabbing her keys on the wood paneling, scoring a line in the two-hundred-year-old oak.

"Ed Wheeler."

"This is John Marshall's mother," Alicia said. "I suppose you know who I am?"

"His mother," the editor repeated. "Miss Harper?"

"No," Alicia retorted, furious. "I'm John Marshall's mother. *John Marshall.*"

"Oh," he said. "I see. Sorry." There was a pause. "What can I do for you?"

"Your paper tonight. The front page."

"Yes . . ."

"Where is he?"

"I'm sorry. Who?"

"John. My son," she snapped. "It says in the paragraph that the boy's been transferred to London for his transplant. If he's getting the transplant, they must have the donor."

Light seemed to dawn in the editor's mind. "Oh, no," he said. "My apologies if that's misleading. The hospital says that was the reason for the transfer, but I don't think they've found his half brother." There was another pause. "But you would know that," he said.

She stared at the receiver, incensed. "Quite," she said. "*I* would know. *I* would know before anyone else."

"Yes, I—"

"And so don't print a story with half the facts," she said. "Don't imply things that aren't true. They haven't found him. If anyone could find him, it would be me."

The words were out of her mouth before she could stop them.

The editor almost jumped down her throat. "You could find him?" he asked. "You know where he is?"

She bit her lip. Anger had propelled her this far: she rapidly tried to backtrack. "I simply want to make the point that there is more than one mother who has lost a son in this," she said. "That's what all you people forget."

"Do you know where he is?" the editor repeated.

She slammed the phone down.

She went into the sitting room, still furious. Not sixty seconds passed before the phone rang again. She looked back. It went on ringing.

She walked out into the kitchen, gritting her teeth. Opening the fridge door, she took out a bottle of wine. She poured out a glass and drank it down in one go.

Everything she had had fallen part.

Everything she had had fallen apart.

The phrase blasted through her mind and wouldn't be put away. She was a wealthy woman, she was well respected, she was influential. And yet she couldn't control her own life. *She never had controlled her own life. It was all an illusion.* Once thought, the idea wouldn't go away. She groaned inadvertently, went back to the sitting room, and slumped down in the nearest armchair, switching on the TV with the remote.

It was the local evening news program. She watched dully, uninterestedly, with the volume turned down, as the news items scrolled on. Other people's small, insignificant lives. Some woman opening a fete. A child with a rosette held proudly in her fist. A road accident, the reporter on the roadside, the flashing blue lights of police vehicles behind him.

She passed her hand over her eyes, irritated by the triumphs and tragedies of the rest of the world. When she took her hand away, Doug's face was looking back at her.

She took a small intake of breath, pressing down hard on the volume switch.

". . . distinguished professor at Blethyn College, who died just over two years ago . . ."

Alicia sat forward in the seat.

Jo and Sam came on-screen. Jo sitting underneath the lilac tree, Sam in her arms. The voice-over went on.

"Sunday's screening of the TV appeal has produced the most astonishing response to the James Norberry Bone Marrow Trust. To date . . ."

The breath seemed to have stopped in Alicia's body.

Unable to look at Jo, she stared at the child, the little boy. He looked so very like John at the same age: he even had the same mannerism, that lopsided look to his mouth when he was concentrating, that so resembled a smile.

But the boy in Jo Harper's lap was not really smiling, she saw. His eyes were fixed on his mother, as if she held an important answer to something. As if to take his gaze from her would send him into oblivion. She looked at his fingers, knotted in Jo's.

Alicia switched off the set and leapt to her feet.

Going out into the hall, she wrenched open the front door and went out into the drive, taking deep drafts of air. She was shaking from head to foot. Forgetting the still-idling car, she walked away across the long lawn.

The garden was in full bloom. Stopping suddenly up short, she stared at the flowers that she had tended all year. Splashes of luminous orange and yellow. The backdrop of the lane, the fields.

She dropped to her knees on the closely mown grass.

"Oh, God." She moaned. "What have I done?"

All her life she had fought to make things happen. She had fought to get Doug; she had fought to keep him. She had cheated him into marriage. She had kept John near her when Doug became ever more the absent partner, emotionally suffocating her child in the process. She knew she had done that. Kept John apart. Kept him inside when other children played. Prevented him mixing. She had insisted upon meeting him from school, even when he was in his teens. She had discouraged him from staying with other boys. Discouraged other boys visiting him. Smothered him with so much emotional blackmail that eventually he dropped his plans of any other university but Cambridge.

And she had nagged him. God, how she had nagged him. She stared now at the colors ahead of her, at their almost savage brilliance. She felt as if her heart were ablaze like that, consumed by its own intensity. Burning up.

Burning out.

She had used to phone John daily. Insisted on knowing where he had been, and who he had been with. And when he started to break away—when she could feel him straining to get himself free of her, when she could see how much he wanted his father's attention, not hers—she had pressed down all the harder to make him feel guilty.

And now she had lost them both.

Husband, son.

All that she possessed was the sum total of her years of pressure. She had what she had made for herself with all her pleading and sulking. Total isolation.

And fear. All the days filled with fear. Loathing the world that she thought had taken John from her. Loathing another woman who had been given Doug's love. Vindictively hating a small, sick child. That was what she was, with all her so-called loving. That was what she had become. Kneeling, she bent double, nausea rushing into her throat.

Jo Harper had a life, a real life. She had friends. She was admired and respected. Look at the girl Catherine, Alicia told herself in despair. Look how that girl had stood by her. Look at those television pictures. Even the doctor seemed struck with Sam's mother. The TV crew, the people at *The Courier*, the local radio stations. There was nowhere you could go that didn't show how strongly people felt for her.

Because she was loved. That's what it was.

Genuinely loved.

Doug had loved Jo as he never loved her. It had been written plainly in his face. And now he was alive again in his son. Sam. Two years old and the spitting image of his father. In twenty years' time there would be another Doug Marshall walking around. Looking exactly the same. Smiling exactly the same. Samuel Douglas Marshall . . .

If he lived.

If he lived.

It was some time before Alicia roused herself to a sitting position. She eventually looked back at the house. Painfully she got up and walked slowly back to the hall, body sagging with defeat. She sat down in the cool shadows of the house. Listened for a long time to the silence.

She opened the drawer in the front of the hall table and took a bundle of papers from it.

In it were John's only two letters to her in the past two years. And a photograph of John, herself, and Catherine. She shook her head at it now, smoothing out the picture, where she had folded it to take Catherine from the image and leave just John and her standing together. Reinstated, she saw for the first time how the photograph was not a trio at all. John and Catherine stood with arms linked, their body language relating only to each other. Alicia was standing at John's side, but it was she—not Catherine—who was the outsider.

Reflectively now, Alicia refolded the photo so that Catherine and John stood together, and she was excluded.

She shuddered.

In the same pile of papers was a small, cream-colored card. She extracted it, looked carefully at it, and then put it, with John's last letter, in her handbag. Then, grimacing, she wiped her eyes and stood up. She picked up the car keys and went out of the house.

Thirty-six

IT was midnight at Great Ormond Street.

Gina had gone home; Jo was asleep on the sofa bed at Sam's side. The lights in the corridor and in the side ward were turned down.

Jo had been dreaming of John.

He stood in the center of a white space. Hard to see what, if anything, was around him. There seemed to be no ground, no sky, no horizon. She was trying to get to him, but whatever it was underneath her feet only pulled her down. She was fighting with all her strength to lift her body, but she was sinking deeper. She was choking for air, while the outlines of John's body and the details of his face faded.

That evening had been the worst few hours of them all.

As Gina and Catherine and she had come back into Sam's room— they had only been out for ten minutes, and he had been sleeping—it was Catherine, going in first, who noticed that something was wrong.

Sam had been awake, his back arched, the gauze vest rucked up under his armpits, and blood seeping from his chest.

"Oh, my God!" Jo had cried. "What's happened!"

At once Gina turned on her heel and rushed back to the ward desk, to fetch the nurse. Jo scrambled to Sam's side of the bed.

"It's the Hickman line," Catherine said. "He's pulled the line out."

"Oh, Christ." Jo gasped. "What do we do? What do we do?"

Instinctively she pressed on the exit site, hard. She looked up at

Catherine. "Where's it all coming from?" she asked. "Is it from his heart? It must be from his heart. Oh God, oh God . . ."

Up to now Sam had seemed shocked into silence at his own unexpected strength, and at the size of the tube that had escaped his chest. Now, seeing their panic, he began to scream.

"Don't do that," Jo begged. "Sam, Sam . . . ssssh . . ."

She gaped at Catherine in horror. The blood was flowing freely between her fingers.

"No!" Sam cried. It was a deafening, high-pitched, inhuman noise. The sound seemed to slice through the room.

The nurse came in, pursued by Gina.

"Where's the blood coming from?" Jo stammered. "I can't stop it. . . ."

The nurse pulled her fingers back a little. "It's only from the skin tunnel," she said.

"We only left him a little while . . . he was asleep. . . ."

The nurse turned Jo to her. "He's pulled out the line. It's not from his heart. It will stop in a minute. It's all right," she said, pointedly, slowly, making sure that Jo heard her above Sam's unearthly screaming. "It's going to be all right."

All right . . .

Jo surfaced slowly, now, from sleep.

For a moment all she saw was the pool of moonlight on the floor, and the blurring of the reflection from the window with the dimmed night-light over Sam's bed.

And then she sat bolt upright.

Alicia was standing at the door.

The other woman was in complete shadow, seeming more ghost than reality. Then she stepped forward. "Hello, Jo," she murmured.

Jo stumbled to her feet.

"He's such a little boy," Alicia said. "I didn't realize . . . so small. . . ."

Jo followed Alicia's gaze. Sam was sedated now. He lay peacefully, looking for all the world like an angel, hands crossed demurely at his waist, his face smoothed by sleep. Only a few tiny specks of blood on the very edge of the pillowcase gave any clue to what had gone on just three hours before.

Alicia stretched out her hand and touched Sam's face.

In an automatic gesture of protection Jo went to Sam's side, and took hold of his hand. "What are you doing here?" she said.

Alicia still hadn't taken her gaze from Sam. "I drove down," she murmured.

"What time is it?"

"Midnight," she said.

And then she looked up.

Jo couldn't read her expression at all. She had never seen a true, uncomplicated emotion on Alicia's face. She had always thought that whatever was in Alicia's eyes was the product of some theatrical lie—not quite real, not quite true. It had been impossible to fathom Alicia's true feelings under all the posturing.

But now there seemed to be none of that left. Alicia's face had been stripped of all its defenses.

"I brought something," Alicia said.

She fumbled with the catch of her handbag. At last she brought out a card. She gave it to Jo.

The James Norberry Trust, said the lettering across the top.

And John's name.

And the number. *AZMA 552314.*

Jo didn't need to go to her own bag to know that this was the number that Ben Elliott had given her. John's donor number. The final proof of the match. She didn't need to check because she had carried that number in her head, knowing that if she ever saw it again, it would be a kind of talisman. A charm to ward off evil.

"There's something else," Alicia said.

She had a letter in her hand. She had taken it, with a trembling hand, from a creased envelope.

"John wrote to me," she whispered. "I went down to see him. He was leaving, I couldn't stop him. I—" Her voice broke. She took a breath. She held out the handwritten page. "If it would help you," she said, "this is where he's gone."

Richard Sibley's' office number and address were printed along the top.

Jo took the page. She gazed at it.

Quite suddenly Alicia turned away. She got to the door again before stumbling against it, only just managing to hold herself upright.

Jo rushed around the side of the bed, John's letter still in her hand. She touched Alicia's shoulder, and just for a second the two women stared into each other's faces.

Then Jo flung her arms around her.

"Oh, forgive me," Alicia wept. "Please forgive me."

Thirty-seven

WHEN he got to the rock, Gus was too tired to sit. He lay down, with his face on the ground and his arm resting on the stones. There was no more snow, no sleet. Not even the wind laden with the fine grains of ice. In fact, the temperature was above freezing, and there had been rain the night before. Gus stared out over Simpson Strait.

They had left the ice behind and had emerged, last week, close to latitude sixty-eight. The sea was unfrozen here. It moved at a sluggish speed, carrying its burden of floes, gray-blue on the deeper blue of the water. Dirty ice, old ice. Ice from the great choked fields where they had left the ships. So many miles south, the ocean had at last freed itself of that solid, suffocating embrace. King William was an island. The Northwest Passage existed, flowing out in front of them. But there was no one to care. Least of all the four men of the *Erebus* and *Terror* who were left alive.

At last Gus managed to raise himself and pull one or two of the larger stones toward him. He pulled and pushed them into place: lifting them was beyond his strength. Then he got the canister out of his pocket. They hadn't even been able to seal it—they had nothing to make a fire, nothing to solder with. So they had rolled the message and pushed it into the canister and wound a piece of leather around the top, and bound it.

He put the canister on the flat top of the larger stones and scraped the pebbles up and over it. The effort made him want to weep. His naked fingertips stuck to the rain on their pitted, granular surface.

Soon the container was covered, but by such a pitiful little heap of rock that he knew no one would ever find it. So much for the final cairn that Franklin's crews would ever make, he thought.

Two hundred yards away, down the shard-strewn slope, they had pitched their last tent. Looking back now, Gus could see how badly it had been done, now that he was away from it. The tarpaulin was not taut, and it moved. The edges had not been weighted properly: one corner had escaped the stones.

Slowly, Gus raised himself onto his elbow. He scraped at the closest rock with his fingernail. The thin, acid-green covering came off in dry flakes. He opened his mouth and put it on his tongue.

His mouth hurt badly; even the lichen flakes were hard to move around. Yesterday they had shot a bird, but the act of walking out to where it had fallen, and bringing it back, had exhausted them. They had sat crouched over it, using a table knife to cut through the flesh. They tried to chew, but their gums were swollen so much that as soon as they chewed, their mouths bled fiercely.

Gus got to his feet. He set off down the slope at a snail's pace. He hadn't walked very fast for weeks. When he had summoned up the courage to look at his feet then, he saw that the toes were black, and he had put his boots back on and not looked again. He had lost sensation from just below the ankle in the right leg; the left was better. He still felt the anklebone there.

At the tent on the shoreline he shuffled down to a kneeling position, hunched against the salt breeze. He didn't want to go into the tent. He didn't want to know what was being said in there. He didn't want to be part of the final conversation. Those prayers and absolutions.

Last night there had been an electrical storm. They had sheltered in the tent, huddled together, wet through as the sleet penetrated the tarpaulin. The lights around them had been truly fantastic, slicing across the water, visible for miles, blue shafts of energy that raced off the sea and swung up the land like racing horses, stallions pounding their hooves.

He'd hoped the devil was coming for him.

He'd hoped it would be quick. If the devil was what sinners deserved, then Gus would no doubt see the devil's face soon enough. He would know what it was to be swept out of one life and plunged into hell. But the thought didn't terrify him as it would have done once. Hell at least would be full of fire. He thought that he could exist in an eternity of boiling heat. Heat as penetrating as ice. Heat to set the blood alight. Heat to melt his heart, char his flesh. A burned body would have no desires and have no capacities. Least of all would he think of his starvation. There would be nothing left of him to feel that scourge.

Hunger was not the empty belly of his childhood. He had once thought so—thought he had felt what it was not to have eaten—but now he knew that every other bodily sensation had been just a shadow of this one. Hunger was a rattling drum, coating the throat with saliva. It was a fist squeezing your stomach. It was an invasion, a deprivation. But it was nothing to the last ten days without food.

Starvation was something else entirely. The pain bent you double with its probing shock. It was a knife in the muscles. Eventually you stopped thinking of the meals that would be waiting for you when you reached home. You stopped thinking of the stews with the flour dumplings floating in their delectable grease and gravy. You stopped thinking of potatoes and beef. The smell of fish cooked in port, off braziers right on the dock. You stopped thinking of it, because you forgot what the smell was. You forgot the feeling of food in your hand, your mouth, your gut. Your thinness became wooden, not flesh. You became dry, cracked through like meat smoked for days on end. You were like pemmican, or beef jerky. And, last of all, your heart died inside you.

When men recovered from scurvy, the old skin dropped off their faces in peeling lumps. They unwound, like layers of onion, like the peel from an apple. The skin underneath would be babylike, hairless, fragile.

But that wouldn't happen to them. They weren't going to recover. They would die in a few days, even if they took the offering that was being made, and being accepted no doubt, at this moment.

Gus couldn't remember the name of the man who had died last. He thought it might have been Abraham. Abraham, like in the Bible. Abraham Seeley, from the *Erebus*.

What had Abraham done, in the Bible? Gus wondered.

He tried to think. Offered to sacrifice his own son, Isaac.

There had been no Isaac on the ships.

There was no one, then, to sacrifice, but that man, who may have been Abraham, or may have been one of the others who had come with them from Point Victory. Daniel Arthur, quartermaster. William Goddard, captain of the hold. George Kinniard. Reuben Male, captain of the forecastle in *Terror.*

Any one of them.

Or, none of them.

Because all those men had ceased to exist. They were not men, now, the four of them. They were just shadows of men. They were the very essence and manifestation of their own starvation. Images only. Ghosts in a frosted glass.

He looked across the water, at the blur of gray beyond the sea. Across the strait was Canada. Hundreds of miles away in that direction were the Hudson's Bay outposts. Fort Churchill, Fort York, Severn Fort, Albany, Moose Fort, East Main, Fort George. They called that country Moosonee, Manitoba, Rupert's Land. There was a Little Whale River there, and a Great Whale River. The natives spoke Sakehao and Ketemakalemao. His uncle's ship had gone down that coast once, driven by storms. There were settlements there. At Albany Station there were eighty families. The missionary had told them so.

But he would never go to the Bay again. He would never get on a whaler, or any ship, again. He felt glad of it. He felt glad at the prospect of ceasing to exist. Never walking again. Never breathing. Never hearing, never listening, never waiting again to see the last dying flicker in a man's eye.

God would not forgive him.

Then, across the strait, he saw movement.

For a while he thought his eyes were deceiving him. He thought it was just the endless ice, turning over in the current. He thought it was the sea itself, at first. And then he saw that it was men. He sat up on his haunches, staring hard.

Just for that second he wondered if it were the crews. The dots of the bodies on the shoreline flickered and altered like a mirage. Perhaps it was the men they had left behind, he thought. Perhaps it was the dead. Perhaps, in the last few minutes since trying to build the cairn, he had actually died, had his prayers answered, and this was the result—the long, slow shuffling across the sea, the lines of the dead crew coming to meet him.

He knuckled his fists against his eyes.

They were clearer now. Closer. How many weeks was it since he had seen such a number of men? There were more than ten out there. Ten, perhaps twelve. How many weeks ago would that be? Not many. Perhaps two. Fourteen days. Fourteen days of dying. It was the men who had fallen behind them along this strait that were coming now, with their emaciated faces, their coats wrapped around them, their caps pulled down over the cuts and sores on their scalps. Gus struggled to his feet.

He had a sudden, burning desire to be saved from this last terrible spectacle. If they were coming for him, he couldn't look in their faces, see their eyes. How could he manage that? Those that he had cut himself. Those that he had helped to cut. Those that they had sectioned out like gutted fish, dried in the thin trickle of sun, to feed the sick.

At Crozier's insistence they had split the thighbones and emptied them. He had taken a piece . . . it was only a portion, sickly warm in his hand. He had not wanted to swallow it. How could he? How could he not? It was the very warmth of it that made it unbearable. He couldn't forget that it was a man.

They had wept over those remains.

He didn't know if Crozier ate or not. He didn't think so. Yet, as they had sat in the half-circle today—and the third man already sleeping with that familiar rasping of pneumonia—Crozier had touched Gus's arm.

"Look at me," he'd whispered.

Gus met his eyes. He saw his own horror reflected there.

"Do you know what this is?" Crozier asked. "What you see here, behind us?"

"I don't want to see," Gus had told him.

Crozier had got hold of his arm so tightly that the grasp burned. "This is not for any man to know about," Crozier said. "When you are free of here, when you have survived . . ."

Gus had snatched up the canister that Crozier had taken so long to painstakingly fill and seal.

"Wait a moment," Crozier said. "Listen to me."

Gus didn't look in his face. He turned the copper cylinder over and over in his palm, sick with the futility of the final message.

August 11th 1848.
HM Ships Erebus *and* Terror.
1 Officer, 3 crew remaining.
Final cairn constructed Lat 68 degrees 15' Long 97 degrees 30'
Awaiting Hudson Bay scouts.
F.R.M. Crozier, Captain and Senior Officer

Crozier's faltering script ran haphazardly over the Admiralty pre-printed page.

The man was gripping his own hand now. In a spasm of frustration he took the canister from Gus and threw it down at their side.

"Gus," he murmured, "you must listen."

"I don't want to see what we did," Gus repeated.

"I know," Crozier said. "But God is merciful. Hold on to that truth."

Gus, at last, looked up at him. His heart broke to recognize the last flame of life burning down in Crozier's face. "There is no forgiveness for us," he whispered.

Crozier's grip on Gus's fingers was still firm. "There *is* forgiveness," he told the boy. "There is mercy in heaven. Those that died forgave us. They blessed us and instructed us. Each man told us what we must do. Is God's heart less than a man's?"

Gus shook his head. "I can't do it," he said.

"You can do it," Crozier retorted. "When you are left alone, it is the one thing you must do."

"No," Gus sobbed.

"Promise me," Crozier said.

The boy began to cry in earnest. It was not an oath he could make. It was not an order he could obey. He had obeyed all the others. He had followed Crozier to this hellish place. He would follow him into the mouth of true hell itself. But he could not do this final thing that Crozier demanded. If he were left alone, what body would be left, but Crozier himself? The man who had been more of a father to him than any man.

"Gus," Crozier said, "listen to me. The bone marrow—"

"No, sir. No—"

"The bone marrow has the most nourishment, Gus. Remember that. If nothing else you must take the bone marrow."

Gus covered his face with his hands, weeping with utter despair. He hardly felt the touch of Crozier's hand on his shoulder.

"I forgive you, Gus," Crozier murmured. "Do you hear me? I forgive you."

Gus had shaken his head. He wanted to do what Crozier asked him. He would have done anything else at all. The solution had struck him in that moment, and he opened his eyes and raised his head.

"Let me go first," he said to Crozier. "Let me be first, for you."

Then, Crozier, too, bowed his head. A groan came out of him, dredged up from the depths, screwed out of his soul.

And this was the worst, the worst of all, the sound of this final groan.

As the Esquimaux approached the camp, they had both a scent and a premonition. They wheeled in a half circle, wondering, listening to the fragments. A voice. Two voices, mixed with the great insistence of the sea alongside them, the rattle and grunt of ice.

The men in front glanced at each other. They were tempted to pass by.

The four had come some distance to hunt seal on the rapidly breaking floes. They knew, as all natives knew, that white men came into this country, but none of those who stood on the shoreline now had seen white men before.

Tooshooarthariu stepped a little way forward. There was something alongside the tent that intrigued him. He could see a man on the ground, and an older one standing above him.

He lifted his hand.

The standing man slowly returned the gesture. Then he walked toward him.

At his side Teekeeta and Owwer shrank back, and Mangaq, who had not moved until that moment, turned swiftly on his heel, ready to run. He signaled his wife; they hauled the sledge around.

Tooshooarthariu could see that the hunger that had plagued his own family all winter had struck hard in the man before him. But before him was an illustration of something more horrible than mere hunger. Tooshooarthariu had heard that white man's skin was lighter, but the man coming toward him was a strange color, not lined by the weather, but patched and jumbled, like badly sewn skins. His forehead was cross-hatched with different shades: a curious, ugly blue, a gray, dead white. His cheekbones, too, looked white. But the mouth was black, and too horrible to look at for long. The lips, the gums, were the same dark color; the teeth long, yellow, flecked with blood.

The man began to speak.

Tooshooarthariu watched his hands. He didn't understand the language—so many harsh, short sounds—but he understood that he had come from the north—he waved his arm behind him. And that there were boats. Large boats. The man picked up the melting rim of ice at the edge of the water and held it toward him. Made a crushing motion with both hands. Then, with the same fingers, he counted off himself, holding up one finger and then pointing back at his chest. He repeated the gesture. One man. Two, three. The hands flew. Many men.

The Esquimaux looked disbelievingly at the tent. There were not many men, that was obvious. How could there ever have been many men walking from the ice? Native families even did not move in great numbers together. To do so was dangerous. They existed in small communities of two or three families. Even at great summer meetings there were never more than forty or fifty. Tooshooarthariu shook his head. You couldn't bring many men—what was he saying, hundreds?—you couldn't bring hundreds of men through the ice.

The white man was thin. You could see that, even if you didn't look at the awful face. He didn't stand straight. The younger one behind him was standing now, and was a little taller, but even he bent over from the waist.

"They're hungry," Owwer whispered at his back.

The Esquimaux walked away, back to the women.

The first thing that his wife, Ahlangyah, said was that there was not much seal. It was as if she had read her husband's mind.

In spring they spent countless hours chasing the sea ice for the right places to hunt. On sunny days, when the seals lay on the floes, they looked easy enough targets, but for a hunter to get within range took time, patience, practice. Seal had acute hearing, and the approach to the ice or the breathing hole was slow, wormlike. Sometimes the hunters rested on the ice for hours, waiting for the sound of a seal coming up to its breathing place, approaching it by fits and starts. This was the moment of greatest skill, to listen to the sound of the seal blowing under the ice and to estimate the exact time that it would flex its muscles for the leap upward. The hunter would plunge his spear, hopefully into the skull, and enlarge the breathing hole, and land his kill, all the while with the seal straining on the line.

They never landed huge quantities. They didn't store them by great numbers. They killed only when they needed them, and they bagged the bones, and took them back to the sea, and dumped them in the water, because to do anything else, to behave in any other way toward the seal, would be bad luck for other hunting.

"They have killed birds," Owwer said. "Let them wait for more birds."

Tooshooarthariu looked back at the older man.

"We haven't enough to feed them," Ahlangyah told him.

He didn't know how many there were. He stared at the tent. Maybe there were other men in there. How many would it hold? Maybe ten. If they gave them enough meat for ten men they would have nothing left for themselves. If the white man saw that they had food at all on their sled, he might want it all.

Tooshooarthariu had been told that when men called Parry and Lyon had come to Igloolik in their ships twenty winters before, their grandfathers had been on the white men's ships. They had talked to them, stayed with them, hunted with them. A man called Artungun, a child at the time, had even been told that he could travel with Parry back to the white man's country. Artungun could count in their language, and sing songs that they had taught him, and said that he had been brought back to life by Parry's shaman, by letting blood from his arm. And Artungun could show the scar on his arm to prove that what he said was true.

But the stories of their grandfathers had something else in them that was more worrying. The white man carried sticks that could kill animals. They carried them across their shoulders, and they used a black powder with them that was very fine, and could ignite.

Tooshooarthariu, looking back still at the older man, wondered if any of this powder, and any of these curved sticks with iron in them, were inside the tents. If they offered the white men food, and it was not enough, even if they gave them all they had, would they use their powder and their weapons to ask for more, to kill them if there was not more?

He looked at Ahlangyah. She leveled his glance with her stony gaze. "What is the sickness?" she asked.

"I don't know," he told her.

She inclined her head to their children. "We don't want their sickness," she said. They had lost a child five months before, and she was thinking of that, he knew. Yet even while he looked around the other men, Ahlangyah's gaze trailed back to the white boy, who could not have been more than sixteen. She gave a half smile before lowering her face and covering it with her hand. Despite his mottled skin, she could see that he was fair. He reminded her of the thin ribbons of lights in the sky.

Owwer crossed his arms. "They're dying," he murmured. "Giving them our meat won't stop that. It only makes the dying longer."

Tooshooarthariu hesitated. Owwer was right. But he couldn't walk on with the meat in the bags. He couldn't walk past with meat, and leave them. He looked again at the sorrowful little tent, and he wondered what ships the men had come on, and where they were. He wondered if they were lying. Hundreds of men. Tall sailed ships.

If they were telling the truth, where were the rest of them?

Perhaps the answer was that they were waiting for others. Perhaps the hundreds of men were coming to them. Perhaps tomorrow they would see them. Perhaps they had left their sick here and were returning for them. And perhaps they wouldn't die if they were given a week's food, because it would be all that was needed.

He wished he knew. He wished he understood them.

The older white man sat down suddenly on the shore, as if the breath had been knocked out of him. Tooshooarthariu met his muddied gaze, saw the blunt hopelessness in his eyes.

Whatever had happened, whatever was to happen, he thought, it came down to the same fact.

He couldn't walk past them with seal in their own packs.

"Give them meat," he said.

Two mornings later there was a brighter light. The sea looked very blue. The air was amazingly sweet. Just for a second Gus thought of gardens.

At his side was the pack of seal meat that the Esquimaux had left.

The night before, he and Crozier had barely eaten a half dozen mouthfuls. It had been too rich, and very hard to chew. They had tried their best, each facing the other. The long evening had faded, but not quite into darkness.

They had said nothing.

There was nothing left to say.

Francis Crozier died early in the morning.

It took Gus a very long time to get the blankets from the tent and wrap the body. The effort exhausted him.

At the very end he couldn't remember a single prayer, and he couldn't weep. He sat with his hands resting on the body, watching the water.

Then, he lay down at Crozier's side, and waited to follow him.

Thirty-eight

THE rain had stopped. The day was dull, but visibility was clear.

The bear lay on her stomach, all four legs splayed out, her head propped up slightly on the stones. She felt easier that way. There was more air.

She had been dreaming for hours.

There was more than one world, and she had lived in them all.

She had swum under ice ceilings swept clean of snow, that filtered light through the ocean, filling the depths with curtains of color. She had filled her senses with the power of the current, the fierce cold beauty of the ice-covered sea. In Lancaster Sound in the Arctic summer the sea was filled with millions of ctenophores, fringed with pulsating tendrils; thick with tiny, translucent copepods, so small that they looked like luminous dust in the refracted light. To dive under the ice was like diving into the stars—an unmapped eternity where whole galaxies rushed by.

She dreamed of the whales; belugas and bowheads who, after wintering along the southern edge of the pack ice, migrated back each spring. They came before any other traveler, returning through leads and cracks, moving northward. If the ice froze over and the leads closed, the beluga could submerge itself for twenty minutes and travel up to two miles under the pack. If there were no breathing holes, it would simply rise to the surface and push the pack upward, and take air from the pocket it had created between the unbroken ice and the sea.

She had seen them swim past her, their backs and blowholes scarred from colliding with ice ridges.

She had heard the whales singing, sounding their way through the oceans. The beluga was the rhythm, its series of clicks rattling through the current. The bowhead, so decimated and slaughtered by man, almost to the point of extinction, truly sang—a low, long, slow-frequency melody.

She had been part of the sea, and the other worlds of high summer. She had tracked hundreds of miles along shoreline, and seen the irrepressible return of life each year: the bearberry, whose leaves turned bright red in the autumn. The crowberry, that stayed on the plant even through the frozen winter. The cloudberry, with its thick, creamy consistency. The lichen—the oldest plants on earth, and virtually indestructible. The flush of wildflowers—pink-flowered fireweed, poppies, white mountain avens, blue forget-me-nots.

She had been part of the air, living on the messages transmitted through scent, carried for uninterrupted miles. She knew the huge concentrations of birds: the four hundred thousand snow geese on southwest Baffin; the two hundred thousand Ross's geese of the Queen Maud Gulf; the long-tailed jaegers; the killer hawks; the black-legged kittiwakes.

She knew the changing patterns of the sky, the dazzle of brightly lit snow reflected on the underside of clouds. The blue-white of arctic haze, carrying ice crystals; the optical illusions of sun dogs, sun pillars and haloes—displays of light caught between the sun and ice and fog.

She had their image in her head and heart. And so many others.

A million stars in the light-filled water.

Sun streaming over snow.

Storms.

Silence.

They carried her now, on her final journey.

The helicopter swung low over the beach, making its fourth run along that section of coast.

"There!" Richard Sibley shouted. "There, by the gravel ridge!"

It was four days since he had got back to the office in Winnipeg. He had been filming grizzly above Khutzeymateen, and returned home to find his sister snowed under with e-mails, and John Marshall sitting among the chaos, a single duffel bag at his feet and a cup of coffee in his hands.

An Inuit guide had spotted the bear from a freighter canoe. He had come back to Gjoa to spread the word of the adult female, apparently dead, a wound showing at the base of her throat. The Swimmer still wore her collar, and the side turned to the sky still carried the black-painted number of the tagging team.

Within minutes the message had gone down to Sibley.

We have the Swimmer onshore here.
Do you want a last picture?

He surely did.

He had originally planned to come north to Gjoa Haven in the summer, to shoot the arctic char fishing. He had said when he invited John Marshall here again, that he would be on King William Island around August, and that he would maybe try to get to the trout fishing farther south, at Chesterfield Inlet.

Marshall had sent him one letter in reply. It had contained the date of his arrival and the flight number.

He hadn't had much time to talk to the boy, and in truth, it seemed to him that Marshall was no conversationalist. He kept to himself, habitually wrapping his arms tightly to his chest. Sibley had plenty of time to observe this pose, as John sat next to him on the long journey up to Gjoa, changing down to smaller and smaller aircraft until they at last circled above the small settlement, perched on the edge of a wide sweep of bay.

John had liked Gjoa on sight. The grid of wood and prefabricated blocks rising out of the limestone lowlands. The regularity. The closed look of it, he'd said, face almost pressed to the plane window.

They had come out yesterday but seen not a single trace of the bear, even with the guide alongside them.

Sibley had woken this morning in a bad temper, irritated at the expense of a second flight.

"She'd better be there this time," he'd told John over breakfast. He had dug a heap of letters and notes from his bag and was sifting through them rapidly. At one he stopped and raised his eyebrows.

"Know someone called Gina Shorecroft?" he'd said.

"No," John told him.

Sibley passed the message across, a handwritten note taped to an e-mail by Sibley's sister. "Says it's urgent," he'd said.

John looked at it, then put it in his pocket.

"Who is Jo Harper?" Sibley asked. He quoted the e-mail. *"Jo Harper needs to talk to you."*

John got up. "She's talked to me before," he murmured, pulling on his coat. Seeing Sibley's puzzled expression, he shrugged. "I'll ring tonight," he said. "It's the middle of the night there now."

The helicopter came down a hundred yards from the shore. Their guide, Mike Hitkolok, got out first. They ran forward from the rotors, before Mike stopped them.

"You stay behind me," he said. "We see what she's doing, okay?"

They nodded their agreement.

Richard had handed a pack of equipment to John, and they both edged onward with the cameras. When they got to the first of the gravel rises, Mike went below. They watched him carefully. There was no sight of the bear from this angle.

"I feel like I know her," John murmured.

Sibley looked at him. "We've followed her for four years," he said. "She's some beast. You know what they've put on the Web site now? *Pihoqahiaq,* her Inuit name. The Ever-Wandering One."

John nodded slowly.

"Not supposed to do that," Sibley murmured. "Supposed to have contained habitat, you know? Few hundred miles this way or that. But not her. Not this one."

The sweat was springing up along his neck, nerves more than heat. Whenever he got this close to bear, he itched. He had never quite lost the awe of them, the fear of their capabilities.

"John," he said softly, "if she's not dead, if she moves, you run, okay? We're back in that machine. Don't look back, get in it."

"Okay," John said.

"Saw a piece in the *Nunatsiaq News* a while back," Sibley murmured.

"Australian hiker just east of the Soper River. A female bear and two cubs chased him for seven miles." Sibley laughed, almost a hiss of anxiety. "Probably not hungry, just curious," he added.

Down the slope they saw Mike wave to them.

They went down cautiously, to within twenty yards.

Mike stood guard on top of the nearest rill.

"She dead?" Sibley called.

"Dead, yeah," came the reply. "No movement."

They eased on, until at last they saw her, curled in almost a fetal position. Blood stained her chest; her back legs were drawn tightly up. Sibley flexed out the tripod and took some time to position it.

When he had done so, he was surprised to see that John had moved forward.

"Hey, son," he said.

"Hey," Mike called, almost at the same moment.

John was walking at a steady pace.

"What the hell?" Sibley muttered. He had set the handheld video running.

"Stay up," Mike shouted, meaning stay upwind.

Just in case.

Just in case . . .

Through the lens Sibley barely saw what happened next. The flash of movement was so sudden that the shock sent the video slithering in his grasp. It slipped from his eyes, and while automatically raising it again—even then the photographer's instinct for the picture got the better of him—he saw Mike Hitkolok raise the rifle to his shoulder in one swift, smooth-running movement.

John didn't cry out at all. He didn't run.

As the bear launched itself forward, he remained exactly where he was, as if frozen to the ground.

The sound of the shot was earsplitting. The bear staggered, a ghastly sight, paws extended, coat stained with blood, teeth bared. Sibley had a split second to think, *What a size, Jesus, Jesus. . . .*

Before she fell, dead, barely six feet from John.

It was only then that Sibley dropped the camera. He started to run full pelt down the slope, stones shifting under him, threatening to unbalance him.

Mike was ahead, shouting John's name.

They got up to him and spun him around.

"You fucking shithead!" Sibley yelled. "You shithead fool! What did you think you were doing? You got a death wish, or what? I told you to stay clear of her, I said to you . . ."

But the words glanced off the boy like weightless blows.

John Marshall was staring past them, past the body of the female, to the pit where she had lain.

"She's got a cub," John whispered. "Look . . . she was protecting the cub."

Thirty-nine

THEY picked Jo up at midday the next day, outside Great Ormond Street Hospital.

As Jo walked out under the white canopy of the front doors, Gina and Mike got out of the taxi to exchange places with her. Jo stumbled a little as she walked forward, and almost fell into Gina's arms.

Catherine got out of the cab. "You don't have to come with me," she told Jo. "Stay here. I'll get to Heathrow by myself. It's okay."

"You won't," Jo said.

"You're a wreck," Gina agreed. "Look, I'll go with Catherine and see her to the flight."

Jo put up her hand to stem any further comment. "Look," she said. "If I could, I'd go all the way with her. Not just the airport."

"We know," Gina murmured.

"I'll be back with Sam as soon as I can," Jo told her. "By teatime."

"We won't stray," Gina replied. "I've got the number of your mobile phone. Go."

Jo kissed her and hugged Mike. She and Catherine got back into the cab. They waved out of the back window, then, as the cab pulled away from the pavement, Jo turned to Catherine.

"You've got everything?"

"Yes, don't worry."

"What time does the flight leave?"

"Three-thirty. Plenty of time."

"And from Calgary . . ."

"To Edmonton," Catherine said. "From Edmonton to Yellowknife."

"What time are you in Yellowknife?"

"Ten forty-four P.M."

Jo nodded. "And the next day you go on to Gjoa Haven."

"I'll be there at half past one in the afternoon," Catherine confirmed. "I'll ring."

"And your father takes another day?" Jo asked.

Catherine nodded. "He's in Nunavut already, but he has to come via Iqaluit, to Yellowknife, to catch the same First Air to Gjoa. He'll be there twenty-four hours after me. It's a long way."

Jo suddenly gripped her hand. "I can't believe this is happening," she said. "First John's there. Then he's not." She squeezed Catherine's hand. "Where's the end to all this, Cath?"

Cath put her arm around her shoulder. "There is an end," she said. "We'll find him."

"For God's sake, even if the weather doesn't seem that bad when you get there, even if they've tracked him, promise me. Promise you won't go out after him without your father, and this Mike Hitkolok. Don't do anything dangerous."

Catherine smiled. "I promise you," she said.

They locked hands.

Gina had got a call yesterday evening from Richard Sibley. He had rung his sister in Winnipeg to confirm the phone number he had seen on John's copied e-mail, the one he had stuffed into his pocket. Yes, John had come to Gjoa Haven with him, he told her. Yes, it was true that they had found the bear. Yes, John had survived the attack, and they had come back to Gjoa together, and from there he had run the news item through the wires.

But, no, he didn't know where John was.

"I'm sorry?" Gina had said, afraid she had misheard him over the crackling static of the line. She had been at home, with Mike, getting ready to go down to the hospital.

"We came back. He went to his room," Sibley shouted down the line. "When I'd done the item for the news, I went to find him. The e-mail with your number was on his bed. But John had gone."

"Gone?" Gina had echoed. "Gone where? Where is there to go to, for God's sake?"

"He'd taken a freighter canoe," Sibley replied. "And, Mrs. Shorecroft . . ."

Gina had waited, eyes squeezed shut.

"Somebody here from CBC told me. They told me about Sam. I'm sorry."

"You didn't know?" Gina breathed, her heart sinking like a stone.

"There was nothing on the e-mail to tell us."

"It was on your national network!" she protested.

"We never saw it," Sibley replied. "We were nowhere near a TV. When we came back, we flew straight to Gjoa. We didn't even have dinner," he said, and the pale little joke fell horribly flat over the thousands of miles of line.

"I can't believe this," Gina murmured. "First you have him, then you don't have him. . . ."

"I don't know why he would go," Sibley told her. "The bear was a shock, but—well, in all honesty, Mrs. Shorecroft, he didn't seem too struck by it. Didn't seem upset at all. I mean, I was carried out of there in a bucket, I have to tell you, but John . . ."

Gina pressed her hand to her mouth. She could guess what was coming next.

"He seems like he's got a heavy burden," Sibley said, at last. "You know what I'm saying, Mrs. Shorecroft. A heavy burden . . ."

"I know," Gina replied, eventually. "It's a long story, Mr. Sibley. A very long, sad story."

The taxi was coming down toward Whitehall now.

On their left was the beginning of the great string of London parks: St. James's, Green Park, Hyde Park, Kensington Gardens. Jo and Doug had walked along the Serpentine dozens of times to Round Pond. And come down the Mall. Always to the same place, of course. The Franklin Memorial at Waterloo Place, near Admiralty Arch. The bronze plaque that showed Crozier reading the memorial service over Franklin's body.

Jo ran a hand over her face. The taxi was stifling. Next to her Catherine let down the window, and the dusty, diesel-fumed air rolled in. London was sweltering. The traffic was hellishly sluggish. Catherine looked at her watch and sat back, her arm resting on the door handle.

Strange, Jo thought. Less than three years ago she had never heard of Franklin. Never wanted to hear of Franklin, or anyone like him. The endurance of the *Erebus* and *Terror* crews had meant nothing to her. And yet here she was, on the same kind of journey into white space.

There were no maps for where she was going. There was no one to show you the way as you stood at the door of an isolation unit and went through it with your son's hand holding your own. People told you there was a way through, but no one knew for sure. You had to just go, make the leap. What was there behind you? No way back. No side routes. No detours. There was only this impossible, seemingly insurmountable course ahead of you. You pushed yourself forward into the unknown, sick with fear. Because there was nothing else to do.

And somewhere now, on the other side of the world, a boy was making the same journey as Franklin, because he had become hooked on the idea that absolution was somewhere down that line. He couldn't know what he was doing any more than she did. He was just as lost. He had no idea of the outcome, and no idea of what consequences his actions might have. And she and Sam were tied to him, being dragged forward into that landscape.

A place of death.

God no, she thought, as her stomach turned over. *Don't think that way. Don't even let that thought come into your head. It won't be a place of death anymore. It will be a place where they come to life. John, Doug, Sam. You. Catherine. All of us.*

We'll all come to life there.

Jo shut her eyes, the familiar names of the dying crew fixed in her head. Doug had told her the story in greatest detail in the weeks when they negotiated the contract for the new program. They had sat down among their packing cases, nearly ready to move into Lincoln Street, and roughed out the treatment for the first few episodes together.

Names had become ingrained then. Names she had pushed to the back of her mind for months after Doug died. They had resurfaced again recently. She thought of them as she sat, unable to sleep, at Sam's side. Heard the litany of them echoing down the corridors.

McClintock, searching in 1859 along the coast of King William Island, had found the body of Harry Peglar, captain of the foretop in the *Terror*. A few miles east of Cape Herschel, Peglar had been found lying on a small ridge, facedown. They could still make out his double-breasted jacket of fine blue cloth edged with silk braid, and the great-coat, a blue-and-white comforter around his neck. He had marched in ordinary uniform. Around his skeleton lay personal fragments: a comb; coins; a pocketbook. A large stone lay behind the skeleton, and McClintock's interpreter decided that Peglar had sat down, resting his back against the stone, and, trying to get up again, he had fallen forward. Perhaps dead. Perhaps simply exhausted. Whichever was the case, Peglar had not stirred from that pitching-forward fall. Nothing had disturbed the body in eleven winters.

Another searcher, Lieutenant Schwatka, found a grave at Point Victory, on the northwest coast of King William, opposite to where *Erebus* and *Terror* had been abandoned. Canvas had been sewn around the body, and a medal was found lying on the ground. It belonged to John Irving. The same searcher found bones scattered all down the King William coast.

Jo opened her eyes now and stared out at the road. The taxi had picked up speed; they were headed out of the city.

She thought of the site where they had planned the first program to be filmed. It was on the eastern coast of King William, about sixty-five miles from the ships.

Doug had thought that the ships' crews had split up somewhere around here. That probably over half of them had been left behind because they were too sick to travel. He thought that one of the surgeons would have been left in charge of what was effectively a tented hospital. Eskimo said that many bodies had been found here. More than thirty or forty. And the boat, of course. Such a famous boat that forever afterward, the part of Erebus Bay where it had been found was known simply as the Boat Place.

The search crew of the steamship *Fox*, commanded by Leopold McClintock, found a lifeboat resting on a sledge in 1859. The boat was pointing north, as if it had been left there as the few remaining men marched back toward the ships. Perhaps they were the last remnants of the hospital tents, the last few who had not died. Doug thought that a decision had been made to try to get back to the *Erebus* and *Terror*, because at least there was greater shelter there, providing they had not been broken up by storms. And because some provisions were still on board. Better to try to get back, they must have decided, than to wait out the whole winter on the shoreline, under canvas. A small band had started to retrace their steps.

But they didn't get far.

At least two men were dying. And the boat was ridiculously heavy. By now all reason and logic had deserted the survivors. They were hauling an enormous weight, and the boat, when found, was filled with incomprehensible rubbish. Inside it, beside two skeletons, were boots, towels, soap, sponges, combs, a gun cover, twine, bristles, saws, files, wax ends, bullets, shot, cartridges, knives, needles and thread, bayonet scabbards, two rolls of sheet lead, silk handkerchiefs, and books. *The Vicar of Wakefield. A Manual of Private Devotion. Christian Melodies.* A Bible. A Church of England prayerbook.

In the back of the boat worse was to come. McClintock unearthed spoons, forks, teaspoons, plate, watches, paddles, tins, tobacco, tea, and chocolate. There was no meat or biscuit of any kind, and no fuel.

Writing about the discovery afterward, McClintock had said that everything in the boat was a mere accumulation of deadweight, of little use, and likely to break down the strength of the sledge crews.

No one ever knew who the two men were that had been left with the boat. One, McClintock said, was crouched in the bow. He had been a young man. His bones were in a jumbled state. Large and powerful animals, probably wolves, McClintock wrote, had found the body and torn it limb from limb.

Under the after-thwart lay the second man. Older and larger, he sat propped up, swathed in furs and cloths, with a double-barreled gun on either side of him, both loaded and cocked, and leveled muzzle upward against the boat's sides.

These two had always fascinated Doug.

An older man and a younger man, he said. Relics of the sick whom Crozier had left behind. Trying to get back to the ships. Left on the shore, with a boatful of books but no food. And the jumbled bones at the older man's feet. What kind of wolves, Doug had asked her, ripped a body to pieces, and then carefully rearranged the uneaten bones back in a heap in the same boat they had dragged them from?

And then there was Crozier himself. This shadowy figure that John seemed to be chasing. All that had ever emerged from that devastated wasteland was the testimony of the Inuit natives, the people that had once been called Esquimaux. There were plenty of legends among them that Crozier had survived for years, living among the natives, and eventually working his way westward toward Hudson Bay. There was even a story that he had almost got to an outpost when he was killed by a rival tribe. Stories abounded of Crozier being nursed back to life over the winter of 1849, and of him eventually making his way up Back's Fish River, or out toward Repulse Bay, in the east. Some Inuit women even teased the Europeans years later by saying that they had children who were descended not only from Crozier but from Franklin himself.

What was certain among all this mixed testimony and hearsay was that Crozier had been seen on the southernmost tip of King William Island in the summer of 1848. He had met a group of Esquimaux then, and begged for seal meat for his starving men. The meat had been given, but during the night the natives had left, because they were afraid of the sight of the Europeans. Their faces were black, they said. Their teeth were discolored, their gums bleeding. They were terrified that whatever sickness the Europeans had would be infectious, and they were almost starving themselves after a winter and spring of intense cold, and a summer that never seemed to come.

Crozier was left on the shores of Simpson Strait, possibly among the small islands off Point Tulloch.

What was absolutely certain was that neither he, nor any of his crew, were ever seen again after that last meeting. The ships—those huge technical masterpieces of Victorian Britain—had sunk, or been driven onto shore by the storms of subsequent years, and broken up. They, like the men aboard them, had disappeared as if they had never existed.

Jo shuddered involuntarily as the taxi pulled into the airport terminal. Beside her Catherine was grabbing her hand luggage and already leaning forward to open the door.

What if John never comes back? Jo thought, watching Catherine's profile intensely. *What if you don't find him? What if no one ever finds him?*

Lady Jane Franklin had mourned for nearly thirty years after Franklin disappeared, she knew. Suddenly she wished desperately that Catherine should never know what it was to live the rest of her life, like Franklin's wife, without knowing what had happened to the man she loved.

Not for her, Jo thought.
Not for this girl.

As they got out of the cab at Heathrow Airport, they were in for a shock.

The first person Jo saw was a news reporter, running toward her, with a cameraman, and other figures, in close pursuit.

"Meridian News," said the woman. "Have you heard any more about John Marshall?"

"No," Jo said, flinching at the brightness of the camera light.

"But he's out there?"

"Yes."

"How is Sam, Miss Harper?" Another voice.

"He's okay. Stable."

"Have you spoken to John's mother?"

"Yes," Jo said.

"Are you going out there?"

"No," Jo said. "Miss Takkiruq is going. She knows the area."

The microphones turned in Catherine's direction.

"If he's there anywhere, we'll get him," Catherine said.

Jo reached out a hand toward the reporter. "I just want to make one thing clear," she said. "John Marshall doesn't know why we're looking for him." She tried to steady her voice. "If we find him, and he decides to come back, that'll be great. That'll be wonderful." She raised her chin and looked directly into the nearest camera. "But if we don't get him in time, or—or whatever happens," she added, "it's not his fault. Please remember that."

It was two-fifteen before they got Catherine's luggage checked through. She stood at the departure gate in the Heathrow concourse, gripping her tickets.

"Hug Sam for me," she said.

"I will."

"His count was better today."

"Yes."

They stared at each other.

"Will you tell John," Jo whispered, "will you tell him . . ."

Catherine nodded. "I know what to tell him. I know. It's okay."

Jo glanced up at the computer screen over their heads, where the number of Catherine's flight showed green. *Boarding, Calgary, Gate 79.*

"I wish I could be with you."

"It's all right," Catherine reassured her.

People were pushing forward. A few glanced in their direction, picking up the tension in their body language, looking twice at the faces, occasionally nudging one another as they recognized them.

Jo wrapped her arms around Catherine. "Please take care of yourself," she whispered.

"I'm going to bring him back, Jo," Catherine said. "Soon, okay? You'll be standing right in this airport, right here. We'll walk back through those gates. I promise you."

She kissed Jo's cheek and walked away.

Watching her, Jo felt an almighty wrench in her chest. She knuckled her hand against her heart, trying to draw breath. She wanted so much to run after her, to go with her, to step off that plane in Calgary. To come down into Gjoa Haven. To walk out with her wherever she was going. She wanted to do that. She wanted to help.

And she wanted to be in Great Ormond Street. She wanted to watch the next transfusion, to will the blood through the lines, to stare at Sam's vein, the little vein showing blue in the crook of his elbow, the pulse. She watched it with a kind of obsession. Not the Hickman line, where the drugs pumped. But just that little blue spot under his skin on his arm. That was her signal of life. While the vein there flickered, he was still with her.

God, it was so much to ask for. So much to demand. The life of a child. The life of John Marshall. Two lives, in a world of daily destruction. Two survivals where so many others did not survive.

The weight of it pressed down on her. The sight of the departure gate swam in and out of focus. She could just see Catherine, her tall frame, her dark hair. She was so frightened that Catherine should be going alone. That she wouldn't come back.

And then, she saw him.

Doug was just to the left of Catherine. Jo saw him in profile, his gray bag slung over one shoulder. He was gazing around the crowds, looking for someone.

"Doug," she whispered.

He turned. First to Catherine. Then, he looked toward her.

She met his eyes, saw the message in them.

I'm going with her.

I'll be there.

She blinked; he vanished. Catherine looked back, once, and raised her hand as she walked on. Then, she was lost in the crowd.

Jo stared after her. She stared at the place where Doug had been.

"Dear God," she prayed, letting go of all her previous bitterness, "dear God, please. Please help us."

An overwhelming feeling suddenly swept through her. A warm sensation, a flood of light, just like that she had felt two years ago in the garden, when she took Sam there, a few days after he was born. That same strange, unmistakable note of connection. She felt Doug so close to her that she had the touch of him, his lips on her face.

Far off in the distance she thought that she heard the reporter's voice, and others, at her side. But their tone of concern hardly registered with her. Colors flew and mixed; the ground flipped under her feet.

Rolling, it took her down into the dark.

Forty

STARVATION Cove. Maconochie Island.

He had seen it before in his dreams.

Although his dreams had always been high with color. Stark blues and orange, backlit ice that glowed in low light; green-blue ocean, Arctic poppies, saxifrage.

In the last two days John had realized that all his dreams had been the same, even those of the *Jeanette*. There had always been such shade and detail. Disko Fjord under McClintock's feet in August 1857, with blue campanula blazing among the wildflowers. The haloes around the sun. McClintock's Christmas aboard the *Fox* in 1858, with the luxury of candles at the table, and their light falling on the scrubbed white pine table, while outside the snow drifted and the temperature fell to eighty degrees below.

But, after all his dreams, there was no color here.

John stood on the highest piece of land he could find. It was probably raised no more than thirty feet above sea level. It was midday. There was nothing at his back but the moonscape of the peninsula, flat and smooth except where it was broken by the occasional small ridge of larger stones. Water was everywhere. Runoff from the ice had left hundreds of pools among the rock. Under the cloudy sky they showed as flat gray circles.

Monochrome, not color.

He looked east. The land was perfectly flat for as far as the eye could see. There was no movement at all on it: no animal, no vegetation. As he turned his body, every muscle in it protested. He had walked thirty-five miles in three days, and his legs and back burned. He had pitched his tent, but he could see now, looking back at it, that he had made a poor job of it. The tent door flapped. He felt an overwhelming urge to pull it down. He wanted to leave everything behind. Everything. He wondered if he would bury the tent, along with the rest of his belongings.

Out there, to the east, the inlet broadened. Maconochie Island was probably a half mile away. He narrowed his eyes, trying to make out any sort of alteration to the monotonous landscape ahead of him. On the map that had been pinned to his wall in Cambridge, the island was a small white oval, fringed on its western side with sand and gravel dunes. White oval on a colorless chart.

And it was the same today. Exactly the same as the map he could have drawn from memory. A bleached horizon, with fog rolling. White on gray, gray on white.

John sat down on the shore. The rock under him made a grating sound, like broken china, a sound to set the teeth on edge. He curled up on the ground, the last of his energy gone, oblivious to the temperature and the ever-present thick cloud of mosquitoes. On the first day of his walk he had tried to pull his hood down over his face, and keep his gloves on, because the insects settled on him as soon as he stopped. They coated the leeward side of the tent, thriving in the relative heat of seven degrees. But he hadn't tried to stop them lately. His face was swollen with bites.

It didn't matter. The pain was no longer anything real. Like his thirst, like the pain in his joints and muscles, it had become background buzz. Static on a radio, the blur of white noise with a missed transmission. The unobtainable signal on a phone. Just background buzz. The indistinguishable, useless buzz of the world.

He rolled onto his stomach, closed his eyes.

He plunged his hands now into the stones underneath him. Ran his fingers over the rough edges, some as sharp as knife blades. A cool salt breeze blew over him.

Schwatka had called this Starvation Cove when he came looking for Franklin in 1879. He thought he had found survivors then. He listened to the Esquimaux and heard them tell him about finding bodies, and watches, and guns, and gunpowder. The Esquimaux children hadn't known what the gunpowder was. They had thought it was black sand. They'd taken it into a tent, and it had ignited, singeing their eyebrows and hair and frightening the hell out of them.

Some said Crozier had got as far as Montreal Island, at the very mouth of the river, but John had always doubted it. It was another thirty miles, and he couldn't see Crozier getting thirty more miles after begging for the seal meat. No . . . it was here. He had died here.

Right here.

John turned on his side and opened his eyes.

He supposed he had been waiting all along. After leaving the boat from Gjoa on the coast, the walk had been pure, cleansing. He was grateful for the hardness of it, because it filled his head. It had rained the second night. Water got into the tent somehow; and he had found that he was wet through when he woke up, the clothes sticking to his skin. He had got up and moved on, aware of the labored sound of his breathing. He had plowed on, seeing ice far out in the channel, noticing crystals of it lodged in the pools on the shore. Another month, and the weather would start to close in again.

He pushed himself to a sitting position now, and waited.

He had thought he would see him. Or something of him.

But there was nothing to see here.

Nothing at all.

Suddenly his father sprang into his mind. His father in that room, the big bay-windowed room of his flat. Piled on the couch with his leg in plaster. Talking about this woman from the paper. Only two visits, and that had been the sole topic of conversation, Jo Harper. Not him. Not John. He remembered the day; rain drying on the window. Sun breaking through. Doug's weather-lined face going into a smile. Light in the eyes.

John had wanted to tell him about Catherine. Never could. Never could put it into words. That was his problem. Words closed in his throat. Couldn't get them out, couldn't reveal himself. Only Catherine had seen the face he hid. Knew his desperation, wanted his love. Love from the real person. Took the obsessions, accepted him. Not like Amy, forever asking him to drop the idea. Catherine worked with him, going along. Hand in his hand. Eyes always searching his face.

He couldn't look into hers after Doug had died. He couldn't bear the patient forgiveness and understanding. He didn't understand himself. He didn't forgive himself. Why should she? He had nothing to give anyone. Nothing to give his mother. Nothing to give Catherine.

And yet she would have walked with him this far.

He put his hand up to his face, and wondered where the water had come from, and realized that it was tears.

The day rolled down toward evening.

The ocean at last gave up a color: a deep, deep indigo. It was so beautiful that he laughed at the magic of the trick, the water turning color in the reducing light. The cobalt and indigo of a paintbox. Add water to the dry paste. Watch it bloom. Indigo on a paintbrush, sinking into cartridge paper. Colors of childhood, names on a paintbox. What were they called? Burnt sienna. Violet. Titanium white. And this—this beautiful blue racing past his feet.

The light of the perpetual day barely faded at first, and then the rain came suddenly, thicker than the mosquito, thicker than darkness. From light to dark in a matter of minutes, the wind picked up and drove the needles of cold into his face. He could no longer see the ice on the ocean. He could no longer see the pitted terrain at his back.

Finally, disorientation took hold of him.

He had found himself on his hands and knees, and he couldn't remember what he was looking for until he closed his eyes and conjured the shape again. He had somehow cut himself on the palm of one hand. Looking for something. The rounded, cylindrical shape he thought he'd felt. Irregularity in the rock. Smoothness. Thought he felt it, then lost it. Hands and knees, hands and knees, air scouring at the top of his lungs.

He lay in the door of the tent now, motionless, gazing back the way he had come.

Somewhere out there in the sea was *Erebus*. She would have drifted. Perhaps she brought the *Terror* with her. The Inuit said that one of the ships had been broken up on the shore of King William, pushed there by ice. They had found the other almost intact, farther south, and they had boarded her, and found a man's body, and a ladder stretching down to the ice, and the footprints of two other men. Afraid at first, and building courage little by little, they had gained access by tearing away part of the hull. They carried off what metal they could, and then found that the ship was sinking, because they had weakened the hull around the waterline.

She went down fast, within the day. For months afterward, only part of her could be seen, then even that disappeared. Somewhere at the bottom of the sea that John was staring at were the remains. Somewhere on the bottom were two steam locomotives. They would remain when everything else was rotted. Somewhere down there. Somewhere *out* there.

His father had always said what a coup that would be. What a dive. The dive of his life. To go down to the wreck of *Erebus* or *Terror*. Worth all the other dives of his life rolled together.

And John thought of the silence when he had dived in Turkey. The rattle of air, the fragile fix of oxygen. A repeated drumming, like the drumming he thought he heard now above him. A drumming like a boat's engine, the noise you could hear when you were below the water, waiting to come up. Waiting, hearing both that and the perfect, suspended silence when you stopped breathing. He thought of *Erebus* suspended, not dead, not alive, on the bottom of Victoria Strait.

Not dead.

Not alive.

He got to his feet and stared out at the ocean. He looked at the blue-on-gray, and the light sky devoid of stars.

The sea writhed at his feet.

Remorseless current.

Empty day.

"Dad," he said, the word drowned by the sound of the water. He sank to his knees in the broken, grainy shale of the beach.

"I can't find you," he whispered. "Dad, help me. I can't find you."

The sound of the boat came late, very late at night.

They had come too far down the coast, and the rain was driving them in to the shore.

It was only the persistence of one person that had brought them this far. The boat ground up on the shingle. Three people got out, two immediately hauling the canoe up onto land, the outboard slumping the hull to one side. They turned their faces from the onslaught of the wind, shoulders hunched. He heard their voices—surely ghost voices— torn and scattered by the gale. The third figure looked up the slope, and began to walk, then run, toward him.

He strained through a fevered sleep to see her, a fragment of his hopes, coming through the torrent toward him.

She was not there, of course.

She was only what he longed to see.

As she knelt beside him, she pushed back the hood from her face, and he saw the water, the driving rainfall of the storm, streaming through her hair.

That hair. That hair, black in his hand, that rope of hair . . .

"John," she called "John . . ."

He closed his eyes, grateful that she had come to him in this most terrible of dreams.

She put her arms around him. She lifted his head.

"It's too far," he said. "Too far to go back."

"It doesn't matter how far it is," she told him. "We'll go there together."

Forty-one

IT was silent in Great Ormond Street Hospital.

Six o'clock in the evening, and silent.

Catherine had been gone five days.

Gina was standing in the corridor by the window, in the same place that the three of them had been only a week before, and the surprise of the sudden stillness made her catch her breath. She glanced at her watch, and then up and down the corridor, puzzled. A hospital was never really silent; there was too much going on. The changing of equipment, the ringing of phones, the hushed but persistent opening and closing of fireproofed doors. Voices in corridors. The hum of the lifts. The monitors by the beds.

And yet, in that moment, it *was* silent.

Even the traffic noise outside seemed to have been smothered.

Gina turned around. A nurse was coming along the corridor.

"Did something stop?" Gina asked.

"Excuse me?" the nurse asked.

"Did something stop?" she repeated. "Did the air conditioning go off or something? The heating?"

The nurse stopped to listen. "No. I don't think so. Sounds the same." She gave Gina a quizzical look.

Then, a terrible conviction hit her. Quite suddenly Gina felt that she knew exactly what the silence meant. She promptly pushed past the bemused nurse and ran to the doors to the ward.

They had put Sam in a screened-off bed; Jo was next to him,

propped up in the big green armchair. She was asleep, her head on one side, and Sam's teddy bear was in her hand. The trolley that had held Sam's supper had been pushed away, the plate barely touched.

The way that Jo had positioned the chair, parallel to the bed, had effectively obscured Sam from anyone standing at the door. A terrible bolt of sick apprehension slammed into Gina, a sense of the world having entirely halted. It was like the moment in an accident when realization slurs forward on slow motion, and minor details become unnaturally clear.

She noticed the ring that Jo always wore on her wedding finger, a slim platinum band, whose delicate decoration of vines seemed to be picked out in high relief. On Jo's wrist was a plastic hospital bracelet. Jo had written her own name around it, so that Sam could see that he wasn't the only one to have this marker. The lettering looked vivid.

Gina strained to hear Sam breathing.

She could hear nothing.

Then, movement in the corner of the room caught her eye.

The TV set was on, but with the sound turned down.

Gina stepped forward, momentarily drawn by the image. She frowned as she looked at it. The familiar BBC logo of the *Evening News* had been replaced by the face of the newscaster, and an overlaid image in the top left-hand corner of the screen. It was of a helicopter hovering above a gray landscape, and a knot of people on the ground below it.

She looked away, and stepped forward.

At the very second she did so, Jo woke up. She stared at her friend.

"What is it?" she asked.

Her eyes widened as she read Gina's expression. For a second her gaze fixed on the floor, too wary to turn around. Then she looked at Sam, pushing back her chair.

The boy was lying still, arms by his sides.

He was awake and looking at the television.

Following his steady gaze, the two women turned back to the screen.

"My God," Jo breathed.

It was now a camera shot taken from a moving plane. They could see the Twin Otter shadow on the shoreline below, mirroring the plane as it flew. The first snatched image showed a patch of blue against the gray. It was a small tent, pitched between pools of water, stranded on an isthmus of land.

Jo stood up.

Next image, a green freighter canoe pulled up on shore, abandoned, the Johnson outboard motor on its stern touching the slope of broken limestone.

A map. Gjoa Haven marked as a red spot in the north; Pelly Bay to the east; Cambridge Bay to the west. The long stretch of King William in between, shaped like a heart lying on its side. And the tent again, closer this time, the plane flying lower.

Then, faces.

Catherine, mobbed on an airport strip, her father at her side. Joseph Takkiruq's brown face and piercing black eyes. Catherine lifting her hair out of her eyes with one hand, grinning, and holding up the other hand, as if fending off questions.

Jo leapt forward for the volume.

". . . found alive after five days' search in this most unforgiving of landscapes, and a worldwide publicity campaign lasting more than two months . . ."

The crowd was parting. Behind them was a Medevac stretcher.

"Oh God, oh God!" Gina cried.

The commentary swept over them. They heard probably half of it. At that same moment both phones on the head nurse's desk down the corridor began to ring.

". . . this double rescue, on the same day that the polar bear cub was airlifted to Manitoba . . ."

Now there was Catherine again on-screen.

A barrage of demands.

"Miss Takkiruq! How is John?"

"He's okay," she replied, trying to find a way through the crowd. "Exhausted. But okay . . ."

"Can you show us what was found?"

"I surely can," she said. They saw Catherine dig into her parka pocket. She brought out a small copper canister, almost greened over with verdigris.

Jo uttered a small, astounded cry. She stepped forward and laid her hand flat on the screen for a second.

"It was underneath him," Catherine was saying. "Under his arm."

The noise swelled to a deafening pitch.

"Is it real?"

"Miss Takkiruq . . ."

Catherine pressed the canister briefly to her forehead, and closed her eyes. Then she smiled broadly as she opened them, and looked at the item in her hand. "Francis Crozier," she murmured, "captain of Her Majesty's Ship *Terror*, August eleventh, 1848."

In the hospital room Jo and Gina flung their arms around each other.

On-screen they saw Catherine put her hands over her ears in renewed protest at the volley of noise around her.

Jo rushed to Sam's side and kissed him.

Catherine had grabbed the nearest microphone. "Can I say something?" she asked. "Can I just say one thing? I have a message. A message for Jo Harper in London."

The room around her fell silent. As silent as the moment that Gina had felt not two minutes before. Across the bed Gina gripped Jo's arm.

They saw Catherine hold up the canister. "Hey, Jo," she said softly, to the camera, "miracles do happen, after all. Tell Sam his brother is coming home."

Postscript

"... we dream more of bears than of any other animals ... when we find him roaming over drifting fields of ice more than a hundred miles from land, we are filled with wonder ... when there is no ice, we find him swimming, and we are scarcely less astonished. ..."

Admiral Sir F. Leopold McClintock
From The Voyage of the Fox in Arctic Seas

"... the tracks were not fresh, but had been made some time ... the footprints appeared to have been made when the snow was soft ... and subsequent gales had swept the impacted snow around the foot prints away leaving them raised ... the men had come from the land to the northward and westward [of Christie Lake] ... some of the Inuit thought that they would find the white men who had made these tracks. ..."

Reported conversation with Inuit of 1850
Charles Francis Hall

THE Tundra Buggy in Churchill Bay, Manitoba, was raised ten feet from the ground, but the bear, stretched to full height, still reached the window.

Those in the vehicle moved back instinctively, seeing the massive head intruding almost into the cab, its teeth fastened on the window edge.

But the child did not move.

Of all those in the buggy perhaps his mother should have been the most afraid, and reached forward to take him away. But Jo Harper stood back with Bill Elliott, with bated breath, to watch this most extraordinary meeting.

It was finally John Marshall who stepped forward. He sat beside his half-brother, taking him on his knee, next to Catherine.

"What shall we call him, Sam?" he asked, wrapping his arms around the four-year-old boy.

"Swimmer," Sam replied.

"You think he can swim?" Catherine said, smiling.

"Miles and miles," Sam told her.

"Like his mother," John agreed.

The bear turned away and dropped onto all fours on the snow-swept plain. It seemed to hesitate for a while, and then it moved away, walking northwest, without once looking back. The first great white bear to be released from captivity back into the wild.

John stood up with Sam. They followed the Swimmer as far as they could see it along the observation deck. Then John turned to Jo, and held out his arms, and hugged her. They stood there for some time, Sam wedged between them.

"Do you think it'll survive?" Jo murmured.

"Yes," John replied, with conviction. "The impossible happens here."

Running back to the window, Sam pulled off his mittened gloves and pressed his palm to the cold pane. As he took his hand away, a perfect impression was left. Taking off his own glove, John superimposed his hand on Sam's. Over John's, Jo placed her own.

When they took their hands down, three interwoven prints patterned the window.

And beyond them the track of the polar bear stretched away.

Footprints were still visible near Christie Lake in the spring of 1850. But they did not belong to Eskimo, Chipewyan, or Cree.

Whoever the white man was who had walked there in the winter, he had done so when the snow was soft and freshly fallen. The snow froze and the winter gales came, and all that was left of his journey now, in the April daylight, were these clear and raised imprints.

His foot was longer than Eskimo, and the track passed onto the ice of the bay from the northwest. There were no heel prints, and the track toed out in a way that native tracks could not. The southern Eskimo who discovered them worked their way through to Lyons Inlet in the hope of finding him.

Some say that the strange traveler passed to Ignearing, northeast of Igloolik. Some say that the white man went east, farther still, to Fort Hope, to the still-standing buildings of John Rae, who had come there three years before, looking for Franklin survivors.

Some said that he passed down that coast and married an Inuit woman, and that he made for Fort Churchill, five hundred miles to the south.

It was possible to travel from this most northerly point of Hudson Bay down to the Fort. There was a chain of Inuit camps in that direction, at Depot Island and Fort Fullerton and at Nuvuk, south of Wager Bay, and they led to the Hudson's Bay trading post where the annual supply ships called, and they said that perhaps from there he went back the way he had come in 1845, and crossed the ocean to his own people.

And some said that the white man had reached Fort Hope, and stood at the ruins of Rae's house for several days with the woman Maliaraq, and looked for a long time at the water of the Bay, before he turned back, and went again westward. Because no man in his own country would believe him.

Or, worse still, his own country would believe only too well what he had done, and yet not understand it. And they would never let him alone for the rest of his life. And he could not shoulder that burden, the burden of being the only man to come back to them, when all the others were lost, and lay unburied behind him.

And some said that it was all invention, the whisper of legend and fantasy, and that there had never been footprints in the spring of 1850, and that the Eskimo families of the Great Fish River, which the white man called Backs River, had never returned to take the one surviving boy with them.

And that he never grew into a man with them, or lived among them, or walked to Fort Hope before he turned back.

* * *

Some stories are true, and some fantasy.

Some journeys are dreamed of, but never made.

And some, like Sam Marshall and Augustus Peterman, travel a long way through the dark, on paths that no other man could ever know.

To reach the light at last, and survive.

Author's Note
and Acknowledgment

"What I fear is that from our being so late we shall . . . blunder into the ice. . . . James, I wish you were here, I would then have no doubt as to our pursuing our proper course. . . ."

THE *Ice Child* began with Francis Crozier.

I had already heard of the Franklin expedition of 1845 when I read the above letter in the Scott Polar Research Institute in Cambridge. It had been sent from the Whalefish Islands on July 19, 1845, by Crozier to Sir James Clark Ross. The faded script of this single letter, so full of both misgiving and good humor, struck me with its incredible poignancy. Crozier had sailed many times with Ross, and his attachment to the great commander shone through the text.

The more I read about this doomed journey, the more admiration I felt for the endurance and courage of the crews of HMS *Erebus* and *Terror*. I hope I have done them justice. Every man on the two ships died; but their qualities—their astonishing loyalty and love for each other— could not die. It reaches out to touch us now, an example to all those who find themselves making their way through the dark.

It hardly matters whether Franklin found the Northwest Passage, though the Passage was determined by those who searched for him in the years to come. Franklin left a much greater legacy and example, as did all his men.

Those who know the Franklin story will see where the facts end and the fiction begins. I have kept to fact wherever possible, but all the conversations described can only be conjecture. No ship's logs or journals were ever found. Similarly, only one copper canister was ever found. That Crozier proposed to Franklin's niece is a fact; that he mourned her loss can only be a guess.

Another guess is the meeting with Eskimos on Cape Felix; however, the final conversations at Starvation Cove are pretty well accepted. The Inuit did give meat to white men in this location at this time.

Traces of the death march are well documented. The classic reference for both the march and the entire expedition is Richard Cyriax's book, *Sir John Franklin's Last Arctic Expedition.*

It should be noted that, although many relics of the death march have been found, no one knows the exact sequence of deaths. We know that Fitzjames wrote the fateful message on April 25, 1848, but we do not know whether he was already ill. We do not know if Goodsir and Stanley were left in charge of the hospital tent. And we do not even know if Crozier was one of the last survivors—though some Inuit reports do suggest this.

There was no one called Augustus Peterman on the *Terror.* There were no boys below the age of seventeen. Yet boys of Gus's age were regularly taken on other vessels, particularly whalers. I wanted to develop the tragedy through a child's perception, so I hope this slight stretching of the facts will be excused.

To the best of my knowledge the ships were designed, built, and loaded exactly as I have described. Controversy will probably always rage as to whether or how much the crew were poisoned by Goldner's provisions, and Victorian England was horrified by the suggestion of cannibalism. My own opinion on both issues is represented in *The Ice Child.*

Although the date of Franklin's death is accurate, the cause of it is unknown. It might well have been natural causes. It might also have been, as is portrayed, botulism. The only thing that is known for sure is that it was sudden.

The autopsies of the bodies on Beechey Island actually happened, and I am indebted to John Geiger and Owen Beattie for their amazing book, *Frozen in Time.* John Torrington's fate especially touched me, and the picture of his long-fingered, delicate hands, shown in Beattie and Geiger's work, was an image that never left me.

I am similarly indebted to John Macdonald and John Harrington for allowing me to refer to their research on *The Franklin Trail* Web site, and to their Web master Karis Burkowski. Johns Macdonald and Harrington endured a positive snowstorm of e-mails from me, and always replied with great patience.

My gratitude also goes to Dan Moore for the information he provided about Gjoa Haven, and to R. K. Headland, the archivist at the Scott Polar Research Institute. Similarly, I acknowledge the great detail of Franklin supplied in Scott Cookman's *Iceblink*, which I read with interest.

David C. Woodman's book, *Strangers Among Us*, presents the tantalizing theory that some of the crew may have survived—returning to the abandoned ships for another winter, or traveling eastward toward Hudson Bay. There is plenty of Inuit testimony that points to these possibilities, but, sadly, nothing concrete or material to support it.

I retrieved many polar-bear facts from Ian Stirling's book *Polar Bears*, Kennan Ward's *Journeys with the Ice Bear*, and Barry Lopez's *Arctic Dreams*. They will all be only too well aware of the near impossibility of releasing motherless cubs back into the wild. But there is always hope. Especially in fiction.

As regards the modern-day story, I received an incredible amount of help on the theme of aplastic anemia.

First and foremost I would like to thank Paul Veys, the transplant surgeon at Great Ormond Street Hospital, who advised me on the possibility of John matching Sam as a bone-marrow donor.

Secondly, my heartfelt thanks go out to two families who have had firsthand experience of this illness: Stuart and Karen Heaton, and their amazing daughters Emma and Beth; Shaun and Sheila Burrowes, and their sons Elliott and Nathaniel. Both families were kind enough to meet me and offer all kinds of detail. They were generous to a fault in the most difficult of circumstances. Their combined courage reminded me so much of the Franklin crews—that same solidarity, and superhuman determination to face down a nightmare. If you have been touched by Sam's story at all, please remember the real-life families who need bone marrow donors right now.

Linda Hartnell at the Anthony Nolan Bone Marrow Trust in London gave me hours of her valuable time, explaining the intricacies of donor matching, for which I thank her.

Also Bryony Dettmar, of the Aplastic Anemia Support Group in the UK, who put me in touch with the Heaton and Burrowes families. And Denise Curtis, who spoke to me about her children David and Hannah.

Those who have experienced the devastation of aplastic anemia will realize that Sam's illness and treatment proceed at a possibly faster rate than normal, and Bill Elliott's attraction for Jo leads him to reveal more than might usually be the case. I ask those who know far more about this experience than I do to please excuse the shortened time scale in the story.

If there are errors in any of the above themes, that error is mine, and not due to any of the sources quoted above.

Lastly, I would like to give my deepest thanks to all those who have supported me through the writing of this book:

My agent, Sara Fisher, fellow traveler and friend on the extraordinary roller coaster that was the year 2000.

Barbara Rozycki, for her confidence in me. Ursula Mackenzie and my editor, Francesca Liversidge, and all the team at Transworld. Carole Baron and Brian Tart and the Dutton team in New York. The votes of confidence and kind messages from so many involved in the publication of *The Ice Child* worldwide.

Julie Goddard, who made sure I didn't sink.

Stu Blunsom and Dale Patfield, Astrid Gessert, and Anne Corbin, for helping me to visualize the future. The Thursday Group, for their selfless enthusiasm and support. Stuart Heaton, my researcher when the going got tough.

Ken McGregor, who always believed the time would come.

And, most important of all, my daughter Kate.

ABOUT THE AUTHOR

Elizabeth McGregor lives with her family in Dorset, England.